Availab...
from Mi...

Chris... ...e in Colorado
by Cassie Miles
&
Nick of Time
by Elle James

Christmas Awakening
by Ann Voss Peterson
&
Beast of Darkness
by Lisa Renee Jones

Safety in Numbers
by Carla Cassidy
&
Christmas Confessions
by Kathleen Long

Classified Christmas
by BJ Daniels

Guardian's Keep
by Lori Devoti

Mission: Christmas
by Lindsay McKenna & Susan Grant

CHRISTMAS AWAKENING

He'd waited ten years for this…

When he'd last made love to Marie she'd been a girl. Now the naked body before him was that of a woman. And she kissed like she had in his dreams. She was so precious to him, so perfect. He wanted to hold her forever, never wanted to lose her.

To lose her…

He pushed the morose thought away, trying to be happy for once in his life. But he knew he wouldn't be, not if something happened to Marie. Not if he lost her. In his arms he had everything he wanted – right here, right now – yet he was more conscious than ever of how quickly it all could be taken away. How quickly Marie could be taken away.

In his mind, the eerie voice spoke again. *All that you love will die…*

BEAST OF DARKNESS

"My world is different from yours, Sarah."

Something in his voice drew her gaze to his. "I'm not like other humans." His hand flattened on hers with more force. "But I'll fight to my death to protect you."

For the first time in years, Sarah trusted someone at their word. She looked into Max's tormented hazel eyes, and she let herself be lost. Lost to him, to the moment, to the whirlwind of emotions taking hold of her.

"I believe you," she whispered. Max felt the brush of Sarah's lips on his and it was all he could do to remain still, to hold back. But he had to hold back. Had to. Attached to him, mated to him, she would not be protected. She would share his destiny, his potential hell.

"Sarah…"

She pressed a finger to his lips. "Don't talk. I need you, Max. Make love to me."

First published in Great Britain 2009
Harlequin Mills & Boon Limited,
Eton House, 18-24 Paradise Road, Richmond, Surrey TW9 1SR

Christmas Awakening © Ann Voss Peterson 2008
Beast of Darkness © Lisa Renee Jones 2008

ISBN: 978 0 263 87337 5

46-1109

Harlequin Mills & Boon policy is to use papers that are natural, renewable and recyclable products and made from wood grown in sustainable forests. The logging and manufacturing processes conform to the legal environmental regulations of the country of origin.

Printed and bound in Spain
by Litografia Rosés S.A., Barcelona

CHRISTMAS AWAKENING
BY
ANN VOSS PETERSON

BEAST OF DARKNESS
BY
LISA RENEE JONES

MILLS & BOON®

CHRISTMAS AWAKENING

BY
ANN VOSS PETERSON

Ever since she was a little girl making her own books out of construction paper, **Ann Voss Peterson** wanted to write. So when it came time to choose a major at the University of Wisconsin, creative writing was her only choice. Of course, writing wasn't a *practical* choice – one needs to earn a living. So Ann found jobs ranging from proofreading legal transcripts to working with quarter horses to washing windows. But no matter how she earned her paycheque, she continued to write the type of stories that captured her heart and imagination – romantic suspense. Ann lives near Madison, Wisconsin, with her husband, her two young sons, her border collie and her quarter horse mare. Ann loves to hear from readers. E-mail her at ann@annvosspeterson.com or visit her website at www.annvosspeterson.com.

To Rebecca, Norman and Patricia and our wonderful time exploring Maryland's eastern shore.

Prologue

Edwin Leonard's heart beat hard enough to break a rib. He adjusted his reading glasses and studied the sketch's deft lines. So much detail. So much planning.

This was proof. Proof of murder.

He slipped his glasses into his pocket. He'd been butler at Drake House since he was a young man, yet he never would have guessed such hatred pulsed within the borders of his beloved estate. Such a malicious, *murderous* force. The paper rattled in his shaking hand, fear adding to the tremor he'd acquired with age.

He needed to hide the sketch. Stash it away until he could get it to the police. If the killer found it and destroyed it, the only evidence of murder would be Edwin's word.

And that of a ghost.

He circled Drake House's south wing and followed the freshly laid oyster shell path through the south garden. The soles of his shoes crunched with each step. Too loud.

He paused, scanning the area, making sure no one had heard. The old mansion's grounds were quiet; only the lap of waves on rock along the shoreline reached him. He was alone. Even so, he found himself holding his breath.

Stepping along the edge of the path, he continued. He had to stash the sketch and get back into the house before anyone noticed his absence. He knew just the hiding place. A spot where no one would think to look.

He quickened his pace, following the white shells into the redesigned east garden. He stopped at a bench nestled among holly bushes and grasped the seat. Grunting with effort, he shifted the seat to the side, exposing a hollow space in the concrete base.

A space just the right size.

He rolled the sketch in trembling hands and slipped it into the crevice. He shifted the seat back into place.

It would be safe there. Safe until morning when he could turn it over to Police Chief Hammer. Still, something didn't feel right. Maybe it was nerves. Maybe it was some sort of sixth sense. Maybe it was related to what he'd experienced in the candlelit room in Sophie's attic. Whatever caused the feeling, it bore down on him, thicker and more invasive than the humid, late autumn night.

Anger. Evil.

He had to get a hold of himself. Straightening, he combed his hair into place with his fingers. He brushed off his suit, pulled a linen handkerchief from his pocket and dried his palms. Extracting his timepiece from his pocket, he tilted the face to catch the light of the moon.

Mr. Brandon would wonder what had happened to him if his bed wasn't turned down when he chose to retire. That certainly wouldn't do.

Edwin slipped the watch back into his vest pocket. It clinked against the skeleton key he'd stolen along with the sketch.

The key. He'd forgotten to stash the key. Turning back toward the bench, he reached into his pocket.

The blow hit him before he could react. The force shuddered through his skull and down his spine. He dropped to his knees on the sharp shells.

Another blow brought darkness. He couldn't move. He couldn't think. He felt his legs being lifted, his body being dragged down the path. Out of the garden. Over the lawn. To the pier jutting out into the bay.

No. Not the water.

He tried to move, to fight, but his body wouldn't obey. Rough hands pushed him. He rolled into the water. Salt filled his mouth. Cold lapped at his body. His head went under.

Then he felt nothing.

Chapter One

"When a loved one dies, it's normal to want answers, Miss Leonard," the police chief drawled. He stopped near the break in the boxwood hedge that opened to the Jenkins Cove Chapel's redbrick walkway, as if he couldn't wait to get out of the graveyard...or maybe just away from Marie. "But sometimes you got to accept that accidents happen."

Accept? Marie gripped a damp tissue in her fist. Maybe she could accept, *if* her father's death really *was* an accident.

She focused on the arrangement of holly and poinsettia draping Edwin Leonard's casket. It was all wrong. The sunny day and cheery Christmas greenery. The sparsity of the black-clad crowd that wandered away from the graveside now that they'd offered their condolences. And most of all, the words coming from the chief's mouth. "I know you've ruled my father's death an accident, Chief Hammer. I'd like to know what led you to that conclusion."

"What led me?" The police chief drew up to his full height, what little there was of it.

A squat, bulldog of a man, Charles Hammer had

struck Marie as lazy, ever since he'd poo-pooed her report of boys smoking marijuana back when she was a sophomore at Jenkins Cove High. His quickness to dismiss her father's death as an accident before he knew all the circumstances just underscored that impression. Obviously nothing had changed in the ten years since she'd left Maryland's Eastern Shore. "Why do you think it was an accident?"

His mouth curved into a patronizing smile. "The evidence of accidental death is pretty clear in your father's case. In fact, nothing suggests it was anything *but* an accident. He was walking on the dock at night. He slipped and hit his head on the rocks along the shoreline. Accidental drowning. Pure and simple."

"It couldn't have happened that way."

"I know." He shook his head slowly, his bald scalp catching the sun's rays. "It seems so random."

Tension radiated up Marie's neck, fueling the headache that throbbed behind her eyes. "No, that's not it. It couldn't have happened the way you said. It's not possible."

He peered down his pudgy nose. "That's what our evidence indicates."

"The evidence is wrong."

"Evidence is never wrong."

"Then the way you're looking at it is wrong."

He drew in his chin, making himself look like an offended old lady. Or a turtle. "What do you do for a living, Miss Leonard?"

"I'm a philosophy professor."

He grinned as if that explained everything. "Well, I'm a police chief. I deal in hard evidence, not silly theories. I've investigated deaths before. Have you?"

She let out a frustrated breath. Her father had always warned her about her lack of tact. She should have tiptoed around the chief's ego. Flattered him. Buttered him up. Then he would probably be more open to her ideas. Instead, she'd turned him into an enemy.

She stared up at the spire of the gray stone church she'd attended as a kid. "I'm sorry. There's just something you don't understand."

"I understand the evidence. And in your father's case, that evidence clearly says accidental drowning."

She leveled her gaze back on the chief. "That's what I'm trying to tell you. My father never would have accidentally drowned."

"Your father hit his head. Even Olympic champions can't swim when they're unconscious."

"My father couldn't swim. Not a stroke."

"Then how can you find accidental drowning impossible?"

She tried to swallow the thickness in her throat.

"Because he was deathly afraid of the water. He never would have gone near it."

The chief looked unimpressed. He edged closer to the redbrick path between the boxwood. "I'm sorry, Miss Leonard. Facts are facts. Your father did go near the water that night. The case is closed. I'm sorry for your loss."

The finality of his words struck her like a kick to the sternum. She watched him amble down the path and join the last of the funeral-goers milling along Main Street.

The man from the funeral parlor eyed her from beside her father's casket, waiting for her to leave so he could lower Edwin Leonard to his final resting place beside her mother.

Marie pulled the collar of her black wool coat tighter around her shoulders. She didn't know if murder victims truly rested or not, but she sure wouldn't. Not until she knew what had happened to her father.

Not until she made his killer pay.

MARIE FORCED HER FEET to move up the loose gravel walk to the kitchen entrance of the sprawling white antebellum mansion. Drake House. An uneasy feeling pinched the back of her neck. The feeling she was being watched.

She spun around, searching the grounds. Waves danced on Chesapeake Bay and the mouth of Jenkins Creek, a body of water ironically broader and deeper than many lakes. Evening shadow cloaked the mansion's facade, transforming it to a dark hulk against the gleam of sunset on water. It looked austere, empty. The Christmas decorations that blanketed every house and shop in town were nowhere to be found here. No evergreen swags draping the balconies. No wreaths adorning the doors. Dark windows stared down at her like probing eyes.

She was home.

A bitter laugh died in her throat. She might have grown up in this house, but it wasn't home. Not without her father.

A gust of wind blew off the water, tangling her funeral-black skirt around her legs. Even though it was early December, the wind felt warm to Marie. And the shiver that ran over her skin had nothing to do with temperature.

Was someone watching her from the house? Brandon?

A flutter moved through her stomach. She gritted her

teeth against the sensation. The last time she'd seen Brandon Drake, she'd been a teenager with delusions of true love. She'd changed a lot since then. Grown stronger. Wiser. Her heart had shattered and mended. Still, she'd been relieved when Brandon Drake hadn't attended her father's service. She didn't want to see him. Not when she was aching from her father's loss. Not when her emotions were so raw. Not when she was feeling less than strong.

Unfortunately, if she wanted to find the truth about her father's murder, she had to start at the place he'd lived…and died. Drake House.

She tore her gaze from the mansion's upper floors and the balcony that ran the length of the private wing. Setting her chin, she increased her pace. The quicker she could get into her father's quarters, look through his things and get out, the better. It was all over town that Brandon had become a recluse since his wife died. He didn't take visitors. If she entered through the kitchen and dealt with the servants, maybe she could find enough to convince Chief Hammer to reopen her father's case as a homicide without ever having to face Brandon Drake.

At least she could hope.

Unease tickled over her again, raising the hair on her arms. She looked up at the house, beyond to the boat-house, then turned toward the carriage house. A man with the flat and misshapen nose of a prizefighter stared at her from the other side of a long black car. He nodded a greeting, then resumed rubbing the hood with a chamois.

The chauffeur. She recognized him from her father's funeral. At least someone from Drake House had come.

She gave the chauffeur a little wave, circled a gray

stone wall surrounding the pool and clomped up the wooden steps. Pressing the doorbell, she peered through wavy glass and into the kitchen where she'd once had milk and cookies after school.

It looked so much the same. Too much the same. A dull ache throbbed in her chest.

A woman with the thin, strong look of steel wire bustled across the kitchen and opened the door. Penciled eyebrows tilted over curious eyes. "Yes?"

"I'm Marie Leonard."

"Of course. Miss Leonard. I'm so sorry about your father." She opened the door with one hand, using the other to usher Marie inside. "I'm Shelley. Shelley Zachary. We talked on the phone."

Marie nodded. The cook, now housekeeper. The woman Brandon Drake had promoted to take over her father's job before he was even in the ground.

"It's nice to finally meet you. I worked side by side with Edwin for the past eight years, and a day didn't go by that he didn't mention you. I'm so sorry I wasn't able to make it to his funeral. Running a house like this in addition to cooking is very demanding."

Marie forced a smile she didn't feel. "I'm here to go through my father's things."

"Of course. Isabella can help you, if you need it."

Marie followed the housekeeper's gaze to the corner of the kitchen where a young woman with huge blue eyes and luxurious, auburn hair polished a silver tea service. She wore a uniform of black slacks and blouse with a white apron, more covered than the stereotypical French maid, yet because of her bombshell body, nearly as sexy.

"Isabella? This is Edwin's daughter."

Isabella continued with her work as if she couldn't care less.

At one time, the servants at Drake House were Marie's family, and a caring and tightly knit one at that. Not just her father, but everyone who'd worked at the house back then, from the maid to the cook to the chauffeur, liked to read her stories and bring her treats. They watched out for her, and she never questioned that each cared about her and about each other.

Clearly that family atmosphere had deserted Drake House in the past ten years.

That was fine. Marie didn't need a surrogate family. She needed answers. She focused on Shelley Zachary. "Do you have my father's keys?"

"Of course. I'm running the house now."

"May I have them? Or at least the keys to his quarters?"

"You don't need keys. Isabella can assist you."

Marie pressed her lips together. She didn't want someone looking over her shoulder. "I can handle it myself."

"You'll need help. Your father lived here a long time. Cleaning out his quarters is going to be a big job."

She was sure it would be. Especially since she intended to do a little snooping while she was here. "Really, I'd rather be alone. You understand."

Shelley Zachary didn't look as though she understood at all, but she nodded all the same. "Fine. But before I give you keys, I'll have to clear it with Mr. Brandon."

The name zapped along Marie's nerves like an electric charge. "No, that's not necessary."

Shelley frowned. "Excuse me? He's the master of the

house. He certainly has a say in who can and cannot have keys to his property."

There she went again, speaking without thinking, making enemies where a little tact might have made her an ally. Marie held up her hands, palms out. "That's not what I meant. It's just that I know he's busy. And I hear he's not taking many visitors lately."

The severe line to Shelley's mouth softened slightly. "No, he's not. Not since he lost his Charlotte."

A pang registered in Marie's chest at the sound of Brandon's wife's name...even after all these years.

"He never minds a visit from me." Isabella tossed Marie a smug smile. "I'll ask him."

"Ask me what?"

Marie's heart stuttered. She looked to the dark doorway leading to the dining room for the source of the deep voice.

Brandon Drake emerged from the dining room shadow. His shoulders filled the doorway. The dying rays of the sun streamed sideways from the kitchen windows and fell on his face.

Marie gasped.

A scar ran from his temple to the corner of his mouth, slick, red skin slashing across his cheek. He stepped forward, leaning on a brass and teak cane. "Hello, Marie."

Chapter Two

Brandon could see Marie stifle a gasp as she took in his face, his limp. The thought of her seeing his weakness hurt more than the burns themselves. He tore his eyes from her, not wanting to witness more, and focused on Isabella. "What were you going to ask me?"

The little vixen didn't answer. Instead, Shelley piped up. "Miss Leonard is here to clear out her father's things. She asked for keys to the butler's quarters."

"Give her the keys."

"You're hurt." Marie's voice was almost a whisper, as if she was murmuring her thoughts aloud, not intending for the rest of them to hear.

He kept his gaze on Shelley, careful not to look in Marie's direction. Her hair was a little shorter than it had been ten years ago, only jaw length now, and her face had lost its teenage roundness. But she was still Marie. He couldn't take seeing horror on her face as she scrutinized his injuries. Or worse, pity. "Where are those keys, Shelley?"

"I'll get them, sir." Shelley bustled off into the pantry.

Marie stepped toward him. She raised her hand.

Brandon wasn't sure what she intended to do. Touch

him? Soothe him? Heal him? He stepped back, removing himself from her reach. "It's nothing, Marie. I'm fine. Charlotte was the one who was hurt."

Pink suffused Marie's cheeks. She dropped her hand to her side and clutched a fistful of her black skirt. "I know. I mean, I'm sorry about your wife's death."

Guilt dug into his gut. He was such an ass. Sure he had to keep his distance from Marie. He owed Edwin that much. Just as he owed Charlotte. And when it came right down to it, he owed Marie. But he could have kept away from her without slapping her down. Just one more bit of proof that he didn't belong anywhere near someone as decent as Marie Leonard.

"My father didn't tell me you were hurt as well."

"Like I said, it's nothing." He glanced at the pantry. Where was Shelley with those keys?

"It's not nothing. If I'd known, I would have come...I would have—" She let her words hang as if she suddenly recognized the inappropriateness of what she was saying. She dipped her chin, looking down at his hand gripping the cane, at the wedding ring still on his finger. "Anyway, I'm sorry."

He nodded, hoping she was finished. "You don't have to put yourself through all this, Marie. Isabella can pack up Edwin's things and send them to you."

"No. I want to do it myself. It will...it will make me feel closer to him."

Brandon gripped the head of his cane until his fingers ached. The thought of Marie spending time in Drake House threatened to unhinge him. Even two floors up and in another wing, he'd be aware of every move she made. But what could he say? That she couldn't pack her father's things? That he refused to let her into the house where she'd grown up? That would make him more of an SOB than he already was. He forced his head to bob in a nod. "Take all the time you need."

"Thanks. You won't even know I'm here."

Fat chance of that.

Silence stretched between them, each second feeling like a minute. From outside he heard waves slap the shore and a yacht hum on Jenkins Creek, probably his uncle taking advantage of the unusually warm December.

Weather. That would get his mind off Marie. Sure. Where in the hell was Shelley?

Brandon cleared his throat. "I'm sorry about Edwin. He was a good man. I don't know what I'm going to do without him."

Tears glistened in Marie's eyes, but they didn't fall. "Thank you."

A car door slammed outside.

Isabella looked up from the tea service she was buffing.

Brandon held up a hand. "I'll get it." He headed for the kitchen door, trying not to lean too heavily on his cane. He was sure the maid was wondering what was going on. Since Charlotte died, he'd refused visitors whenever possible. But right now he had to get out of the cramped kitchen. He had to get away from Marie.

How on earth was he going to handle having her in his house the next few days?

IN THE PAST TEN YEARS, Marie had imagined countless times what it might be like to see Brandon again. But even in her worst nightmares, she'd never pictured things going so badly.

"All right. Here you go." Shelley Zachary emerged from the pantry with a set of keys jangling in her hand. "There's a key for this kitchen door and one for the butler suite. That should be all you need."

Marie nodded. She was hoping for her father's set, which held keys for everything on the estate, just in case she needed to follow up on anything she found. But she didn't see how she could ask for that without raising more than a few eyebrows. She'd just have to figure out another way to snoop. "Thank you."

"Where is Mr. Brandon?"

"Talking to Doug Heller." A tray with the tea service in her hands, Isabella nodded in the direction of the kitchen door, then disappeared through the arched hall to the dining room.

Marie peered through the windows to the porch. His back to her, Brandon was talking to a man dressed in jeans, work boots and a rough canvas coat. The name sounded familiar to her, as if her father might have mentioned it at some point. "Who is Doug Heller?"

As if sensing her scrutiny, the man talking to Brandon raised his weather-beaten face and stared at her through watery blue eyes.

A chill raced over her skin.

Shelley crossed the kitchen. "He works for Drake Enterprises. Operations manager."

"I thought Brandon was running the foundation. Is he back working for the company?"

Shelley plopped the keys into Marie's hand. "No, no. Brandon's uncle is still running Drake Enterprises. Mr. Brandon has his hands full with the foundation."

"Then why is the operations manager here?"

"Oh, I'm betting he's not here about Drake Enterprises. It's probably about that developer again. Ned Perry. He's trying to buy up waterfront property. More tenacious than a terrier."

"Developer? Brandon isn't thinking of…" She couldn't finish. The thought was too abhorrent.

"Selling Drake House? Turning it into condos?" Shelley laughed. "Mr. Brandon would rather die."

A morbid thought, but one that inspired relief. At least he still loved the historic old mansion. And though it might not feel like home without her father here, Marie had to admit being inside these walls made her feel grounded for the first time since Chief Hammer had called to break the news of her father's death. "I'm glad to hear he's not selling. It's just when I saw no Christmas decorations and then you mentioned a developer…"

"Mr. Brandon has canceled the Christmas Ball, I'm afraid."

Marie frowned. The annual Christmas Ball and charity auction was an institution in Jenkins Cove. "That's too bad."

"He said there's no point without Charlotte here. Oh, and your father. He doesn't even feel like celebrating Christmas."

"I'm sorry to hear that." Marie was. Brandon had always embraced Christmas, especially since the annual ball and auction brought in a lot of money the foundation could distribute to people in need. Brandon had always believed in spreading his good fortune to others. It was the reason he'd devoted his life to the foundation instead of taking his spot at the head of his family's company. It was one of the many things she'd admired about him.

Marie shook her head. She couldn't afford to nurse good feelings about Brandon and Drake House. Not unless she wanted to forget herself the way she had when she'd first seen his scarred face. She had to remember things were different than they were the summer before she'd gone to college. And even then, things between her and Brandon weren't really the way she'd imagined them to be.

Marie let out a heavy sigh. Her father had always said the old-money Drakes were different from working people. That even though she grew up in Drake House, she didn't belong in their world. That summer after high school graduation, when Brandon had given his mother's diamond ring to Charlotte instead of her, she'd finally realized her father was right.

"…to Sophie Caldwell."

Marie snapped her attention back to Shelley. "I'm sorry. What did you say?"

The woman blew a derisive breath through her nose. "I said, you should talk to Sophie Caldwell."

It took a second for her to process the name. "The woman who runs the bed-and-breakfast down by the harbor?"

Shelley nodded. "The House of the Seven Gables. Word was Sophie and Edwin were quite the item."

Her father? Seeing a woman? "He never said anything to me."

"That might not be something a father tells a daughter."

Marie didn't appreciate the woman's gossipy tone, but this time she managed to hold her tongue. As unlikable as she found Shelley Zachary, the woman was the best source of information she had when it came to her father and the goings-on at Drake House. "I wish he'd told me. I always worried he'd been lonely."

"He didn't have time to be lonely. Just ask Josef."

"Josef?"

"Our chauffeur. Josef Novak. Poor Josef. Another man who lost his love. She died in the hospital. An illness, just like the way your mother went. He used to drive Edwin to the Seven Gables several times a week. He doesn't talk much, but he probably understood your father better than anyone, except Sophie, of course."

Of course. Marie pictured the man who'd been buffing the car outside, the man who'd waved to her and had attended her father's funeral. Josef. She couldn't imagine her father having many heart-to-hearts with the quiet chauffeur, no matter how much they had in common. Better to go straight to the source, Sophie Caldwell.

She glanced at Brandon through the kitchen windows. The manager, Doug Heller, was still stealing glances at her that gave her the creeps, but judging from the men's body language, their conversation was drawing to a close.

And that meant Brandon would be returning to the kitchen.

"I think I'll run over to talk to Sophie Caldwell right now. Will you pass my thanks to Brandon for the keys? I'm parked out front, so I'll just scurry out through the foyer."

"Fine." Shelley looked pleased to be rid of her. Maybe that was her intent all along.

"I'll be back later tonight to start on my father's things."

"Fine. Don't park near the kitchen. This is a busy house."

Late at night? Marie doubted it, but miraculously held her tongue. The decision to leave and come back later was looking better all the time. Later, after the servants were gone. And after Brandon had retired to his third-floor suite.

When she could be alone.

Chapter Three

It didn't take long for Marie to drive into the town of Jenkins Cove and wind her way through its quaint little streets. She parked in a lot off Royal Oak Street and walked the rest of the way to the bed-and-breakfast.

Connected to the harbor area by a narrow, concrete bridge, the House of the Seven Gables perched on the edge of the water. Masts of sailboats jutted into the twilight sky. A few yachts docked at a seafood restaurant nearby, and the scent of crab cakes teased the air. Christmas music mixed with the lap of the waves.

Unlike Drake House, the bed-and-breakfast was already decked out for the season. Wreaths adorned every door. Ropes of holly wrapped the porch posts and draped the balcony above. Marie climbed the steps to the front and rang the bell.

Footfalls approached, creaking across a wood floor. The door swung inward and a pleasantly plump, gray-haired woman peered out. A broad smile stretched across her Cupid's bow lips and crinkled the corners of her eyes. "Merry Christmas. Please, come in." She wiped her hands on her apron and gestured Marie inside with a sweep of her arm.

Marie couldn't help but return the woman's smile. She looked familiar, and Marie was fairly certain she'd seen her at the funeral.

"Are you interested in a room? We have one left overlooking the harbor."

"No, thanks." Was this the woman her father had been seeing? She hoped so. The woman seemed so gregarious and kind. Marie would like to think her father had someone like this caring about him and sharing his life in his final months. "I'm Marie Leonard."

"Of course. Edwin's daughter. I'm sorry I didn't recognize you right away." She opened her arms and engulfed Marie in a soft hug. When she finally released her grip, the woman had tears in her eyes. "I'm so happy to meet you, dear. I wanted to talk to you at your father's funeral today, but I…" She fanned her face, unable to go on.

A stinging sensation burned the back of Marie's eyes. She blinked. Getting her emotions under control, she met the woman's blue gaze. "I need to ask you some questions about my father, Ms…"

"Sophie. Please, call me Sophie." She took Marie's coat and led her into a parlor with windows gazing out onto the garden and the water beyond. She gestured to the corner of the room where an easel propped up an artist's canvas. The scent of paint thinner tinged the air. "And this is my niece, Chelsea."

Marie started. She hadn't even noticed someone else was in the room. She looked beyond the canvas and into the beautifully haunting face of a blue-eyed blonde. "Nice to meet you."

The young woman nodded. Quietly, she set down her paintbrush and glanced out the window as if her thoughts were far away.

Marie couldn't put her finger on it, but there was something about her…something disconcerting. As if when Chelsea looked out over the water, she could see things Marie couldn't even imagine.

Sophie ushered her to a grouping of white wicker near the canvas. "Please, sit down and feel free to ask me whatever is on your mind, honey."

Marie lowered herself into a chair across from Sophie. Staring at the cameo necklace around Sophie's neck, Marie searched for the right words to lead into her questions. "About my father…you two were close?"

The woman nodded her gray head. "Your father was a light in my life." Again, her eyes filled with tears.

Marie fought her own surge of emotion. Silence filled the room, making her feel the need to break it. She wanted to ask if Sophie knew who would murder her father, but how was she supposed to do that? The woman was obviously as grief-stricken as she herself. Throwing around suspicions of murder might send Sophie over the edge. Tact. Marie needed to use some sort of tact. To tread carefully for once in her life. "How did the two of you meet?"

Sophie smiled. "We met through your mother, in a way."

Marie looked askance at the woman. "My mother? My mother died of cancer when I was eight."

Sophie nodded as if she was perfectly aware of that fact. "And your father missed her horribly."

"She was the world to him. Well, along with me and Drake House. I was worried about him being lonely after I left for college." She'd mostly been worried about him devoting every waking moment to the Drakes, exactly what he hadn't wanted for her. She wished he would have told her he'd met a woman. It would have made her feel so much more at ease. "But I still don't understand how the two of you met through my mother."

Sophie and Chelsea exchanged looks.

"What is it?"

Chelsea shrugged to her aunt and let out a resigned sigh. "You might as well tell her."

"Your father came to me because he believed I could help him communicate with your mother."

"Communicate?" The ground seemed to shift under Marie's feet. "What are you? Some kind of medium?"

"No. Not me. Chelsea has more talent in that area than I have."

Chelsea shot her a warning look. "We don't need to go into that. She's here to learn about her father."

"Yes, your father. He wanted to use a room I have upstairs."

"For what?"

"As a portal to reach your mother."

"A séance?" Marie wasn't buying any of this. Not one word. She couldn't imagine her father holding some sort of séance. If Chelsea wasn't here, looking so serious and grim, she'd chalk up Sophie as a bit of a kook.

"Not exactly a séance. A portal to communicate."

"A room upstairs?"

She nodded. "A special room I've constructed. A room that acts as a door to the spiritual world."

A laugh bubbled through Marie's lips. She covered her mouth with a hand.

"This isn't a joke." Chelsea crossed her arms over her chest. "And my aunt isn't off her rocker, or whatever it is you're thinking."

"I wasn't…" Marie's cheeks heated. Fact was, she'd been thinking exactly that. She focused on the older woman. "I'm sorry. Please explain. I need to understand my father. I know you can help me do that."

Sophie's smile didn't change, as if Marie's disbelief didn't bother or surprise her in the least. "Have you ever heard of a psychomanteum?"

"A what?"

"It's based on a phenomenon we first see in Greek mythology. A psychomanteum or oracle of the dead."

Marie had studied Homer as an undergraduate. "The pool of blood in Odysseus."

Sophie's face brightened with the glow of a teacher who had just broken through to a lagging student. "Exactly. Odysseus dug a pit and filled it with animal blood. Through the reflection in the blood, he could communicate with spirits."

Marie suppressed a shiver. What kind of strange things had her father gotten involved in? "Your attic is filled with blood?"

Now it was Chelsea's turn to cover a smile.

"Oh, heavens, no." Sophie laughed. "You must really think I'm a nut."

Marie's cheeks burned. Her face must be glowing red. "I'm sorry. I didn't mean…I'm just trying to understand."

Sophie laid a comforting hand on Marie's arm. "Of course you are, sweetheart."

"My aunt uses mirrors, not blood," Chelsea explained. "Communicating through a psychomanteum really has quite a long tradition, and it crosses cultures. Africans, Siberians, Native Americans…they all used different forms, whether they were gazing into water or blood. There's even a story about Abraham Lincoln seeing his future reflected in a mirror."

Marie had heard of some of these traditions. It had never occurred to her that they were anything but super-stition and myth. "And my father believed he could look into mirrors and contact my mother?"

Sophie's smile widened. "He didn't just believe it. He did it."

"He did it? He contacted my mother?" Marie shook her head. This was impossible. Ridiculous. "What did my mother say?"

"She didn't *say* anything. The psychomanteum ex-perience isn't like some séance you see in a movie, dear. A ghost doesn't just appear and recite his or her life story. Not usually, anyway. It's a bit more subtle than that."

"How does it work?"

"It's more like meditation, opening yourself to stimuli we don't pick up normally."

"So my father meditated by staring into a mirror, and he spoke with my mother?"

"He sensed your mother. He could feel she was there. He could feel her happiness that he'd met me."

So that's what this was about? Sophie was worried Marie wouldn't approve of her relationship with her father and she thought some spiritual mumbo jumbo would help her cause? "I don't know about any psycho-whatever, but I'm glad he met you. I really am. I was worried about him after I left for school. Worried he'd be lonely. And he was. For years."

"That means a lot to me, honey." Sophie's expression shifted. "But your mother's acceptance wasn't all he ex-perienced in the psychomanteum. There were other things. Not-so-pleasant things."

"About my mother?" A shiver raced along Marie's nerves. Weird. She didn't believe any of this, yet Sophie's comment and tone of voice left her cold.

"Aunt Sophie…" Chelsea's voice held a warning ring.

Her aunt splayed her hands out in front of her. "She needs to know what Edwin experienced. She's here to look into his murder."

Marie's chill turned to shock. "How did you know that? Did the police chief—"

"Police Chief Hammer?" Chelsea rolled her eyes. "All that man cares about is making his job as easy as possible. A murder might mean that he has to do some actual work."

That certainly jibed with Marie's assessment of the man. "Then how did you know why I'm here?"

Sophie leaned forward and placed her fingers on Marie's arm. "You know your father. He wasn't one to enjoy walking the shoreline."

"Exactly." At least Marie wasn't the only one to recognize something very wrong with the police's accident theory.

Sophie nodded her head, her gray bun bobbing. "Contacting your mother was a good experience. A peaceful experience. The unpleasantness didn't have anything to do with your mother. It had something to do with Drake House."

"Drake House?" Marie's head spun. She held out her hands palms out, trying to physically push back all these bizarre claims and confusing twists of logic.

"Your father learned things in the psychomanteum. Things that upset him."

"What?"

"He wouldn't tell me. He said he didn't want to endanger me, especially after all I went through with Chelsea and her fiancé, Michael."

"Aunt Sophie…" Another warning from Chelsea.

Sophie gave Marie a conspiratorial look. "I'll fill you in on that story sometime." She glanced at Chelsea.

"When I'm not around to stop you?" Chelsea shook her head. "My experiences don't have anything to do with your father, Marie. My aunt just likes telling stories."

Sophie harrumphed at her niece, then returned her focus to Marie. "I wish I could tell you more about what your father experienced, sweetie. All I know is that it upset him greatly. And he said it led him to a dangerous secret."

"A dangerous secret?" The secret that got him killed?

Chelsea nodded as if reading her thoughts. "Your father was murdered to keep him quiet about what he learned."

"How do you know that?"

Chelsea shifted in her seat and glanced at her aunt.

Sophie smiled. "You mean are we basing that theory on fact or on some sort of vision in a mirror?"

"Well…yes."

"*I'm* basing it on what he told me before he died. Edwin was scared for me. He was also scared for his own life."

Sophie's words wound into a hard ball in Marie's chest. She couldn't picture her father frightened. He'd always been so strong, so in control. The only times she'd known him to be truly worried was when her mother was sick…and after he'd witnessed the way she looked at Brandon the summer before she'd left for college.

"I can't reach him in the psychomanteum. I've tried every day since he died, but it's no good. Maybe he's still trying to protect me. Or maybe I'm not the one he needs to communicate with."

The older woman stared at Marie so hard, Marie couldn't fight the urge to shift in her chair. She didn't want to ask what Sophie was getting at. She had a feeling she didn't want to know. "It's getting late. I'd better get back."

"He always talked about how he hadn't seen you in so long, how he had so much he wanted to tell you, so much he needed to say…."

"Aunt Sophie, if she doesn't want to—"

"If your father will communicate with anyone, it will be you, Marie. He loved you so."

Marie shook her head. "I can't possibly. I don't even believe."

"It won't hurt to try."

Marie grabbed the handles of her bag in one fist and thrust herself out of her chair. "I really have to go." She picked up her coat from the sofa arm where Sophie had draped it.

"It's not ghostly, Marie. Forget about all those movies you've seen. That was horror. This is real life."

"I'm sorry. I don't mean any disrespect, Sophie, really I don't. Talking to ghosts might be your real life, but it's not mine." She pulled on her coat and hurried out the front door and down the steps, nearly tripping over her own feet in her rush to get away.

THE MAIN FLOOR of Drake House was dark by the time Marie drove back through the gate, down the winding drive and parked in the empty servants' lot next to the carriage house. Dinner having been served, the servants had no doubt returned to their own homes. She looked up at the light in the private eastern wing of the house. The master suite, among other rooms. Brandon was home. She couldn't help but wonder what he was doing.

Thinking of her?

Pushing away that idea, she started through the east garden to the kitchen entrance. After recovering from her experience at Sophie's and grabbing a dinner of crab cakes at one of the harbor restaurants, she'd debated skipping Drake House and heading straight for the bed-and-breakfast off Main Street where she'd reserved a room. In the end, she'd decided she wouldn't be able to sleep, anyway, not after her conversation with Sophie and her niece. If she did slip into sleep, she'd spend the night hashing out their strange ideas in her dreams.

Better to get to work on her father's suite and keep her mind off both ghosts *and* Brandon Drake.

Marie followed the curvy path made of loose white shells. The night was dark, but she didn't need light to see where she was going. Even after ten years, she knew Drake House the way she knew her own heart. Even though some details had changed, there was something about this house and its grounds she recognized deep inside. Something that would be with her forever. Like the tune her mother always hummed. Like the almost imperceptible twinkle in her father's dry smile.

She swallowed into a tight throat. She missed him so much. Her father was so much a part of Drake House, she could still feel him, even outside on the grounds. The next few days, being in his rooms, sorting through his things, weren't going to be easy. But at least she'd feel closer to him. Just being back on the estate made her feel closer.

The night was warm for December, yet pockets of cold, still air dotted the path, raising goose bumps on her skin. She rubbed her arms and quickened her pace. She probably could have parked in the lot near the grand entrance and cut through the inside of the house to the butler's quarters. But somehow that felt presumptuous, as if she thought she belonged at Drake House or was some sort of honored guest. Here in Jenkins Cove, she was the butler's daughter, pure and simple. In the past ten years, she had learned her place.

She circled the corner of the east wing and approached the back entrance. A light glowed from a set of windows off the kitchen. Her father's quarters.

Her steps faltered.

The light dimmed and shifted. Not lamplight. More like a flashlight beam.

Was someone searching through her father's rooms?

A flutter of nerves made her feel sick to her stomach. Who would gain from searching her father's quarters? A murderer trying to cover his tracks?

The light flicked off. Darkness draped the house.

Marie pressed her lips into a hard line and covered her mouth with her hand. Whoever it was, the last thing she wanted was for the intruder to know he'd been spotted. She stepped off the path and slipped behind a holly bush. Reaching into her purse, she grasped the keys Shelley had given her, threading them between her fingers so they protruded like spikes from her fist.

The kitchen door closed with a click. Marie peered through spined leaves. A figure wearing a boxy rain slicker crossed the porch and descended the steps to the path. The hood covered the intruder's face, and the size of the slicker made it impossible to discern the size or shape of the person beneath. The figure turned in her direction.

Marie pressed back behind the bush, hoping the night was dark enough, the evergreen bush thick enough to hide her. The rhythmic crunch of footsteps on oyster shells approached...slowed...stopped.

She drew in a breath and held it.

Suddenly darkness rushed at her. Hands grabbed her shoulders. A fist slammed into her jaw. Leaves clawed at her like frantic fingers.

A scream tore from her throat.

Chapter Four

Brandon relived it almost every night. Fighting his way into the blazing car. Choking on smoke and gasoline. Charlotte's scream ringing in his ears. Helpless to save her.

He jolted up from the window seat, surprised he was in his room, no fire around him. No choking smoke. No Charlotte.

The scream came again.

Not Charlotte. Not a dream.

"Oh my God. Marie."

He thrust to his feet. His leg faltered, folding under him, and he grabbed the window molding for balance. He snatched his cane. Willing the damn limb to function, he bolted for the door. Clutching the carved railing with his free hand, he thundered down the back stairs and sprang into the parlor. He moved through the dining room, half hopping, half galloping. He had to move faster.

He raced through the kitchen and burst out the door. The night was dark, no moon, no light. He couldn't see a thing. Couldn't hear a thing but the rasp of his own breath. He held the cane out in front of him like a weapon. "Marie? Who's out here? Marie?"

A quiet groan emanated from a tall hedge of holly near the path leading into the east garden. "I'm here. I'm okay."

Pressure bore down on his chest. Her voice sounded small, shaken. Not at all okay. He followed the sound. He couldn't see her at first, but he could feel her. He could smell the scent of her shampoo. Something both spicy and sweet. Something that reminded him of a warm summer and good times. "Where are you?"

"Here." Holly leaves rustled. She sat at the bush's base, struggling to free herself from sharp leaves.

As he reached for her hand, his heart felt as if it would burst from his chest. "Can you get up?"

"I think so...yes."

She grasped his fingers, and he pulled her to her feet. "What happened?"

She focused on him, round caramel-colored eyes in a pale face. "Someone was sneaking around in the house. An intruder. He saw me."

"He attacked you?"

She lifted her fingers to her jaw. "He hit me...I think."

Brandon tried to discern the discoloration of a bruise, but it was too dark.

"I saw a light in my father's quarters. When I heard the kitchen door close, I hid."

"In a holly bush?" He could see something dark on her cheek, feel something slightly sticky on the hand he clutched in his, probably blood. No doubt the sharp edges of the leaves had scratched her up pretty good.

"I hid behind the bush, not inside the bush. When he hit me, I fell."

"Let's get you inside." Still gripping her hand, he led her toward the open kitchen door.

"What are you going to do?"

"Call the police."

"What are you going to tell them? I didn't see his face. I don't even know if it was a him."

"I'll take care of it." He hurried Marie up the steps and into the house. Closing the door, he locked it behind them. He didn't know what the police could do, but he wanted them there. If nothing else, they could check out the grounds and make sure the bastard who attacked Marie was gone.

He turned to look at her. In the light of the kitchen, he could see the pink shadow of a bruise bloom along her jaw. The holly had scratched one cheek as it had her hands. Beads of blood dotted the slashes. Snags and runs spoiled her black tights. "You're hurt."

"You should have seen the other guy." She tried for a smile, but it turned into a flinch of pain.

"Let me see." He brushed her hair back from her cheek with his fingertips. Her skin was soft. Her hair smelled like…cinnamon. That's what it was. Like the cinnamon gum she'd chewed as a teen. He took a deep breath. In the back of his mind he recognized the clatter of his cane falling to the floor.

"Does it look bad?"

He forced himself to focus on her injuries. "Not too bad. I'll get some ice for that bruise. And there's a first aid kit here somewhere. I'll get those scrapes cleaned."

"I can do it."

He met her eyes and swallowed into a dry throat. What was he thinking? He was having a hard enough time touching her skin and smelling her hair without doing or saying something he'd regret. Playing nurse-maid would send him over the edge. "Of course. I'll find the kit for you."

Her lips trembled. "I can get it. My father always kept it in the same place."

"Yes, all right." Come to think of it, he had no idea where Edwin kept the first aid supplies. He had even less of an idea what he thought he was doing hovering over Marie. He needed to step away from her, to focus on something other than the way her hair smelled and the warmth of her body and the tremble in her lips. But right this minute, she was all he could see.

He bent down and picked up his cane. Pulling in a measured breath, he stepped to the burglar alarm and punched in the activation code.

"Do you usually have the alarm on at night?"

He nodded, but didn't allow himself to look at her. He'd only be back to hovering if he did, noticing things he couldn't let himself notice. "I told Shelley to leave it off for you."

"So Shelley knew it was off. Who else?"

"Isabella. Maybe Josef. Anyone who knew you were planning to come back tonight, I guess. I doubt any of them would be looking to break in. They're in and out of here all day."

"The man you were talking to when I was here earlier? Did he know the alarm would be off?"

"Doug Heller? Maybe. Yeah, he was probably still here when I talked to Shelley." Something was going on. Something Marie didn't want to tell him. Despite his better judgment, he turned around and eyed her. "What are you getting at, Marie?"

"Do you think it's just a coincidence someone broke in the one night the alarm was off?"

"Good point. I'll mention it to the police. But I can't

see the staff involved in some kind of break-in. Or Heller, for that matter."

She shrugged a shoulder, the gesture a little too stiff. She was working on some sort of theory about the break-in. A theory she obviously didn't want to share with him.

Not that he could blame her. She'd trusted him with more than a theory before, and he'd thrown her to the dogs. She'd be smart to never trust him again.

"I've got to make that call. Whoever attacked you could still be out there." He made his way to the household office and plucked the cordless phone from its charger. He stared at the receiver in his hand. He didn't want the hoopla of calling 9-1-1. But he didn't even know where Edwin kept the phone book. Without Edwin, it seemed he couldn't handle a damn thing.

Glancing back to the kitchen, he let the idea of asking Marie sit in his mind for less than a second. The feeling he'd gotten when near her still vibrated deep in his bones. When she was close, she was all he could focus on. When he was touching her, the sensations were so strong they were painful.

After Charlotte's death, he'd wished he could no longer feel. Not the torment of his injuries, not the guilt in his heart, not the emptiness that hadn't been filled in far too long. Now that Marie was back, now that she was here in Drake House, he couldn't do anything *but* feel.

He had to keep control of himself. And if that meant staying away from her, he'd find a way.

He called up the directory feature on the phone. Sure enough, Edwin had programed the police department's nonemergency number. His butler had saved him yet again. If he wasn't so shaken by everything that had happened tonight, he'd find that ironic.

"Jenkins Cove Police Department," an official-sounding woman answered. "What is the nature of your call?"

"I'd like to report a possible burglary at Drake House."

"Mr. Drake?"

"Yes."

"Will you hold, Mr. Drake? The chief is here right now. He'd like to talk to you himself."

"Sure." Brandon frowned into the phone. It wasn't unusual for the chief to personally handle anything having to do with Brandon or his uncle Cliff. He supposed that was what happened when your family had nearly single handedly established and nurtured a small town like Jenkins Cove. Parks were named after you. Statues of your father and grandfather and generations back graced the town square. And the chief of police personally handled your crime reports. Still, it was awfully late for the chief to be in. It must have something to do with the state police's investigation of the mass grave that had been found just down the road.

"Brandon," Chief Hammer's voice boomed over the phone. "I hear you had a break-in. I hope no damage was done."

Damage. Brandon had been so absorbed with Marie he hadn't even looked for damage. He stepped out into the kitchen and swept it with his gaze. "None that I've noticed."

"Glad to hear that. We've had problems with some teens in the area. Vandalism. You might have read about it in the *Gazette*."

Brandon had read about a lot of wild things in the *Gazette* lately, with the coverage of the mass grave, the doctor who was rumored to be responsible and his lackey the state police had hauled off into custody. A lot more excitement than usual in Jenkins Cove. The teen delinquent stories must have been buried on a later page. "I know my uncle Cliff has had some problems with vandals. Let me look around to be sure there's nothing damaged."

Getting a grip on himself, he made his way to Edwin's suite. The door was open and Marie stood in the sitting room, her back to him. He forced himself to notice the room's condition and that of the two bedrooms beyond, not the curve of her hips in the skirt and sweater, now that she'd taken off her coat. "Notice anything missing or damaged?"

Marie shook her head. "No. I don't think so, anyway."

He nodded and forced his attention back to the phone. "The rooms we think the burglar entered don't seem disturbed."

"We?" Hammer repeated over the phone.

"Edwin Leonard's daughter, Marie, is packing up his things."

"I see."

"She saw the light on in the butler's quarters. The burglar attacked her trying to get away."

"Is she all right?"

"Just a bruise and a few scratches."

"This is going to seem like an odd question, Brandon, but are you sure someone was in the house?"

Brandon paused. "Of course I'm sure."

"Did you see anything yourself? Hear anything?"

"What are you getting at, Chief?"

"Nothing. I'm just a little concerned about Marie

Leonard. I had a talk with her today at the funeral, and she seemed to be having a bad time of it."

Brandon cupped a hand over the phone and stepped out of the room. He wasn't sure what Hammer was getting at, but he knew he didn't want Marie to overhear. "Her father died. Of course she's upset. You think it's more than that?"

"I'd call her paranoid."

"Paranoid?" Not a word he would associate with Marie. If anything she'd seemed too calm, too in control. But then, he'd been so turned inside out since he'd first seen her this afternoon, maybe she was just controlled in comparison. "What is she paranoid about?"

"She seems to think someone killed her father."

His words probably should have surprised Brandon, but they didn't. They explained a lot. "Why does she think that?"

"You'll have to ask her. I'm afraid it isn't based in reality. I've found no evidence that Edwin Leonard was murdered."

Of course, knowing Hammer, he hadn't expended much effort looking. "Thanks for the heads-up, Chief. But no matter what is going on with Marie, I don't think she imagined this attack."

"I'm not saying she did. I'm concerned about her. That's all."

"Well, if you could send someone out here, I can guarantee Ms. Leonard would feel a whole lot better. And so would I."

"Soon as I can, Brandon. I only have two officers on tonight, and one is securing the state police's dig site. It might be the state's investigation, but you wouldn't believe the monkey wrench it's thrown into our day-to-day operations."

Brandon grimaced. Apparently the chief hadn't had a good few days, either. "Send someone out as soon as you can. I want to make sure whoever it was is gone."

"In the meantime, stay inside, make sure your doors are locked and turn on that fancy alarm system of yours just to be on the safe side."

"Already done." He turned off the phone. The only problem with the chief's advice was the idea of locking himself in with Marie. Still, he couldn't see how he was going to find it within himself to let her leave, not when whoever had attacked her might still be outside.

"Is an officer on the way?"

Something jumped in his chest at the sound of her voice. He looked up to see her standing in the doorway to Edwin's quarters. "It might take a while. You have a place to stay?"

"A B&B in Jenkins Cove."

"How long are you planning to hang around yet tonight?" Edwin Leonard was an impeccably neat and organized man. Still, he'd been the butler of Drake House since before Brandon was born. Cleaning out his rooms was going to be a big job.

"I'll be here a few hours at least. I don't think I can sleep after all this."

He was sure he wouldn't be sleeping, either. But at least he had the sense not to offer to help. "Why don't you stay?"

She raised her brows.

"In your old room. Edwin would have insisted. And I would feel better if you didn't go back outside. Not until the police have a chance to check out the grounds."

He had to be crazy, inviting her to stay under his roof. Drake House was big, but not big enough to keep him from listening for her all night long and noting her every movement.

At least that way he could keep her safe. Edwin would have insisted on that as well.

"Thanks."

"Chief Hammer is concerned about you."

She twisted her lips to one side. "I'll bet he is."

"Why?"

She waved her hand in front of her face as if trying to erase the words between them. "Nothing. Never mind. It's just been a long day, that's all."

"He said you believe your father was murdered."

She held his gaze but said nothing, as if waiting for some kind of prompt.

"I take it you do. Why?"

"My father never walked near the water. You know that. He was deathly afraid of water."

"So he couldn't have accidently fallen in."

He wasn't sure if she'd nodded or not. She just watched him as if waiting for him to discount her theory.

"Hammer says there's no evidence."

"Because he's too lazy to find it."

That was the Charles Hammer he knew. If the answer wasn't easy, Hammer wasn't interested. "So that's why you're here."

"I'm here to pack up my father's things."

"And look for evidence he was murdered. And that's what you think our burglar tonight was doing, too, don't you? Looking for something incriminating. Something that ties him to Edwin's murder."

Again she didn't react. She just seemed to be sizing him up, watching, waiting. For what? Did she think he was going to tell her she was wrong? Hell, it should have occurred to him earlier how unlikely it was for Edwin to venture close to the water. He should have been looking for explanations himself. "Talk to me, Marie. Maybe I can help."

She didn't look convinced.

"Well, there's no reason for you to tie up a room at the B&B during Christmas shopping season. You can stay here as long as you need. Shelley gave you keys?"

"Just to the kitchen entrance and my father's quarters."

Leave it to Shelley. The day he'd promoted her to fill Edwin's job, she'd collected keys from all employees, doling them out only when she deemed necessary. The woman wielded her new power with a closed fist. "I'll get you a complete set."

"Thanks." Her lips softened. Not quite a smile, but an acknowledgment. Something.

"It's the least I can do. Your father meant a lot to me." *And so do you.* The words stuck in his throat. Not that he would ever say them out loud. He'd hurt too many people the last time he'd given in to that indulgence. Himself, Marie, and Charlotte most of all. He deserved the pain. But Charlotte... He couldn't erase what he'd done to her. Nor would he risk hurting Marie again. No matter what happened, he had to protect her. He owed Edwin. And he definitely owed her. "I'll go wait for the police. Good night, Marie."

MARIE LAUNCHED into the fifth drawer of her father's personal desk. So far she'd found nothing. No questionable photos or letters or anything that even hinted why someone might want him dead. But she had gone through almost a half box of tissues wiping the tears that continuously leaked from her eyes.

What she wouldn't give to have him back.

She closed her eyes, her lids swollen and hot. She didn't know what she'd do without him. Ten years ago, he'd helped her put her life in perspective. He'd hugged away her tears in that stiff-backed way he had. He'd encouraged her to get away from Drake House and make the life she deserved.

She hadn't lived with him for over ten years, but she knew whenever she had a question, whenever she needed to know if she was making the right decision, he was only a phone call away. Without him, she felt lost.

If only she could talk to him about her stirred-up feelings for Brandon.

She rubbed her eyes. She knew what her father would say. He would tell her to go home. To get away from Brandon, from Drake House. The same thing he'd told her ten years ago.

Too bad she couldn't follow his advice this time. Not until she found out who killed him. Not until she brought his murderer to justice.

She reached to the top of the desk and snapped on the ancient transistor radio she remembered her father using to listen to his beloved Orioles on summer nights. She turned her attention to the last desk drawer. "I'll Be Home for Christmas" drifted over the airwaves.

Great.

Here she was. Home for Christmas. Except the only person she had to come home to was gone. Taken away forever.

She turned the dial. Static took over.

Fabulous.

She twisted the knob. Now she couldn't get a signal at all. She rubbed a hand over her eyes. She was too tired for this. Maybe she should get some sleep and finish going through the desk tomorrow. She reached up to switch the radio off. Shadows of a voice rustled among the white noise. "Murder."

Marie jerked her hand back.

"Murder."

There it was again. A whisper rising from the static.

Marie frowned at the radio. It had to be a news report. Maybe something about the mass grave the state police were investigating, the one the waitress in the crab shack had been buzzing about last night. Marie gave the dial a twist, moving the needle back and forth, trying to get better reception. The static fuzzed on.

"Marie."

The whisper again. Saying her name?

She snapped the radio off. Sophie Caldwell's theories about communicating with ghosts flitting through her mind, she thrust herself to her feet and walked into the bathroom. She was tired and she was imagining things. That was all it was. All it could be.

Turning on the water to warm, she fished a hair band from her bag and pulled her bob back from her face. She looked into the mirror.

Sophie and Chelsea believed mirrors were like oracles. A way to see into the spiritual world. A way to communicate with loved ones lost.

The only image in her mirror was herself with her hair in a hair band. Not her best look.

She thrust cupped hands into the warm water and

lifted it to splash her face. She froze before the water reached her skin.

That scent.

Marie took a long breath. She knew the smell. The fragrance was faint, but she recognized the exotic notes, a blend dominated by jasmine.

She let the water drain between her fingers.

Pressure lodged under her rib cage, hard as a balled fist. Glancing around the bathroom, she dried her hands on a towel and turned off the tap.

The scent had to be caused by soap or air freshener. But look as she might, she didn't see a source. As she searched, the scent grew stronger. She could swear it was coming from the other side of the bathroom door.

A tremor moved through her chest. Her pulse thrummed in her ears.

She'd remember that scent all her life. And the woman who wore it. So exotic, so sophisticated. And so much more than little Marie Leonard. More beautiful, more accomplished. In every way, more.

No wonder Brandon had made her his wife.

But Charlotte had died six months ago. Why was Marie smelling her scent now? Here in the butler's quarters?

Sophie and Chelsea had talked about spirits communicating through images in mirrors, not voices carried on radio static, not scents. She was freaking herself out over nothing…wasn't she?

Pulse thrumming in her ears, she stepped out into her father's sitting room. The room was as vacant as before. She tested the air again. The scent was stronger, but it didn't seem to be coming from this room, either.

She followed her nose to the door leading to the estate office and kitchen area. The cloud cover had cleared outside, and stainless steel and stone counter-tops stretched long and cold in ribbons of feeble moon-light shining through window blinds. The scent was even stronger out here. It teased the air as if Charlotte had just walked through the room.

Ridiculous.

More likely Brandon had the furnace filters treated with the scent to remind him of Charlotte. Or Shelley used jasmine air fresheners to memorialize the mistress she adored, à la Mrs. Danvers from Daphne du Maurier's *Rebecca*. A giggle bubbled up in Marie's throat. She was being absurd, letting her imagination run away with her—first to ghosts and now to char-acters from novels. Silly or not, she followed the scent.

Marie wove her way through the kitchen and veered through the hall and into the dining room. She circled the grand table and stepped quietly across the parquet floor and oriental rugs in the first-floor sitting room. A hint of moonlight filtered through draperies, creating misty images on leaded mirrors. Images that almost looked like ghosts.

"Marie?" Brandon's voice boomed from the shad-ows. "What is it?"

Marie started. She whirled around to see him jolt up from a sofa in the sitting room.

His eyelids looked heavy, as if he'd just awakened. He reached for his cane and walked toward her. He stopped just inches away. Close enough for her to trail her fingertips over his stubbled chin and the slick, scarred skin of his cheek.

Marie's nerves jangled. For a moment she couldn't think.

His dark eyebrows dipped with concern. "Is something wrong?"

Something? *Everything* was wrong. Him standing so close. Her need to touch him, to hold him, to pretend the past ten years had never happened. She shook her head. "Don't you smell that scent?"

"What is it? Something burning?"

"No. It's like perfume. Jasmine." Maybe Brandon was used to it. Maybe he didn't even detect it anymore. Marie took another deep draw. The fragrance had faded, but the whisper of it was still there. "I noticed it in my father's room and followed it out here. Don't you smell it?"

"Jasmine?"

"It was the scent Charlotte used to wear."

His mouth flattened in a hard line. She could see him moving away from her, withdrawing, even though he hadn't physically moved an inch. "Why are you saying this?"

Realization hit her with the force of a slap across the face. She'd blurted out what was in her mind without any thought about who she was talking to, how bringing up his dead wife would make him feel. Her lack of tact knew no bounds.

She took a step backward as heat crept over her cheeks. "I'm sorry. I got carried away."

"Carried away by what?"

"My imagination, I guess. The house. The conversation I had with Sophie Caldwell."

"You talked about Charlotte?"

She shook her head. "We talked about ghosts."

If she'd thought he had given her a cold look before, she was mistaken. The temperature in the room dropped twenty degrees.

She'd better at least try to explain. "They wanted me to try to contact my father."

"That crazy psychomanteum of theirs?"

"I guess." She wished she could crawl under a rock. "I'm sorry for bringing up Charlotte. I just heard a voice and smelled that scent and my imagination went a little wild, I think."

"A voice?"

She shook her head again. She didn't want him to get the wrong impression. "On the radio. It was nothing. Like I said, just my imagination."

His lips softened. "You've been through a lot. Don't worry about it."

His kindness did more to rattle her than even his anger. "I didn't mean to… I'm going to go to bed now."

He leaned toward her, as if he wanted to touch her but didn't quite dare. "Let me help you."

Help her go to bed? She knew that wasn't what he meant, but another giggle bubbled up inside her, anyway. Fatigue. Hysteria. She choked it back.

Brandon didn't seem to realize her struggle. He looked at her with that same concerned look. A look that made her want to curl up in his arms and cry.

Finally he let out a heavy breath. "There's no reason you have to look into Edwin's death alone. I know people. I can help."

All she could manage was a nod.

"Has Hammer given you a copy of the accident report?"

"Yes." She forced a word out. A miracle.

"How about the autopsy?"

"No."

"What do you say tomorrow we go to Baltimore and have a talk with the medical examiner?"

"You can do that? I called, and his secretary or assistant or whatever gave me the runaround."

"I'll give him a call. He'll make time."

"Of course." The world worked differently for Brandon than it did for her. There were perks to being a Drake.

"Like I said before, Edwin was important to me, too. Very important." He gave her a controlled nod. "Tomorrow morning, then?"

Marie took a deep breath. The scent was gone. Even though the desire to touch Brandon still pulsed through her veins, she felt focused once again. Focused on her father, on finding his killer, on bringing his murderer to justice. As long as she could remember why she was here, she could handle the rest.

Even being around Brandon Drake. "See you tomorrow."

Chapter Five

By the time Marie ate Shelley's wonderful breakfast of crab benedict and rode to Baltimore in the quiet comfort of Brandon's chauffeured car, she was beginning to understand just how different Brandon's life was from her own. And when the Maryland medical examiner was actually waiting to talk to them, she knew accepting Brandon's help had been the right thing to do.

Or at least she hoped.

She concentrated on the harsh disinfectant and repulsive fleshy smells of the morgue. Staff bustled through the halls clad in baggy scrubs, some wearing stiff long-sleeved aprons over top. The distraction didn't work. She didn't have to look at Brandon to feel him next to her. She didn't have to smell the leather of his jacket to be aware of every move he made.

His almost black hair glistened in the fluorescent light. His black leather car coat accentuated his broad shoulders as if it were made for him alone. Of course, it probably was. Even his cane only played up the aristocratic air about him.

No wonder she'd fallen so hard when she was a

teenager. Good thing she knew better than to trust the emotions he brought out in her now.

The medical examiner was waiting for them when they entered his office. An older man with skin that resembled a wrinkled brown paper bag, he motioned for them to take off their coats and sit in a pair of chairs facing the desk. Brandon made introductions, and Marie shook the man's hand.

After the formalities were finished, Dr. Tracy started flipping through a pile of file folders lying on his bland, government-issue desk. "I'm sorry I haven't had time to pull your father's records from the recent cases. This will just take a second. Your town has been keeping us awfully busy lately, what with the state police excavation site."

After reading the first few articles back in Michigan, Marie had avoided the story of the mass grave, even though it was in papers and on news channels all over the country. The whole thing was too upsetting. Too depressing. The thought that all those people were victimized just because they wanted a better life. The thought that a doctor who'd sworn to do no harm had forced them to give up organs in return for their passage into the country. The thought that many had given their lives through no choice of their own, their hollow shells dumped into mass graves.

She shuddered. "They caught the men responsible for that, didn't they?"

"One is dead and now the other…" Dr. Tracy peered over his reading glasses at Marie, his hands still shuffling through a stack of reports. "You haven't heard."

"Heard what?"

"Franz Kreeger, the one who was jailed. They found him dead this morning."

Brandon's eyebrows dipped low. "Suicide?"

"I don't know. But I guess I'll find out."

Marie nodded, realizing that what the doctor said was literally true. He would find out, personally. Or at least he would with the help of his staff. Just as his staff would examine each of the bodies buried outside Jenkins Cove. "Have they recovered all the bodies from the mass grave?"

He shook his head. "They're bringing in new ones every day. Very old ones. Fresh ones. It seems like they'd need more than two men to do all that damage. Not that I'm speculating." He pulled a file from the pack and set the others aside. Adjusting his glasses, he flipped open the folder. "Now, how can I help?"

She paused, waiting for Brandon to speak. Instead, he gave her an encouraging nod.

She cleared her throat. "The police told me my father's death was an accident."

"And you want to know if it really was?"

"Yes."

"I can't tell you that."

"Can't tell me?" Marie slumped against the back of her chair. How could that be? "Don't you determine cause of death?"

"Yes. That's exactly what I try to do. And your father's cause of death was drowning."

Marie's throat tightened. Her father had always hated water. He'd always been scared to death of it. The fact that he'd drowned was unspeakably cruel.

"The police believe Edwin hit his head and fell in the water," Brandon said. "Is that possible?"

Marie pressed her lips into a grateful half smile. At this moment, she wasn't sure she could talk. Not unless she wanted to start bawling.

"Yes. He had an injury to the back of his head that could be considered consistent with that theory."

Marie tilted her head to the side. It sounded as though the medical examiner wasn't quite sure the police were on the right track.

Of course, that could just be what she wanted to hear. She forced her voice to remain steady. "Could it have happened differently?"

"Yes. When I say something is consistent with the police's theory, that doesn't mean their story of the death is the only one possible." The doctor glanced down at the report and then pointed to his own bald head. His finger stopped near the top. "The bruising occurred right about here."

"Did he have other bruising that suggested he fell on the rocks? Like on his back or shoulders?"

"No. He had some scrapes on his legs, but that could have been caused by the rocks after he was in the water."

Marie swallowed into an aching throat. She knew the doctor was trained to look at her father's death—any death—in an objective and emotionless way. But it was impossible for her to listen to these details with the same detachment. She was just glad, once again, that Brandon was with her.

Brandon narrowed his eyes on the doctor's head as if trying to visualize what had happened to her father that night. "So he would have had to fall nearly upside down. As if he went off the pier in a somersault and didn't make it all the way over."

The doctor nodded. "That could explain it."

Marie shook her head. That wasn't how she imagined it happening. That wasn't it at all. "He was hit from behind."

The doctor looked down at the report, then back to Marie. His expression was matter-of-fact, as if her statement didn't surprise him at all. "The bruising is such that he could have been hit from behind."

A trill vibrated up Marie's backbone. This was what she had come to find. Something that would prove he was murdered. Some kind of evidence Chief Hammer would have to acknowledge. "Will you tell the Jenkins Cove police chief that?"

Dr. Tracy's forehead furrowed. His lips took on a sympathetic slant. "Just because it's possible doesn't mean it happened that way."

"But it's more likely than my father walking along the water and doing a somersault onto the rocks."

The medical examiner waved his hands in the air between them, as if clearing out the words they'd spoken. "What I'm saying, Ms. Leonard, is I can't tell exactly how your father hit his head before he drowned. It could have happened exactly the way the police said. If you're looking for evidence he was murdered, this is not going to do it."

Marie lifted her eyes from the document in the doctor's hands and stared at the overhead lights. She couldn't let herself cry. She knew her father was murdered. The ambiguity of the autopsy results didn't change that. She'd just have to find better evidence. She'd have to dig harder.

But where to look next?

"Thank you for your time, Doctor." Brandon thrust out a hand. The men shook.

Marie stretched her hand out as well. Swallowing the emotion welling inside, she forced her voice to remain steady. "I appreciate your candor."

The doctor enfolded her hand in his. His graying brow furrowed in concern, as if he could sense how close she was to losing control. "If you have any further questions, you know how to reach me."

"Yes." She turned away and made for the door, needing to escape the smells, the emotion, the doctor's concern more than she remembered needing anything. Brandon slipped a gentle arm around her waist, and at his tender touch, her tears started to flow.

BRANDON HANDED Marie the pressed handkerchief Edwin always insisted he carry and guided her out of the morgue. He'd been amazed she'd been able to hold back her grief this long. While he hated to see her cry, he knew it would be better for her to let it out.

He spotted Josef waiting on a side street and flagged him to bring the town car over. The car sidled up to the curb, and Brandon helped Marie inside.

They were humming down the interstate skirting Annapolis by the time Marie composed herself enough to talk. "I'm sorry."

"Don't apologize. If Edwin was my father, I wouldn't be holding it together half as well as you are."

"That's not true. I'm a mess."

He wiped a tear from her cheek with his fingers. Despite his better judgment, he let his fingers linger, soaking up the satin feel of her skin, the warmth. Both he and Marie had lost their mothers when they were young. Ten years ago they'd connected through their shared experience. Even then he'd been impressed how strong and accepting she'd been of her mother's passing. And he knew how much she loved her father. "You're a lot of things, Marie. A mess isn't one of them."

"I don't know about that. I feel like I can't think straight."

That's how he felt, too, at least when he was this close to Marie. And he knew it had nothing to do with grief.

"I can't stand to think of him as just some case in a… It's just so hard."

He moved his fingertips over her cheek to her chin.

She tilted her face up to him. Her eyes glistened. Tears clumped her lashes. Her lips parted.

He leaned toward her. Kissing her right now felt like the most natural thing in the world. As though it was meant to be. Yet that didn't make it any less impossible.

Especially now.

He dropped his hand from her chin and stared straight ahead through the windshield. The Bay Bridge stretched in front of them, twin ribbons of steel curving high above the wide blue of the Chesapeake.

"Can you do me a favor?" Marie's voice sounded pinched.

"Anything."

"When we get back to Jenkins Cove, will you drop me at Thornton Garden Center? It's over—"

"I know where it is." She must want to see Lexie Thornton. Lexie had decorated Drake House for the annual Christmas Ball every year since she'd started working in her parents' business. And just this fall, Edwin had hired her to redesign the east garden. Brandon had forgotten she was Marie's childhood friend. He was relieved Marie still had a friend in the area. No doubt she needed a shoulder to cry on. He only wished it could be his. "Josef?"

The chauffeur nodded. "Thornton Garden Center. Yes, sir."

Chapter Six

Located on the edge of town in a redbrick building off Main Street, Thornton Garden Center was decked out like a Christmas wonderland. Pine bough swags and wreaths were draped dark and fragrant behind clusters of red, white, pink and blue poinsettias. Gold and silver ornaments filled baskets and decorated sample trees. And a variety of holiday-themed and other sun catchers filled wide windows, sparkling like curtains of colored and sculpted ice.

Marie pushed back memories of past Christmases amidst the grand decor of Drake House and entered the center. More decorations cluttered the inside, competing with flower pots, garden orbs and birdbaths waiting for spring. "Carol of the Bells" tinkled in the pine-scented air.

A man in jeans and a heavy sweater looked up from a stack of boxes he was unpacking. Ornate sleighs made of gold wire scattered the countertop in front of him. He held a price gun in one work-roughened hand. "Can I help you?"

"Is Lexie around?"

"She's in the back room working. If you wait just a second, I'll get her for you."

"You look busy. I'll just peek in myself, if you don't mind. I'm Marie Leonard. We're old friends."

His rough brow furrowed. "Any relation to Edwin Leonard?"

"My father."

"I'm sorry. I did some work for him at Drake House. He was a good man."

Marie gave him what she hoped was a grateful smile and nod. After the emotional upheaval she'd gone through in the morgue and in the car with Brandon, she didn't trust herself to talk. The last thing she needed was more tears. "I'll just go back." She turned away before he had the chance to say anything more. Reaching the small workroom, she peeked her head inside.

Lexie stood at a table strewn with pine boughs and ribbon. She attached a luxurious gold bow to a Christmas wreath.

Only a day had passed since Marie had seen Lexie at her father's service, but after all that had happened, she was so relieved to see her friend, it felt as if it had been weeks. "You told me to stop in. I hope my timing is okay."

"Marie. Your timing is perfect. I'm just finishing these up to bring to a client." Lexie set the wreath down, circled the table and took Marie's hands in hers. "Are you okay?"

Marie tried her best to smile. After her latest bout of crying, her nose was sore and her eyelids felt like overfilled sausage casings. She must look horrible. "I'm fine."

Lexie looked doubtful. "I'm not buying it."

The hazards of having a best friend. Even after all this time, Lexie could see right through her. Once again, tears threatened to break free. She shook her head. "How much can one person cry?"

Lexie surrounded her in a hug. "You lost your dad, Marie. Grieving is normal."

Marie nodded, her cheek snug to Lexie's shoulder. If anyone knew about grief, it was Lexie. Marie and Brandon could never be together, but at least she knew he was living his life, albeit without her.

And that was precisely why she'd needed to see Lexie this afternoon.

She pulled out of her friend's embrace and looked her straight in the eye. "You might think I've lost it, but I have a favor to ask you."

"I would never think you'd lost anything."

"Wait until you hear the favor."

"Okay, shoot."

"Do you know anything about the woman who owns House of the Seven Gables?"

"The bed-and-breakfast? Sure. Sophie Caldwell. She comes into the shop. I helped with some of the decorating for their big holiday open house. What about her?"

"She has a way to communicate with people who have died." She told Lexie about the psychomanteum.

Marie waited to see the skeptical look sweep over Lexie's features. It didn't. Instead, she nodded. "You want to try to speak to your father."

Marie teared up, this time with relief. "You don't think that's weird?"

Lexie shrugged. "Weird? No. I'm not convinced it will work, but I think it's natural for you to want to talk to your dad, to say goodbye."

"That's not all I want to say."

"You want to ask him how to handle Brandon Drake?"

Marie choked back a bitter laugh. She could still feel the heat of Brandon's fingertips on her cheek, her chin. And her chest still ached from the way he'd pulled back. She didn't know if she wanted to talk about Brandon. Not even with Lexie. "My father would tell me to handle him by staying far, far away. And he would be right."

Lexie nodded to a nearby window. "I saw his car drop you off. And I heard you were staying at Drake House. It doesn't seem like you're staying very far away."

So much for avoiding the subject of Brandon. She'd forgotten how quickly news could travel in a small town like Jenkins Cove. "Where did you hear I'm staying at Drake House?"

"Shelley Zachary. You gave her something to gossip about, something besides Brandon's reasons for canceling the Christmas Ball." Lexie shook her head.

"You didn't tell me he was hurt when Charlotte died."

"I'm sorry, Marie. Your father asked me not to. He was afraid you'd come back. And I have to admit I agreed with him. The last time you were around Brandon, things didn't turn out so well. Be careful, won't you?"

Marie nodded, but she could tell by Lexie's expression that her friend wasn't convinced. "I'm just staying there to see if I can find some kind of evidence my father was murdered."

"That's another reason you're thinking about going to this psychomanteum thing at Sophie Caldwell's, aren't you? You want to ask about his death."

Marie nodded. She'd told Lexie her suspicions the morning before her father's funeral. Now after hearing what the medical examiner had to say, she felt she was on the right track. If she could learn something from the psychomanteum, anything at all, it would be worth it. "What do you think of the idea?"

Lexie shrugged. "Try it. What's to lose?"

"Will you come with me?"

Lexie shifted her work boots on the floor. "To hold your hand?" It was meant as a quip, but judging from Lexie's discomfort, she knew what Marie was about to say next.

"To contact Simon."

Lexie started shaking her head before the words were out of Marie's mouth. "Simon died thirteen years ago, Marie. There's no use trying to relive the past."

"Why not? Like you said, it might not work, but there's nothing to lose."

"There's nothing to gain, either. Simon's dead. Let's just leave it that way."

Marie nodded. She didn't want to press her friend. Lexie had gone through enough after Simon had died on that Christmas Eve they had planned to run away together. She'd raised his daughter alone. She'd thrown herself into her family's business. She'd pulled her life together. The last thing Marie wanted to do was make her feel as though she had to revisit those dark times. "You're right. You've moved on. You've done an amazing job with Katie."

Lexie pressed her lips into a smile. "Thanks. Although you might not agree when you meet her. She's got a pretty good preteen snit going on these days."

"I hear her mother and her mother's friend were pretty good at that preteen snit in their day."

Lexie smiled. "My mom always told me she hoped I had a daughter like me. Now she reminds me of that regularly."

At the mention of Lexie's mom, the tears misted Marie's eyes. She was all alone now. Now she didn't even have her dad. "I want to see your parents before I go back to Michigan."

"They would have your hide if you didn't." Lexie laid a hand on Marie's shoulder. "But now why don't you go ahead and try to contact your father? I have to deliver these wreaths to a client who lives near the harbor. I'll drive you to Sophie Caldwell's place."

MARIE FOLLOWED SOPHIE up the staircase to the third floor of the old bed-and-breakfast. She'd been chattering nonstop since Marie and Lexie had shown up at the door. Fine with Marie. The more Sophie talked, the less Marie had to. And right now she was so nervous, she doubted she could string three words together that made sense.

"The best way to do this is to spend a day meditating and centering yourself, honey. But nowadays, I know people just don't seem to have the time."

Unease fluttered in Marie's chest. "No. No time."

"I know you think I'm a little crazy with all this stuff, but you don't have to believe in ghosts, if you don't want to. Think of this as meditating. Just relax and open yourself to your deepest thoughts. That's all you need to do."

All? Right now she felt as though relaxing was the

toughest thing in the world, and she was trying to avoid her deepest thoughts.

"I use breathing exercises. In through the nose, out through the mouth. Count slowly while you're doing it. It calms me." Sophie reached the hallway at the top of the steps and spun to face Marie. She breathed in and out, moving her arms with each breath as if conducting an orchestra. She kept it up until Marie joined in. "That's it, sweetheart. In and out. In and out. Starting to feel better?"

"Strangely enough, I am."

"Good. Now follow me." Sophie pushed through a door and led Marie into a darkened room. She flicked a light switch.

Even with the overhead light blazing, the room still felt dark. Black-curtained walls, black ceiling and dark carpet made the space feel smaller than it probably was. Marie eyed the single chair positioned in the room's center. It faced a large gold-framed mirror. "That's the oracle."

"That's right."

Even though she knew the mirror was merely silvered glass, it felt deeper, as if it were calling to her, drawing her in.

She pulled her gaze away and scanned the rest of the items in the space. Antique chests and small tables dotted the carpet, the surface of each one covered with equally antique candelabra holding tapers and other holders cradling fat column candles.

"You built this place?"

"With the help of my handyman, Phil. Phil Cardon. I'm determined, but not exactly strong. Not physically strong, anyway." She pulled a long lighter from one of the tables and bustling around the room, she lit the candles. Once she'd finished, she snapped off the overhead switch. A gentle, flickering light filled the room. "I made my own candles, too. Sometimes scent is part of the experience we get from the other side. Perfumed candles can mask that. So all these are one hundred percent fragrance free."

Marie thought of the jasmine she'd smelled in Drake House. Maybe she was right to think of ghosts when she'd experienced that scent. Not that Brandon would agree.

Pressure assaulted her chest at the thought of him.

She pressed her hand against her breastbone and looked into the mirror. Her emotions were so jumbled where Brandon was concerned. That was part of why she was here. The part Lexie had guessed.

Her father loved Brandon like a son, yet he'd warned Marie about him ten years ago. About his need to be in control of his emotions. About his choice to marry Charlotte. Marie's father had helped her break her ties with Brandon and start a new life. She needed him to help her sort through her feelings now. "I sit in the chair, right?"

"That's right, dear. Look into the mirror and relax. Use those breathing exercises."

"How long will it take?"

"There's no telling. Sometimes communication happens right away. Sometimes it can take hours to open yourself up enough."

Marie lowered herself into the chair. Hours. She couldn't see herself staring into a mirror for hours. She didn't even like looking at her face for the five minutes it took to put on makeup in the morning. "I hope it's faster than that."

"You have to be patient." She could hear Sophie rustle toward the door behind her. "Concentrate on your father. How much you love him. How much you miss him." The woman's voice faltered. Clearly she was talking about her own feelings as much as Marie's.

Before Marie could turn around, the door closed, and she could hear Sophie's footsteps receding down the stairs.

Marie turned back to the mirror and looked into her own eyes. Tears sparkled at their corners in the candle-light. She did love her father. She did miss him. She ached at the prospect that she'd never again see his smile.

She scrutinized her own smile in the mirror. She wasn't ugly, but she was a far cry from the glamorous Charlotte. She didn't need a picture to remember Char-lotte's wavy blond hair and flawless skin, her vibrant laugh, her sparkling, intelligent eyes. That was the woman Brandon had chosen. And that was the image she should keep in her mind, especially after what had happened today.

Or *almost* happened.

She let her eyes stare and become unfocused. Relax. That was what Sophie had said. Drift. Her image blurred, obscured by clouds of light and dark. This was better. At least now she didn't have to stare at herself, compare herself to Charlotte. She could just drift…open herself…love her father….

At first she didn't identify the scent. Exotic. Slightly spicy. Pleasant.

She pulled in a deep breath. It was that jasmine blend, all right. The same scent she had followed through the halls of Drake House. Charlotte's scent. She breathed in again, but the scent was gone.

She shifted in the chair.

"Marie." The voice was light as air.

Had Sophie returned? Marie twisted to look behind her.

The door was closed, the room empty.

"Murder." The voice again. The same one she'd heard in the radio static. Or was it?

A tremor seized Marie's chest.

"Murder."

There it was again, faint, indistinct. Marie could swear the sound was coming from the mirror, yet it was all over the room at the same time. "Daddy?" Even as she called out, she knew the whisper wasn't his. She stared at the center of the gold frame, waiting to see something, anything. But only her own reflection stared back. Candlelight danced behind her. "Who's there?"

The scent tickled her senses again. Jasmine.

"Charlotte? Is that you?"

The scent grew stronger.

This was crazy. It couldn't be happening. She must have fallen asleep in her chair. She must be dreaming.

Cold moved over her. Penetrating deep like the first cut of a blade. She gripped her legs and dug fingertips into the muscles of her thighs. "Charlotte? If it's you, answer."

"Marie." The voice hissed like a steam radiator. The scent grew overpowering.

Marie forced herself to stay in the chair, though every cell in her body clamored to run. "Charlotte? What is it? Why are you communicating with me?"

"Love." The hiss trailed off, but the word was clear.

Charlotte loved her? She found that impossible to believe. "You love Brandon. That's why you're speaking to me?"

"Love."

"Are you trying to warn me away from Brandon? Is that it? Are you staking your claim to him even from the grave?" Marie's inside shook. With fear, with anger, she wasn't sure which. She was getting tired of playing this guessing game. She wanted answers, and she wanted them now. "Out with it, Charlotte. What are you trying to say?"

The cold deepened. The tremor inside her grew until her whole body shook.

The hiss came again, barely loud enough to hear. "All Brandon loves will die."

Chapter Seven

Marie was still shaking when she arrived at the Jenkins Cove Police Station, only a few blocks from the B&B. After she heard the voice, she'd panicked, bolting out of the attic room. She'd escaped from the House of the Seven Gables without explaining to Sophie anything of what she'd experienced. What was she going to say? That Charlotte's ghost had spoken to her? That Charlotte said she was murdered? That the entity had suggested Brandon was responsible?

All Brandon loves will die.

Charlotte's ghost hadn't come out and said Brandon was responsible, only that those he loved would die. But what did that mean? That Charlotte's ghost would kill anyone Brandon loved? Was she warning Marie away?

Marie gathered her wool coat tight at the neck with one hand and clutched her bag against her side with the other. She didn't know what to believe. Heck, she didn't even know what she'd just experienced. But one thing was clear. She needed to know more about Charlotte's death. And save asking Brandon, the only place she could think to get that kind of information was the Jenkins Cove Police Station.

She set her jaw and mounted the steps of the remodeled old house that served as home to the police department. She wasn't sure how she was going to explain her questions to Chief Hammer. He'd probably think she was some kind of paranoid conspiracy nut, seeing a murder behind every accident.

She'd be happy if paranoia was all it was.

She stepped into the entry. Still sporting its original hardwood floors, the station looked very little like a house on the inside. Instead of a foyer, a high desk squatted about ten feet from the door, making it impossible to get into the rest of the station without being seen. A heavy woman wearing a trim polo shirt emblazoned with the Jenkins Cove PD seal looked up from the bank of three computer screens surrounding her. "Can I help you?"

"I was wondering if I could talk to someone about an accident investigation."

"Miss Leonard." Chief Hammer's voice vibrated off the hardwood floors. He poked his head around a corner and gave her an insincere smile. "Are you still *investigating* your father's death?"

She couldn't help note his patronizing tone. "Yes, I'm still looking for answers. But that's not why I'm here this afternoon. I was wondering if you could answer some questions I have about another matter."

Chief Hammer looked relieved. He actually gave her a friendly smile. "Come on in, then. We're pretty shorthanded around here, but I'll see what I can do."

He led her into a surprisingly large office just around the corner from the dispatcher. "Have a seat."

Marie sat, though she'd rather stand. At least she remembered her manners this time. No reason to get the chief defensive about her refusing his offer of a chair before their chat even began. "I was wondering if you could fill me in on another accident that took place at Drake House in the past year."

His relieved look melted like an early snow. "Charlotte Drake."

"Yes."

He groaned and shook his head. "A horrible, tragic accident. But I'm not sure what you expect from me. If you want to know more about Mrs. Drake's accident, why don't you ask Brandon Drake himself? I hear you're staying out at Drake House."

It seemed the entire town knew she was staying at Drake House. Of course, Chief Hammer had learned of it from last night's break-in, not Shelley's gossip. "Brandon is still grieving. I don't want to upset him if I can help it." At least that was the truth.

"Of course." The chief leaned back in his desk chair and tented his fingers. "I'll do my best to answer, within reason. What do you want to know?"

"What happened that night?"

"Charlotte, er, Mrs. Drake was drinking. Late in the evening she got into her car. She lost control, and her car collided with a stone wall on the property. The gas tank ruptured, and the fuel ignited."

"And Brandon?"

"Oh yes. Brandon was badly burned trying to pull her out of the fire."

Marie loosened her grip on her coat. She set her bag in the chair beside her. Brandon had risked his life to save Charlotte. So he couldn't have been responsible, could he?

Murder.

The word popped into Marie's mind, carried on a whisper as it had been in the psychomanteum and on the radio. If not Brandon, could someone else have killed Charlotte? "Was there any evidence of foul play?"

There was the expression she knew was coming. The expression that said Chief Hammer thought she was out of her ever-loving mind. "You're kidding, right?" He glanced around his office as if Marie were setting him up, and he was searching for the camera that must be recording the joke.

"No. I'm not kidding. I'm asking. Was there any chance Charlotte's death wasn't completely accidental?"

His gaze finally landed back on her. "It was an accident, Miss Leonard. Just like your father's death was an accident. Neither of them was murdered."

"I can understand why it seems far-fetched for Drake House to see two unrelated murders in the span of six months, Chief. But two accidents in that time span seems odd, too." She paused, weighing her words, careful not to offend Chief Hammer. "What if my father found out something about Charlotte's death? What if he was murdered to keep him quiet?"

A bushy brow crooked toward his nonexistent hairline. "Are you sure you're not some kind of murder-mystery writer?"

"I'm serious, Chief."

"I'm serious, too, Miss Leonard. I don't know what you're after here, but this is ridiculous. And it's starting to get on my nerves. We're very busy around here with real life. I don't need to spend any more of my time on your silly theories."

Obviously she had no talent for diplomacy. "Really, if you hear me—"

"I'm done here, Miss Leonard." Hammer rose to his full modest height. "If there's anything rational that we can do for you here at the police department, let us know."

"Would it be possible for me to see Charlotte Drake's accident report?"

"Why would you want to do that?"

"I need to understand what happened."

Hammer puffed out his bulldog cheeks. He didn't move.

"Accident reports are public record, aren't they?"

With a grunt, he thrust himself from his chair and stalked to the office door. "I'll get them for you. It might take a while. Half my staff is assisting the state police." He closed the door behind him, leaving her alone in the office.

Time ticked by, and Hammer didn't return. Finally Marie left the office to find out what had happened to the chief and his promise. Rounding the corner, she stepped into the dispatch area.

The last person she expected to see was Brandon. But there he was, powerfully sexy in his black leather coat, taking a sheaf of papers from the chief himself. "Hello, Marie."

"CHIEF HAMMER CALLED you, didn't he?" Marie stopped stock-still on the police station's front porch and stared a hole through Brandon.

Brandon's gut ached. "What does it matter? You needed a ride back to Drake House, anyway." He looked out across the street where his car idled, Josef waiting patiently for them. Clouds hung low and ominous in the sky. The air smelled like coming rain.

"You could have waited until I called. You could have sent the car. Why did he call you? Because I was asking too many questions?"

"Because you were forcing him to work too hard, I think."

Marie and he had found common ground when he'd mentioned Hammer's laziness last night. Now her expression darkened and she clamped her jaw tight. "What did he say to you? Be honest."

Brandon should have known Marie wouldn't let him get away with ducking the subject. He used to like that about her. Her directness. Her doggedness. Now he wasn't so sure. "He said you were asking a lot of questions about Charlotte. Questions he thought I could do a better job of answering."

"Or a better job of avoiding?"

She was right. The last thing he wanted to do was stand here in the rain and talk about Charlotte. Especially with her.

"You rushed over here to get me to back off, didn't you?"

"Yes."

"You don't want to talk about Charlotte."

"No."

Her lips tightened. She clutched the top of her coat, pulling it protectively around her throat.

"What do you expect me to do? Lie? I don't want to relive Charlotte's death, especially not with you." He gripped the head of his cane until his fingers ached. His wedding band dug into his flesh. Having Marie around had been a struggle from the first moment. Between his old feelings for her coming to life and his need to keep from hurting her again, he'd tied himself in knots. But he really couldn't stomach dredging up his past with Charlotte. His failure. His guilt. Scars so much deeper than the ones on his face and leg. "Why are you asking about Charlotte? What could you possibly need to know?"

"I think she was murdered."

He took a step backward, his heel hitting the base of the porch railing. He'd been ready for her to say a lot of things, but not that. "Why on earth would you think she was murdered?"

She rolled her lower lip inward and grasped it in her teeth. "Something Sophie Caldwell said."

"What?"

"She said my father discovered something right before he died. Something he told her was dangerous."

"Why do you think whatever it was he found has anything to do with Charlotte's death?"

She searched his eyes, her gaze moving back and forth as if she wasn't finding what she was looking for. "Doesn't it seem strange to you? I mean, two fatal accidents at Drake House in a six month time period?"

"I already told you I agree your father's death seems suspicious."

"Then an accident and a murder."

"Coincidences can happen."

She stiffened and shook her head. "You're not listening."

"No, you're not listening, Marie. I *know* Charlotte wasn't murdered. I know why she died. I was there, remember?"

She released her coat and balled her fists at her sides, her chest rising and falling with shaky breaths. "No, I don't remember. You haven't told me anything about

Charlotte's death. Neither did Chief Hammer. Neither did my father or Lexie. Everyone seems to be trying to protect me. Well, I don't need protection. And I don't want it. I want the truth. I want some answers."

"Charlotte wasn't murdered."

She held up a hand as if shielding herself from his words. "*I* have reason to believe she was. Not just what Sophie said, but reasons I don't want to talk about. *And* I have reason to believe my father was murdered after he found out who killed her. Probably by the same person."

He drew in a breath to speak.

Marie gestured again with her hand. Her fingers were trembling. "I don't want to hear your pronouncements. If you can't enlighten me, stay out of my way."

God, he hated to see her so upset. And he had no one to blame but himself. He had been avoiding the subject of Charlotte since her death. It was the reason he avoided venturing out into public wherever possible. It was the reason he canceled the Christmas Ball. It was the reason he discouraged the few servants he tolerated around him from even mentioning her name. He even tried to prevent himself from thinking about her, although he failed regularly at that. And since Marie had come back to Drake House…

He waved an arm, directing Josef to swing the car around to this side of the street. Brandon knew that he'd made a royal mess of everything, and that he needed to set things straight. To come clean. At least with Marie. The rest of the damage he'd done could never be repaired. "Marie? Get in the car and I'll tell you everything."

As Josef pulled to the curb, Brandon stepped off the

porch. Drizzle misted the car's windows and felt cool on his cheeks. He opened the back door and gestured Marie inside.

She held his eyes for a second, as if deciding whether he was sincere about his promise. Then she slid into the seat. He followed, settling in beside her. For a moment all he could think about was kissing her, actually going through with it this time and pressing his lips to hers. Tasting her mouth. Feeling her body yield to his, soft and accepting.

He nodded for Josef to drive and focused straight ahead. As they drove through town, he watched the windshield wipers sweep the glass periodically and searched for words that would make this easier.

Nothing would make it easier.

Finally he just spoke. "Charlotte lost control of her car. As she was leaving Drake House, she veered off the drive just before the gate and hit the rock wall. Her car caught fire. I heard the impact. I saw the fire. I tried to pull her out, but she was trapped in the wreckage. She died right in front of me. I heard her last screams." He kept his voice flat, unemotional, but his stomach seized involuntarily at the memory. Charlotte's screams were always in his nightmares. Always lurking in the back of his mind.

Marie shook her head. "A woman doesn't just race her car into a stone wall. A car doesn't just burst into flame."

"I was there. It did."

"Did you see her before it happened?"

The tension in his stomach turned to nausea. And he'd thought this couldn't get worse.

"You said you'd explain. You said you'd tell me everything."

He blew air through tight lips. "Yes, I did."

"So?"

"Yes, I saw her."

"Was she upset about anything? How did she seem? Chief Hammer said she was drinking."

"She was."

"Why?"

For a one word question, that one was about as complicated as a question could get. "She just did. She collected fine wine. I still have the wine cellar to prove it."

"So she always drank?"

"She liked her wine."

"Chief Hammer said there was a vodka bottle."

"Yes. The police found it in the car. He told me that after the accident."

"Did Charlotte drink a lot?"

He couldn't stand this. "I don't think this has anything to do with anything. Sure, she was drunk. Sure, she shouldn't have been behind the wheel."

"Then why was she? Josef could have driven her, couldn't he? Was he working for you then?"

"She could have had him drive her. Back then we used him more as a handyman than a driver. We usually drove ourselves." He looked down at his leg. Those days were over. Now he was lucky to be able to walk, albeit with a cane. His doctor doubted his reflexes would ever be sharp enough again to drive safely.

Marie shook her head. "Charlotte didn't strike me as the type of woman who would—"

"We had a fight, all right? She was upset with me. That's why she was drinking. That's why she got behind the wheel. That's why she crashed."

The click of the turn signal and the swoosh of the wipers were the only sounds as they approached the long, winding drive. The gray stone wall stretched along the highway, opening only for the classic white pillar entrance of Drake House and the ostentatious redbrick and cast iron of his uncle's neighboring estate, The Manor at Drake Acres. Josef slowed the car to make the turn.

Brandon stared straight out the window. He didn't want to witness Marie's reaction to his confession. Getting the words out had been hard enough. Nor could he bear to look out the side window and see the stone wall as they passed.

The wall that still held a shadow of fire.

"It's not your fault, Brandon." Her voice sounded calm, soothing, forgiving.

He shook his head. He couldn't let himself listen. It was enough to undo him. "You still don't understand. It *is* my fault. It's all my fault. Charlotte was a good wife. She was kind and beautiful and so damn smart. She was any man's dream. And what did I do to repay her?" He lowered his head and pinched the bridge of his nose between thumb and forefinger. He couldn't explain. Not to Marie. Never to Marie.

"You had an affair?"

"No!"

"What, then? What did you fight about?"

He promised he'd tell her everything. He promised he'd be honest with her. But how could he be honest about this?

"What did you fight about, Brandon? What was so bad?"

He clutched the head of his cane in both hands.

Avoiding the platinum gleam of the ring around his finger, he raised his eyes to meet hers.

Most men probably wouldn't find Marie as beautiful as Charlotte. But most men were fools. To him, one look into Marie's eyes was more addictive than any drug. It had always been that way. Ever since the summer when he'd come home with his MBA from Harvard and found her all grown up. And try as he might, he hadn't been able to change his response. He couldn't change his response to her even now. "Charlotte and I fought about you."

Chapter Eight

"Me?" The word caught in Marie's throat, almost choking her. She couldn't have heard Brandon right. How could they have fought about her? At the time of Charlotte's death, she hadn't seen either of them for ten years. "I don't understand."

"Of course you don't. You're strong, resilient. After that summer, you moved on."

"After that summer?" Marie's stomach tightened into a knot. There was no question what summer he meant. The summer she'd given him everything she was, and he'd tossed it away. "You make it seem as if moving on was my choice. As if I had a choice at all. After that summer, you got married."

The car's tires popped over loose gravel. Drake House loomed at the end of the winding drive, bright white columns glowing in the dreary weather, gray slate roof glistening with rain. The crunch of the tires slowed. The car stopped in front of the main entrance.

"You were so young, just out of high school. I already had my MBA. I was ready to settle down in Jenkins Cove and run the Drake Foundation. I couldn't tie you down when you hadn't even had a chance to see the world."

"That's what my father told you."

"And he was right. You deserved the chance to live your own life. To see the world beyond Jenkins Cove. To discover who you wanted to be." He lifted his hand. For a moment, he let it hover in the air, as if he wanted to touch her, before returning it to his cane. "It wasn't just that. I had already promised Charlotte. She was a good woman. My age. Already accomplished. Ready to settle down. I thought she was the perfect wife for me. I had no misgivings about marrying her. Not until…that summer with you. That summer made me rethink everything I thought I knew, everything I thought I felt. I didn't know what to trust—feelings that had swept me up in one summer or plans that were years in the making."

So he went with the plans.

Marie stared at the grand house. She didn't want to hear this. Any of it. She'd tried so hard to overcome her feelings for Brandon. She'd tried so hard to forget him and stand on her own. "Why are you telling me this?"

"You asked."

"I asked about Charlotte's death. Not about you and me."

"But it's all linked. It's all tangled into one giant mess."

She focused on Brandon. "How?"

He tore his eyes from hers. "Josef?"

The chauffeur glanced over his shoulder. "Yes, sir?"

"We would like some privacy. Just turn off the engine and leave the car here."

"Very good, sir." The chauffeur switched off the engine and left the keys dangling in the ignition. He climbed from the driver's seat and closed the door behind him, the sound followed by an abrupt and deep silence.

Marie watched him cut across the lawn to the carriage house. With each step he took away from the car, the more panicked she felt. She wanted to call the chauffeur back, ask him to stay, use him to shield her from whatever was coming. She didn't know what Brandon was going to say, but she had the feeling that whatever it was, it would be better for her not to hear.

"Charlotte deserved someone who loved her."

Marie let his words settle into her brain. She felt Brandon's pain in them, his regret. But the shift inside her was more insidious, more dangerous. It was the shift from numbness to hope.

And that scared her more than anything.

She clutched the bag in her lap and held on. She had to get a grip on herself. She was no longer eighteen. She had to remember all she'd learned.

Her father had warned her about Brandon that summer. He'd told her of Brandon's childhood. Of the heartbreak Brandon suffered when he'd lost his mother and the tightrope he'd had to walk to please his demanding father and grandfather. Her father feared Brandon had been damaged. He feared all the trauma he'd suffered as a boy had combined to make him afraid to open himself to love. To vulnerability.

Even with a woman as amazing as Charlotte.

And that's what she had to keep foremost in her mind. Her father's warning. Her father's fears. Not the way Brandon had looked at her that summer as if she were beautiful. Not his tenderness when they'd made love, when she'd given him her virginity. And certainly not the kiss he'd almost given her this morning, the kiss she still longed to claim.

"That night..." Brandon's voice cracked. He drew a

deep breath. "The night Charlotte died, she asked me for one thing. Something I couldn't give."

Marie wrapped her arms around her middle and held on. She needed to stay in control of her feelings, her fantasies. She didn't want to go back to that raw, painful place. The place it had taken her years to escape.

Brandon reached into his pocket and pulled out a leather wallet. He flipped it open and slipped something free. He handed Marie a small photograph.

She tilted it toward the car's window. Her high school graduation picture stared back at her, long hair, freckles, goofy smile and all. "My senior picture?"

"Charlotte found it the night she died. She asked me to get rid of it. I couldn't."

Marie looked up at him. She didn't want to know…she didn't want to ask…but she couldn't help it. "Why?"

"I don't know."

She closed her eyes. She'd dreamed for years that someday Brandon would tell her he loved her. That he'd made a mistake. That he wanted her instead of Charlotte. Now even though he'd admitted to arguing with his wife about her picture, he still wouldn't say those special words.

And the worst part of it all, the part that made her feel sick inside, was that she still wanted to hear them. "That's what you fought over? My picture?"

"Yes." He shook his head, the movement slow and sad. "I never should have asked Charlotte to marry me. It wasn't fair to her. But I didn't know that. Not until after I'd proposed. Not until that summer."

That summer. Their summer. Marie watched the drizzle bead up and slide down the window like tears.

Now that he'd put his regrets out there, she had to know the rest. "Why did you go through with the wedding?"

"I didn't know how to break it off. There were so many reasons not to. My promise to her. Our families. And she suited me. At least I thought she should. My feelings for you were so new. So overwhelming. I'd never experienced feelings like that before. I didn't trust them. And because I was weak and indecisive…" He pinched the bridge of his nose once more, as if he thought doing so would push back the tears. "And because I was weak and indecisive, Charlotte paid the price."

Marie wrapped her arms tighter. She felt cold. Colder even than the Michigan winter. Suddenly what he'd been trying to say about Charlotte's death dawned on her, what he'd been trying to tell her all along. "You think she committed suicide."

He looked past her, past Drake House. Pain etched his face. His eyes looked more flat and hopeless than the overcast sky.

She had to go on. She had to know. For so long she'd kept a glimmer of hope alive…the wish that she and Brandon would find a way to be together. She'd tended it like a flicker of fire in the hearth, but with his confession, Brandon had doused the flame. "You think she killed herself because of you. Because you couldn't love her the way she needed. Because of the feelings you had for me. That's why you feel so guilty. You blame yourself for her death."

He looked down at his hands, knuckles white, clutching the carved head of his cane. He didn't speak. He didn't nod. He didn't answer at all.

He didn't have to.

MARIE STOOD in the darkened foyer of Drake House and stared up at the majestic twin staircase. For the first time she could remember, she felt truly relieved to be away from Brandon. After disabling the alarm and instructing her to lock the door behind him, he'd said something about wanting to check the boathouse. Promising to be back soon, he'd left her in the house alone.

Understandable that he wanted to be alone with his thoughts. With his regrets. She wanted to be alone, too, but not to think. She would be just fine if she never had to think of this evening again.

She mounted the steps. When she reached the first landing where the staircase split, each branch leading into opposite wings of the mansion, she paused. To the right, the stairs climbed into the house's grand ballroom and outer sitting rooms. Usually this time of year, the wing would be humming with activity as servants and outside contractors like Lexie readied it for the annual Drake House Christmas Ball. It would smell of pine boughs and cinnamon and jingle with music. Instead the space felt vacant and dead. No festive decor. No bustling energy. Just a forlorn sadness that made Marie miss her childhood Christmases even more.

But she wasn't here to relive Christmas memories and mourn the demise of Drake House tradition.

She turned away from the public west wing and started up the stairs that led east. She wasn't sure how Brandon would feel about her snooping in the house's private wing. Especially after what he'd just confessed. But just in case he didn't like the idea, she wasn't going to wait to ask permission. Better to ask forgiveness, as the saying went. Better still to find some evidence of murder—either Charlotte's or her father's. Then she wouldn't have to ask for anything.

Climbing the steps, Marie moved out of the light of the foyer and into the dark, enclosed portion of the staircase that led up to the rooms on the third floor. She groped along the wall. She had no idea where the light switches for the stairs and halls were located in this wing. She had only been in this area of the house a few times when she was young. The last time she'd ventured this way, she'd been exploring the house with Lexie. When her father had discovered them in the private wing unaccompanied and without permission, he'd grounded her for a week and called Lexie's parents. After that, they'd confined their exploring to the ballroom, parlors and guest quarters of the public wing.

She gripped the banister, feeling jittery in the dark, as if her father were going to jump out at any moment and demand to know why she was there. She smiled at the thought. She wouldn't mind being grounded for a week if she could see his face once more. She wouldn't mind at all.

Reaching the third floor, she stopped and tried to get her bearings. The rain sounded as if it was coming down harder now, its patter a constant din on the roof a full floor above her head. Located on a jut of land, Drake House offered views of the water on three sides. She peered through an open door facing the forest side of the house. The nursery. Big enough to house half a dozen children, it stood empty now, the whimsical carving of animals along the ceiling molding merely a reminder of the next generation of Drake children who would never occupy this space. She passed several locked doors she remembered were the nanny's quarters and various other rooms before reaching the back staircase that led to the third floor.

If she remembered correctly, Charlotte's study overlooked the east garden, which would put it at the end of the wing. When her father was first working up plans with Lexie for redesigning the garden's landscaping, he'd mentioned how enthusiastic Charlotte had been, since her rooms overlooked that part of the property.

Unfortunately, she'd died before work on the garden began.

Marie forced her feet to move down the dark hall. A door facing the water side of the house stood open. Despite a shimmer of unease at the back of her neck, she stopped in front of an open door and peered inside.

The wet glisten of rain and water shone through windows unencumbered by draperies. Heavy, masculine chairs clustered in the sitting area. The scent of leather hung rich in the air. She stepped farther into the room, to the next open door and the chamber beyond. A bed big enough for five people faced a window overlooking Chesapeake Bay.

The master bedroom suite.

Marie's pulse pounded in her ears. It didn't take much imagination to see Brandon in that bed, leaning back against the pillows, his bare chest gleaming in the first glow of the morning sun.

She shook her head. Blocking the image in her mind's eye, she returned to the hall. She felt like that girl again, exploring places she shouldn't, indulging in feelings she had no business feeling. She needed to forget what she and Brandon had together all those years ago. Forget the hurt. Forget it all.

Hearing Charlotte's voice and smelling her scent in the psychomanteum might or might not qualify her as insane, but going through the same thing over and over with Brandon and expecting a different outcome was the *definition* of insanity. She needed to wipe Brandon from her mind…and her heart.

Swallowing into a dry throat, she walked farther down the hall. She passed the open entrance to Brandon's study and skipped the door she knew led up to the widow's walk on the roof. At the eastern-most end of the wing, she stopped at a locked door and pulled the ring of keys from her bag. Trying each, she finally found the one that fit. She let herself in and flicked on the light.

Lamps artfully positioned around the room gave off a soft glow. The room was as feminine as the master suite was masculine. Dainty antique chairs covered with silk damask gathered around a fireplace. Built-in bookshelves flanked an ornate antique desk. Pillows decorated a floral sofa. And the scent…jasmine.

She drew in a deep, slow breath. Sure enough. The same scent she'd noticed last night. The same one she'd smelled in the psychomanteum. This wasn't her imagination. She wasn't crazy. This was real.

Like last night, she let the scent lead her across the study, toward the windows and the desk positioned underneath.

If Charlotte's spirit was responsible for the scent of jasmine and the voice she'd heard in the psychomanteum, maybe she was trying to tell Marie something now. "Charlotte? Are you here?"

There was no reply.

"Is there something to find here?"

Again, silence answered.

Great. Now she was talking to herself. At least there was no one home to hear. She could just imagine how Brandon would feel about her wandering through the house calling out his dead wife's name. "Charlotte, if that's you, did you commit suicide?"

A sharp thud came from somewhere in the house.

Marie jumped. Was that an answer? Or was the wind kicking up outside? "If that was you, Charlotte, it wasn't clear enough. You talked to me in the psychomanteum. Why not talk to me now?"

No sound. Just the scent.

Marie eyed the antique desk under the window. "Is it the desk? Is there something inside?" She didn't wait for a response this time. She pulled open the top drawer.

Empty. The second was empty as well, and the third. She moved to the closet, then on to the built-in wall units. There was nothing to be found. Brandon might have left the furniture in the room, but he'd cleaned out all Charlotte's personal things. Marie wondered what he'd done with them.

A creak sounded from the hallway. The soft, slow beat of footsteps.

Brandon.

Marie turned away from the empty wall units and walked to the door, her skin prickling with nerves. She told herself she was being ridiculous. There was no reason to sneak around, no reason to hide what she'd been doing. If Brandon didn't want her looking through the house, he wouldn't have given her the full set of keys. Still, the thought of facing him again after what he'd revealed in the car left her a little shaky.

No matter. She wasn't going to hide from him the rest of her time in Jenkins Cove. She needed answers, starting with what had happened to Charlotte's personal papers and possessions. She was going to get to the bottom of Charlotte's and her father's deaths, and she wasn't going to let anything get in the way. Especially not the past.

She crossed the room and opened the door. The hall was dark, and for a moment all she could see was a shadow.

A shadow without a cane. A shadow too short to be Brandon.

Suddenly the shadow rushed toward her and an arm clamped around her throat.

Chapter Nine

Rain spattered cold on Marie's cheeks. She could feel hands gripping her under her arms, pulling her. Her feet dragged over something rough.

She must have passed out.

She remembered the shadow, remembered the arm across her throat, bearing down. Her head throbbed. Her stomach swirled. Her throat burned like fire.

But she could breathe.

She scooped in breath after breath of cold, moist air and tried to fight her way to consciousness. She tensed her muscles. She forced her eyes open.

Color exploded in her head. Her vision swirled, dark and light. The night closed in around her. She saw the water far below, and white lines stretching on either side of her. They were the rails encircling the widow's walk.

She was on the roof.

She gritted her teeth and tried to clear her head, tried to think. Hell, she didn't have time to think. She had to move. She thrust her arms up, lashing out at the hands dragging her. She bared her fingernails like claws, trying to dig her stubby nails into flesh.

A blow rained down on her head, and rough hands pushed her into the railing. The top rail hit low on her thighs, but her upper body kept moving, flipping, carrying her over.

She hit the sloped roof. Air exploded from her lungs. She coughed, gasped, tried to breathe. Her body started to slide.

She scrambled to find a handhold, a foothold, but wet with rain, the shingles felt slick as ice. Her fingers slipped. Her feet thrashed.

And still she kept sliding. Closer to the edge. Closer to the three-story drop to the ground.

Her hand hit something. A roof vent. She grabbed on, the steel cutting into her fingers. Her legs jutted out over the roof's edge.

She stopped.

She clung to the vent, afraid to move. Rain pattered on her back. Water sluiced around her, beneath her and emptied into the gutter that ran under her legs. Her heart pounded against the wet slate. She slowly, carefully scooped in a breath. Then another. Her lungs screamed for more.

She peered down, past her dangling legs. She could see the gentle lighting of the east garden through the misty rain below. The concrete bench glowed pale against dark leaves of holly. So far down…so far…

She grew dizzy and closed her eyes. The edge of metal cut into her fingers. Her muscles trembled and ached. Her fingers started slipping.

Oh God. She was going to fall.

Pressure closed around her wrist and held her fast. Not cold like the rain, like the slate and steel she clung to, but warm as a human hand.

She looked up into the night. Through the rain the widow's walk railing gleamed white against a black sky. She was alone. Totally alone. And yet she could feel a hand on her wrist, a hand that kept her from falling, a hand that kept her safe.

"Marie?" a woman's voice screamed. Not from the roof, but from below. "Oh God, Marie! Hold on! We'll be right up."

Marie didn't know how long she clung there, the unseen hand binding her wrist, before she heard a clatter on the roof.

"Over here. This is where I saw her." A thump came from above. "We're here, Marie. We're coming for you."

The same woman's voice. A voice Marie recognized. "Chelsea?" What was Sophie Caldwell's niece doing here?

"Hold on, Marie."

Something scraped against the slate shingles above her head. A large hand encircled her wrist, replacing the pressure that had stopped her fall. "I've got you."

She looked up into a man's eyes. Rain sparkled in his dark hair. He gave her a reassuring smile. "It's okay. You can let go now."

She forced her fingers to obey.

He pulled her up, slowly, gently, until the two of them reached Chelsea on the widow's walk.

"Thank God," Chelsea said. "It's a miracle you held on. It took a few minutes to rig a rope. We were afraid you'd fall before Michael could reach you."

And she might have.

Marie looked out over the wet slate. Her whole body trembled. Her legs felt like loose sand. "Something held me. A hand. It kept me from going over the edge, but I couldn't see anything there. It was like…" She searched for the word, but her mind balked. Even after the experiences she'd had lately, she didn't want to say it out loud.

Michael gave a knowing nod. "A spirit?"

"Yes."

Chelsea and Michael exchanged looks. "Let's go inside," Chelsea said. "We have a lot to talk about."

WHEN BRANDON MOUNTED the steps to the kitchen entrance of Drake House he was surprised to see the lights still on in Edwin's quarters. He'd sat in the boathouse for hours and listened to the rain patter on the roof, trying to process what had happened with Marie, trying to get his head straight. And even though he didn't feel any better than he had when he'd left, he thought by now it would be safe to return to the house. He thought she would be asleep.

He unlocked the kitchen door and stepped inside. The door to the butler's quarters stood open. "Let me check your eyes again, just to be sure." A woman's voice. Not Marie.

He crossed the kitchen and peered through the open door.

A blond woman leaned over Marie's chair. She directed a flashlight to the side of Marie's cheek and peered into Marie's eyes, one after another. "Looks good. I think you're going to survive."

Alarm prickled along Brandon's nerves. He stepped forward into Edwin's sitting room. "Survive? Survive what?"

"You must be Brandon." A man nearly as tall as

Brandon with the build of an athlete pushed himself up from a chair. He stepped across the room and offered his hand. "Michael Bryant. This is Chelsea Caldwell."

Brandon made the connections in his mind while shaking the man's hand. He nodded to the blonde. "You're related to Sophie Caldwell?"

"My aunt."

So they'd made their introductions, but no one had answered his initial question. He focused on Marie. "What happened, Marie? Are you hurt?"

Marie wrapped her arms around herself as if she was cold. She looked so small sitting on the love seat. Small and fragile.

"Marie had an accident," the blonde supplied.

Something inside him seized. He struggled to keep himself steady, to stay calm and wait for the details instead of racing to Marie and gathering her into his arms. "What kind of accident?"

Marie glanced from Chelsea to Michael. "Thanks so much for everything you've done. And everything you told me. I think it's better if I talk to Brandon alone, if you don't mind."

"Yes. That's a good idea." Chelsea exchanged looks with Michael. Brandon led them to the front entrance of Drake House. "Thank you," he said as they plunged out into the rain and ran to their vehicle. Brandon locked the door and set the alarm behind them.

When he walked back into Edwin's sitting room, Marie was still huddled on the love seat. She looked as if she hadn't moved a muscle. A welt rose on her scalp, just above her right ear.

"You're hurt."

"Just a bump and a headache. I don't have a concussion. Believe me, Chelsea has been checking me every hour. I guess I just have a hard head."

His gaze moved down to her neck. Although she had a throw blanket wrapped around her shoulders, he could see a bruise starting to purple on the pale skin of her throat. He swayed a little on his feet. "And that?"

"I'll tell you about all of it. But first, you'd better sit down."

Brandon didn't move. "Who did this? Have you called the police?"

"They were already here."

"And a doctor? You need to see a doctor. We need to get you to a hospital. I'll call Josef."

"A paramedic was here, too. I'm just bruised. I'm going to be fine. Now sit down."

He couldn't. He needed to do something. Sitting felt too passive. Besides, the only place he wanted to sit was in the love seat beside her. More than anything he wanted to take her in his arms and keep her safe. "I'll stand."

"Fine." She explained how she'd been looking through Charlotte's study, how she'd thought she'd heard him return from the boathouse, how she'd been attacked. When she got to the part about being thrown off the roof, he started pacing, a habit he'd broken since he'd injured his leg. A habit that saved him now. "Why didn't I hear any of this? I should have heard something. I should have known. You could have died." Damn him. Marie had already been attacked once since she came to Drake House. Why in the hell had he left her alone? What had he been thinking?

"Chelsea found me. She and Michael saved me."

He managed a nod. What he wanted to do was smack himself in the head…or worse.

He ran a hand through his hair before walking back the length of the room. He hadn't been thinking. Not about anyone but himself, anyway. He'd simply wanted to get away. Far away. Where he didn't have to see the pain and disappointment in Marie's eyes. Where he wouldn't be tempted to take her in his arms and make promises he feared he could never keep.

At least Chelsea Caldwell and this Michael had been here. Brandon eyed Marie. "Why *were* Chelsea and Michael here? And how did they find you on the roof?"

"Chelsea sensed I was in trouble."

"She *sensed* it?"

"She sees things other people don't see."

"Like what? The future?"

Marie watched him. A little too closely for his comfort. "She sees ghosts. They communicate with her."

His stomach felt as if he were cresting in a roller coaster and hanging in midair. "You're joking."

"You know the mass grave we've been hearing so much about? Do you know how the police discovered it?"

She'd lost him. "What does the mass grave have to do with what happened tonight?"

"A spirit named Lavinia appeared to Chelsea. Michael saw her, too. The spirit led them to the graves. She helped them figure out the truth."

"Let me guess, Lavinia was one of the people buried in the mass grave."

"Yes."

He massaged his forehead with his fingertips. What kinds of stories had Chelsea and Michael been telling? "You don't believe all this stuff, do you?"

Marie watched him a long time. Rain and wind beat against the windows and whistled over the chimneys of the old house. He was about to ask again when Marie finally spoke. "Yes. I do."

"You're kidding."

She narrowed her eyes to caramel-colored slits. "You don't believe there are things in this world that we don't understand?"

"Things like ghosts?" He couldn't even believe they were having this conversation, and he still had no clue where it was leading. "I've never really thought about it."

"Would you believe if you saw one? Or heard one?"

"I don't know. I suppose I might."

"Would you believe if I told you that a ghost has contacted me?"

An uneasy feeling knotted deep in his gut. "How did this go from a story Chelsea told you to this? What are you trying to say, Marie?"

"Just that. I've been contacted by a spirit. I didn't want to believe it myself at first. But it's real."

He shook his head.

Marie slumped back in the love seat. "You don't believe me. You haven't even heard what I have to say, and you don't believe me."

"I'm just trying to get this straight." He didn't have a clue what to think. This whole conversation was so unlike Marie. She had a romantic streak, yes. But she always seemed to have her feet firmly planted in reality. She was like her father in that way. "The ghost you saw. It was your father?"

"I didn't *see* a ghost. I heard a voice. I smelled a scent."

He went cold inside. Memories of their argument at the police station popped into his mind. The way Marie had insisted Charlotte had been murdered. She couldn't be leading where he feared she was. She wouldn't. "It was your father, right?" *Please let it be Edwin.*

"I tried to contact my father. I couldn't reach him."

"Then…" He couldn't ask. He didn't want to know.

"Brandon, it was Charlotte."

"The jasmine."

"Exactly."

"It was a scent, Marie. Just a scent. Charlotte lived here for ten years. It isn't unheard of that the house would still smell like her."

"I didn't just smell it here. I smelled it in Sophie's psychomanteum."

"How do you know the scent was Charlotte? How do you know it wasn't from some other source? Jasmine isn't common, but it's not rare, either."

"I heard her voice, Brandon."

His heart stuttered. "You're sure?"

"Yes."

Even though he had an idea of what Marie's answer would be, he forced the question from his lips. "What did she say?"

"She said she was murdered. She said, 'All Brandon loves will die.'"

He stared at the wall, the moldings on the ceiling, anything but Marie. The part about Charlotte saying she was murdered, he'd guessed. The other part…*All Brandon loves will die.* What did that mean?

"You still don't believe." Marie's voice trembled.

Something inside him broke at the sound. He met her eyes. "It's not that I don't want to, Marie. I just…"

"You can't."

"I don't know. I'm trying to absorb it. That's all." He turned away from her and strode the length of the room, the extra beat of his cane on the parquet making his footfalls sound as unbalanced as all of this felt.

Murder. Charlotte murdered. As much as he wanted to believe Marie, as much as he wanted to believe Charlotte hadn't killed herself, that he wasn't responsible for his wife's death, he didn't know if he could. "Who would murder Charlotte?"

"You tell me. Did anyone stand to gain from her death?"

"You mean financially?"

"Sure. Or other ways."

He walked back to where Marie sat. The answer to her question was obvious and inevitable. "Me."

Marie shook her head. "Who else?"

"No one else." He thought for a moment. This whole exercise was so foreign to him. Murder? Motives? For crying out loud, *ghosts?* It was as if he'd fallen down some surreal rabbit hole. "Her mother is still alive. But she isn't in need of money. And she adored her daughter. She was crushed when Charlotte died."

Marie stared into the empty fireplace, deep in thought. "What if you died without having children? Who would inherit?"

"My uncle. He's not in need of money, either." Brandon took several steps and stopped. The words Marie had repeated, the ones she said had come from the ghost, whispered through his mind.

All Brandon loves will die.

His fingers tightened on his cane. Charlotte had died, only he hadn't loved Charlotte. Not the way a man should love his wife. But… "What about this attack tonight?"

She met his eyes, unflinching. "I'm pretty sure my father was killed because he found something, something that proved Charlotte was murdered. Maybe the killer thinks I've found whatever that is. Or maybe he or she is afraid I will."

There was one other possibility. One Brandon didn't want to entertain. That a ghost's warning was real. The ghost of his dead wife.

He finished his trek back to the love seat.

Arms wrapped around herself, Marie peered up at him, so pale, so fragile. Even though he knew she was strong as steel inside, he still had the urge to sweep her into his arms and take her far away. Somewhere she would be safe.

He wasn't sure he could believe any of this. But maybe he didn't have to. Maybe his role was simpler than that. "I don't know what's real and what's not, Marie. But I know one thing. Whoever attacked you tonight, I won't let him hurt you again. I promise you that."

Chapter Ten

Marie had heard all about the ostentatious redbrick mansion Clifford Drake had built on the jut of Drake family land right across the small inlet from Drake House. She'd even seen it across the water. But none of that was the same as having it looming before her now, up close and personal.

Josef held the car door. Brandon climbed out and joined Marie on the sidewalk. "Here it is. The Manor at Drake Acres. Uncle Cliff's answer to the fact that my father inherited Drake House."

"It sure is big." And red. The rich color of the brick glowed in the morning sun. His tall white pillars and three and a half stories' worth of windows stretched up to the gabled roof.

"Big. Yes. I think that's what he was going for. Bigger than Drake House, at any rate."

Marie had to turn her head first fully to one side, then to the other just to take in the length of the place. Not easy with a sore neck. And she wasn't even counting the garages and guest house and cabana. If she turned far enough, she could see stables, too, a few hundred yards beyond. The gardens surrounding the house were equally opulent. Last night's rain and the humidity still hanging in the air made even the late autumn garden smell alive and lush.

"It might be big and fancy and new," Marie said, "but it doesn't have the beauty of Drake House. Nor the class."

A smile flickered over his lips.

A corresponding flutter seized her chest, despite her efforts to clamp it down.

"What?"

She shook her head. "Nothing, really. I just...I think that's the first time I've seen you smile since I came back."

The smile faded.

She wished she hadn't pointed it out. But it was probably better this way. His smile only reminded her of better times. Times she couldn't afford to think about now. She focused on the sprawling house. "Maybe you're right. Maybe Cliff has all the money he needs."

"I was thinking about that. Maybe it's not about money. Maybe it's about the one thing I've got that he doesn't. Drake House."

Chills trickled down Marie's spine. Could that be it? It seemed to make sense. "If you and Charlotte had children, Drake House would pass to them. But if you died without heirs, Cliff would finally get what he feels should have been his inheritance all along."

Brandon nodded. "It's hard for me to believe Cliff would take things that far, but I suppose it's possible. He and my father defined the term *sibling rivalry*. Maybe it's more about that than anything else."

Unfortunately Cliff wasn't home. After a brief exchange with the servant who answered the door, they followed his instructions and circled to the boathouse and long pier that reached into Chesapeake Bay. A lethal-looking speedboat bobbed in the water. A lethal-looking redhead lounged inside the craft.

"Brandon!" Isabella shouted from the yacht's deck. She flipped her hair over one shoulder and sat up in the boat, giving her employer the benefit of her full attention and her electric blue eyes. She artfully ignored Marie. "What a wonderful surprise. Are you coming out with us?"

Marie did her best to ignore the twinge of jealousy. Even in jeans and a leather bomber jacket, Isabella had the pin-up potential of a swimsuit model.

"*We* are here to have a word with Cliff."

"You can chat with Cliff on the boat. Really, Brandon, it's not an imposition to have one more. Cliff won't mind, I'm sure. I feel like I haven't seen you very much in the past few days." She leaned forward in her seat. Her unzipped jacket parted to reveal a low-cut top framing ample cleavage.

Marie tried her best not to let Isabella get to her. It was obvious she had the hots for Brandon. And likely his uncle Cliff, or she wouldn't be here on her day off. But whatever games she was playing with the Drake men, it wasn't any of Marie's business. She had to remember that.

Cliff emerged from the redbrick boathouse, a miniature mansion in itself. Dressed in a Burberry windbreaker, a cashmere sweater and perfectly tailored slacks, he looked every inch the wealthy playboy he was. His thick hair had gained some gray since the last time Marie saw him, but the new look only served to add sophistication to his list of charms.

He nodded to his nephew. "Brandon." Judging from his tone of voice, he wasn't as excited to see his nephew as Isabella was. He eyed Marie. "And…Marie Leonard, right?"

Marie nodded. Cliff had always intimidated her growing up. He'd seemed so confident, carefree and in control of his life. A man who lived big and wasn't ashamed to let the world envy him for it. He was the opposite of everything her humble, decorous father had instilled in her, and more than once she'd been totally bowled over by his presence. She could only hope now that she was an adult, she'd be able to handle him better. "Hello, Mr. Drake."

"Call me Cliff, please." He managed to look her up and down in a manner that was more flattering than intrusive. "You've grown up since the last time I saw you."

Marie held his gaze. She wasn't sure if Cliff's once-over was meant to bother Brandon or Isabella or both. But whatever was going on, she wanted no part of it. "I have a few things I'd like to ask you."

He raised his brows. "Sure. I'm glad you stopped by. I heard you were visiting Drake House."

"Visiting? My father died."

"Yes. A great loss. I'm so sorry."

Surprisingly, his tone sounded sincere. Maybe there was more to Clifford Drake than she'd ever guessed. Or maybe he was just trying to throw her off balance. "Thank you."

"You should come out on the boat. Racing over the water at high speed tends to take your mind off your problems. And it promises to be a lot more fun than hanging around old Brandon."

"We came to ask you some questions," Brandon said.

"Questions?" Cliff kept his gaze glued to Marie. "About what?"

"The recent deaths at Drake House. My father and Charlotte."

Cliff finally glanced at Brandon, as if gauging his nephew's reaction to his dead wife's name.

Brandon didn't move a muscle. Wavelets lapped against the pier's pilings.

Cliff looked back to Marie. "Tragedies, to be sure. What makes you think I can tell you anything?"

"You're part of the family. You live nearby."

"I do live nearby, but if you hadn't figured this out yet, the Drake family isn't exactly close."

Marie looked past Cliff to where Isabella was climbing out of the speedboat and onto the pier. Apparently she'd grown tired of being out of the spotlight and intended to take it back.

Marie gave Cliff a businesslike smile. "I know you have plans, so I'll make this short."

A lazy grin spread over Cliff's lips. He glanced in Brandon's direction and lowered one lid in a wink. "What can I say? I'm in demand."

"What are you men talking about?" Walking up behind Brandon, Isabella slipped her hands onto his shoulders and started kneading his muscles.

Brandon stiffened.

Cliff's easy smile faded. He shot Isabella a warning stare.

Isabella withdrew her hands and wormed her way into the circle, Brandon and Cliff on either side.

Marie shook her head. Let Isabella play her games. Marie had more important things to focus on. "Mr.

Drake? Did you see either Charlotte or my father around the time of their deaths?"

"I told you, it's Cliff. And yes, I saw your father a day or two before he died."

Of the two, Marie would have guessed it more likely for Cliff to have seen Charlotte. Or at least to have noticed her. But six months was a long time. Maybe he didn't remember, provided he didn't have anything to do with killing her. "Where was my father when you saw him?"

"Near the harbor. You know that bed-and-breakfast called The Seven Gables or some such?"

"Sophie Caldwell's place? Was he with her?"

"No. He was talking to that pain-in-the-ass developer. Perry. And let me tell you, your father didn't look too happy."

Marie could imagine. Shelley had said Ned Perry was trying to buy waterfront, including Drake House, and build condos. No idea would insult her father's sensibilities more. "What about Charlotte? Did you see her before her death?"

"No."

Marie and Brandon exchanged looks. He seemed to be as uneasy with Cliff's answer as she was. The abrupt answer felt a little too quick, a little too pat. "You're sure?"

"Absolutely."

Brandon eyed his uncle. "Charlotte died six months ago. That's a long time."

"You want an alibi?" Cliff chuckled, the sound more taunt than real laugh. "I was sailing. A regatta in the U.K. Stop by the yacht club. I'll take you on the yacht that won and show you the trophy."

Marie's stomach sank. Beyond Cliff, she didn't have much of a list of people who could benefit from Charlotte's death. She had no leads. All she had were the words of a ghost. Words Brandon didn't even believe.

Cliff narrowed his eyes on his nephew. "So why are you playing like this is some sort of murder investigation? I know about the vodka bottle. You might have been able to keep that part out of the papers, but I have my sources." He shot Isabella a little smile.

The maid tilted her chin up and gave Cliff a frown. She laid a hand on Brandon's arm. "I'm sorry, Brandon. I didn't mean to say anything. Really I didn't. I was just so upset that she would do that to you. She didn't deserve what she had. Drake House. You. She didn't deserve any of it." Flirty lilt gone, Isabella's voice rang with a hard edge.

Brandon's lips flattened. "Isabella, stop."

"It's true. I was hoping you'd see it after she died." The maid tilted her head in Marie's direction. "And if you think this one deserves you, you're going to be disappointed all over again."

BRANDON HAD NEVER BEEN as glad to leave a place as he was walking back to the car from Cliff's boathouse. Every moment of that encounter had been awkward and painful and teeth-grindingly frustrating.

"Did you hear the venom in her voice?" Marie asked.

"Isabella has a few issues." To put it mildly.

"Issues like she wants to be the lady of Drake House."

"Or The Manor at Drake Acres. I don't think it matters much to her." He let out a pent-up breath. "I think we're going to need to keep an eye on her."

"Do you think she might have killed Charlotte?"

"I don't see it. She couldn't have gotten Charlotte into the car and crashed it by herself." He still wasn't sure how anyone could have done that except for Charlotte herself. But since he wasn't about to get into a debate with Marie about the existence of ghosts, he'd let that part slide for now. "Isabella could have gotten someone to help her. She's good at convincing men to do things for her."

"Men? Like who? Cliff was racing one of his yachts."

"There are men besides Cliff." They rounded the far corner of the house and started toward the circle in front of the house's grand entrance where his car waited. Josef spotted them and climbed out of the car. Brandon kept his voice low. "Take Josef. He lost his fiancée about a year ago. He's got to be lonely. And he knows his way around cars."

"You think Josef—"

"Or Phil Cardon."

Marie frowned, as if searching her memory for the name. "The guy who works at Thornton Garden Center?"

Brandon nodded. "He has done some work at Drake House from time to time. And he worked on the gardens with Lexie. He was pretty interested in Isabella."

"I can imagine. But was he interested enough to help her commit murder?"

Brandon shrugged.

"How about the guy from Drake Enterprises? The one who came to Drake House?"

"Doug Heller? I could see it." Truthfully, he couldn't see it at all. Any of it. He still couldn't wrap his mind around the idea that Charlotte was murdered. That someone he knew was responsible. Maybe he was just in denial, but this whole conversation with Marie didn't seem real to him. More like a guessing game played purely for amusement. He was much more concerned with finding who had tried to kill Marie. "Do you think Isabella could have been the one who tried to throw you off the roof last night?"

Marie's steps slowed. "Maybe. She's taller than I am. And strong. I don't know."

"Maybe that's what we should focus on."

"I told you, I think it's all related."

He nodded. He was waiting for her to say that. "Think and know are two different things. And until we know it's related and know who wants you dead, we need to keep our options open. I don't want to overlook anyone."

They walked for a moment without speaking, the click of their shoes on the brick path the only sound. The sun beamed down from a sky that seemed shockingly blue after the dreariness of the day before. Too bad their situation wasn't as clear and pleasant as the weather.

"So what do we do?"

He wanted to suggest buying her a plane ticket, sending her back to Michigan where she'd be safe…and away from him. But he knew what her reaction would be. "Set some traps and see what happens."

As they approached the car, Josef opened the back door. Marie climbed inside. The chauffeur circled the car and opened the opposite door for Brandon. When it came to his job, Josef was precise and efficient. Could he be as precise and efficient when it came to killing someone? Especially if a young redhead, beautiful beyond his dreams, seduced him into it?

Brandon lowered himself into the car and waited for Josef to take his place behind the wheel. "Josef?"

"Yes, sir?" His accent was thick and warm and tinged with respect. Just the right tone.

"Take us back to Drake House. Then you can have the rest of the day off. And the night. We'll see you again tomorrow morning."

"Sir? May I ask why?"

"I've been asking a lot of you the past few days." He paused for dramatic effect...he hoped. "And we've learned something very disturbing about Isabella Faust. I'd like to handle it myself. If we need to go anywhere, we'll use Ms. Leonard's rental car."

Josef nodded and pulled away, leaving The Manor at Drake Acres behind. "Very good, sir."

SITTING IN A CRAMPED RENTAL CAR with a leg injury was not a good idea. Too bad Brandon hadn't realized that before he and Marie had jumped in her car in a damn fool attempt to follow Isabella's little yellow sports car when she'd returned from her day with Cliff. The trap he'd set for Josef turned out to be nothing. Nothing at all. The chauffeur had made no move to warn Isabella of their suspicions. He hadn't gone anywhere, and a call to the phone company had proved he hadn't made any phone calls.

Brandon shifted his leg into a more comfortable position. "I feel like an idiot spying on my employees. Especially since they don't seem to be doing a damn thing out of the ordinary."

Eyes on the road and the yellow car in front of them, Marie let out a sigh. The lights from the dash cast her face in a green glow, a color that would make anyone look like death warmed over. But not Marie. She looked as vibrant and determined as ever.

God help him.

"What is it?" he asked her.

"Nothing, really. I'm relieved Josef isn't tangled up with Isabella, but his life seems kind of sad."

"How so?"

"I don't know. Just what Shelley told me. Moving to a country where he doesn't know anyone. Losing his fiancée. He seems so alone."

Brandon nodded. Widowed. Alone. As Brandon himself had been before Marie had returned. As he would be again after she left.

He shook his head. If only he could forget all that, accept it. But it was impossible with her sitting only inches away. The scent of her, warm and spicy, wrapped around him, and he longed to feel the softness of her skin again.

Riding around with Marie in this cramped little car wasn't one of his best ideas.

He gripped his cane in both hands and remembered the bruising hidden under the high collar of her coat. He couldn't have Marie. He couldn't even let himself want her. But he could protect her. He could keep her safe.

"I finally got a hold of Lexie." Marie kept her focus on the road. "She said her records show Phil Cardon was working with her on a garden in Easton when Charlotte died. She said they were on the job site until sunset every night. There's no way he could have driven all the way to Drake House before the time of Charlotte's accident."

Another name off the list. "Doug is stopping by Drake House for a chat tomorrow. But I can't imagine he has anything to do with this."

Marie piloted the car down Main Street and into the heart of town. Shops and cafés lined the street, festooned with wreaths and lights and tinsel.

Christmas.

An ache settled into Brandon's gut. From the time he could remember, Christmas had been centered on the ball and charity auction. He remembered his mother presiding over the decoration. Then Edwin and, to a lesser extent, Charlotte. When he'd lost all of them, there had seemed no point to go on. He hadn't even felt bad about letting the tradition die. Or maybe he'd felt so bad about everything else that he hadn't noticed.

But now?

The time Marie had been here had been filled with turmoil and pain. Still, by comparison, he felt more alive than he had in years. And for the first time, the thought of Jenkins Cove going through a Christmas season without the charity ball felt...not right.

As the yellow car reached the outskirts of town, it slowed and turned into a lot. Brandon glanced at Marie. "Did you see that?"

"Yes." Marie drove to a spot near the street where Isabella turned, and pulled to the curb. Beyond a small parking lot sat a little restaurant and bar known to the locals as the spot for soft-shell crab in season and cheap booze all year-round. The Duck Blind.

"Does Rufus Shea still own this place?"

"I think so." Brandon frowned. Even though Rufus Shea had cleaned up his act and his tavern in recent years, the former town drunk wasn't the type of man Brandon could picture Marie having anything to do with. "How do you know Rufus Shea?"

"I knew his son."

Brandon nodded. He'd known Rufus's son, Simon, too, though not well. The kid had been younger. The quintessential troublemaker from the wrong side of the tracks. Brandon had been at Harvard when he'd heard about the kid's death. A lifetime ago. "I wonder what brings Isabella here?" He nodded out the window as the auburn-haired beauty pulled the door open and slipped inside.

"Should we find out?" Marie took the key from the ignition and got out of the car.

Brandon followed. They entered in time to catch Isabella stride past the counter and bar stools and turn into the restaurant. They followed. Sturdy round tables covered with red and green tablecloths dotted the modest-sized room. A good crowd of people filled the place, dining on plates of crab cakes and passing bowls of stewed tomatoes and lima beans served family style. The din of conversation bounced off paneled walls, and the sweet and tangy scent of seafood hung in the air.

Isabella made a beeline for a table in the far corner. She slipped into a chair beside a man.

A man Brandon recognized immediately.

He grabbed Marie's arm, stopping her before she was spotted. He leaned close and spoke into her ear. "Ned Perry. She's meeting with Ned Perry."

Marie looked toward the table, eyes wide. "The real estate developer? Do you think this might have something to do with Drake House?"

"I don't know. But I aim to find out."

MARIE SNUGGLED her coat tight around her shoulders against the cool morning. Kneeling down beside

Brandon's town car, she examined the tire. The white chalk line was still there, untouched.

She'd gotten the idea from her parking hassles in college. It was a trick the parking authority used. Mark the tire with chalk. If the chalk is still there, the car hasn't moved. In this case, that meant Josef hadn't moved. Not the entire night.

At least they could cross him off the list. Cliff as well. And probably Phil Cardon. But Isabella seemed to be neck deep in whatever was going on. And Marie was betting Ned Perry was helping her.

Marie wound through the east garden and back to the kitchen. Frost sparkled on the concrete bench, the fountain and the white shells that covered the path. Not quite like snow at Christmastime, but the extra sparkle lent Drake House a little magic of the season. Magic that was sorely lacking.

She found Brandon in the kitchen, sitting at the stone counter where she'd eaten cookies as a child. He sipped a cup of coffee and watched Shelley sauté vegetables for one of her extravagant breakfasts. Mouthwatering aromas and thick steam wafted from the pan. Brandon looked up at Marie and arched his brows in silent question.

She shook her head.

He leaned back in his chair, relieved.

One more name off the suspect list. Marie took a cup of coffee and tried to concentrate on drinking it without burning her lips and tongue.

A knock sounded on the kitchen door.

Marie jumped at the sound. She glanced through the mullioned glass. A pair of watery blue eyes stared straight at her.

Shelley wiped her hands and scampered to open the door.

The operations manager of Drake Enterprises stepped inside. "Brandon?"

Brandon nodded and stood, leaning heavily on his cane. "Thanks for coming, Doug. We'll talk in the office." Giving Marie a glance, he led Doug Heller from the kitchen. Brandon had told her he planned to pump the manager for information about Perry. And, of course, he wanted to ask a few questions of Heller himself.

As soon as they disappeared into the household office and closed the door behind them, Shelley made a tsking noise under her breath.

Marie focused on the housekeeper. "What is it, Shelley?"

"I can just imagine. Probably Ned Perry again."

Marie nodded vaguely, not wanting to let on that Shelley's guess was right on the nose. "Does this Mr. Perry stop by often?"

"No. He hasn't for a while. He doesn't have the nerve. But then he doesn't have to when he has someone already in the house lobbying for him."

"Someone in the house? Who?"

"Isabella."

Marie's pulse launched into double time. She didn't know why she hadn't thought of asking Shelley about this sooner. The woman seemed to know everyone's business. And she had no qualms about spreading the news around. "Why would Isabella lobby for Ned Perry?"

"They have a deal."

"A deal?" This was getting better all the time.

"She says she's buying one of the condos down by

the yacht club. But I think she wants a piece of Drake House. She's always wanted Drake House, you know. Although I don't know how she thinks Ned Perry is going to get his hands on it."

It hadn't occurred to Marie that Isabella wanted Drake House, not until her performance yesterday. What other secrets could Shelley tell her? "Why do you think Isabella wants Drake House?"

"Just ask her." Shelley pulled a knife from the block and started dicing shallots with more gusto than called for. The knife made a sharp snap each time it hit the cutting board. "When she first came to work here, she told me that one day she'd be lady of the house. 'It's only a matter of time,' she'd say. Hogwash. Mr. Brandon saw nothing in her. He only saw his Charlotte."

Shelley shook her head. Scooping up the shallots with the flat of her blade, she feathered them into the sauté pan and turned up the heat. An onionlike tang flavored the air. "After Charlotte died, Isabella got more aggressive. I told her it was no use. And it wasn't. Mr. Brandon is heartbroken. He lives only for his foundation and this house. He'll never marry again. Charlotte was the only woman he could ever love. She was perfect. You'd do well to remember that, too."

"Me?" If Marie hadn't been sitting, she would have stepped back under the assault. "What does this have to do with me?"

"I've seen you with him. Trying to make him smile. Trying to make him do things for you. You'd be better off leaving him alone." Shelley gathered a handful of dirty utensils and carried them to one of the huge sinks. She pushed up the sleeves of her blouse, revealing muscled arms. "I'm not trying to be mean. I'm telling you for your own good. He belongs to Charlotte. No other woman is wanted around here."

Marie stared at Shelley, not sure she heard the woman right. Hadn't she joked to herself about Shelley's resemblance to the fictional Mrs. Danvers? And now this on the heels of Isabella's comments yesterday? "Anything between Brandon and me is in the past, Shelley. It's over. You don't have to feel threatened by me."

"I'm just telling you the way things are. You seem like a nice girl, and I always respected your father. I wouldn't like to see you get hurt."

Marie nodded, not sure if Shelley's words held more motherly concern or threat.

Shelley thrust the utensils under running water. The scent of dishwashing soap mixed with the aroma from the stove. "While we're on the subject, I've talked to a handyman who occasionally does work around here. Phil Cardon. He has some hours free later today, so I hired him to help you pack up your father's things."

So Shelley was shoving her out of the house. Protecting Brandon's honor and Charlotte's memory, no doubt. Unless she had a more personal agenda. "I have time. I'm on personal leave from my job. There's no hurry."

"Well, you aren't the only one this affects, Marie. We have to think about Brandon. He likes his privacy. Having a guest in the house is tough on him."

Marie pushed herself back from the counter and picked up her coffee. She was getting a little tired of being in Shelley's crosshairs this morning. And while Marie knew her presence wasn't any easier on Brandon than it was on her, she wasn't going to let the housekeeper chase her out before she got her answers. "Maybe we should ask Brandon."

"There are other concerns, too." Shelley smiled, backpedaling.

Marie should just walk out of the room, leave Shelley stewing. Unfortunately she was never one to leave a leading comment hanging in the air without asking the question that went with it. "Such as?"

"It's very difficult to run the house when I'm not living here."

Now it was becoming clear. "You want to move into my father's quarters."

"Those rooms are for the person who is running Drake House. They aren't your father's personal property."

Marie couldn't argue with that, even though her father had lived in those rooms for forty years. "As soon as I finish tying up some loose ends, you can have your rooms."

Shelley nodded her graying head. "Good. I'm glad we understand each other."

Marie gave Shelley a broad smile. "Yes. We understand each other. But I don't need your handyman's help. No one is to touch my father's things but me."

Shelley didn't answer.

Marie clenched the hot mug. The moment she left the house, Shelley would probably have an army of handymen erasing her father's presence from Drake House. She'd have to ask Brandon to make sure that didn't happen.

"Perhaps you'd do a favor for me now."

The woman was asking for a favor? After everything she'd thrown at Marie in the past few minutes?

"I need you to move your car to the parking area

next to the carriage house. I have a decorator coming in to take measurements, and your vehicle will be in the way."

Marie had the sneaking suspicion Shelley thought everything about her was in the way. But as much as Shelley's grasping annoyed her, she had to admit life went on. An old and important mansion like Drake House needed a full-time caretaker, and Brandon had given the job to Shelley. With the job came the living quarters. She couldn't deny Shelley that.

But that didn't mean she'd let the woman push her out before she'd exhausted every lead. Finding her father's killer, and Charlotte's as well, came first. "Measure all you want, Shelley, but don't touch my father's things. Do you understand me?"

Shelley pursed her lips and raised her chin. "As long as you clear out the rooms in a timely manner. Now will you move your vehicle? My decorator will be here any minute." She glanced at a clock on the wall for emphasis.

Marie plunked her mug on the countertop, grabbed her keys and coat and gladly left the kitchen to Shelley Zachary.

Out in the cool morning, her car started on the third try. She'd have to take it in to the rental agency. Have them replace the battery or give her a new car.

She piloted the rental around the kitchen entrance's circle drive and joined with the drive leading to the carriage house, curving along the edge of the water.

Steely waves echoed the color of the sky and pounded rocks edging the shoreline. She approached the turn to the carriage house. Although the land around Drake House was fairly flat, this part of the drive dipped slightly, making her car accelerate. She pressed her foot to the brake pedal. It gripped, then softened.

Then plunged to the floorboards.

Marie tried the brakes again. Again they pushed to the floor. She didn't have time to think. Didn't even have time to panic. Blood rushing in her ears, she gripped the wheel and steered. The car canted to the side. Tires skidded on loose gravel.

The car jolted over rock and plunged into water.

Chapter Eleven

Marie hung forward in her seat belt. The air bag softened in front of her like a limp balloon, only dregs of air left. Her ears rang. Her already sore head and neck ached. Her feet felt so very cold.

Pushing down the air bag, she fought to clear her mind. Water sloshed over the car's hood. It covered the pedals and crept up the floor mat, swamping her feet to the ankles.

What a mess.

She looked out the driver's window. The car balanced on the gray rock that lined the shoreline, preventing erosion. Even though the nose tilted down into the water, the back end of the car was still high, if not totally dry.

She was lucky. If she had been going faster, she'd be out in the bay right now. As it was, she might have to do a little swimming, or at least wading, but she still had time to get out.

Trying to steady her trembling fingers, she found the buckle of her seat belt and released it. She groped the armrest, locating the controls for the power windows. She pressed the button to lower the driver's side.

Nothing happened.

She tried again. Damn. The water or the impact must have shorted out the car's battery or jostled the wires free. Not that it hadn't been half drained before she'd even gotten behind the wheel.

There was no reason to panic. Although the water seemed to creep higher by the second, she still had time to escape. But she needed to move.

She grasped the lock and pulled it up, releasing it manually. Fitting her fingers into the handle, she pulled it and shoved her shoulder into the door at the same time.

The door didn't budge.

A sob caught in her throat. She tried again. Again, it wouldn't open. Water bore down on the door, sealing it from the outside.

What was she going to do?

She closed her eyes and focused on her breathing. In and out. In and out. She couldn't let herself panic. There had to be a way out. She just had to stay calm enough to think, stay calm enough to find it.

If water pressure from the outside was forcing the door closed, then equaling the pressure would free the door. She just had to wait for the car to sink. The slight odor of fish clogged her throat. The relentless lap of waves drummed in beat with her pulse.

She'd never been afraid of water. Her father had insisted she take swimming lessons so she wouldn't suffer from the fear as he had. But the thought of letting the car sink, letting herself be trapped underwater…she didn't know if she could go through with it.

The car listed farther forward, the heavy engine dragging it down. The water rose to her knees. It crept over the seat.

A shudder came from the back of the vehicle. Marie twisted in her seat. Sore muscles in her neck protesting, she strained to see where the movement had come from.

Behind her, the shoreline seemed to move away.

The car jolted again. Oh God. She knew what was happening. The back wheels were thunking down the rocks along the shoreline. Without brakes to stop them, they would keep rolling, pushing the car farther into the bay.

Where the water was deep.

A sound came from her throat, an involuntary whimper.

She pulled the emergency brake. The lever moved easily. Too easily. It wasn't working, either.

She tried to breathe, struggling to remember the way Sophie had showed her. All she could think about was the car's nose diving deep. The car flipping over. Would she be able to get out if that happened? Would she even be conscious by the time it settled on the bottom?

She couldn't wait. She had to do something now.

She pulled her feet up out of the water. Twisting out from behind the steering wheel, she aimed the heels of her boots at the driver's window. Pulling her knees up to her chest, she gasped in a lungful of oxygen and kicked with all her strength.

Glass exploded into tiny pieces.

CURSING HIS LEG, Brandon raced for the edge of the water. He'd been walking Doug Heller to the door when he'd seen Marie's car go over the edge. For a second, he'd been stunned and confused. His body had burst into a run before his brain had caught up.

Marie was in the water. Maybe trapped in her car. Maybe hurt. He had to move. He had to reach her in time.

Pain clawed through his damaged tendons with each stride. He gripped his cane, stabbing it into the ground, pushing his legs faster.

He wouldn't lose Marie.

He reached the crest of the shoreline. Water stretched in front of him, waves lapping on rock. A light mass showed through the undulating waves. The car. It was submerged.

He stumbled on the rock, almost going down to his knees. She couldn't—

"Brandon."

He turned to the sound of her voice.

She huddled on the sharp rock, ten yards down the shoreline. Her clothing was soaked, her hair dark with water. She struggled to stand.

He scrambled over rock. His cane slipped from his hand and clattered into a crevice. He didn't care. He kept going. The only important thing was reaching Marie. The only important thing was that she was safe.

He wrapped her in his arms.

She clung to him, wet and cold and shaking. She looked up at him, her breath warm on his face.

He brought his mouth down on hers. Needy. Devouring the very life force of her. She tasted just the way he remembered. Warm and strong and oh so alive. He moved his lips over her face, her neck. Taking in all of her. Soaking in the feel of her body, the beat of her heart against his. He felt he'd waited forever for this. Wanted it. Dreamed about it. Pushed the dreams away. But he didn't deny himself now. He couldn't. It didn't matter that it was all wrong. That they'd get hurt in the end. That it could go nowhere. He'd almost lost her, but she was here. She'd almost died, but now she lived.

And God help him, whatever happened next, he didn't know how he'd ever let her go.

MARIE PULLED her big wool sweater tight around her shoulders and shifted closer to the fire. Her neck had changed from painful to stiff and painful. And although she was now dry, the chill hadn't left her bones. It felt as if it never would.

"Here." Brandon pushed a fresh cup of hot tea into her hands.

"Thanks." She wrapped her fingers around the cup's heat. He'd been hovering over her since he'd found her on the rocks, having escaped from the car and swum to shore. And even though she hated to admit it, she loved him taking care of her. It had been a long time since someone took care of her. Since she'd last lived at Drake House with a father who took care of everybody.

But Brandon wasn't anything like her father.

She could still feel the desperate press of his body against hers. She could still taste his kiss. It had been everything she wanted, the passion between them unleashed, the barriers broken. But even though he looked at her now with the same fire in his eyes, she knew their moment had changed nothing.

And that was what confused her the most.

Brandon lowered himself into a nearby chair.

How she wished he'd sit closer. How she wanted him to wrap his arm around her and kiss her again. She knew he'd do it if she asked. After that kiss she was even pretty sure he still loved her. Not that he'd admit it. Not that it mattered.

Brandon blamed himself for loving her. He blamed his feelings for causing his wife's death. And unless she proved to him Charlotte hadn't taken her own life, there was no way he'd forgive himself. Not enough to find happiness. At least not happiness with Marie.

And there was no way she wanted to suffer that kind of heartbreak again. She knew better this time.

Brandon checked his watch. "Hammer should be here any minute."

Marie almost groaned. "I'm not looking forward to explaining this to Hammer. He already thinks I'm making things up. My father's murder. The break-in. Even the roof. He's going to think I drove into the water myself. He's going to be more convinced than ever that I'm a crackpot."

Brandon didn't disagree. Instead he leaned forward and looked her in the eye. "Don't mention your father's murder. Or Charlotte's."

She wanted to protest that it was all related, but she'd told him that too many times before. "I won't. He'll have me committed for sure."

"Just focus on the attempts to hurt you. That's all we can do. It's all Hammer can help with, anyway."

And it was all Brandon believed.

A heavy feeling settled into the pit of Marie's stomach. This whole thing was a no-win situation. Finding evidence that didn't exist. Falling in love with Brandon all over again when she could only hope for more of the same pain.

Brandon shifted in his chair. "Where were you going this morning? The last I saw, you were having coffee."

He looked up at her again, this time his expression less insistent and more filled with worry.

"I wasn't going anywhere. Shelley asked me to move my car."

"Why?"

She explained about the decorator and Shelley's pressure to clean out her father's things. She wanted to tell him the rest, too. The way Shelley worshiped Charlotte. The way she'd warned Marie to stay away. But it all seemed too close after the kiss. Shelley was more perceptive than Marie had given her credit for.

Brandon groaned. "I should have been more on top of that. You'll have as much time as you need."

"Thanks."

He kept his eyes on her face. His brows dipped low. "What else?"

"I'm going back to the psychomanteum." She hadn't known that was her plan until she said it. But once the words were out, she knew it was what she needed to do.

"Are you sure?"

The thought made her nervous. But not more nervous than the idea of never finding out who killed her father and Charlotte. Not more nervous than waiting for the police to track down whoever was trying to kill her, especially when Chief Hammer seemed determined to chalk it up to her paranoid imagination. And it didn't make her more nervous than the growing feelings she had for Brandon and the certainty that she was heading for the same anguish she'd suffered ten years before. "I'm sure."

It seemed to take a lot of effort for Brandon to nod this

time. "Then I'll take you. I'm not letting you out of my sight until you're safely on a plane back to Michigan."

The cold settled deeper into her bones.

"Mr. Brandon?" Shelley called from the doorway. "Chief Hammer and Officer Draper are here."

Marie took a deep breath and braced herself for another round with the Jenkins Cove police.

MARIE STARED at the flickering candlelight reflected in the mirror. She tried to clear her mind, to relax, but a jitter circulated through her bloodstream like too much espresso, and she didn't seem to be able to focus on anything. After more than an hour, she'd given up trying to reach her father. Now she'd switched her focus to Charlotte. If this didn't work, she was out of options.

She breathed deeply, as Sophie had instructed. In and out. In and out. But all she smelled was the dusty odor of an old house. All she felt was a light head.

"Charlotte? Where are you?"

No scent. No voice.

"Charlotte? Please. I need your help."

Again nothing.

Marie stared at the mirror. Her own face stared back. She didn't get it. If Charlotte had been trying to tell her she'd been murdered, if she'd wanted Marie to find proof and seek justice, why wasn't she answering? Why wasn't she helping now?

"I can't find anything to prove your murder. I don't know where to look." She buried her head in her hands. If Charlotte couldn't communicate anymore, all this was no use. She might as well go back to Michigan. At least that way, she'd get far away from Brandon. She'd save herself the heartbreak of loving a man who wouldn't let himself love her back.

Tears stung the back of her eyes. She drew in a shuddering breath.

Jasmine.

Marie raised her head. Swiping at her eyes, she stared at the mirror. She felt something. A pressure. A presence. Candlelight flickered from behind her. Her vision became unfocused. "Charlotte? Tell me who killed you. Give me some kind of sign."

The scent of jasmine faded. Another odor took over the room. Something harsh. Sharp fumes stung her eyes.

Gasoline.

The whoosh of flame stole the air from her lungs. Heat seared her skin. Pain. Burning.

A scream ripped from Marie's throat. She shielded her face with her hands. She wasn't on fire. It wasn't real. She knew it…and yet the brightness flooded her vision, the roar of flame deafened her, the heat made her feel as if she were dying. "Charlotte, please. Who did this? Who did this to you?"

Footsteps thunked up the stairs.

She dragged her hands from her face and stared into the mirror.

The image was faint, like a cloud on her vision from the pressure of fingertips against closed lids. Petals. A stem. A single leaf.

A childlike etching of a simple flower took shape. A flower with cupped petals. A tulip.

The door flew open behind her. Brandon's reflection filled the mirror. Broad shoulders, dark brows, worried eyes. "Marie! For God's sake, what happened?"

Marie stared deeply into the silvered glass, but the

image had faded and was gone. All she could see was candlelight and shadows playing over Brandon's face.

Sophie joined him in the doorway. "Sweetheart? Are you okay?"

She felt weak. Sick. And although the burning sensation had stopped, she felt numb as if she were now covered with thick scars. "No, I'm not. I'm not okay at all."

Chapter Twelve

"I know you don't believe me."

Brandon's throat pinched. He followed her up the stairs that led to the upper floors of the east wing. Swallowing what she'd experienced in the psychomanteum was definitely a challenge. He'd never been one to believe in things he couldn't see with his own eyes, hear with his own ears, touch with his own hand. "I've never had experiences like that, Marie. I'm trying to understand."

She stopped on the landing and spun to face him. "Go to the psychomanteum. Obviously Charlotte is trying to contact you. She's just using me to do it."

"I don't need to sit in Sophie Caldwell's room, Marie. I know what Charlotte went through. I was there."

Even in the dim light he could see her gaze flit over the right side of his face.

He clutched the head of his cane. He hated the thought that Marie could see his scars and imperfections every time she looked at his face or witnessed his limp. He wished he could be the same man for her that he'd been that summer ten years ago. Despite the raw emotion still between them, he knew damn well it was too late for that.

Just as it was too late for Charlotte.

"What are you looking for up here?"

Marie resumed climbing the stairs. "The other night I smelled Charlotte's scent near the window in her study. I looked around, but couldn't find anything."

"I had Edwin give Charlotte's personal things to her family and the rest to charity. He wanted to auction off the furniture at the Christmas Ball."

"Shelley said you canceled the ball."

"Edwin and Charlotte put on the ball. It just didn't seem right to do it without them. And to tell you the truth, I didn't feel up to having people in the house."

"My father loved the ball. He loved Christmas."

"Which is why I can't see having it without him."

Reaching the top of the stairs, she paused once again to face him. "I think he would like it to go on. I think it would be a fitting tribute, to both my father and Charlotte. Besides, the Drake Foundation does wonderful things with the auction money, things that help a lot of people."

Leave it to Marie to see past the pain, to focus on the people in need and a tribute to the memories of those gone. "You are a strong woman, Marie." He wanted to touch her, to run his fingers through her hair, to kiss her the way he had by the water. He wished he could kiss her like that every day for the rest of his life. He gripped his cane in both fists.

"Thanks. I don't feel very strong."

"Well, you are. That's probably why Charlotte has contacted you instead of me. She knows you can handle it. She knows you're a fighter."

"You're a fighter, too." Her wide, caramel eyes looked straight into his, as though she believed what she was saying, as though she meant every word.

"I like the man I am in your eyes. I always have."

"You are that man, Brandon."

How he wished he could believe that. How he wished all the mistakes he'd made in his life would disappear and he could be as pure and strong and righteous as he'd felt when he'd fallen in love with Marie all those years ago.

But even then he'd already given Charlotte his mother's ring. Even then he hadn't lived up to Marie's image of him. "I'm not. I don't know if I ever was. But when you look at me, I can pretend. And that will have to be enough."

She reached out and took his hand.

He clasped her fingers. Her skin felt impossibly soft, her bones fragile. But it was all an illusion. Marie was strong and tough and unflinching in her caring for others and in her belief that good would win in the end. She was everything he was not. Everything he'd lost over the years. Everything he'd never had. It was impossible to go back, impossible to change things. But at least for the moment, he could hold her hand and pretend. "Lead on."

"DO YOU SMELL IT?" Marie leaned close to the desk where she'd smelled the jasmine before she'd been dragged to the roof. The scent tickled her nose, light and sweet. Barely there, yet every bit grounded in reality.

Brandon tilted his head and gave the air a sniff. "Where?"

It grew stronger. She gestured for him to move closer. "Right here. All around."

He stepped beside her. Almost close enough for her to feel his body heat. Almost close enough that if she shifted to the side, their arms would touch.

Breathing slowly, he finally shook his head. "Where does it seem to be coming from?"

She leaned toward the window. Sure enough, it was stronger here. "Not the desk. Maybe the window."

He followed, breathing deep, a frown still lining his brow.

Marie stood still. Cold flowed over her, digging deep and sucking the warmth from her skin. She glanced back at Brandon. "Do you feel that?"

"The draft?"

"A few days ago I would have thought it was a draft, too." She raised her palm to the window. The air felt still. "This is not coming from outside. But the scent is strongest here." She gestured to the mullioned window.

"I...I can smell it." Brandon's voice rang low and steady, not questioning anymore, but sure.

Goosebumps peppered Marie's skin. "Do you feel her?"

"I...maybe. No. I don't know."

Marie peered through the rippled glass. The faint light of a slivered moon reflected off the waves of Chesapeake Bay. Below the window, the east garden nestled, ready for winter.

The garden where she'd first felt the still cold that was surrounding them now. "The garden."

"Edwin had that garden redesigned this fall."

Yes. She remembered that. But she hadn't put it all together. A trill reverberated along her nerves. "Maybe that's it. Let's go down to the garden." It didn't take them long to retrace their steps down the staircase. They wound through the dimly lit house to the kitchen and headed for the exit.

"Mr. Brandon?"

Marie jumped at the woman's voice.

Brandon spun around. "Shelley? Isn't it kind of late? What are you doing here?"

Shelley smiled sweetly at her boss. "Just taking care of some loose ends. Can I get you something?" She glanced at Marie, at their joined hands. The smile faded.

"No. We're fine. It's late." Brandon gave Marie's hand a little squeeze, then slipped his fingers free.

A weight shifted into Marie's chest.

"It's a big house. A lot to do," Shelley rattled on. "I can see why Edwin lived in the house. It's the only way to get everything done. And he didn't have anything to do with the cooking."

Marie knew Brandon wasn't going to offer the butler quarters, not until she was done with them. But she half expected him to let Shelley move into one of the guest rooms. And she had to admit, having someone else living in the house would make it easier for him to keep his distance, easier for them both.

"You're right, Shelley," Brandon said. "You are trying to do way too much. We'll have to start interviewing for cooks. Let me know when you have some good prospects lined up."

"Cooks?"

"Unless you'd rather take applicants for the butler's job."

"I'll get some cooks lined up right away, sir." She glanced at Marie, and gave her a somewhat apologetic smile.

"Good night." Brandon gave Shelley a nod. He held

the door open for Marie, and she slipped through into the night.

Oyster shells crunched under their feet. The night was cool, but even so, it felt balmy compared to the frigid air in Charlotte's study. Marie had heard cold spots were thought to be caused by spirits' attempt to manifest themselves. But she hadn't really connected those dots the first time she'd passed through the east garden. She wouldn't miss it again.

They wound their way to the garden. Holly and boxwood flanked the path. A plastic-covered fountain hulked near the house, its musical trickle silenced in preparation for the freezing temperatures of winter. The white concrete bench she'd spotted from the window glowed in the artful landscape lighting, nearly as bright as the shells at their feet.

"What are we looking for?"

"Search me." Brandon jabbed the fountain's covering with the tip of his cane. "This garden was redone after Charlotte's death. What was your father's favorite feature of this garden?"

Marie glanced at him. Did he now believe? She didn't know. Maybe he didn't, either. But at least he was trying. He was keeping his mind open. He was supporting her.

"My father. What did he like?" Marie blew a breath through tense lips. "I have no clue. My father was never into nature."

"Charlotte loved the rose garden on the west side of the house. And the gardens around the boathouse."

Marie shook her head. "I have a feeling it's this garden." The scent tickled Marie's senses, as if a confirmation of her belief. "Jasmine."

"Where?"

She turned around slowly. It seemed to be everywhere, faint in the outside air. Too faint. "I can't tell. I can hardly smell it."

"There must have been something about this garden that your father liked. He was the one who had it redesigned. I left it all up to him. I couldn't have cared less at the time."

What did her father like? "I don't know what it would be. I didn't know him to ever be passionate about gardens. Drake House, that's all he really cared about. He loved Drake House."

"That doesn't tell us anything."

"Wait. Maybe it does. I have an idea." She took the side path and wound her way through loosely mulched plants. She stopped at the concrete bench and sat down facing the house.

Landscape lighting shot upward, highlighting the house. The dark bushes stood out in sharp relief against the mansion's snow-white siding. Columns soared up to the third floor where the slate roof took over, all sharp angles and graceful slopes. In the summer, the fountain's magic would play against the backdrop of it all, its music adding to the mansion's grandeur.

Brandon sat down beside her.

Shivers prickled over her skin. "This is it. This is my father's favorite part of this garden."

He squinted at the bushes, the fountain, the smaller plants protected by mulch. "What is it?"

"My father loved Drake House more than anything, except maybe me. You have to admit, the house looks spectacular from this vantage point."

Brandon didn't look up. His eyes were still locked on the mulched plants at the bench's base. "What's this?" He reached into a patch of ivy and pulled something out. He held it in the air for her to see. A barrel key.

Marie's pulse fluttered. "Any ideas where it's from?"

Brandon shrugged and held it up higher to catch the landscape lighting. The key carried the patina of age and had a leaf-shaped end. "There are a few of the old doors in the house that use a key like this, but this looks like the wrong size."

"Where else could it have come from?"

"Lexie Thornton had a crew here working on the garden. Maybe it belongs to one of them."

Of course. Lexie had designed the garden. Her family's landscaping company had provided all the plants, the fountain and the bench. "Maybe Lexie could tell us more, not just about the key. Maybe she can help point us to whatever it is we're looking for."

"How late is too late to give her a call?" Brandon glanced down at his watch.

"I don't know. She works so hard, I'd hate to wake her. Maybe we should look around a little more first, try some of the doors in the house."

"Sure. I'll ask Shelley if she knows anything about the key, if she's still here."

"And Isabella?" Marie couldn't help thinking the key had to be related to something that had been going on. And Isabella seemed to be hiding the most secrets of anyone at Drake House.

Brandon nodded. "Right."

They pushed up from the bench at the same time.

Beneath them, the concrete shifted. Brandon grabbed Marie's arm, steadying them both.

"What was that?" Marie said.

Brandon gripped the top of the bench and pushed. It moved under his hand.

For a split second, Marie thought she saw a hollow space in the base of the bench. A space with something that looked like paper tucked inside. "Wait. Do that again."

Brandon lifted the edge of the bench.

Marie leaned close, her pulse racing. This had to be it. She peered into the dark space. "The legs of the bench are hollow. And there's something…" She dipped her hand inside. Her fingers touched the edge of a rolled piece of paper. She pulled it out.

Brandon lowered the bench's seat back into place. "What is it?"

Marie unrolled the paper. At first she wasn't sure. All she could see were penciled lines. "This is strange. It looks like a drawing of some sort."

Brandon studied it over her shoulder. He guided her hand, positioning the paper to take advantage of the landscape lighting. "It looks like a diagram. A sketch of the undercarriage of a car."

Sure enough. She could make out the wheels and the axles, the engine area and the gas tank. "What is this?" She indicated a pointy object near the gas tank.

"Some sort of spike?" He raised dark eyes to meet Marie's. "It's positioned to puncture the gas tank."

A pop split the air and echoed off Drake House.

Marie's heart jumped. "What was that?"

Brandon stiffened. He spun around, looking for the source of the sound.

Another pop. The bench made a snapping sound and something hit Marie in the leg.

"Get down!" Brandon threw his arms around her. His body slammed into her, and both of them tumbled to the ground.

Chapter Thirteen

Brandon could feel the air rush out of Marie's lungs as he came down on top of her. He raised himself up on his elbows, trying to lift his weight off her. "Marie, are you okay? Say something." He held his breath, willing her to speak, to be all right.

She coughed, gasped, nodded her head. Her breath sputtered and caught. Scooping air into her lungs, she looked at him with wide eyes. "I'm fine. I'm... What *was* that?"

"A gun."

"Someone is shooting at us?"

"Yes." And Brandon had to get Marie out of here. He had to get her someplace safe. "Can you move?"

"I don't know. I think something hit my leg."

A bullet? Brandon's gut tensed. Had Marie been shot? "Where?"

She moved her left leg under him. "I can't... You'll have to get up."

"Not until you're out of the line of fire." Marie might already be shot. He wasn't going to move aside and risk her being hit again. "Move to the other side of the bench. I'll shield you."

"But you—"

"No arguments." He glared directly into her eyes. She had to listen to him. She had to do what he said. "Go."

She gave a nod.

He lifted his weight off her, balancing on hands and toes, as if he were doing a push-up.

Marie rolled in one place until she lay on her stomach. She started crawling.

Pain screamed up Brandon's damaged leg. Gritting his teeth, he held on, trying to compensate with his good leg and arms.

She moved out from under him. As she cleared his body, he could smell blood. Something dark glistened on one leg of her jeans.

Damn. He hadn't been fast enough. It had taken too long for him to recognize the popping sound, to realize what it was. And his failure had left Marie hurt. Shot.

Reaching the corner of the bench, Marie rose to hands and knees. She moved faster, slipping between the holly bush and the bench.

Another pop echoed off the house. Something hit the concrete bench close to Marie's head. Too close.

"Get down!" Brandon yelled. He struggled to his knees. To his feet.

"Brandon!" Marie screamed. She popped up behind the bench, as if she was going to jump out and save him. "You'll be shot!"

"Stay there."

Another shot cracked in his ear. Again, something hit the bench. The bench. Not him. Even though he was standing in plain view. Even though he was a big, open target. Even though he'd done everything he could think of to draw the fire to him and away from Marie.

"Marie, stay down." He raced for the bench. He climbed into a spot next to her. He brought his hand down on her head, physically pushing her head lower, under the protection of the bench. He laid his chest on top of her and he wrapped his arms around her body.

She hunkered down, making room for him. She trembled all over.

Brandon held her tighter. Anger balled in his chest like a hard fist. Marie had almost been hit again. She'd almost died. No matter how careful he'd been, no matter how hard he'd tried to shield her, protect her, she'd come so close to losing her life he could hardly breathe. "Why didn't you get down? Why didn't you do what I said?"

She shuddered, as if letting out a silent sob. "I thought...I thought you were going to be killed."

He forced a breath into tight lungs. She didn't understand. In true Marie fashion, she'd thought only about saving him. Only about making sure he was safe. "Whoever is out there, he's not gunning for me."

She shook her head, as if she didn't want to believe the obvious.

It didn't matter. Not now. Now the only thing that meant a damn was getting Marie out of this mess. And the first thing he had to do was douse these lights.

He peered over the bench. His cane lay in the center of the path, its wood dark against the oyster shells. Too far to reach. Even if the shooter wasn't gunning for him, Brandon couldn't chance it. He didn't dare move that far from Marie.

He looked down at his feet. What he wouldn't give to be wearing hiking boots about now. Or a pair of the steel-toed work boots Doug Heller preferred. His Bruno

Maglis would have to do. Any luck and their sheer expense would make up for what they lacked in heft. Yeah, right.

Forcing his arms to release Marie, he slipped one shoe off.

"What are you doing?"

"Giving us some cover. Stay down." He slid between Marie and the prickly wall of holly. Using his hands and one foot, he pulled his body forward until he reached one of the landscape lights, a canister pointing up toward the siding of Drake House. Holding the shoe by its toe box, he brought the heel down hard against glass.

The lense protecting the light cracked but held.

He struck it again. And again.

Finally it shattered. One more blow and the light went dark.

He moved to the next light, the only one left that illuminated the bench area where they hid. He pulled back his shoe, ready to strike again.

A gunshot split the air.

Brandon ducked. His heart pounded; his breath rushed in his ears. He twisted back to check on Marie. She hadn't moved. "Marie?"

"I'm okay."

Had that bullet been meant for him? He didn't think so. The other shots had been fired close to Marie, too close. If the shooter had aimed at him this time, he should have been able to do a better job of hitting his target than that.

Unless he was just trying to scare Brandon. Trying to get him to abandon breaking the second light.

Hands clammy, he grasped the shoe and brought it down on the lens. Two more blows and the bulb was broken. The area was dark.

He scrambled back to Marie. The shells around the bench dug into his hands, his good knee. Now that the would-be killer had lost his spotlight, Marie was safer. But he still knew where she was hiding.

Brandon scanned the garden, searching for another spot to hide. But most of the garden was young, the plants still small. Only the holly and boxwood were left from the old east garden. Only they were large enough to conceal two adults. And only the bench could stop a bullet.

There was nowhere else to go.

Brandon looked down at the shoe still clutched in his hand. Maybe Marie and he didn't have to find a new hiding place. Maybe they only had to make the shooter think they had.

He dragged the shoe against the shells, making a shuffling sound. After several seconds of that, he flung it into a far section of the garden. Slipping off the second shoe, he flung that one as well.

Now to get back to Marie.

He moved slowly, careful to make no sound, careful to avoid rustling against the bushes. When he reached Marie, he slipped his arms around her as he had before. Lying flat behind the bench, he held her back tight to his chest. He brought his lips to her ear, her hair like silk against his cheek. "Shh."

She nodded. She didn't move. She barely seemed to breathe.

A minute passed. Two. It seemed like forever. Finally Brandon could hear the crunch of oyster shells underfoot.

He listened, struggling to hear the sound, to track it, over the beat of his own pulse, the hiss of his own breathing.

It came closer. Closer. It stopped.

Beneath him, Marie trembled. He could feel the rise and fall of her chest cease as she held her breath.

He wrapped her close, shielding her. If only he had a weapon. His cane. Even one of his shoes. Anything. He'd fight. But he'd used everything he could think of. Everything he had. And all that was left was to wait and see if it was enough.

A siren screamed from the direction of the highway.

The police. Thank God.

Footsteps crunched on shells. But this time going away, getting faint.

The siren drew closer. Red and blue light flashed from the other side of Drake House, radiating out from the corner of the east wing like an aurora during an eclipse.

Unless the gunman was an idiot, he had kept running and was long gone by now. Brandon closed his eyes and scooped in a deep breath of Marie's scent. He lay there for several seconds, soaking in the feel of her, the knowledge that she was safe.

Finally he forced his arms to release her. He forced his body to move away. Cold air filled the warmth where she'd been. His chest ached with it. It was all he could do to keep himself from gathering her against him again.

He looked at her, wanting to make sure she was okay. His gaze landed on her bloody jeans. "Let me see your leg."

She sat up. Grimacing, she pulled the leg of her jeans up to her knee. A red stain darkened her calf.

He moved to the side to get a better view of her wound. He could see a cut. He could see blood, but not as much blood as he'd expected.

"It's not too bad," Marie said. "I think it's just a cut. Maybe from a fragment of the bench."

She was probably right. In everyday life, the size of the cut and amount of blood would have horrified him. After all Marie had faced in the past few days, it seemed like nothing. She was alive, after all.

She was alive.

He could hear footsteps circling the house from either side, and low, official voices. The police. Josef must have called. Or Shelley.

"Whoever was shooting at us must think I found something. That I know something. That's why he's trying to kill me. To keep me quiet. Like he did my father."

Marie had voiced that theory before. And it made sense. But to Brandon, it didn't feel right. He'd been asking as many questions as Marie. He'd been with her, in her father's quarters, in Charlotte's study, in the garden fishing the sketch from the bench. So why didn't the shooter see him as a threat, too? Why wasn't the shooter just as eager to kill him?

The words Marie heard in the psychomanteum filtered through his mind. *All Brandon loves will die.* And who did he love? Who had he always loved?

Marie.

To Brandon's relief, it didn't take long for the police officers to secure the house and grounds and lead Brandon and Marie safely inside. A few minutes later, Chief Hammer joined them. Dressed in jeans with what little hair he had left plastered flat to one side of his head, he obviously hadn't been at the station this time. He'd no doubt been sleeping comfortably in his bed beside Mrs. Hammer. And although Brandon didn't have unshakable confidence in the Jenkins Cove Police Department or their leader, he was unspeakably glad they were here.

They'd saved Marie's life.

He answered the door himself, ushering the chief inside. "Thanks for coming personally, Chief. I know it's late."

"Not a problem. You know that, Brandon. It's a good thing your housekeeper called about the gunshots. I'm glad we were able to get here in time."

"Your men did a good job."

"Glad to hear it. They're good boys. I just had a word with Benson over by the carriage house before I came in."

Guilt jolted through Brandon with the force of an electric shock. He gripped his cane in both hands. He hadn't even thought to check on Josef. "My chauffeur. Is he all right?"

"Seems okay. Pretty scared. Poor guy was shaking."

Brandon would have to find a way to make it up to him. Extra vacation time. Trip to Florida. Something. Shelley, too. She'd kept her head and called the police. Interesting that the one employee he couldn't account for was the one he and Marie had the most reason to suspect. "You might want to send a car over to my maid's house. Isabella Faust."

"Why is that?"

"She's been acting a little strange lately. And I have reason to believe she might be out to get Marie."

"Marie? You're sure she was the target in this incident, too?"

"She was the target. Believe me, if whoever was

shooting that gun had wanted me dead, I wouldn't be talking to you now. He was gunning for Marie."

Brandon tried to read the chief's eyes. Hammer didn't like Marie, and he didn't believe much of what she said. He'd made that much clear. Maybe once she showed him the sketch they'd found, he'd reassess her theories.

Brandon sure had. At least he wanted to.

Hammer finally nodded. "All right. I'll have someone check up on Ms. Faust. Anyone else I should know about?"

Brandon thought for a moment. "Ned Perry, the developer."

Hammer nodded. "So he's been after you, too? I should have known. The man is a making a nuisance of himself. Badgering folks all around town to sell their waterfront."

"I think he and Isabella might be doing a little scheming to get their hands on Drake House."

"Scheming? How would shooting at Marie Leonard help them get Drake House?"

"Marie thinks they want to cover up something she has found."

"Marie thinks, eh?" The chief didn't look impressed. "And what do you think?"

Good damn question. Brandon shifted his feet on the thick oriental rug. He gripped the head of his cane. Marie's theory still didn't feel right to him. But what was the alternative? The words of a ghost? Words he hadn't even heard himself? "I'm with Marie."

The chief smiled in an unsuccessful attempt to cover up his skepticism. "All right, then. I'll hear Ms. Leonard out. Any more ideas about who might have declared target practice tonight?"

None that had panned out. "Come on in the kitchen. Marie's in there and she has something to show you. It might make everything more clear." At least Brandon could hope. He led Hammer through the halls, past the formal dining room and into the kitchen.

Marie and Shelley stood in the food preparation area, leaning on opposite countertops. Even though Brandon had helped Marie bandage her leg and had given her instructions to keep it elevated, she was back on her feet, probably still feeling too shaken to sit for long.

Hammer focused on Marie. The lines in his jowly face deepened with concern. "How is it you were involved in two life-threatening incidents in one day, Miss Leonard?"

Marie met his eyes. Her back stiffened just a little. "Not by choice, Chief."

"Brandon said you have something to show me?"

"I do." She pushed away from the counter and held out the rolled paper. "We found this hidden in the hollow base of a bench in the east garden. I think my father stashed it there."

The chief unfurled the roll. Plucking a pair of reading glasses out of his pocket, he slipped them on his pudgy nose and squinted down at the sketch. "A car?"

Shelley inched closer, craning her neck to see. She cradled a tea cup in her hands, a sweet scent wafting over the brim.

"The undercarriage of a car," Brandon said. "And look at the spike positioned by the gas tank."

Hammer frowned. "What is this supposed to be?"

"The evidence you wanted." Marie's voice was low but rang with conviction.

Brandon hoped Hammer would see it the same way.

The chief focused on Marie. "Evidence of what?"

Marie didn't miss a beat. "Charlotte Drake's murder."

A choked whimper came from Shelley's throat.

The chief held the paper at arm's length, as if suddenly afraid it would bite him. "Is this real?"

Marie's eyes flashed. Her hands tightened to fists by her sides. "You mean did I quickly draw it up?" she said sarcastically. "Of course it's real. It's just what I told you it is."

Brandon moved to Marie's side. He knew she was frustrated with her push and pull with the police. But if she wanted Hammer to look into the case, if she wanted him to switch the deaths from accidents to murders, if she wanted him to call in the state police to investigate, she had to be more diplomatic. He rested a hand on her arm.

She let out a pent-up breath. "I'm sorry, Chief. I've had a tough day."

"No offense taken, young lady. I'll take this back to the station and look into it along with the rest of the leads we find."

"No." Marie reached out to grasp the paper.

Hammer pulled it out of her range. "What do you mean, no?"

"I want to see your photos of the vehicle," Marie said. "The one Charlotte died in."

Brandon was aware of Shelley stepping closer behind him.

Hammer kept his eyes on Marie. He shook his head. "I'm sorry. I can't let you do that."

"Why not?"

"You aren't family. You don't own the car. You're not

part of the investigation. In short, I have no reason to show you anything."

Brandon took a deep breath. "Then maybe you can show me."

Marie whirled to glance up at him. Turning back to Hammer, she nodded. "You can't say Brandon doesn't have reason to look at the photos."

Hammer watched Brandon intently, as if trying to read his thoughts.

Strange. Brandon hadn't felt scrutinized like this by a police officer since he'd been caught drinking beer underage during his first year of college. A lifetime ago. He was more used to the chief of police handling his routine calls personally, not searching for the truth in his eyes.

Finally the chief nodded, as if he'd made up his mind about something. "There are no photos."

"No photos?" If it was possible for Marie's eyes to grow wider, they did. "What do you mean? Aren't they part of the accident report? Isn't taking pictures of a car involved in a fatal accident routine?"

"My officers must have overlooked it."

An uneasy feeling crept up the back of Brandon's neck. That could be true, except an officer hadn't overseen the accident report. As with most of the things involving the Drakes, Chief Hammer had hovered over the incident personally. And although Hammer had a reputation for being lazy, Brandon couldn't believe he was this lazy, not about something as serious as a death, accidental or not. "Why weren't pictures taken, Chief?"

Hammer looked down at the tile floor, the overhead lights reflecting off his scalp. "I thought…I thought it might get…inconvenient."

"Inconvenient?" Brandon parroted. "What in the hell does that mean?"

Hammer raised his eyes. "I don't think you want me to spell it out."

What was he getting at? Brandon had no clue. And he wasn't sure he wanted to know.

"You don't need pictures of her car," Shelley said.

All of them turned to look at the housekeeper.

She gripped her tea, her hands shaking so badly the steaming liquid sloshed over the edge of the cup and onto reddened fingers. She stared from Brandon to Marie, as if unaware she was burning herself. "The car itself. Her car. It's in a salvage yard outside town."

"It's still around?" The chief stared at Shelley as if she were speaking another language. "It was supposed to go to a crusher. It was supposed to be destroyed." He glanced at Brandon, his expression strangely apologetic.

"Shelley, are you sure it's still there?" Marie asked.

The woman nodded her gray head vigorously. "I see it every week."

"You must be mistaken." Again Hammer shot Brandon that strange look.

"I'm not mistaken. Believe me. I pay the rent, and Joey keeps it for me. Just like it was. I visit it every week. It helps me remember. Helps me keep her alive."

Brandon stared at his housekeeper. The woman visited the car in which Charlotte died? She paid someone to keep it for her? The idea was disturbing. Twisted.

Shelley's face crumpled. Tears rolled down her taut cheeks. "That paper, what does it say? What does it mean?"

Marie stepped toward Shelley. She laid a gentle hand on the woman's arm. "Charlotte didn't die in an accident, Shelley. I'm so sorry."

"What are you saying?"

"That paper and the car you've been caring for prove that Charlotte was murdered."

"Just a minute, Ms. Leonard," the chief boomed. "It doesn't prove any such thing."

"It will when we examine the car," Marie insisted. "We'll know then."

Shelley's tears gushed harder. The woman's wiry body convulsed in a sob. "Who could have done that?" She focused on Marie, and for a moment Brandon thought he saw a flash of hatred in her eyes.

"Calm down, Shelley," he commanded. "It wasn't Marie, for God's sake. But with your help, we can find out who did it. We're going to find out."

Shelley drew in a shuddering breath and nodded. Blindly she set her cup on the counter, then covered her face and softly cried.

Marie stepped beside her and placed a tender hand on the woman's shoulder. She said something soft in her ear, too quiet for Brandon to catch.

"I'm sorry," Shelley whispered. "So sorry." She reached for Marie, and Marie wrapped the woman in her arms.

Brandon looked back at Hammer. "I think you should call in the state police."

"You really want to do that?"

Brandon frowned. Strange. The chief's words sounded ominous, almost threatening, but his tone of voice was just plain worried. "Why wouldn't I?"

"You want it straight?" Hammer asked in a low voice.

Brandon answered with a nod.

"Because if your wife was murdered, the state's first suspect is going to be the husband, that's why."

Understanding rippled through Brandon. Suddenly it all made sense. The chief's hovering. His laziness in taking photos of Charlotte's car. Maybe even his reluctance to look at Edwin's death as anything but an accident. "You think *I* was responsible?"

Hammer waved off the words. "I don't think anything."

"You do. And you're protecting me."

Hammer didn't confirm or deny, he just held up the paper in his hand. "What do you want me to do with this? I'll handle it however you say."

Brandon shook his head. He'd never needed Chief Hammer's special protection. He'd never asked for it, never wanted it. And although he now realized it was merely part of his birthright, part of being a Drake in a town like Jenkins Cove, he felt a little sick at the double standard wealth gave him.

He looked Hammer straight in the eye. "Give the sketch to the state police. And while you're at it, call them right now and have someone meet us at the salvage yard owned by Shelley's friend. We have a car to examine."

Chapter Fourteen

The sun was starting to pink the eastern sky by the time Marie, Brandon and Chief Hammer met a Maryland state police detective named Randall McClellan at Joey Jansen's Auto Salvage east of Jenkins Cove on Route 43. Tucked into the base of a narrow neck of land clustered with vacation homes, the junkyard consisted of two corrugated buildings surrounded by rusted and twisted skeletons of cars and signs proclaiming Off-Season Boat Storage, Cheap Prices!

Joey, a man young enough to be Shelley's son and with a facial tick that looked to Marie as if he were constantly winking at her, led them to one of the steel sheds. He unlocked the door, apologized that there were no electric lights in the place, then announced he was going back to bed.

Marie let the men lead the way. A mixture of covered boats and a few pieces of farm machinery packed the large shed. The detective led them through the narrow paths between covered hulks with the flashlight he'd brought from his car. Finally his beam shone on a blackened and twisted steel skeleton against the back wall.

Charlotte's sports car.

Even though it had been six months since the fire, the stench of burned plastic and upholstery made Marie's eyes water as she stepped close. Oily and thick, the odor clogged her throat just as it had in the psychomanteum. She could still hear the roar of the fire echoing through her memory.

Marie watched Brandon as he studied the car. Seeing the vehicle where Charlotte had died was hard enough for her. It had to be excruciating for him. Without thinking, she reached for his hand.

He squeezed her fingers and offered a tight-lipped grimace. "I'll look under the rear bumper, see if the spike is there."

His eyes looked tired, empty. Marie knew he was torturing himself by making himself face Charlotte's death all over again. But to what end? To punish himself for past mistakes? To reinforce the wall he'd built around his feelings for Marie? To give him the impetus to push her away again? She couldn't let him do it. Not now that they were so close to resolving this, so close to proving he had no reason for his crippling guilt.

She held his hand fast. "Let the detective look."

He held her gaze for a moment. And for that moment, time seemed to stop. Finally he nodded. "You're right. It's up to the police now, not us. Not anymore." He glanced at the detective and shifted to the side, giving him room to pass.

As if purposely unaware of their drama, Detective McClellan took one last look at the sketch they'd given him and moved to the car's rear. He crouched low and directed his beam under the back bumper, sweeping the undercarriage with light.

Marie forced herself to breathe. If the spike was no

longer attached to the car, she didn't know what she would do. She was out of leads and she was almost out of hope. Tonight, for the first time, the reality that someone wanted her dead had finally penetrated her thick skull. And worse, she understood that in protecting her, Brandon was in danger, too. She wanted to be done with this investigating stuff. She wanted the professionals to take over. She wanted the sketch to be out of her hands, and there be no more reason for fear.

But more than any yearning she had for safety, she wanted Brandon to know Charlotte hadn't killed herself. That for all his mistakes, all the mistakes everyone had made ten years ago, there was still a future for him and for her. Maybe even the promise of happiness.

Detective McClellan straightened, nearly as tall as Brandon himself. Marie searched his face for a clue of what he'd seen, but his flinty eyes were unreadable. He turned to Brandon. "We'll have to take the car."

"Fine with me."

"And I'd like to look around your property. And inside the house. I can have an evidence crew there this afternoon. Is that a problem, or should I call a judge?"

"You don't need a warrant. You'll have free run of the place."

A trill shimmered up Marie's spine. She wanted this so badly, she was afraid to speak, afraid to hope. But she had to know. She forced the words from her mouth. "Does this mean you'll look into Charlotte's and my father's deaths?"

Detective McClellan's mouth flattened to a line. "I have evidence sufficient to believe Charlotte Drake was murdered."

Relief warmed her like a double shot of brandy, making her feel light-headed and unsteady on her feet. "And my father?"

The detective peered down at her, his expression unchanging. "I'm sorry. Unless more evidence comes to light in your father's case, I have no reason to believe a crime was committed."

"I'LL HIRE A PRIVATE INVESTIGATOR. A professional. Someone good. He'll find the evidence the police need." Brandon watched Marie's face as Josef drove them back to Drake House. The morning sun had crept into the eastern sky, but even its warm rays couldn't dispel the darkness of the state police detective's pronouncement about Edwin's case.

Marie shook her head. "I'll keep looking. I still have some of his things to go through. I'm sure I'll find something… Something has to help."

She looked tired. Hurting. And Brandon didn't know what to do about it. He'd never felt so powerless in his life. "Now that the police believe Charlotte was murdered, it's only a matter of time. You know that, right? Edwin had to be the one who hid that sketch. He had to be killed because he knew who murdered Charlotte. When Detective McClellan finds who that is, he'll solve Edwin's murder as well."

"I know." She smiled up at him. "The important thing is that you know Charlotte didn't commit suicide. You know it wasn't your fault."

He let her words sink into him, let them circulate through his bloodstream, warming him to the core. But as good as it felt, he knew it wasn't that simple. Even though he knew Charlotte hadn't killed herself, he wasn't absolved of everything. "I made a lot of mistakes. I hurt Charlotte. I hurt you."

"You hurt yourself."

He nodded. But that wasn't important. Not as important as the burden of knowing he hurt people he cared for, people who cared for him. He looked down at his hands, suddenly aware he was twisting the wedding band on his finger.

He hadn't felt right about removing it when Charlotte died. He'd worn it like a penance. A constant reminder of what he'd done to her, the tragedy he'd caused. But now that he knew he hadn't caused that tragedy, it felt blasphemous to treat a wedding band as punishment. Somehow it felt disrespectful to Charlotte. To the wonderful woman she was.

He slipped it off.

Marie said nothing, but he could feel her watching. He could feel her body close and smell her delicious, spicy scent.

If only he'd trusted his feelings for her ten years ago. If only he'd stood up to what was expected of him and listened to his heart. He still would have hurt Charlotte, still would have been unfair to her. But her hurt would have faded, and she would have had a good life. Marie and he would have had a good life.

Despite the unease still niggling at the back of his mind, he'd like to believe they could have that good life now.

The car slowed and turned. Passing the redbrick and iron gate of the Manor at Drake Acres, it went through the simple white pillars announcing Drake House. Brandon pulled in a breath and peered out the window.

Black soot still stained the gray stone wall. A bouquet of flowers lay at the foot of the small cross Edwin had placed on the site. Flowers arranged by Shelley, no doubt, and placed with the utmost care. "Stop for a moment, Josef. Will you?"

The car slowed to a stop.

Brandon sat still, watching out the window. "I've never looked at that spot. Not since that night. Every time Josef drove me past, I averted my eyes. I just couldn't…"

"It's different now." Marie's voice sounded hushed, respectful and so wise.

"Yes. It looks different in the sun." He thought about placing the ring on the cross. Thought about bringing it to her grave outside Jenkins Cove Chapel. But in the end, he knew neither option felt right. He slipped it into his pocket. Charlotte was a part of him. A part of his past. And even though he would never again wear it, he would keep the symbol of their marriage with him. To remember the good things…and the mistakes.

"Go ahead, Josef."

The car resumed moving down the drive. He didn't remember getting out. Didn't remember walking to the house and unlocking the door. Didn't remember turning off the alarm and ensuring that the house was empty. All he remembered was taking Marie's hand in his and leading her upstairs.

He felt as though he'd waited ten years for this. He supposed he had. He peeled off her coat, her blouse. He pulled off her jeans tenderly over her bandaged leg and stripped her panties and bra.

The soft light of morning glowed through the bedroom window and kissed her skin.

When he'd last made love to Marie, she'd been a girl.

Now the naked body before him was that of a woman. And he couldn't quite catch his breath. "You're beautiful."

She looked down at the floor.

He slipped his hand to her face and tilted her chin up. "You're the most beautiful woman I've ever known."

He brought his mouth down on hers, tasting her, savoring her. She kissed as she had in his dreams, light and caring one moment, passionate and needy the next. Smelling her scent aroused him. Touching her filled him up.

She raised her hands to his shoulders, combed her fingers through his hair. She moved one hand to his face as they kissed, and traced her fingertips over his cheek.

The skin had once been so tender, so sensitive that a whisper of air inspired agony. Back then, after the car fire, he'd wished he couldn't feel anything. He'd prayed for it. Now her touch felt faint, his nerve endings protected by scar tissue. And for the first time he wanted to scrape it off, to dig deep, to feel.

For the first time he wanted more.

Without releasing her lips, he shucked his clothes. She helped him, unbuttoning his shirt, pushing his pants down his legs. He wanted to be as naked as she was. He wanted to feel every inch of her skin with every inch of his.

When the last piece of clothing fell, he picked her up in his arms and carried her the few steps to the bed. It was an old-fashioned move. Something he'd seen in the movies. Something he'd never thought a modern man would do. But it felt fitting. It felt right.

He lowered her to the bed, gently, so gently. He feathered kisses down her neck and over her collarbone. He worshiped her breasts with his mouth, his tongue, his teeth. He'd never wanted another woman this way, only Marie. He'd never felt so powerful and strong and important as when he looked into her eyes.

He kissed her whole body. Her belly. Her thighs. Between her legs. And when shudder after shudder took her, it was the best feeling in the world.

When he kissed his way back to her mouth, she rolled him to his back and smiled. Moving down to his legs, she traced her tongue up the scars on his legs before devouring him with her warm, wet mouth.

She moved her lips up and down his length, stoking his want, drawing out his need. He felt as though he'd explode—with need, with love, with more happiness than he'd ever dared to dream. And when she came back to his lips, he took her mouth, tasting himself, tasting her, wanting more.

She sat up, arching her back. Sun caressed the curve of her breasts, lit her taut, reddened nipples. She moved over him and positioned him between her legs.

Sinking down, she accepted him inside.

He groaned as her slick heat enveloped him. Swallowed him. Claimed him. He covered her breasts with his hands, feeling her softness, reveling in her strength. He didn't know how long they moved like that, her on top, him on top, every way they could invent. Not long enough. Too long. It didn't really matter. Finally pleasure shuddered through her and spread to him as well. Release. Redemption. And when their bodies calmed and the sweat slicking their skin cooled, he cuddled her close. "I love you, Marie. I always have. More than I thought I could love anyone."

She smiled, a beautiful, open smile. "I love you, too, Brandon. And I'll never stop."

Her voice curled inside him. Her scent marked him. Her body melded to his. She was so precious to him, so perfect. He always wanted to hold her. Never wanted to lose her.

To lose her.

He pushed the thought away and snuggled a kiss into the crook of her neck.

Her giggle bubbled through him. Light. Carefree. Just what he wanted. To be carefree. To be untroubled. For once in his life to be happy.

But he wouldn't have those things. Not if something tragic happened. Not if he lost her.

His chest felt tight. His leg started to ache. He was being morose, but he couldn't help it. He had everything he wanted—right now, right here—yet he was more conscious than ever of how quickly it all could be taken away. How quickly Marie could be taken away.

All Brandon loves will die.

The words beat in the back of his mind like a war drum. Matching the beat of his heart. Overwhelming it. He didn't believe in ghosts. Not really. He'd never seen one, never heard one. Why would he believe a ghost's words?

He rolled his shoulders to loosen them. He tried to breathe deep, to draw in her scent, to pull oxygen into his starving lungs, but the pressure was too strong to shrug off. The fear was too strong to push away.

Maybe it wasn't about believing or ghosts or any of that. Maybe it was just about Marie. And if there was even the slightest chance that loving him was putting her in danger, it was a risk he couldn't take.

Chapter Fifteen

Marie didn't want to get out of bed. She didn't want to move away from Brandon. She didn't want to shower and wash off Brandon's scent from her skin. She felt if she disturbed this perfect moment, this perfect scene, the magic they had finally found might slip away.

Chimes rang through the house. The doorbell downstairs. She could hear the click of Isabella's footsteps crossing the marble foyer.

She flinched. "I don't want to move."

Brandon ruffled her hair with his fingers. "Can you see the surprise on Detective McClellan's and his evidence team's faces when they come up to search the master bedroom and find us naked in bed?" Brandon's words were light and joking, but something in his voice made Marie uneasy.

She propped up on an elbow and studied his face. "What's wrong?"

He shook his head, but he didn't meet her eyes.

"Please, tell me." Her voice sounded strained, frightened to her own ears. She *was* frightened. The way he'd avoided looking at her scared her to death.

She was probably overreacting. The last time she'd

made love with Brandon and let herself feel this happy, her whole world had come tumbling down around her. But things were different this time. Weren't they? There was no pending marriage. Their age difference didn't matter anymore. And after this morning's revelation, nothing was in their way. Everything had changed.

Brandon cupped the back of her head in his hand and pulled her snug against him.

Marie leaned her head against the solid strength of his shoulder. She knew there would be tough times ahead. She knew everything wouldn't be magically okay. That was fine. Brandon would never totally put the pain of the past behind him. Neither would she. But now that they had each other, maybe they could move forward. Bit by bit. Day by day. They could be happy together. At least after this morning, she dared to hope. "Whatever it is, you don't have to worry. We'll handle it. Together."

He didn't answer.

She could feel her heart rate rise, beating against his chest. Her throat grew dry. "Brandon?"

"You need to go back to Michigan."

His words jangled through her with the force of an electric shock. She sat up. As an afterthought, she pulled the sheet up, covering her breasts. "What do you mean, go back to Michigan?"

"You'll be safe there."

"I'll be safe here. The police—"

"Don't need your help."

"I wish that was true. But they wouldn't even have looked into this if we hadn't made them."

"But we did. And they are." He reached up and ran his fingers over her shoulder, down her arm. "It's up to the police now. Remember? You helped me see that. You helped me step away and go on with my life. Now let me help you."

"But I don't have to go back to Michigan for that. I'll look for teaching jobs in Baltimore or D.C. My life is here now."

He pushed himself up from the pillow. The soft glow of the afternoon sun lit his bare chest.

"Isn't my life here?" Panic clawed inside her. She struggled to remain still. To not grab him. Shake him. "Brandon?"

He thrust himself from the bed. He stepped to the chair and stood there, naked.

Marie scanned his face. His body. Her focus landed on the long scar marking his leg. Brandon had other scars, not so visible. Scars not totally healed.

"How can you send me away?" Her voice cracked. She sounded hysterical. She felt hysterical. This couldn't be happening. Not now that he knew Charlotte hadn't committed suicide. Not after they'd made love. Not after he'd told her he loved her. "We're supposed to be together. We're supposed to be happy. How can you ask me to leave?"

He grabbed a thick terry cloth robe from the back of the chair. He pulled it on and tied it at the waist, covering himself. "It's temporary. It's for your own protection. Once Detective McClellan finds out who killed Charlotte and your father, you can come back."

She shook her head. She knew what he was saying was smart. It was safe. It made sense. But logical or not, she had the feeling that once she left, what she and Brandon had found would be gone. That once she walked out of Drake House, she couldn't come back again. "I love you, Brandon. I don't want to lose you again."

"You won't lose me."

"If I leave, I will. I'll lose you. I know it. I don't want to leave."

"No, Marie. If you *don't* leave, I'm afraid *I'll* lose *you*."

A wave of cold swept through her and penetrated her bones. She clutched the sheet tighter against her breasts. "What? Why? The police have the sketch. It's out of my hands now."

He shook his head. He raked a hand through his hair. He seemed conflicted. Desperate. As tortured as when he'd believed he was the cause of Charlotte's death.

Now he was really frightening her. "What is it, Brandon? Tell me."

He met her eyes. "'All Brandon loves will die.'"

He didn't have to explain where the quote came from. She'd heard it with her own ears, and she'd never forget. "Did Charlotte speak to you?"

"No."

"Then what has changed since this morning?"

He stared at her as if he wasn't sure how to answer.

"You told me you loved me this morning," she said. "You made love to me. I thought you wanted us to be together."

"I did. I do."

"I told you what Charlotte's spirit said *days* ago."

He raked his hair again. "I know. I just didn't really understand what it meant until now."

Her throat felt tight. As if she could scream and scream and never get the pressure to loosen. "What does it mean, Brandon? What does it mean to *you*?"

"That I could lose you." He tested the belt of his robe, as if it wasn't tight enough, as if he'd felt it coming loose. "What if it isn't just about who killed Charlotte and your father? What if it isn't about you snooping around?"

"What are you trying to say?"

He splayed his hands out in front of him, begging for her to understand. "I've been investigating this, too. I've been asking questions. I even helped you find that damn sketch. But someone tried to throw *you* off the roof. They cut the brakes in *your* car. They shot at *you* alone, even though I was a much easier target."

"All that stuff is about covering up the murders."

"What if it isn't?"

"Are you saying you're afraid I'm a marked woman?"

"No. I'm saying what if by loving you, I've *made* you a marked woman?"

She shook her head. She was hoping things had changed. She was hoping the proof that Charlotte was murdered had taken away Brandon's guilt. Taken away his fear. But she'd failed to realize the fear wasn't really about Charlotte. Maybe it had never been. Maybe it was older than his marriage to Charlotte and his summer with Marie. Maybe it was something rooted deep in Brandon himself.

Tears filled her eyes, making the room blur. She turned away. "You're blaming yourself again. Just like you did with Charlotte. Just like you always do. What are you so afraid of?"

He was in front of her in two steps. He gripped her shoulders, turning her back toward him, forcing her to look into his eyes. "'All Brandon loves will die.' You said you heard Charlotte's spirit speak those words." His voice was hard, almost accusing.

"I did."

"Do you believe in ghosts, Marie? Because it seems like if you believe in ghosts, you should listen to the things they tell you. You should believe the words they say."

Her throat felt thick. Her heart ached with each beat. For him. For her. "Loss is part of life, Brandon."

He released her arms. Shaking his head, he limped to the fireplace and grabbed his cane.

Tears rolled down her cheeks, but she didn't push them away. She understood what he felt. Understood what he feared. "Last week when I talked to my father, our discussion was so ordinary. The snow in Michigan. His plans to visit me at Christmas. The box of ornaments he sent me from when I was a kid. I never guessed I wouldn't hear his voice again. And when he died, all I could think about was all the things I wanted to say that I can never say now. But you know what?"

"What?"

"It isn't about the things I didn't say. It's about the time we spent together. Like every ordinary minute of that conversation. That's the stuff that is life. That's the stuff that makes up love. And if you send me away, that's the stuff you and I will never have."

"I love you, Marie. How can I not protect you?"

"You can't protect me from everything."

He shook his head slowly, as if he could hardly summon the energy. "I can't accept that."

Tears clogged her throat, choked her words. "Everyone will die. It's just the way things are. We don't get to decide. But, Brandon, we do get to decide how we live. Who we share our days and nights with. Who we love."

He paused in front of the mantel, clutching his cane in both hands, leaning on it as if he couldn't stand on his own. "I'll book you a flight for tomorrow morning. That should give you enough time to finish packing your father's things."

MARIE TAPED THE LAST BOX of her father's papers and wrote her address on the label. Shelley would mail the papers, a few family heirlooms and a handful of photo albums to her address in Michigan. His clothing, shoes and most of his furniture would go to charity. And the rooms themselves would finally belong to Shelley.

Marie didn't cry as she looked around the space. She didn't have tears left. Not anymore. Ten years ago, when she'd left this place, she'd thought her heart was permanently broken. Now Brandon had mended it this morning only to shatter it again.

This time she knew it was unfixable.

Her father had been right. Brandon would never open himself to love. If it wasn't his engagement to Charlotte keeping them apart, he'd find something else. And he had. The real issue. Fear.

Marie walked into the bedroom. It had taken her all day, but the room was bare. Only her mostly packed suitcase remained in the corner. The bedsheets and spread were still tucked in neatly on the bed. Her flight to Michigan left in the morning, which meant she'd be sleeping at Drake House one last time.

Sleep. She almost laughed. There wasn't a chance she'd be able to sleep. She might not have any cry left in her, but her heart squeezed with each beat. Her ears kept hearing Brandon's words over and over. Her mind searched for things she could have said or done to make this turn out differently.

Too bad those perfect words and deeds didn't exist.

Shaking her head, she sat on the edge of the bed. Even if she couldn't doze off, she might as well go through the motions. She had nothing else to do. Nothing else to pack. And she could stomach no more goodbyes.

She slipped off one boot, then the other and dropped them on the floor. One hit something, producing a metallic clink. What was that? Had she missed something? She shoved off the bed and peered under the white spread. A watch lay on the rug. One of her father's old pocket watches.

She plunked down on the floor and cradled the watch in her hands. When Jonathan Drake was alive, he'd given his butler a new pocket watch every Christmas, and her father treasured them, wearing a different one each day. The thought that she'd almost left one behind made her stomach twist.

What else might she have missed?

Sniffing back her tears, she flipped the edge of the bedspread back. Crouching on hands and knees, she scanned under the bed. Even though the rug seemed clean, her nose tickled with dust. The edge of a small notebook caught her eye. She grasped it and brought it into the light.

At first it seemed like nothing, just a pad of paper he might have jotted messages or to-do lists on. Then she saw the indentations left from pressing the pencil or pen on the sheet above.

Marie's heart jolted. She scrambled to her feet and

raced into the sitting room. She ripped open the box holding items from his desk and fished out a pencil. Rubbing the pencil back and forth lightly across the indentations in the notebook paper, she started to see the indentations take shape. A short, curved stem emerged on the page…a simple leaf…and finally the U-shaped petals of a tulip.

Identical to the image she'd seen in the psychomanteum mirror.

She squeezed her arms close against her sides to steady herself, to try to keep her hands from shaking. Her father had seen the image, too. He'd copied it. And there was more.

She rubbed the pencil over the other indentations on the notebook page. Numbers formed in her father's abrupt script. No, not numbers. Letters. A name.

JENKINS COVE CHAPEL CEMETERY.

The graveyard where her father was buried.

Chapter Sixteen

Brandon paced the third floor. His leg ached to high heaven, but he couldn't care less. He was doing the right thing. He was. Wasn't he?

He wished tomorrow morning was already here, that Marie was on the plane, that she was safe. Every second that ticked by made him more nervous. Every creak of the old house made him long to run downstairs to gather her into his arms. To protect her? Or to tell her he'd changed his mind? To beg her to stay with him forever?

He didn't know.

The distant sound of an engine hummed from the front of the house. What the hell?

He raced to the door of his sitting room and across the hall to his study. He pulled aside drapes covering the windows facing the forest and driveway at the front of the house. This was where he'd seen the fire that had taken Charlotte's life. A small orange glow through the trees at the stone wall. But he didn't see a fire now. He didn't see a crash.

He saw headlights shining down the drive, moving

away. And immediately he knew the car, even though it had only arrived from the rental agency the day before.

Where did Marie think she was going?

MARIE WRAPPED HER JACKET around her shoulders and quickened her steps up the redbrick path that wound between boxwood hedges. The gray stone church and walled graveyard were smack in the middle of town, right on Main Street. But that didn't seem to matter to her jumpy nerves.

A cemetery was still a cemetery.

She'd tried Sophie's breathing exercises. They didn't work. The only thing she could think of as she was scooping in those big, slow breaths was that she could hear sounds around her. Footsteps following up the path behind her. The creak of someone watching from the willow oaks overhead. Moans from among the gray, lichen-covered stones.

She had to reel in her imagination.

She pulled the notebook from her bag and tilted the page toward the light from the nearby street. Why had her father included both the sketch and the cemetery name on that page? She knew they were related. The two things were grouped too deliberately on the page not to be. Had he seen both the tulip and the name of the graveyard in the psychomanteum mirror? She'd seen the tulip right before Brandon had rushed into the room, responding to her scream. If she hadn't been interrupted, would Charlotte have shown her the rest?

Charlotte.

Charlotte was buried in this cemetery. Generations of Drakes were, as were many of their loyal servants who attended the chapel alongside the family. Would finding Charlotte's grave make the tulip's meaning clear? But how could she locate the grave in the darkness?

Maybe she should have roused Brandon and asked him to come with her. He would be able to lead her directly to Charlotte's headstone. And as painful as it would be to spend her last hours in Jenkins Cove with him after he'd pushed her away, at least she wouldn't be walking through graves alone.

No. He would never have let her come. Not as determined to protect her as he was. Once he made his decision, she knew he wouldn't let her go anywhere but to the airport. He would insist she turn the notebook over to the police. And they would file it away, never knowing what importance the drawing held.

Not that she knew, either. At least not yet.

She glanced around the perimeter of the yard. Just over the redbrick wall, she could hear a car's engine as it buzzed down the street. She could see the night-lights of the stores along Main Street. Some insomniac soul was burning the night oil in a nearby house.

She'd never been afraid to walk around Jenkins Cove by herself. No one was. Half the residents still didn't lock their doors, at least not during the off-season. She didn't need Brandon's protection. And she didn't need his help finding Charlotte's grave, either.

She could do it herself.

She reached an opening in the boxwood. She stepped off the path onto the sparse, winter grass. The dappled glow of nearby streetlights kissed the cemetery, filtered through thick, evergreen leaves of magnolia and wispy branches of willow oak. Tombstones of different shapes and sizes jutted from the ground like jagged teeth. They crowded every space between tree trunks and shrubs, some old as the town itself, some new…like her father's.

Marie hadn't noticed Charlotte's grave during her father's funeral, but then she'd been focusing on holding herself together and on the upcoming discussion she'd planned with Police Chief Hammer. It could be in the same area, and she'd simply missed it. At least she knew some Drakes were buried in that area. It was a place to start.

She wound through the stones, rubbing her arms to ward off the chill. If spirits roamed Drake House, surely they must roam this place. She thought she could feel them. The cold pockets of still air. The hair rising on the back of her neck. The soft beat in her ears that she swore had to be footsteps.

Or maybe the beat of a heart.

She shivered again, tamping down her imagination. She had to focus on the tulip. She had to find what it meant, what connection it had to the cemetery. She rounded a tree and spotted a white spire thrusting into the night.

The marker of Brandon's father, Jonathan Drake.

She remembered the tall column of stone, reminiscent of the Washington Memorial across the Chesapeake in the nation's capital. She couldn't help thinking of Brandon's uncle. When Clifford Drake died, no doubt his memorial would be twice as tall.

A twig cracked behind her.

She whirled around, but all she could see were stones, trees, shadows. She pushed out a tense breath and moved on. One by one, the Drake name started popping up on the headstones around her. Her father's grave was closer to the wall, deeper in the cemetery. But judging by the increased frequency of the Drake family graves, Charlotte's had to be close by.

She scanned each name. Mirabelle Drake, who died in 1933. Samuel Drake, who died as an infant twenty years earlier. William Drake, 1883, possibly one of the first Drakes buried in the yard.

Charlotte Drake.

Charlotte's stone was smooth. No mark of a tulip. No sign of the violence that had taken her life. Just beautiful, flawless, white.

Marie swallowed into an aching throat. She'd never liked Charlotte, but that wasn't due to anything Charlotte had done. It was because of what she had. It was because she was living the life Marie had dreamed of. It was because of jealousy and envy and bitter resentment.

Marie felt ashamed of those feelings now. She felt ashamed she'd been so hard on Brandon's wife. "I'm sorry, Charlotte. I'm sorry things worked out so badly for you. I'm sorry things worked out so badly for me. And most of all, I'm sorry Brandon will never know happiness."

The chill surrounding her faded and the air warmed. Marie blinked back the tears pooling in her eyes and scanned the stones around her. Maybe there was no tulip. Maybe Charlotte was the reason she had to come here tonight. To speak to her one last time. To put everything between them to rest.

Feeling less tense, Marie walked to her father's grave, the earth on top still rough and mounded. She'd felt Charlotte's presence in the graveyard, but she could tell right away her father wasn't there. His stone felt like just a stone. The mound of dirt covering his casket was just dirt. She pressed her lips together and studied the flowers clustered around his grave. "Goodbye, Daddy. Wherever you are. I'll miss you every day."

She turned away from the stone and wiped her eyes. She shed still more tears. A miracle. When her vision cleared, she focused on the brick wall. Concrete squares lined the length of the wall, vaults for cremated human remains. Each one held another name, another loved one who would never come back. The dates they died. The special bonds they had with family and friends and community.

And one held the simple etching of a tulip.

Marie sucked in a breath. She stumbled to the marker and fell to her knees.

She didn't have to compare the image to the one her father had drawn in the notebook. It had been burned into her brain in the psychomanteum. She read the name.

Lala Falat.

A foreign name. Maybe Eastern European.

The story Chelsea and Michael told her after her experience on the roof filtered through her mind. They'd said the doctor, Janecek, had smuggled people into the United States from Eastern Europe. He'd made them pay for their passage by donating their organs. Many had died. The state police were still counting the bodies.

Could Lala Falat be tied to the mass grave? And if so, what could she possibly have to do with Charlotte Drake? And why did her father think her grave was important?

Marie dug into her bag. Her hand closed over her digital camera. She pulled it out and focused the camera on the wall marker.

And the world went black.

"MARIE?" Brandon quickened his pace. He swore he'd heard the low whisper of her voice on this side of the graveyard. "Marie? Are you in here?"

Damn this leg. By the time he'd awakened Josef to drive him, Marie had a substantial head start. He wouldn't even have known where she'd gone if she hadn't parked her car right on Main Street in front of the Jenkins Cove Chapel.

He wound through the headstones, making his way to her father's marker. What on earth would make her so intent on visiting his grave that she had to drive here in the middle of the night? And what had possessed her to come here alone?

He knew the answer. Or at least he could guess. She'd assumed he would nix the idea in an effort to protect her.

And the worst thing was that she was probably right.

He reached Edwin's grave site.

No Marie.

He made his way to the brick wall. Maybe if he walked the perimeter, he could locate her.

His foot hit something in the grass.

He bent down and picked up a camera. And not five feet away lay Marie's purse.

His lungs constricted. His pulse thundered in his ears. She never would have dropped these things. Not unless she was forced to. Not unless she was attacked.

He spun and headed back to the dark, squared outlines of the boxwood hedges. He had to reach the car. He had to find Marie. "Josef!"

The chauffeur didn't answer. Or at least, Brandon didn't hear him. He couldn't hear anything above the roar of his breath and the beat of his heart. "Josef!"

He reached the boxwood. He could move faster on the path's hard, brick surface, but still not fast enough. He approached Main Street and strode through the church's gate.

Marie's second rental was still parked at the curb. The black shadow of his town car hulked behind it. A man stood behind the town car, raised the car's trunk.

"Josef?"

The man bent down and picked up a large object. Something wrapped in a blanket or a bag. The way he strained, Brandon could see it was heavy. The package seemed to move. The man dumped it in the trunk.

No. Not a package… A body.

Marie.

Josef slammed the trunk and looked up at Brandon.

Brandon raced for the car. Pain shot up his leg. He gritted this teeth and pushed faster.

The chauffeur jumped in the driver's seat. The engine hummed to life.

Brandon reached the curb. He slammed into the passenger door and grabbed at the door handle. But the car jolted into gear. It shot away from the curb, tires screeching.

The door swung open under Brandon's hand. He ran, trying to keep up, trying to jump inside. His legs faltered.

The door handle ripped from his grasp. He staggered and fell to his knees in the street.

The taillights faded into the distance.

Chapter Seventeen

She had to find a way out.

Marie pulled in the moist air of her own breath into her lungs. The bag he'd slipped over her head and shoulders clung tightly to her skin. Duct tape cut into her wrists and ankles. She fought the need to scream. It wouldn't do any good. Once he'd taped her hands and feet, he'd stuffed a gag into her mouth and secured it with more tape before replacing the bag. The gag wouldn't allow her to make much noise. Not enough for anyone to hear.

All she could do was thump her feet against the wall of the trunk, and even then she didn't have enough space to get power into her kick.

Josef.

She'd heard his voice when she'd kicked him. His accent. The strange language he spoke with a fluent tongue. She still couldn't believe he was doing this. She couldn't understand it. He'd seemed so meek, so courteous. Why would he want to hurt her? What had she ever done to him?

She could feel the car slow beneath her. She could feel it turn. More driving, over loose gravel this time. Around twists and bends. Finally the motion stopped.

A door slammed. Footsteps moved to the back of the car. The trunk lock clicked its release. Cool air rushed over Marie's sweat-slick skin. The crash of waves against rock whipped on the wind.

His rough hand gripped her arm. He pulled her to a sitting position, strong fingers bruising her flesh.

She didn't know what he planned to do, but she wasn't going to let him do it easily. She twisted her body, wrenching from his grasp. Flopping back down in the trunk, she lashed out with her feet.

She hit something solid.

A grunt broke from his lips, followed by swearing in that other language. He gripped her arm again. His fist crashed down on her neck and shoulder.

Breath shuddered from her lungs. For a moment, she couldn't think, couldn't move. Pain shuddered through her.

He lifted her from the trunk and slung her over his shoulder.

A whimper stuck in Marie's throat. She swallowed it back. She couldn't give in. She wouldn't.

She willed her mind to clear, willed the pain to fade. She wasn't strong enough to fight him. And trying wasn't going to get her anything but hurt…or killed. She had to be smarter. Had to strike when she could make it matter. *If* she could make it matter.

He walked on, her body swaying on his shoulder with each stride. The scent of water rode the wind along with the sound of the lapping waves. Then Josef stopped. She heard a lock rattle. Her body brushed against what felt like the jamb of a door. His heavy footfalls moved over what sounded like a marble floor.

Drake House.

She'd heard Brandon calling her name in the grave-yard, even though she couldn't answer loud enough for him to hear. He must still be at the chapel. Without Josef, without the car, he'd have no way to get back to Drake House. No way to help her until it was too late.

She had to find a way out of this on her own.

Stairs creaked. She could feel the sensation of moving upward. He was taking her upstairs. To do what? She tried to think, tried to stay calm. There had to be a way to escape. There had to.

"You kick again, I beat your head." His voice was low, dead, as if bled of any emotion, any humanity.

He lowered her down, letting her fall the last two feet to the parquet floor.

Oxygen rushed from her lungs. She tried to breathe, but took in dust. She coughed and sputtered.

He pulled her up to a sitting position and yanked the bag off her head. Without saying a word, he strode out of the room.

She blinked against the light. She didn't recognize the room at first, but the molding along the ceiling and the carved woodwork proved they were in Drake House. The room smelled dusty, as if it hadn't been used in a long time. She focused on the trees outside the uncovered window. The room was facing the south side of the house, away from the water. She blinked her eyes. Her vision cleared. Details came into focus. Animals circled the room, carved into the moldings. They rimmed the fireplace mantel. They had to be in the nursery.

Josef thunked back into the room. Rugs and paper and broken sticks of furniture overflowed his arms. He dropped them near the front bank of windows. He walked back out, returning with another armload, as if he was raiding whatever he could find and piling it in here.

As if he was building a bonfire.

Marie's throat constricted. She struggled to breathe around the gag. She had to think. Clearly she couldn't fight Josef. Not only was she tied, but he was twice as strong. She'd found that out the hard way. But maybe she could talk to him. Reason with him. Convince him that she was a person, too, that he couldn't just burn her like trash.

She offered a pleading look and made a noise deep in her throat, words impossible to squeeze past the rag jamming her mouth.

"You have something to say?"

She fought the urge to flinch from the harshness of his voice. Instead, she forced her head to nod.

He stepped beside her. Grabbing the duct tape, he ripped it from her lips.

Her skin burned. The room blurred with tears. She coughed, spitting the rag onto the floor. "Why are you doing this?"

He looked at her as if he didn't understand the question.

"I've never done anything to you," she said. "I never would."

"I am not doing this to you."

Marie stared at him. His words made no sense. "Of course you're doing it to me. You're hurting me right now."

He shook his head as if she were the one speaking gibberish. "I am doing it to him. Like he did to me. I am paying him back." As if that was all he needed to say, he turned and plodded from the room.

There was only one "him" Marie could think of, but

it didn't make sense. Why would Josef want to hurt Brandon? Nothing the chauffeur was saying or doing made sense. She twisted, looking around the room. She had to find a way out.

Her gaze landed on the old radiator along the wall. It was made of metal. Some pieces of it might even be sharp. It was her only chance.

She pushed herself across the floor, a combination of scooting on the wood and moving her legs like an inchworm. Reaching the radiator, she positioned her back against its warmth and felt the bottom edges with her hands.

Her fingers touched hard edges. Not exactly sharp, but if she had some time, if she could stall, she might be able to rub the tape enough to weaken it. She might be able to set herself free.

She just needed time.

Footsteps stomped in the hall, approaching. Josef bulled through the door, his arms filled with another load. More fuel for his bonfire.

He threw the armful on the pile and turned to stare at her. "You moved."

"I needed to lean against the wall. My back is sore." Marie didn't have to act. The muscles in her back were sore. And with her ankles taped, she had a hard time sitting in the middle of the floor with nothing to lean on.

Josef grunted. He started back to the door.

"Wait!"

He stopped and glared at her.

"You said you were doing this to someone else, not me. That you were paying him back. Who? Who are you paying back? Brandon?"

"Yes, Brandon."

"Why? What did Brandon ever do to you?"

A shadow of something passed over his brutal face. Anger. Sorrow. "He took away my Lala."

Lala? "The woman whose ashes are in the wall vault? She has the tulip on her marker?"

"Lala means tulip. She was my tulip. She and I were to be married. Now she is dead. Murdered."

The fiancée who died. Shelley and Brandon had both mentioned the woman, and how devastated Josef was when she died. "But I thought she was sick. Didn't she die in the hospital?"

"An infection. That's what they said. An infection from the surgery."

She couldn't follow. She knew Brandon provided health insurance to all his employees, just as his father had. She'd grown up on that insurance. So how could Josef blame Brandon for his fiancée's death? "I don't understand. It's not Brandon's fault she died."

He stared at her, his eyes hard, his boxer's nose red with the burst capillaries of a heavy drinker. A man who'd tried to forget. A man in pain. "It is his fault."

She kept rubbing the tape. The man looked as though he was rapidly reaching the end of his patience. She didn't have time to waste. "How?"

"He made her have the surgery." He walked from the room.

Now she was really lost. He wasn't making sense. Why would Brandon make anyone have surgery? Maybe Josef was suffering some kind of psychotic breakdown. Maybe Lala simply had a life-threatening illness and Brandon was there helping Josef through it. Maybe that's why Josef blamed his feelings of helplessness and frustration on Brandon.

She rubbed the tape, pressing it against the iron radiator as hard as she could. Moving it as fast as she could. It wasn't working. The tape was weakening a little, maybe, stretching a little. But it wasn't happening fast enough. She was running out of time.

She groped under the radiator again. There had to be a valve somewhere. Maybe that would give her the sharp edge she needed. She touched something circular, ridged like the serrated edge of a knife, but not as sharp. It would have to do.

The heavy footfalls returned. Josef carried an armful of gossamer draperies, something large and red underneath. He threw the drapes on the pile. Then she saw what else he carried. A fuel can. He twisted off the cover.

The sharp scent of gasoline assaulted Marie's senses. She had to delay him. She needed more time. "There's something I don't understand. Why would Brandon force Lala to have surgery?"

"She needed to pay." His voice growled low with anger. It shook with frustration. "She had no money. I had no money. She needed to pay, and I could not help her."

"She needed to pay what?"

"For coming to this country. She needed to pay. Dr. Janecek would not let her come without the surgery. Without giving something to pay for her passage. He would not let her come to me." A sob broke from his lips, deep and low and full of agony.

The pieces fell into place in Marie's mind. "The human trafficking? The mass grave? Lala was one of the people Janecek smuggled? He forced her to give him an organ to pay for smuggling her into the country?"

Josef made a keening sound low in his throat.

Marie's head hurt. She rubbed the tape harder. Faster. Even though she'd tied the pieces together, what Josef was saying still didn't make sense. "It was Janecek who did those things. It was him who forced Lala to have the surgery. It was him who caused the infection. Why do you keep saying it was Brandon?"

He splashed gasoline on the draperies and rugs. "The Drakes. Brandon and his uncle. I break his uncle's things. I try to make him pay. But he does not care about anything like I care for Lala. Brandon does."

She remembered overhearing Brandon talking to Chief Hammer about some vandalism at his uncle Cliff's. That was Josef? None of this made sense. Why would he target the Drakes? "I don't know about Cliff, but Brandon would never do anything to hurt you."

He shook his head. "He would. He did. I saw the ship. I was brought in, too. Before Lala."

"What ship?"

"A big ship. It said Drake right on the bow."

"The ship used for smuggling?"

"Yes."

"Are you sure?"

"I lost my Lala. I must live alone. I will have no children." He looked at the carved moldings at the top of the nursery walls. Tears wet his rough cheeks. "My life is dead, yet I must live on. Well, if I must, then Brandon Drake must, too. He will know how it feels."

The words she heard in the psychomanteum echoed in Marie's mind. *All Brandon loves will die.* Was Brandon right? Were the people who cared about him marked for death? All to serve Josef's need for revenge?

"Charlotte?" She felt the tape give. Not entirely, but

a little. Her hands trembled and burned. The odor of gasoline stung her eyes. She held Josef's gaze and pushed on. She had to know. "Did you weld the spike near the gas tank? Did you crash Charlotte's car into the wall?"

"Lala came here to marry me. He took my wife. He did not deserve one of his own."

"And my father?"

He stuffed his hands into his pockets and stared down at the floor. "I could not let him tell. I am sorry."

"And now me?"

"You most of all. He loves you like I loved Lala. I cannot let him have you."

"You'll never get away with this. The police will know you did this."

He brought his hands out of his pockets, something in his fist. He looked up at her, his eyes dead. "I am not trying to get away. I am going with you. I am going to be with Lala, where I belong." He struck the match and threw it in the pile.

Chapter Eighteen

Brandon noticed the orange glow in the sky before he could see the house. It pulsated beyond the twisted, bare branches of oak, sycamore and wisps of willow, radiating like the eerie light of a coming storm. He pushed the accelerator harder. The engine of Marie's little rental whined. Its tires jolted over dips in the long drive.

A curve in the drive rushed toward him. Gritting his teeth, he forced his leg to respond. He lifted his foot from the accelerator. Hot pain shot through his thigh and hip, pulsed up his spine. He jammed his left foot to the brake. The little car fishtailed around the turn. He steered into the slide. The car righted itself. Remembering to breathe, he hit the accelerator again.

He'd lost so much time rushing back into the graveyard and finding Marie's purse. Time he couldn't afford to give Josef. But at least he'd found her cell phone and the keys to her car. At least he could call for help. At least he had wheels to get back.

At first he hadn't been sure where the chauffeur would take Marie. Then it came to him. Drake House. He could have killed her in the graveyard. It would have been easier. Cleaner. But his focus wasn't simply on killing her. He wanted to kill her at Drake House. The place where he'd tried to kill her the other times. And where he'd chosen to kill Charlotte.

All Brandon loves will die.

The words were true, just as he'd feared. It was all about him. Not Charlotte. Not Edwin. Not Marie. Whatever Josef had against him was personal. He'd want to do it at Drake House. He'd want to bring it home to Brandon.

The only thing Brandon couldn't figure out was why.

He fishtailed around another bend in the tree-lined drive. The trunk of a sycamore rushed at him. The car door missed the tree by inches.

He stomped on the gas.

He'd been so damn stupid. So stupid. He'd pushed Marie away. He'd tried to make her leave. He'd told himself he was protecting her, shielding her from a killer. But all he'd done was leave her alone and vulnerable. And tonight he'd brought Josef straight to her.

He hadn't protected her at all.

The car broke from the trees. Nothing obscured the fire now. It licked from the front windows of the east wing. Black smoke gushed into the air and engulfed the balcony. It carried on the air and made him choke.

He couldn't be too late. He couldn't.

He stomped the brake and the car skidded to a stop. He shoved his way out the door. He pushed as fast as he could go, jabbing his cane into the ground, pulling his legs along.

He shoved the front door open. Smoke hung in the air, making the grand staircase appear dim and gray. The fire was in the east wing. He'd noticed from outside. The nursery.

He raced over the marble foyer. Clutching the banister, he half pulled himself, half ran to the top of the staircase.

The air grew hot. His eyes stung and watered. Smoke thickened, choking out oxygen, making it hard to see.

He groped through the dark hallways. Low. He had to get low to the floor. The smoke would be thinner there. He could breathe.

He crouched down. It was easier to breathe, but he still couldn't see. Tears streamed down his cheeks. His eyes felt as if they were burning out of his head. He groped the wall as a guide and crawled.

He hoped to God Marie wasn't in the nursery. The way the flames were leaping from the front windows, if she was in that room, she was likely dead.

He couldn't believe that. He wouldn't.

A loud thunk shook the house. A cough rose above the crackle and hiss of fire.

A woman's cough.

Not from the nursery. It came from down the hall. He could swear it.

He crawled faster. His leg screamed with pain, but he didn't care. If he didn't find Marie, if he didn't reach her in time, he didn't care about anything. Not his leg, not getting out of Drake House, not living until tomorrow.

UNABLE TO REMOVE THE TAPE that bound them, Marie dragged her useless legs down the hall. She didn't know where Josef was. Didn't even know if he was alive or swallowed by fire. She'd made her move when he'd thrown the match. Adrenaline, survival instinct, what it was she didn't know. But when the fire flared, sucking the oxygen from the room and imploding glass from the windows, she'd finally ripped the tape free. She'd pulled herself out of the room and down the hall. She'd gotten away.

And she'd taken a wrong turn.

Unthinkingly she'd turned down the hall, racing away from the fire instead of turning back for the staircase. And now she had to find her way back to one of the staircases before she was trapped.

Smoke billowed around her, enfolding her in its gray darkness. She was all turned around. She couldn't see, could hardly breathe.

"Marie!"

She gasped and coughed. How had he gotten here? How had he reached her? Tears ran from her eyes, but not from the smoke. "Brandon! I'm here!"

"Move toward my voice. Stay low."

As if she had a choice. She scooched on her stomach, dragging her legs behind. Along the hall, back toward the heat, the fire. *Toward Brandon.*

A shape came out of the smoke. Brandon? Was he here?

Something smacked the side of her head. Hard.

She slumped forward, her eyes blurring, her ears ringing.

"Marie? Are you okay? What happened?"

No. Josef was here. Josef had found her. And now he would find Brandon. He'd hurt him. He'd kill him. "Brandon! It's Josef! It's—"

Another blow hit her and she couldn't say anything more.

Chapter Nineteen

Brandon could see shapes through the smoke. One crouching, like him. One lying flat on the floor.

Marie.

Growling deep in his throat, he launched himself at the larger hulk. He lashed out with his cane.

The blow connected. Its force shuddered up the teak and into the handle. A masculine grunt rose above the din of the fire.

Brandon swung again, fighting his way forward to Marie.

Josef moved back.

Brandon swung again. This time he missed, his cane whooshing through nothing but smoky air.

Josef slipped around the side of the hall. He circled around behind Brandon.

No.

He couldn't let Josef cut them off from the stairs. The man had a death wish. He must. He never would have stayed in the fire if he hadn't intended to die along with Marie. He would do everything in his power to keep them from escaping. And now that he was between Marie and closest the staircase, he might succeed.

Unless Brandon stopped him.

Brandon struggled to his feet. Swinging the cane in front of him, he crouched low, following Josef down the hall, pushing him back. They reached the nursery door. The heat was intolerable, fiery as a blast oven. The smoke gushed out into the hall, too thick to see through despite the blinding light of the flames behind Josef and the blown-out windows all along the front of the wing.

Brandon's muscles ached, but he kept swinging. "Marie! Get out! If you can hear me, get out now!"

Josef backed up under Brandon's assault, retreating into the nursery.

No, not retreating. He darted to the side and grabbed something from the room. Something long. He swung it at Brandon.

Pain slammed into Brandon's thigh. He blinked back the agony.

The gray shape he knew was Josef drew back its weapon, angling to land another blow. Even though the thick cloud, Brandon could see it was a stick of some sort. A broken piece of furniture.

Josef swung again.

Brandon blocked the blow with his cane. He jumped back, out of the doorway. His leg crumpled under him and he fell to the floor.

A larger crash rumbled through Brandon's head, through the whole of Drake House. The orange flames leaped. The nursery's ceiling closed down on them, falling, crashing. A flaming piece of molding landed on Josef, pinning him to the floor.

His scream ripped through the roar of fire, deep, guttural, full of agony. Flame jumped around him. Heat sucked air from the room.

Brandon scurried back. He couldn't help Josef. But he could still save Marie.

Or die trying.

The fire was hot. So hot. Smoke clogged his throat. Sweat dripped in his eyes.

He closed his eyes and felt his way along the hall back to the spot where he'd left Marie. The trek seemed to take forever. His hands touched nothing but smooth floor and wall moldings. The heat seemed to close in behind him.

His fingers brushed something soft. Silky strands of hair. He ran his hands over her, gripping the wool of her coat.

She stirred.

She was alive. Still alive. "Marie? Can you move? I need to get you out of here."

She made a sound, but he couldn't decipher words. She struggled to her elbows. "Feet."

He ran his hands down her legs. Duct tape affixed her ankles. He couldn't get it off, not without scissors or a knife to cut it. He'd have to carry her. "I got you. I'm going to lift you to my shoulder. I need you to hang on. Can you do that?"

He felt her nod.

He hefted her to one shoulder. She helped him shift her body into a fireman's carry position, slung over his shoulders and behind his neck. She locked her hands around his left arm. He threaded his right between her bound legs. They had to move.

Slowly, too slowly, he crawled down the hall. The nursery was engulfed in flame now, the air in the hallway too thick to breathe, the heat too intense to slow down.

Josef's screams had stopped.

Brandon pushed the chauffeur from his mind. He had to focus. He had to get Marie and himself out, or they would suffer the same fate as Josef.

He made his way down the staircase, half stumbling, half falling. He forced his feet to carry them across the marble foyer. He pushed his way outside.

Sirens screamed from the highway.

Brandon staggered to the lawn and fell to his knees. He released Marie's legs and lowered her to the cool grass.

She looked up at him, her face streaked with soot and tears. Her eyes red and swollen. Bruises bloomed on her delicate cheek. "Josef?"

"Dead."

She swallowed, flinching as if the action was painful. Her throat must be as swollen from the smoke as his. No, more swollen since she had breathed it longer.

"Police are on their way. Probably fire, too. Paramedics."

"I'm okay."

"No, you're not. Me, either. But we will be."

"You were right. Josef was trying to destroy everything you love. Charlotte, my father, me, Drake House." Her voice sounded choked. She swallowed hard and went on. "His fiancée was one of the people Dr. Janecek smuggled into the country. She died from an infection after the surgery."

It was a sad story. A tragic story. But it didn't explain a thing. "What does all that have to do with me?"

"He said she was smuggled into the country aboard a Drake ship."

"Drake Enterprises? A cargo ship or the yacht?"

She moved one shoulder as if trying to shrug. Flinching from pain, she aborted the move. "He said the name *Drake* was on the bow."

"Damn. I'll have to talk to Cliff about that. And Detective McClellan."

"Josef tried to hurt Cliff, too. The vandalism."

He nodded. The surest way to hurt Cliff was to destroy his toys. And the surest way to hurt Brandon was…

He felt sick. His throat ached, not just from the smoke. "I brought him right to you. He wouldn't have even known you were at the chapel graveyard except I asked him to drive me there."

Marie reached a hand to him. She traced her fingers over his face, his cheek, his scar. "It's not your fault. You couldn't have known."

"Maybe not about Josef, but I should have known enough to keep you by my side. To never let you go." He hadn't let himself think of it. Not since he'd seen her purse on the cemetery lawn. But he knew that was his mistake. That had been his mistake all along. "I've wanted you so long, Marie, that once I had you in my arms again, all I could think about was losing you. I couldn't let myself believe we could be together. It just felt too…"

"Fragile."

He nodded. And *he'd* felt fragile. Raw. Exposed. Vulnerable. "I didn't see until I lost you. I didn't understand until…"

"It's okay."

He shook his head. He had to explain this. He had to

make her see. "When I lost you, all I could think about was how I threw my chance away. Again. Our chance to be together."

Police cars flew into the clearing and screeched to stops in the yard. Another siren screamed up the drive. Lights flashed red against the bare trees. A fire truck barreled toward the house. Another screamed out at the highway.

He looked back to Marie. He had to finish. He had to make her see that he understood. He needed to know if she could forgive him. If she could trust him again. If she could love him. "I get it now. I understand. I can't protect myself from losing you. If you're here or in Michigan or halfway around the world, it's going to feel the same. It's going to destroy me."

Tears streamed down her face and sparkled in the fire's radiant glow. "You're not going to lose me, Brandon. I'm here. I love you. And I'm not going anywhere."

They were the most beautiful words he'd ever heard, and he soaked them up and held them in his heart. "I want to spend the rest of my ordinary moments loving you, Marie."

"Oh, Brandon. I—"

He hovered a finger over her lips. "Let me talk. I need to say this." It might not be poetic. He was sure it wouldn't be. But he had to say it. And he needed her to hear.

She nodded.

"I want all that stuff you were talking about. All that ordinary stuff, every day for the rest of our lives." He swallowed into a burning throat. "However long that will be."

A smile curved her lips. "It will be long, Brandon.

We'll have children and they'll have their own children. We'll grow old together."

More beautiful words. And looking into her eyes, he believed them. He knew from now on, he always would.

MARIE WATCHED LEXIE'S WORKERS bustle into the ballroom, hauling armfuls of the most luxurious poinsettias she'd ever seen, the first step in getting the room ready for the Drake Foundation's Christmas Ball. She was so glad they were going through with the ball. It seemed right. A fitting tribute to her father and to Charlotte. And a sign of the life and vibrancy she and Brandon intended to bring back to Drake House.

The cleaning crews had been amazing. She could barely smell the smoke from the east wing fire. And Lexie's plan of filling the room with pots of flowers to add more freshness to the air should take care of the problem nicely.

Even Isabella and Shelley had pitched in long hours without complaint. And although Marie was still a little guarded around the two of them, she felt they'd reached some kind of truce. Shelley had even warmed to her after their talk in the kitchen that night. Isabella had focused her romantic ambitions fully on Brandon's uncle Cliff. And even though Ned Perry was still out there buying up land for condos, the fact that he wasn't killing people to get it made Marie feel a lot more charitable toward him as well.

It was the season for giving, after all.

And now it was the season for deciding what she thought of Lexie's new ideas for decorating the ballroom before her friend came down from the balcony and demanded her verdict. But try as she might, she was having a heck of a time looking around the ballroom and making the sketches Lexie had shown her come to life in her mind's eye.

Marie tilted her head to the side, despite the residual soreness in her neck, and studied the mantle of the ballroom's grand fireplace. She just didn't have the talent for design that her friend had. Or the good taste of her father, for that matter. Although Lexie had explained her plans for garlands around the glass doors, a evergreen swag and candles on the fireplace mantel and a lighting effect that would look like snow falling from the sky, Marie couldn't see it. And she didn't want to let her friend down.

Brandon walked up beside her and slipped an arm around her shoulder. "What is it?"

"Lexie wants to know what I think of her plans."

"So what do you think?"

"I don't know. She knows this stuff better than I do. I wish she wouldn't ask me. I trust whatever she decides will look great."

"Then tell her that."

"I tried. She said she always ran things by my father. She wants my opinion."

"Tell her it will look beautiful."

"Unless I can really imagine it, she'll know I'm just saying the words."

"I think it's beautiful. In fact, I think it's absolutely perfect." But he wasn't looking at the mantel or the mirror above. He was staring straight at her.

She backhanded him in the ribs.

"Ow."

"Yeah, that hurt. Sure."

"Okay. It didn't hurt. But I like tickling better. Or kissing."

She let out a sigh. She couldn't help but smile. After all they'd been through, they'd finally found a way to be together. To share their love. To live their lives. Every ordinary minute they had left. "I'm happy."

"Are you?" Brandon gave her a grin. "I'm glad. I'm happy, too."

"I only wish…"

"What?"

"That my father was here. That he could see Lexie's plans. That he could let us know what he thinks."

Brandon's grin softened. He rubbed her arm gently with his fingertips. "You want his approval."

"Yes."

"You're not just talking about the Christmas decorations, are you?"

A tingling sensation stole over her. "No. I guess I'm not."

He leaned down and kissed her, light and gentle, a confirmation of their love and a promise of more love to come. "I have something for you." He took her left hand in his and slipped something onto her finger.

Marie held her breath. She lifted her hand and studied the ring.

It was a marquis solitaire diamond on a platinum band, sleek, classic, beautiful. And bigger than any diamond she'd ever seen. Not his mother's ring, but a new one. A fresh one. A ring just for her. "I love it."

He leaned on his cane. He grimaced as he lowered himself to a knee. "To make it official, you know."

Her throat felt thick. "I would love to marry you."

He shook his head. "You have to wait until I ask."

"Then ask, already." She couldn't help being impatient. She'd waited ten years for this. But the ten years had been worth it to see his smile now. To feel his unreserved happiness. To bask in happiness of her own.

"I love you, Marie Leonard. And I would be honored and humbled if you would agree to be my wife."

Marie smiled and nodded, unsure her voice would work.

He crooked his eyebrows. "Is that a yes? Because my leg is killing me."

She gripped his arm and pulled him to his feet. "It's a yes. Always and forever a yes."

He gave her a peck on the lips and glanced around the ballroom, watching the workers carry in another round of colorful plants. "I think Edwin would be happy. I think he would heartily approve." He kissed her, longer this time, deeper, and when he finished, he held her close against his side.

Marie's eyes misted. They had wonderful days ahead, wonderful years. And with luck, children to fill the new nursery that would rise from the old nursery's ashes. Rebuilt with detail and care to match the rest of Drake House.

She blinked back the tears and looked into the mirror above the mantel. Suddenly Lexie's decorating plans came alive in her imagination. Greenery draped on the mantel. Candles of different heights rose gracefully, their flames reflected in the glass. Light drifted through the ballroom like floating flakes of snow. Perfect.

And deep in the mirror's antique silvered glass, as real as her happiness, she could see her father's smile.

* * * * *

BEAST OF DARKNESS

BY
LISA RENEE JONES

Lisa Renee Jones is an author of paranormal and contemporary romance. Having previously lived in Austin, Texas, Lisa has recently moved to New York. Before becoming a writer, Lisa worked as a corporate executive, often taking the red-eye flight out of town and flying home just in time to make her son's baseball game. Her award-winning company, LRJ Staffing Services, had offices in Texas and Nashville. Lisa was recognised by *Entrepreneur* magazine in 1998 as the proprietor of one of the top-ten growing businesses owned by women.

Now Lisa has the joy of filling her days with the stories playing in her head, turning them into novels she hopes you enjoy!

You can visit her at www.lisareneejones.com.

To DH for the supernatural marathon week of television, videos and books that helped me work through my plot points! And thanks to Jordan Summers for coming up with the name of my ghost town. The name sparked ideas and took my imagination in all kinds of new directions!

Prologue

He'd broken a rule and now he would pay a price. It was as simple as that. Max had taken the life of a human. His reasons didn't matter.

Pulling his Harley to a halt in front of Jaguar Ranch's west-end training studio, he killed the engine, prepared to face the consequences of his actions. His gaze lifted beyond the wooded terrain, taking in the barely visible main house. To its right was a cluster of extra housing where the Knights in training lived. This was home to The Knights of White. And for a short time he had felt he might finally have found his place here, as well. But he'd been wrong.

Dismounting his bike, Max sauntered toward the studio entrance, boots scraping the dirt-and-gravel path, apprehension working him inside out.

He took some comfort in knowing his actions had

saved a woman's life—and not just any woman. He'd saved the mate of one of his fellow Knights. A mate who had healed the stain of the beast inside that Knight.

But regardless of the reasons for his actions, he'd broken a sacred vow by taking a human life. And for that, he would face consequences. Though Max knew this, even accepted it, he was no more at ease as he stepped inside the air-conditioned studio. He shut the door with a thud that was unintended, that screamed of finality. Of hard actions to come. But then, he didn't expect leniency. Max knew how close to the darkness he walked. Four hundred years of battling the stain on his soul had worn him down.

Max felt the lightly padded floor beneath his feet, barely noticing the weapons lining the walls, weapons that were used in the war against the demon Beasts they fought, the Darkland Beasts. The lights were off; meditation candles flickered in each of the room's four corners.

Max's attention focused on the two men standing in the center of the room. He approached them, in awe of the dominating figures they both were, how similar in so many ways. Long, dark hair touched each of their shoulders, powerful bodies spoke of warriors, of Knights. But more than anything, an inner strength radiated from them both.

Max offered Jag, the leader of The Knights of White, a nod. Dressed in jeans and a T-shirt as Max himself was, Jag used his role as horse rancher to disguise his true role as demon hunter.

Though Max was centuries older than Jag, Max respected him no less. For Jag had brought hope to the Knights—even to Max. Jag had been the first to find a mate, to prove that the right woman could tame the beast in all of them. And he'd replaced the leader Max had once known, a leader who'd turned to the darkness inside himself, who'd become a Beast, turning away from the Knights. A leader who had forced his men into hiding to avoid death by his swords.

But Max's attention didn't linger on Jag. His gaze strayed to the man dressed all in white, standing beside him, to Salvador—the one who'd created him. The one who could end his existence with a mere wave of a hand.

Max met the light green stare of his maker with directness. If he were to fall this day, he would do it bravely; he would do it with his head held high. And he felt the touch of those eyes as if they moved inside him, as if they reached to the depths of his soul. Perhaps they did. Perhaps that moment, that look, exposed the truth in him: that Max was so near the darkness, he could almost taste evil with each breath he drew.

Long seconds passed before Salvador spoke. "Leave us," he said softly to Jag.

Jag hesitated. "Without Max's help, we would have lost Jessica. And without Jessica, I have no doubt Des would have succumbed to his inner beast."

Max's chest tightened at the protective gesture from Jag, regret biting at his gut. He'd been alone so very long. Finally, he'd felt a sense of belonging at Jaguar Ranch, and now it was in jeopardy.

But that realization didn't change the facts. He had to live with what he had done. Max knew all too well that he couldn't turn back time. Crossing his arms in front of his chest, he widened his stance. "I'm prepared to face the consequences of my actions."

Jag stepped forward then, pausing to lay a hand on Max's shoulder. "Peace be with you, my friend." And with those words, he departed.

Somehow, Max doubted peace would find him anytime soon. The heavy silence between Salvador and him certainly set his imagination to work, taunting him with the possible punishments he might face.

The sound of the door shutting, of Jag's exit, echoed in the room. Then, and only then, did Salvador speak. "You've been a Knight for how long?"

Max supplied the answer they both already knew. "Three hundred and seventy-one years."

"You've faced much in that time. Made tough choices."

"Yes," Max agreed.

"Fought the darkness and won when others failed. Devoted yourself to protecting humanity."

"Yes."

"Yet you chose to take a human life." It wasn't a question. "Why?"

Max squeezed his eyes shut. He'd dreaded this moment, hated what he had to admit. He forced his gaze to meet Salvador's. "I remember the human charging at Jessica with a knife. I tried to save her, but I saw the blade go into her side. I grabbed him and...I don't remember anything until he was on the ground. Dead."

Salvador studied him, his stare intense, potent. "So you have no idea why you killed him? Or even if it could have been avoided?"

"No." He shook his head, his throat dry. "But I cannot lie. I know I felt fury. And darkness. I was lost to what I felt."

Salvador raised his hand and a sword flew off the wall and into his hand. "On your knees, my son."

Max did as he was told without hesitation, his heart pounding wildly against his chest, his eyes cast to the ground in disgrace. He knew death by beheading would follow and he did not fear it. To take a Knight's head was one of the only two ways to kill him. But he wanted the end to be quick. He wanted this to be over.

"Choose now," Salvador said, the blade touching Max's shoulder. "Choose life…" Metal brushed the other shoulder. "Or choose death."

The words shocked Max and his eyes lifted to Salvador. He could barely conceive of what he was hearing. Was he being given another chance? "I don't understand."

"It's a simple question," Salvador proclaimed. "Life…or death?"

Indeed, it was a simple question. Max didn't want to fail the Knights, to fail his duty. And death meant failure. "Life. I choose life."

"You are certain?" The blade swung upward, above Salvador's shoulder, before slicing through the air. It drew to a halt a whisper from Max's neck. "One sharp movement and you can find the darkness you claim to embrace."

"Life," Max whispered. Though he tried to yell, his voice simply wouldn't come out. "I choose life."

Salvador pulled the blade away from Max's neck and tossed it in the air. It disappeared as if it had never existed. "To your feet, Knight." Somehow Max obeyed, his knees weak. Once he was standing, Salvador stood toe to toe with him. "You will be sent to a place few know of, a place where you will face a great test. There you will need every gift your centuries of life have given you."

Max's response was instant. "I will not fail."

"Make no mistake. This test will push you to your limits. It will force you to face your greatest fears. And you must face this test on your own, my son." He held out his hand to Max. "But you will not face it alone. You are never alone."

Max understood. He knew the Knights were always there for him. He knew Salvador was, as well.

He accepted his creator's hand and repeated his prior words. "I will not fail."

Chapter 1

Destination: Nowhere, Texas. A town with a strange name and no location on the map. Now, that little Nowhere town had managed to scare up stories of real supernatural troubles. Or so the town sheriff seemed to believe, which was exactly why Sarah Meyers and her team were headed that direction. They investigated the paranormal events, the unexplainable and often scary things most thought to be fiction.

Sitting in the passenger seat of the van, Sarah eyed the flatland around them, not a sign of life in sight. She glanced at Edward, a research assistant and friend, who manned the steering wheel on most occasions. He was their driver and electronics expert. "They don't call it Nowhere for nothing," she commented.

He grunted his agreement, which was about all Sarah expected from him. A big black man with the brains of a genius and the sense of humor of a rag doll, he didn't waste words. When he chose to speak, his words either had real value, or they were meant to annoy Cathy, who rode in the backseat for that specific reason. The two had a love-hate relationship, to say the least. At times, Sarah's ability to mediate Edward and Cathy's tiffs successfully felt like more of a gift than her ability to receive communications from spirits.

"What is a five-letter word for a breakfast?" Cathy asked, her voice laced with an Alabama accent despite graduating from the University of Texas. Cathy had an affinity for magic and crossword puzzles. The magic part of that equation had turned her into their field expert.

Edward flicked a look over his shoulder to offer a word choice. "Pizza."

Sarah smiled, not having to see Cathy to know she was rolling those big brown eyes, her brown bob bouncing around her head. Hunting spirits and demons who had nocturnal preferences demanded erratic hours, but it also bred a love of junk food—pizza being Sarah's favorite anytime snack.

Feeling a bit mischievous after the long hours trapped in the van, Sarah decided to aid Edward's efforts to tease Cathy. "I have to agree with Edward on this one. Pizza is—" Her words cut off as pain splintered through her head. "Oh." She moaned and grabbed her head, lacing her fingers through her long blond locks as she prayed the pain would ease.

Suddenly she was in the middle of one of her visions, a spirit communicating with her by making her relive an experience from the past. She was inside an unfamiliar car, seeing through the eyes of the female driver. She reached for the dash, but in her mind, it was the steering wheel. She had become the spirit that was guiding her.

Approaching an upcoming bridge, the rain pounding on the windshield, visibility near zero, she was nervous about the bad conditions, but the butterflies in her stomach were excitement not fear. Eagerness to get home, to celebrate her one-year wedding anniversary, dictated her mood. The special gift for her man waited in the backseat, adding an extra thrill. She couldn't wait to see his face when he opened the big box.

The radio screeched, a terrible sound that bit through her eardrums. She reached forward to turn it off, glancing down for only a moment, but it was a moment too long. Her heart lurched at the sight of an animal in the road—a big black dog of some sort. No. It was too big for a dog, but the rain made it hard to tell.

She honked as she approached but it didn't move; it didn't even seem to hear the sound. And she was close now, unprepared for its stubborn stance. Her foot slammed down on the brakes, pumping them to no avail. The brakes gave her nothing, they wouldn't work.

Her stomach was in her chest as she jerked the wheel to the right to miss the animal, relieved when she didn't make contact. But when she tried to right herself, the car was going too fast. The front bumper hit the bridge's edge with a jolt that shook her teeth. The second before everything went black, she called out to the one she loved. Allen!

Sarah snapped back into reality with a gasp of air, yanking herself to a full sitting position to ensure she wasn't in the water.

"Easy, easy," Edward said, grabbing her arm as if he were afraid she might need stabilizing.

"Are you okay?" Cathy asked, concern in her voice. "I swear, I will never get used to this happening to you. It scares the hell out of me."

"I'm fine," Sarah said, and she was. She had lived with these visions since her teen years just as her mother had before her, and hers before her.

Reality slid slowly into place as Sarah noted they'd pulled over in front of the very bridge she'd had a vision of. She reached for the door and got out. Walking to the edge of the bridge, she noted the skid marks and shivered despite the hot summer day, hugging herself.

Edward and Cathy appeared by her side, but they didn't say anything. They'd been around long enough to know she needed to process and think. Sarah stood there for what could have been seconds, minutes, or much longer.

When she finally turned away from the bridge, she spoke. "A woman was murdered on this bridge."

"How?" Cathy and Edward asked at once.

"Black magic," Sarah answered, knowing the impact the two words would have on her friends, knowing they understood the implications. If there was one thing the three of them knew, it was what kind of trouble the dark arts could bring. Thanks to the university's support and plenty of grant money, they'd seen far too many bad things in their time together. Whatever was going on in Nowhere, Texas, had the kind of roots that festered into hell far too fast for comfort.

Sarah and her team pulled to a stop in front of the two-story town inn, the one recommended by the sheriff when he'd requested her presence. In a small town of three thousand, the 1800s Victorian-style house was the closest thing to a motel they possessed.

"Well, this is quaint," Cathy said. "So far the town looks more fairy tale than nightmare."

"Apparently, it normally is," Sarah commented, reaching for the door and shoving it open. She'd been hunting the supernatural since she was twelve, tagging along with her parents before their deaths. They'd died at the hand of a friend who was possessed by a demon. Sarah knew better than to underestimate a situation because it "looked" safe. Nothing had been safe since their deaths. "Let's size up the place before we haul our equipment inside."

Ten steps led them up to a porch that covered the front of the house. Cushioned chairs and couches sat in various positions, welcoming people to sit down and relax. Several wind chimes dangled from the roof, lifting with the wind. The scent of rain was in the air.

Edward held the door open for Sarah, and she entered the house, her boots scraping against the hardwood floor. To her right was a small dining area where several people mingled around a table, sharing coffee, and to her left, a lounge area with a fireplace and winding stairwell—all part of the inn's cozy allure.

Sarah walked up to the desk directly in front of her and pumped her finger on the bell. A woman came down the stairs mumbling as she rushed forward. "All right, already. I'm coming."

The gruff response took Sarah by surprise, and she turned to see if Edward and Cathy shared her reaction, only to find them arguing, their voices low but laced

with heaviness. A flutter of unease touched her stomach.
The sheriff had spoken of odd, violent behavior in the
townspeople.

"Ringing the bell once was enough," the fiftysome-
thing woman said, as she shoved her glasses on her face
and slammed the guest book down. "Impatience will get
you in trouble, Miss."

In a different situation, Sarah would point out that she
had rung the bell only once. Not this time. Not in this
situation. "Sorry for any inconvenience," Sarah said. "I
should have reservations for three rooms under Meyers."

Before the woman could answer, two men came down
the stairs exchanging heated words. One of the patrons
in the dining area stood up and shoved his chair to the
ground, yelling at the person he'd been speaking pleasantly to. The woman behind the counter screamed and
took off toward them, as if intending to interfere. Sarah
turned to find little five-foot Cathy poking a finger at
Edward's chest, fearless of his towering six-three frame.

The door to the inn opened, and her eyes went wide
at the unexpected sight of the man filling the entrance.
Dressed in jeans and a leather jacket—that had to be hot
considering the Texas summer, but damn he wore it
well—he towered well above six feet tall; his shoulders
nearly reached the width of the entry. His hazel eyes
melted into hers for all of two seconds before he moved.

Next thing she knew, she was lying on her back, the
hot leather-clad man on top of her. A knife zoomed past
her and planted into the wall next to her head.

"You okay?" her stranger asked, near her ear.

"Yes," she mouthed, unable to find her voice. As

okay as she could be with insanity and his rock-hard body surrounding her. Not to mention, the weapon she felt pressed against her leg. And it wasn't the kind meant for pleasure. Whoever this stranger was, he came armed and ready to fight. If he lost control like the rest of them, they could all kiss their tomorrows goodbye.

But he wasn't out of control that she could see. And it seemed they were two sane people, alone in a crowd that seemed to be losing their minds.

A crashing sound put them both into action. He eyed the counter and in silent agreement, they scrambled behind it, taking shelter. They both settled with their backs against the solid surface, waiting for what came next.

But nothing happened. "Do you hear that?" Sarah whispered.

He frowned and rotated to face the counter, squatting beside her, listening. The sound of nothingness filled the air. Complete, utter quiet had taken over where chaos had ruled.

"Let's hope this is a good sign," he said, as he eased upward to check out the situation. But Sarah had a feeling this was only the beginning. The beginning of what?—that was the question.

Max eased from his squatting position, analyzing the reason for the sudden silence. He knew he'd been sent to Nowhere, Texas, as part of a test. The ultimate test that would decide if his soul was worth saving. And as he peered from behind the desk, taking in the sight before him, he had no doubt that the test was not only already in full-blown effect, it was going to be hell.

Scrubbing his jaw, he watched as the faces of the inn's guests filled with bemusement, as if they had been zapped back to reality and struggled for their memories. They had no idea they'd just damn near killed one another.

In his four hundred years of living, three hundred and seventy of it had been spent fighting demon foot soldiers and protecting unknowing humans. He'd stuck to his own kind, The Knights of White; he had no clue what to do with a bunch of humans who'd clearly lost their marbles. But how ironic that he was here, dealing with them now, considering he'd gotten in trouble for killing a human— albeit an evil human, but it still broke the rules.

Beside him, the gorgeous blonde, who had his gut tightening and his heart pounding, peered out from behind the counter. "They don't know what they did, do they?"

"It doesn't appear so," he commented, discreetly inhaling another whiff of her jasmine-scented perfume. He cut her a curious glance. "Why is it you weren't affected?"

She narrowed her eyes on him. "I could ask you the same."

He laughed at that, watching her walk toward a petite brunette and a big black man. She had spunk, this one. Max felt an unnatural desire take hold, to pull her back by his side, to kiss her until she told him what he wanted to know.

There was something deep inside him that seemed to respond to this woman, seemed to call out to him. No woman had ever drawn such an instant reaction. The kind of reaction he'd heard spoken of as a sign of mating. But then, that seemed unlikely. He was inches from being destined for hell. He would not be rewarded with a mate.

Then again, this was the ultimate test he was living, a test that would push him to his limits. Perhaps, facing his mate and being strong enough to walk away, selfless enough to put her needs first, was part of that test. To claim her would mean locking her to him eternally. She would share his destiny, which was uncertain at best.

Of course, there was one other option. She could also be part of some sort of demon trick or manipulation. He couldn't be too cautious at this point.

Max decided whatever her role in this test—and she had one, of that he was certain—he had better keep her close. He stepped forward and joined her and her friends. "How is everyone?" he asked. "No serious injuries, I hope?"

The blond, would-be mate, would-be trickster answered. She had a soft, sweet voice that danced along his nerve endings with sensual results.

"Thankfully, they seem to be fine," she said, her gaze on him, a probing look in her sea-green eyes. "They don't remember any of it, though." She paused and studied him. Something in her probing stare gave him the impression she was looking for a reason to distrust him. "I'm Sarah Meyers, by the way." She motioned to her friends. "This is my research team, Cathy Wilburt and Edward Marshall."

He inclined his head at the introductions. "I'm Max," he announced, not willing to give a last name. He hadn't used one in centuries. His past was his past.

"Nice to meet you, Max," Sarah said, offering her hand.

Max steeled himself for the impact as he reached out to accept Sarah's hand. The minute their palms connected, molten heat shot up his arm. Shock darted across her face, and he knew that she, too, felt what he did. Discreetly, he cleared his throat, withdrawing his hand with regret. "What kind of research do you do?"

Before Sarah could answer, a murmur of concerned voices filled the room as it grew darker inside; the sunlight was no longer shining through the windows. Rain began to beat fiercely on the roof. Someone flipped on several lights as both Max and Sarah looked outside, to the storm that was stealing the attention of the other patrons.

"What the hell?" Max said, half to himself, his voice low. The rain was black. A thick, greasy-looking black.

To get a closer look, Sarah stepped to the window. At the same moment, Max moved, as well, claiming a position beside her. Their shoulders brushed, and for a moment Max felt as if they were one. Neither moved, neither stepped away from the other.

After several seconds, she glanced at him. "Do you believe in supernatural experiences?" she asked.

Max drew in a breath and let it out. "Yes," he said, eyeing the darkness outside the window, the sun having disappeared.

Sarah shivered and hugged herself. "Something evil has come to this town."

Max feared she was right. He knew evil in an intimate way. Long ago, a Darkland Beast had bitten him, turned him into a demon, his soul lost. Though he'd been given back that soul, saved to fight evil, he'd felt that sinister reality—still felt it—inside him. He still possessed the primal side that the Beast had created. Yet nothing he had felt, past or present, nothing he had experienced, came close to the sinister feeling that crawled through the air this day.

Whatever caused that rain, whatever caused the humans to lose control, was evil personified. And Max knew he had to destroy it.

Before it destroyed him, and everyone around him.

Chapter 2

The lights flashed and then went out; the inn was cast, once again, into dark shadows. The room grew silent, the people inside transfixed by the sight of the black rain.

Max and Sarah remained side by side, arms touching, watching the oily-looking substance pound into puddles on the ground. Sarah's presence beside him drew unfamiliar feelings. A desire to keep her close and safe. The way she lingered near him, allowing their physical connection—the touch of two strangers—seemed to indicate that the invisible bond between them was growing without effort, growing from simple exposure to one another.

It was Edward who broke the silence. From behind Max and Sarah, his deep, gravelly voice filled the air. "Shouldn't we call the sheriff?"

Sarah responded by turning to the woman behind the counter. "Can you get him on the phone?" she asked.

Max's eyes remained transfixed on that cursed black rain one more second before he glanced at Sarah, wondering what kind of evil was going to try to thwart his ability to claim his mate. If she were his mate, he reminded himself. She could be part of a trick.

"I doubt the sheriff can help with this," he pointed out.

"Unfortunately, there's truth to that," she said. "That's why he called my team to assist. But he still needs to know what just went on here."

"Phone's down," the front-desk clerk called out, concern lacing her now friendly voice. Gone was the grumpy, gray-haired woman who'd yelled at Sarah, replaced by a sweet woman with fear in her eyes. "Computer, too."

Reaching for his cell, Max checked for service. "Nothing." Max held up the screen for her to see the no-service notation.

"Damn," Sarah murmured.

"I'd say we should get our equipment," Edward said, "but it's outside. And frankly, I don't want any part of that junk falling from the sky."

Cathy interjected, "If they can log our reservations manually, we can get checked into our rooms. Then we'll be ready to set up when it stops."

"If it stops," Edward muttered bad-naturedly, a snort following his words.

Cathy nudged him. "Be positive for once."

"Yes," Sarah said. "Be positive. And grab me a room key, too, please."

Max wondered what equipment they were referring to. "You said the sheriff requested your presence?" he asked, as Edward and Cathy moved out of hearing range.

"Right. Apparently there had been some strange things happening before the rain." His brow lifted in question and she responded, "As in supernatural things." She hesitated and then added, "We're paranormal investigators." She dropped the words into the air with emphasis, much like dropping a bomb. Then she waited, studying him closely, giving him a second to reply. When he didn't, she asked, "No smart remarks? No rolled eyes?"

"I was actually thinking the sheriff was a pretty smart guy," Max commented. "Because whatever is going on here isn't of this world."

"I'm amazed to hear that you believe in the supernatural," she said, surprise in her voice. "Most people either don't believe, or won't admit they do for fear of looking silly."

He eyed the black rain flowing by the bucketful, hard and fast. "If I didn't believe before this storm, I would now."

"There are all kinds of scientific explanations for black rain," she inserted.

"And we both know they'd all be bull crap," he quickly countered.

"Yes," Sarah said, amusement lacing her words as she repeated his statement. "They would, indeed, be 'bull crap.'" She sobered quickly, as her gaze scanned the room. Around them people murmured concerns, fear in their voices. "And clearly these people know that."

"It's in everyone's best interests that we figure out what's going on," Max asserted. "How about I lend you a hand with your investigation? I'll go grab that equipment of yours. And while I'm at it, I'll get my laptop computer. It's got a hell of a battery, and I'm not half-bad with research."

"Aren't you worried about that rain?"

"I've been chin deep in all kinds of sh—er, junk in my lifetime. A little black water isn't going to make me melt."

"You don't think it can hurt you," Sarah said, and it wasn't a question. A hint of suspicion laced her words. "Just like you weren't affected by whatever made everyone start acting weird. Why is that?"

She didn't trust him and he didn't blame her. But he couldn't afford to trust her, either. Not with everything he had on the line. A fool he was not. Sarah could be part of his test. He countered with a reminder. "I believe I asked you that question a few minutes ago and you avoided it."

She seemed to hesitate. "Yes. I guess I did." She paused, and then admitted, "I'm a medium. As in I communicate with the spirit world. Have been since I was about twelve. I assume it must offer me some sort of mental shield."

Interesting. So, she wasn't like everyone else here any more than he was. That supported his theory that she was his mate, the light to his darkness.

A frown dipped her brows. "No comment?"

Max smiled, resisting the urge to reach out and brush his fingers down her ivory cheek. "You want me to say I don't believe you, don't you?"

They stared at each other for several seconds, her eyes searching his. She was seeking something in his gaze, something he didn't understand. But he wanted to. He wanted to understand everything about this woman.

Her lashes fluttered and she turned to the window, her

fingers spreading on the panel. "People don't understand what I am."

The statement, the emotion attached to her words,
took him off guard. He felt pain that wasn't his own. He
felt her pain. It was as if they were one, bound without
the actual mating ritual.

"This isn't my first supernatural experience," Max
confessed, wanting her to know she had found acceptance
in him. "In fact, I have a few talents of my own." *Like immortality,* he added silently. Unless someone sliced off
his head or bled him dry, he wasn't going anywhere. He
could feel pain, he could even get hurt, but he'd heal.

Her head whipped around, body tensing, her attention fixed on him. "Meaning what?"

"You investigate what can't be seen, Sarah," he said,
shoving aside his jacket enough to expose several
weapons. "I hunt things you don't *want* to see. Things,
I can promise you, most people don't want to even know
exist. Let's just hope you don't see them for yourself,
though I fear you might. Something is telling me our
two worlds have come to a crossroads. We need to figure
out what we're facing before it finds us."

Confusion flashed on her face. "I feel the same thing.
It's…unusual."

He continued, "Time is what matters right now. We
need to figure out what this rain means before something else happens. If that equipment of yours will help,
I need to go get it." Max held out his hand. "Keys?"

"Okay," she said, "but I'm not done asking questions. Not even close. If I consider working with you—
and I'm not saying I am—I need to understand who and
what you are."

He inclined his head. "Understood."

She gave him a probing inspection, seeming to gauge his words. Apparently accepting his reply, at least for the time being, she gave him her back, walking over to the front desk where Edward and Cathy were busy with check-in. She whispered to her friends. After a moment, Edward and Cathy twisted around and looked at Max as if he were insane.

A long, hard stare later, Edward reached into his pocket and tossed the keys to Max. "It's your death wish, man."

Max caught the keys and smiled. "They don't call me Wild Thing for nothing," he commented dryly.

Sarah stared at Max, ignoring his joke. She wasn't buying into his nonchalant attitude about the rain. He might have some sort of "gift" as she did, but she was pretty darn certain he was aware he was taking a risk. There was no telling what effect that rain could have on what it touched.

The idea of Max risking his safety bothered her. Not that he couldn't take care of himself. Still, for some reason, she fought the urge to insist he not do this. She also knew herself well enough to know her feelings were a bit over the top. She had to assume her emotions were getting mixed up with those of the female spirit making contact. It was clear this spirit worried for her husband. That could happen. At times, she felt the spirits so intensely, they almost became her.

The fact that she was attracted to Max probably aided her sensitivity to the spirit's emotions. This wasn't the time or place to be distracted by a man, not to mention her libido, but she couldn't seem to turn off her attraction to him.

Suddenly, she realized she was not only still staring at Max, he was staring back. She swallowed, feeling the heat of his hazel eyes all the way to her toes. Something about him got to her in a big way. A way that defied the circumstances, which were quite serious. People's lives could be on the line, she reminded herself.

She drew her spine stiff and delicately cleared her throat, afraid she wouldn't find her voice otherwise. "At least take an umbrella," she suggested, needing some semblance of comfort that he had protection.

The front-desk clerk was quick to assist. "I'll get you one, and we have a carport 'round back. Pull around there and you can unload under the shelter."

Max looked as if he would refuse, which wasn't okay with Sarah. When his gaze found hers, she made sure he saw the determination in her expression. He sighed with resignation and walked to the desk.

The front-desk clerk headed toward a closet as an elderly man approached the desk. He placed several lit candles on it as he called to the clerk. "Hold up, honey," he said, and eyed the rest of them, but she didn't listen. She grabbed an umbrella before returning to the counter. The man lowered his voice. "You're the people the sheriff called in from that Austin University?"

"Yes," Sarah said. "That's us."

"I hope you got answers that don't require fancy equipment 'cause nothing's working. Not even battery-powered."

Sarah grimaced with that news. "No need to risk the rain for equipment that doesn't work."

The man's lips thinned, his expression grim. "I don't want to scare the guests, but we got us big trouble here in Nowhere, Texas. We got us a ghost or a demon or something evil like that."

The clerk swatted his arm, and he shot her a mad look. "You know it's true, Helen," he said. "Tell 'em."

"Actually," Cathy said, doing one of the things she did well—calming people's fears. "There's a long list of scientific explanations."

"Name one," the man said.

Cathy was quick to respond, drawing them into conversation, Edward assisting her. He never showed his cranky side to the public, saving it for Cathy and Sarah.

Thankful for the escape Cathy had offered her, and concerned about the newest developments, Sarah motioned to Max. Discreetly, they moved away from the group. "Look," she said softly, the sense of unity she felt with this man like that of a longtime friend, not a virtual stranger. "If you have any idea what we are dealing with, please tell me now. Don't avoid my questions. Who called you here and why?"

Max hesitated and Sarah narrowed her eyes on him. She wanted to know about this man. About why he was here and what made him different from everyone else here. Because he was different and they both knew it.

As much as her instincts said he was worthy of her trust, her past history told her to be concerned. She'd learned the hard way with her parents' death that, in the world of demon hunting, trust could lead to destruction. She wouldn't give Max, or anyone, her blind trust, ever again. "Did the sheriff call you?" Sarah asked, pressing Max for answers when he offered none.

"The sheriff didn't call me. I work for a covert operation called in under extreme circumstances. I'm told where to go and I show up—sometimes, like now, with very little information. All I know for certain is that my boss is selective about what I deal with. I wouldn't be here if the situation wasn't bad. Real bad."

Sarah wanted to press for more details. Turning her attention to the view outside the window, she processed what she'd just been told. He'd basically admitted to hunting the supernatural, just as she did. Only he hunted a different breed. Perhaps those who bore fangs?

Without looking at him, she said, "I know you aren't telling me everything there is to tell." She cast him a sideways look. "Since we're the only two people who seem unaffected by what's going on, it appears we might have to work together. I can't do that if I don't trust you. I can't trust you if you talk in code. I need to know who sent you and why."

Several people walked past them and Max hesitated. "Now isn't the time or place for unveiling deep, dark secrets."

She drew a labored breath, her chest expanding with effort. He was right, of course. And her instincts told her to trust this man. For now. "Fine." She narrowed her gaze. "But soon."

"Fair enough," he agreed.

Sarah considered her next move. The best thing they could do now was to start researching. That meant interviews, since they were cut off from technology. "As much as I don't want to go out in that mess," she admitted, referring to the weather, "I need to talk to the sheriff and get some answers. I need to do something productive while we wait for our equipment to work again."

"I'm all for that," Max inserted. "It beats the hell out of standing here in the dark, waiting for some invisible bomb to explode."

"Yeah, it does," she said, searching his face, surprised at how accurately he described what she felt, and how in tune they were with each other. How in their own world. These people around them were scared, her team included, but no one else seemed to sense the ticking clock that she and Max did. "I'll get that umbrella."

She started to turn away and his voice called her back. "Stay here where it's safe. I'll go and bring the sheriff back."

It was a gentleman's offer, and she appreciated it. She just couldn't accept. "I don't know if I'd call here, or anywhere in this town, safe," she said, not one to worry about her own safety, anyway. Risk was part of this job, as she suspected he knew from his own work. Demon hunters made bad lovers; they were always knocking on death's door. "Besides. I'm not the type to sit and wait."

"I'd feel better if you stayed," he said.

"I wouldn't." She gave him a smile. "But thank you, anyway."

"What if I insist?"

"I'll go anyway, and you can't stop me," she said sternly, turning away with decisiveness this time, and as expected, facing an argument with her staff over her decision to go out in the storm. But they knew what Max was starting to learn. She made her own choices.

Sarah returned to Max's side with an umbrella and a few supplies. "Ready?"

He gave her a nod and pulled the door open. They stepped outside, the wind gushing with sudden force as if it were warning them to turn back into the inn.

Sarah was about to step off the porch when Max grabbed her arm. "Not until I do a test."

She rolled her eyes. "Macho is so not appealing."

"Humor me," he said, and started to hold his hand out.

Instinctively, she yanked it back. His brow arched. "Sorry," she said. "That water just looks so damn evil."

"But you want to go out in it," he said flatly. "I told you I can go and get the sheriff."

"I'm going," she said, her voice firm.

"You're very stubborn," he declared.

"Yep," she said. "I am."

"Then I guess we better try my test again," he suggested as he eased her fingers from around his wrist, which she was holding tighter than she realized.

She crossed her arms in front of her chest so she wouldn't be tempted to grab him again. "If you insist."

"I do," he said quickly.

She held her breath as he reached into the rain. The dirty-looking substance ran over his skin, through his fingers, splattering on his leather jacket. But nothing more happened. No pain. No insanity. No demon possession. Not that she could tell, anyway.

Sarah let the air slide from her lungs. "Thank God."

Still, he held his hand under the water, apparently not quite satisfied it was safe. It was hard for Sarah to shake the fear of demon possession after watching a demon take over a friend and turn him into a killer. A killer who had murdered her parents. The thought had her studying Max with renewed concern.

Yet she was attracted to Max in a way she didn't remember ever being attracted to any other man—in a way that went beyond his physical beauty. She thought she'd shut off that part of herself when she'd lost her parents—the part that connected beyond the surface, that allowed emotion to flare—but somehow Max had slipped under her guard. And she couldn't help but wonder how and why.

She drank in the vision he made, his face so full of character, full of strength. A dimpled chin. A long scar across his right brow. She wondered how he got it. Would he tell her if she asked?

He was different from anyone else she'd met, she concluded. Could she actually have found someone who she didn't have to fear would be possessed by a demon? Did she dare hope?

She stiffened. That was a dangerous thought that would only lead her to destruction. She couldn't let down her guard. "You still feel okay, right?" she asked, needing that verbal confirmation.

"Same as I always do," he said, shaking the water from his hand. He popped the umbrella open and offered her his arm. "Shall we?"

The air around them crackled with menace, and Sarah gratefully slipped her hand beneath his elbow, welcoming the warmth and security of that deliciously muscled, well-armed body. A strange thing for her. She preferred to stand alone, not depending on anyone.

She prayed that the feelings that urged her to trust Max were genuine. She prayed she wasn't being lured into some dangerous charade by some evil spirit.

But deep in her core she felt Max was part of her

journey in this town. He felt familiar in some odd way. And her gut said they were headed for a fight, and it was going to require both of them to win.

Something was here, around them, near them. She could almost feel it watching. Something that could strike at any minute. She didn't know much about Max. Nor did she know what she would face in the next minute, the next hour. Only that danger seemed to surround them, to blanket them in warning.

Determination formed in Sarah. She didn't like defeat. She didn't like allowing things to spin out of control. She was going to learn Max's secrets, to dig beneath the surface of the sexy stranger who'd pulled her under some sort of seductive spell. And she was going to find out the source of evil in this town and what killed that woman on that bridge. Sarah couldn't turn back time and prevent that woman's death, but she could help her rest in peace. And she could stop anyone else from dying the same way.

Chapter 3

Demon Prince Vars fed on human desires and emotions, created each person's personal destruction by delving into their innermost thoughts and feelings. Until he was cut off from his connection to the earthly realm, imprisoned in the Underworld beneath a magical barrier created by the Archangel Raphael. For centuries, he had been without his powers, weak and pathetic.

That had all changed when Kate and Allen Walker had chosen the land above his hell hole, his prison, as the place to build their home. Their presence had delivered to him the power to find escape, had allowed Vars to create a tiny hole in the magical barrier of his prison and begin controlling their lives.

Vars stepped to the top of a boulder, the highest point inside the confines of his prison, and looked down at the fiery caverns he would soon depart. Satisfaction filled him. Everything was going as planned. Stage one had been Kate's death, which had led to Allen's interest in the dark arts and his study of black magic. An amateur at his craft, Allen had accepted the mental push Vars had given him, and foolishly tried to subordinate demons as his servants, demanding they resurrect his wife. All part of Vars's plan, of course.

Unknowingly, Allen evoked the most powerful of Vars's demon legions, Vars having guided him to their names. When Allen found the demons too weak to do his bidding, he attempted to send them back to hell, but he was too inexperienced to succeed. Instead, Allen had set them free to roam the earthly planes, to aid Vars's efforts at escape. But escape for Vars would not be as simple as it had been for the lesser demons who reported to him. To break the binding spell of an archangel, Vars would require a source of great magical energy. A source Allen would now bring to him.

When Allen became brave enough to call on him, Vars would promise him his wife, in return for a few little favors and a blood oath of service. Once he had that oath, he would be powerful enough to contact the Underworld. Most importantly, he could contact Cain, the king who oversaw the Darkland Beasts. Cain hated Raphael and his army of Knights even more than Vars did. He would aid Vars's escape, and together they would crush all that Raphael valued. They would crush humanity.

Vars laughed. Yes. Allen would deliver all of this to him and more, in exchange for a promise of his wife's return. Not that Vars had ever kept a promise in all his centuries of existence.

* * *

Power flowed through Allen as he stepped to the edge of the magical circle drawn in the center of his living-room floor. Candles flickered at four points outside the circle's boundaries. He drew a breath, claiming his magic, feeling it flow through the long black robe he wore and the sheathed black dagger he clutched in his right hand.

Each time he used his craft, he grew stronger, more capable of mastering his skills. A rush of adrenaline poured through him as he thought of what was to come, what would happen when he stepped inside that circle. He'd come to crave this high magic that was delivered to him; he devoured the feeling of ultimate control it offered, and he hated himself for that.

Deep down he knew Kate would hate it, too, that she would not approve of his touching the dark arts. But he had tried her way, turning to the church, praying for her return. All they'd offered him was a promise that the pain would ease. That Kate would always be in his heart if not by his side. He refused to accept a promise that left him without his wife.

Besides, he knew his Kate. She would want to be with him. She knew how much he needed her. She was all he had, all the love he'd ever experienced. After a life of foster homes and loneliness, she had brought him joy. The church wanted him to forget, but damn it, he didn't want to forget. He would *not* forget.

His hand tightened on the dagger, his jaw clenching. This path he'd chosen had been for one purpose and one purpose only: to get his wife back. Kate would understand why he had to do this.

New resolve formed and he stepped inside the circle. Tonight, he would evoke an upper-level demon, the one that lesser demons had called "Vars." And he was ready. He could feel the tingling of electricity dance along his nerve endings, the surge of his own energy rippling through his veins, charging the air.

He unsheathed the dagger and sliced his hand, dropping the blade to the ground as he let the blood trickle from his skin to the floor. In a low voice, he began the evocation spell, willing Vars to show himself. Evil crackled in the air almost instantly; the hair on the back of Allen's neck stood on end. Fire flickered within the triangle, and Allen felt the heat as if he were on fire, but still he chanted, still he continued. He had to do this. He had to get his Kate back. A vague shape within the fire began to take solid form.

"I command the demon known as Vars to show himself!" Allen shouted.

The man, or rather demon, that appeared in the center of the triangle stood a good six feet five, his long black hair in a braid that disappeared between broad shoulder blades. He wore a black shirt and pants and boots that covered his calves.

The demon lifted his hand, fingers pointing at Allen. Suddenly, Allen's legs gave out on him, and he fell to his knees. The demon closed his hand into a tight fist, and Allen felt his chest tighten, as if the demon were squeezing the breath out of him. Fear shot through Allen's body. The precious control he'd reveled in moments before now gone. The lesser demons he'd summoned had not wielded this kind of power.

"Prince Vars is my name," the demon said. "Address me with respect or do not dare address me at all."

The invisible grip Vars held on Allen's chest disappeared, he gulped for air. Desperate to escape, Allen tried to get to his feet, but his legs were still frozen in place, as if they were glued to the hardwood floor.

"Those who serve me, bow to me," Vars bellowed.

No! Allen screamed the word in his mind, silently beginning a spell meant to subordinate the demon.

Vars laughed. "You cannot control one such as me, Allen," he said, making it clear he knew Allen's name and what he was attempting to do. "I am royalty in the Underworld, one of the great powers. You will bow to me or you will not get what you seek." His lips twisted sardonically. "You do want your precious Kate back, do you not?"

"Yes!" Allen said, too anxiously. He could not help himself, could not contain his urgency. "I want my Kate back."

Vars tilted his head and studied Allen. "I can help you, but only when I have my freedom. I am bound beneath the earth, my powers bound with me. Free me and you shall have your wife."

"How?"

"I will guide you, human." Vars pointed at the dagger and it flew through the air into his hand. He sliced his hand and black liquid poured from his palm. "Vow a blood oath and give yourself to me. Within our blood, I will be connected to you. I will lead you on your path. A path that will deliver you to your wife."

Allen pushed to his feet, free to move now. He didn't hesitate, determined to find his way to Kate. A second later, he stood on the edge of the triangle and extended his bloodied hand across the line. Vars grabbed his palm, pressing it to his own.

The instant their blood mingled, a current of electricity dashed through Allen's body. He felt numb, shaken, scared. He cried out. The pain, the pain was too much... and then it was just gone.

In its place, he felt calmness, peace; a sense of magnificent energy flowed through him. In his head, he heard Vars speak the name of three great sorcerers. *Bring me their souls, and I will give you Kate.*

Allen smiled, knowing he would not fail, aware he now wielded great magic, borne of his connection to Prince Vars. Yes. He would deliver those souls, and he would have his Kate.

Chapter 4

Max and Sarah didn't speak as they walked toward the sheriff's office, both watchful, the edginess they shared as evident as the puddles of ominous black rain splashing around their feet, its mere existence seeming to scream with silent threat. But there was a connection between them that didn't need words, an understanding that what they faced would be faced together. Not to mention a charge of awareness, of attraction, that seemed to heat his arm where her hand rested.

In Sarah, Max found a brave, feisty female; she was bold and uncompromising about being different, about being a medium. A woman who accepted his admission about hunting the supernatural. He had no doubt she had questions about who and what he was; yet, she had still accepted him. She even wanted to trust him, though she was fighting that desire. If she were, indeed, his mate, she would instinctively trust him. But she had baggage of some sort telling her those feelings were wrong. He could feel it in her, feel the worry, the hesitation.

Still, there was something surreal about finding a mate in this time of judgment for himself, a time that might well forge his demise.

He shoved that thought aside as the sheriff's office came into view, noting the pitch-black interior. "It looks as if no one is home," he commented. "If the entire town broke out in rage like the hotel occupants did, I imagine they're out trying to clean up the aftermath."

"Either that or they don't have any candles," Sarah said, indicating her bag. "Glad we brought our own."

They took the stairs and found cover from the rain beneath a small overhang. The meager space demanded they stay close, bodies touching. Which is where Max wanted Sarah, anyway—close and safe.

He dropped the umbrella to the ground beside the stairs as Sarah tried the locked door and then knocked. No one came to the door, no one called out in response. "We still have to go in," Sarah said. "He was expecting me. It seems logical he'd have a file with notes to hand over."

He slanted her a sideways look. "Are you asking me to break into the sheriff's office?"

She didn't look even mildly ashamed of her request. "Desperate times require desperate actions."

A smile touched his lips at that and he reached into his pocket, withdrawing a small leather case he kept there for just this type of situation. In about sixty seconds, Max had the lock popped.

"Impressive," Sarah commented. "Not sure I want to know where you learned that."

"You never know when a skill might save a life," he said, thinking of the many things he'd encountered in the four hundred years he'd lived. "I like to be prepared." Besides being a fairly capable locksmith, Max could hack into just about anything electronic in existence, a skill he'd put to use for the Knights on more than one occasion.

He shoved open the door and surveyed the interior, before letting Sarah enter. Max's instincts reached well beyond that of a normal human, and they told him the building contained no threats, but caution dictated he do a walk-through just to be safe.

Once Sarah was inside the lobby, he locked the door to keep out unannounced visitors. He turned around to find himself almost toe to toe with Sarah, her gaze locking with his. The setting was dark and intimate, the attraction between them hot and heavy. The desire to claim Sarah, to possess her, burned him inside out. Flaring to life without warning, threatening his control. This was like nothing he'd ever experienced before. The primal side of him, the part touched by a Darkland Beast, a demon, cared nothing about time and place, about danger. It simply wanted Sarah.

"It's very dark in here," she murmured, her voice washing over the rawness of his nerve endings and calming him a bit. Ironic how one woman could cause the same rawness that she could calm.

Before he could stop himself, he reached up and caught a soft strand of her hair between his fingers, the desire to touch her too intense to resist. Her eyes widened with surprise, and he saw the flash of uncertainty in her gaze. As if she wanted to pull away but couldn't. Damn, how he could relate to that feeling. This woman was going to be his undoing if he wasn't careful. If she knew how much he burned to taste her, to feel her softness against his body, she'd likely run for cover.

Her soft scent lifted in the air, insinuating into his nostrils, and Max felt his willpower sliding away. He knew he had to distance himself. "Stay by the door while I have a look around," he said, but he didn't move. He was too transfixed in the awareness between them, by that desire to taste her that wouldn't let go.

Her teeth scraped her bottom lip as if she were thinking the same thing. The action drew his gaze, tempting him further, pushing him to take what he wanted. The beast clawed and pressed, devouring his willpower.

"You might want a candle," she suggested, reaching for her bag.

Her words helped jar him back to reality. "I don't," he said a bit abruptly, as he reached for the control he'd been about to lose. He turned away from her, starting his inspection of the office.

As for the candle she'd offered, the truth was that his night vision was as good as his day vision. And staring into those deep-green eyes of Sarah's was driving him insane with want, a feeling he shook off, reminding himself of the need for a clear level head, ready for battle. Ready to protect Sarah and defeat an enemy.

That thought helped him step into duty mode. It didn't take long for him to finish his scan of the few small offices he found and confirm the building was secure. On the way back to the lobby, he grabbed a roll of paper towels from the bathroom in case Sarah wanted to clean off a little.

* * *

Sarah was grateful for a few minutes alone as Max inspected the offices. Her emotions were reeling as she lit the four candles she brought with them from the inn. She'd wanted Max to kiss her. Wanted it in such a desperate way, she'd darn near grabbed him and pulled his mouth to hers. This was so not like her. Not one bit. She didn't get distracted from her work. Didn't get close to people, especially not strangers, not men. But something about Max had her twisted up with need. Had her wanting things she'd long ago decided her work made impossible.

Before she had time to analyze her feelings, Max was back. "We're good," he said, stopping in front of her. "I need to check out the computers and see if I can get anything working." He was close. So close she could feel the heat of his body. She reached for the paper towels in his hand, needing a distraction, a reason to avoid eye contact.

"Thank you," she said, taking a step backward to give herself some distance from Max and then busying herself cleaning her boots. "I'm getting mud everywhere."

"I'm sure the sheriff will understand."

She tossed the dirty towels in the trash. Her hands went to her hips, and she blew hair out of her eyes. "It's strange he's not here. And what about his staff? Where are they?"

Max leaned on the desk, casting his ruggedly handsome features in candlelight. "Based on what I saw as I looked around, there's only one deputy. I assume there's a secretary. And if the violence that broke out at the inn occurred all over town, maybe someone got hurt. If so, I'm sure they had their hands full with the aftermath."

"Good point," Sarah said, agreeing. "And since no one seems to remember what happened, I'm sure there's a lot of confusion." She paused, thinking a moment. "I wonder if the sheriff even knows what happened."

"I'd venture to say he is as confused as everyone else, and still trying to deal with any chaos caused by today's events. Everyone but you and me were affected at the inn."

"Everyone but you and me," she repeated, feeling torn about that similarity between them. Should she be relieved or suspicious to find someone else who couldn't be touched by this thing—whatever it was?

Abruptly, he pushed off the desk again, but not before she saw a flash of understanding in his gaze. He knew she wanted answers and he wasn't ready to give them. "Let's check out the sheriff's office," he said. With those words, he turned away, shutting her down before she could begin questioning him.

Sarah grabbed a candle and followed him, but she wasn't letting him off the hook. Because she was going to demand they clear the air, that he start talking. Feeling this kind of intense attraction to someone she didn't know made her vulnerable. She didn't like vulnerable. Despised it, in fact.

She took a step forward, when a sudden awareness of a spiritual presence took hold—it was the woman from the car accident. Sarah forgot Max, focusing on the connection to the spirit, trying to understand any message that might be sent to her. What Sarah felt in that moment was urgency, an urgency to find out more about that car accident. Driven for answers, she headed toward the back offices.

Max had already grabbed several stacks of files and was setting them up on top of a table in the break area. She set her candle down, as well. "Are these all the case files?"

"From what I can tell," he said. "But I'm going to check the deputy's office. Anything particular you need?"

She sat down at the table and reached for a file. "Yes, and this would be so much easier if the sheriff were here. He could find what I'm looking for right away, I'm sure. It's a car accident on the bridge leading into town. It's somehow related to what's going on."

He leaned a shoulder on the doorjamb. "What's the name?"

She shook her head. "I only know the husband's name. Allen. And before you ask, I know this sounds crazy, but I had a vision as we drove across that bridge. Sometimes that happens. The spirit wants me to know something, and it makes me relive the event."

"Relive the event?" he asked, his voice holding surprise. "What exactly does that mean?"

"One minute I was talking with Cathy and Edward. The next I was transported into that woman's car, living through her crash." She paused and let out a heavy breath. "And her death."

"Holy shit," Max murmured, stunned. "How often does that kind of thing happen to you?"

"Not often," she assured him, "but the experience isn't something you get used to. It's a bit like how I've heard seizures described. I completely zone out. Everything around me disappears."

"What if you were driving, or doing something dangerous when that happened? You could be killed."

She shrugged. "I don't think the spirits are trying to

kill me. Just communicating. My mother had the same thing, and it never happened at a time when she could get hurt. And, like I said, that type of experience is rare. Usually I just hear whispers in my head, and I have to decipher their meaning. Or I have a vivid dream. Often I dream about a case before I'm officially involved. That's what happened with this town. I dreamt about it and the next morning the sheriff called."

"Okay," he said, scrubbing his jaw, obviously thinking aloud. "Let me get this straight. You dreamt about this town. You had a vision of the car accident." He cast her an inquisitive look. "Are we thinking the woman who died on that bridge is haunting this town?"

A couple of files flew off the table onto the floor and a book pounded down on top of them. Max pushed off the doorframe. "What the—?"

"She's here, and no, she's not the one causing havoc." She smiled. "And obviously, she doesn't like that you suggested otherwise. She wants to help us."

Max mumbled to himself and then motioned toward the stuff on the floor. "The woman from the bridge did this?" Sarah nodded. "And I suppose she thinks it's funny to throw things around like that? To try to spook someone?" He didn't wait for an answer. "Tell her I'm not laughing," Max said, bending down to grab the files. He paused to glance up at her. "That is, if you can talk to her. Can you? Obviously she can communicate with you."

"It's a one-way conversation. They do all the talking," Sarah said. "I just listen."

Still kneeling by the fallen items, Max balanced his weight on his heels, hands on his muscular thighs. "How do you know she isn't tricking you? What if she *is* the one doing all of this?"

"She's not tricking me," she said. "I can't explain it, but I get a real sense for who these spirits are. Especially when I am in one of those visions. This woman is worried about her husband. He's involved. We need to find out who he is and talk to him."

Max grabbed the files and the book from the floor and then joined Sarah at the table, setting the materials down in front of him. "Okay then. You trust her, I trust her. "Maybe this spirit was telling us something by throwing these specific items on the floor." He reached for the book. "This is the town history. I'll read through it and look for anything that might help. Maybe a myth or a legend of some sort. Usually there is some distorted truth to those things. Maybe something about that bridge." He inclined his chin to indicate the files. "Hopefully, one of those is your car accident."

Sarah blinked with surprise. She simply couldn't get over how easily Max accepted her world. "The way spirits talk to me doesn't freak you out at all, does it?"

"Macho guys like me don't get freaked out," he said, smiling as he referred to what she'd called him earlier at the inn. But as quickly as that smile had appeared, his expression turned serious. "I accept easily what others don't, because I've seen a lot of things, Sarah. A lot of them ugly. Things you might not want to know about."

She did want to know. Had to know, in fact. But before she could say as much, a sound at the front of the office had her pushing to her feet.

Already standing, gun in hand, Max said, "Stay

here." He didn't wait for a response, rounding the corner, gun stiff-armed in front of his body.

Max entered the lobby just as a big burly cowboy in uniform charged through the door, a 9 mm pistol in his hand. Though Max had no doubt this was the sheriff, he also didn't know what the man's state of mind was.

"Put the weapon down, son," the sheriff ordered. "No reason anyone has to be hurt."

"Normally, Sheriff," Max drawled cautiously, "I'd be happy to comply. You are wearing a badge and all. But forgive me if I'm cautious. We haven't exactly been received by a welcoming party."

"Who is *we?*" the sheriff asked.

Sarah appeared beside Max, carrying a lighted candle. "Sarah Meyers, Sheriff Jenson. And this is Max."

A flicker of recognition sparked in the sheriff's eyes. "I was expecting you, Ms. Meyers. Will you be kind enough to tell *Max* it's not smart to draw a gun on the sheriff, and it's downright stupid to do it in his own office?"

"Max," Sarah said, her hand touching his arm.

"Where's that deputy of yours?" Max asked, not ready to lower his gun quite yet. After what he'd seen back at that inn, he couldn't be cautious enough. *He* wouldn't die from a bullet wound, but Sarah would.

"I'd like to know, too," the sheriff said. "But it appears we have no phones."

"Max, please," Sarah whispered. "Put down the gun."

Slowly, Max complied, easing his gun to his side, finger still on the trigger. He stepped in front of Sarah as he shoved the Glock into his holster, protecting her with his body until he was sure she was safe.

"Now you," he ordered the sheriff, sidestepping as Sarah tried to get around him.

The lawman looked as if he might refuse, but after a second he blew out a breath and harnessed his gun. His finger slid over his long mustache and then tapped his cowboy hat back on his head. "I hope the two of you are really here to help, because we need it."

"We *are* here to help," Sarah said, casting Max an irritated look, as he finally let her step to his side. Her gaze caught on the sheriff and then went past him, to the window. "The rain stopped."

"For now," Sheriff Jenson agreed. "Still cloudy as hell, though." He flipped the light switch. "And no power yet. No phones or Internet, either. Truck worked, though, and so did my flashlight. Hope that's a sign some of this has passed."

Sarah glanced at her wrist. "My watch is working again. From my best estimate, it rained a couple of hours at the most. I expected six hours of rain." Her throat bobbed as she swallowed hard, her eyes lifting and catching on Max's. "Today is June 6. The sixth month, the sixth day. I'm wondering if there is a third *six* we haven't identified."

"As in the sign of the devil?" Sheriff Jenson asked. "Just what are we dealing with here, Ms. Meyers?"

Devil. Demon who received power from the devil. Max didn't know the answer, but he'd seen plenty of bad stuff. He'd fought demon soldiers by the hundreds. Winning those battles had been a matter of raising a sword. A Darkland Beast died when its head was cut off. Max had a damn bad feeling this spirit stuff was a lot more complicated than that, a lot nastier. That Sarah appeared quite rattled didn't comfort his worries. This was familiar territory to her, and her obvious unease wasn't a good sign.

"Whatever it is," he assured her softly, "we'll beat it."

"Ms. Meyers?" Sheriff Jenson said, his tone more demanding this time. "What *are* we dealing with?"

"Call me Sarah, Sheriff," she said, turning to face him. "I don't know what we're dealing with yet, but things are looking really bad. I need some information and I need it fast. I had a vision about a car accident on that bridge coming into town. About a woman who died there. I need to see the case file." The sheriff's face noticeably paled.

Sarah studied him. "What is it, Sheriff?"

"I'm sorry," he said, obviously flustered. "I've never been a believer in ghosts and all the paranormal junk—"

Sarah interrupted him. "But you invited me here."

"Right," he said. "I'll be frank. I didn't want you to prove I had ghosts or spooks. I wanted a scientific explanation for all of this. Which brings me back to that car accident."

Max could tell Sarah wasn't pleased over the sheriff's admission. "What about it?" Max prodded.

Sheriff Jenson scrubbed his jaw again. "A woman died in that accident. Since then, her husband's behavior has become a bit of a concern to folks around here." He eyed Sarah. "The fact that you bring up the same incident is a bit disconcerting."

Sarah stiffened and Max remembered her words. She had claimed that the husband was involved in all of this. "What's wrong with the husband besides the obvious grief of losing his wife?" Sarah asked.

The sheriff held up his hands stop-sign fashion. "Before I go on, let me say this. Small towns breed superstitions and rumors." He motioned to the back room. "This is a long story. Why don't we go sit?"

Sarah and Max exchanged a look as they followed him back to the break room; they sat down on either side of him. There was no doubt Sarah was concerned. Max saw it in her eyes, in the tension in her body.

"Here's the thing," the sheriff said. "I've had reports that Allen has been acting a bit suspiciously for quite some time now. Long before the strange stuff started happening 'round town. So when it did, he was already on the town radar." Sarah and Max nodded their understanding, and he continued, "Since Kate died—that was his wife—Allen's been a real recluse. Before that, he was a real friendly guy. In church on Sundays. At all the town events. That kind of thing. But after Kate's death, he didn't show his face in town for months."

"That's understandable," Sarah commented. "That had to be a hard time for him."

"I agree," Sheriff Jenson offered quickly. "Allen and his wife grew up here together. For him to have a hard time with this was expected. The chatter didn't start until he ventured out again. He'd changed. Wouldn't make eye contact, wouldn't speak. Then, he bought some rather odd supplies, and the rumor mill split wide-open."

Sarah frowned. "What kind of supplies?"

"Candles, incense, knives. Some say he's messing with black magic. One of the neighbors' kids snuck onto the property and saw a big circle and triangle drawn on his living-room floor."

"That doesn't sound good," Max inserted, eyeing Sarah.

"It would be used for evoking spirits," Sarah confirmed, her eyes full of concern.

"The kid could be lying," Max offered.

Sheriff Jenson agreed. "That's what I thought but the parent pressed and I checked it out. I stopped by and visited Allen, and I didn't see anything. But then, he has a rug on the floor. I couldn't rightly lift it up."

Sarah sat back in her chair and drew a breath. "He wants to bring his wife back," she said softly.

The sheriff looked stunned. "Is that possible?"

Max's brow inched upward, surprised at Sarah's statement. But he wasn't a fool. He'd seen things. Lived some miracles himself. After being turned into a demon and saved by Salvador, he knew anything was possible.

"In theory," Sarah admitted, her lips thinning. "But we are talking black magic, which Cathy will know more about." She seemed to get lost in her thoughts a moment before she refocused on the sheriff. "Tell me everything you know about Allen and Kate."

The conversation continued and Sarah drilled the sheriff about every detail of that car accident on the bridge—and the events and people involved.

Max thumbed through the town history book as he listened, scanning for anything of importance. He had almost skipped a half torn-out page, when he paused to study the text. "Excuse me, Sheriff," Max interrupted, reading enough to know the page was important. "What can you tell me about this legend?" He slid the book toward the man. "Part of the story is missing."

Sheriff Jenson glanced at the page and sighed. "I'd have said it's an urban legend, but now, I don't know."

"What is it?" Sarah asked, grabbing the book to take a look.

"It's the legend of a powerful demon doing battle with an archangel," Sheriff Jenson explained. The minute he said *archangel,* Max went on alert. This might just be the piece that tied him to this town, the explanation of why Nowhere held his destiny. The sheriff continued, "The demon was defeated and sentenced to prison deep beneath the earth. That location is said to be directly below Nowhere, Texas."

"This makes sense," Sarah said quickly. "It's not uncommon to evoke the aid of a demon when using black magic. If an unskilled practitioner performs an evocation, the demon could easily take control of the human."

Max hardly heard her; he was focused on one thing. On a critical point that impacted his mission, his test. "Any idea which archangel?" Max asked.

The sheriff frowned. "Hmm. Michael. No. That's not it."

"Raphael?" Max prodded.

The sound of the front door opening filled the air. "Sheriff?" It was a female voice.

"That's Mrs. Carmillo," Sheriff Jenson said. "She lives alone. I imagine she's scared." He started to get up.

Max grabbed his arm, halting his departure. "Was it Raphael?"

The sheriff looked surprised at Max's urgency. "Yes. Yes, that sounds right."

Max let the man go, his mind racing with the implications of what he'd just learned. Now Max knew the connection between himself and Nowhere, Texas. Raphael. The archangel who had created The Knights of White had imprisoned the demon that Max was now destined to face in battle.

This was a demon so powerful, it had taken an archangel to defeat it. Max inhaled. Salvador would not have sent him here alone if this were more than he could handle. He could defeat this demon. Though, clearly, not with a sword. Salvador had said he'd need every life experience he had lived to do this.

Sarah's fingers brushed his hand, a soft touch that shook him to the core. "What is it, Max?"

Her question, her presence, somehow brought back Salvador's words. *You must face this on your own, but not alone.* Max's gaze lifted to Sarah's beautiful green eyes. Eyes that seemed to reach inside and touch his soul. He felt that connection, that moment, in every inch of his body. He knew now that Sarah was, indeed, his mate. Whatever evil was here, they were to face it together. And that evil was nothing like the Darkland Beasts. Nothing like the demons he knew how to slay with a sword. This evil used humans to do its deeds. Humans whom Max existed to protect.

Max was headed to war, and he had everything on the line. His future as a Knight of White. And his mate, Sarah. A mate he may well have found too late. A mate he could not claim. Because if he didn't pass this test, if he didn't save this town, he was doomed to eternity in the Underworld. And he wouldn't take Sarah with him.

Chapter 5

"**M**ax," Sarah said, willing him to look at her and tell her what was going on. Something about that town legend had him rattled. In turn, it had her rattled. No, if she were honest with herself, the way Max made her feel had her rattled. There was a weird connection between them. Even now, she could feel his distress almost as if it were her own. That had only happened with spirits until now. "Max, please. Talk to me."

His gaze lifted, locking with hers, the look in those soulful hazel eyes grim, matching the feelings he'd somehow been feeding her. He opened his mouth to speak, but paused as the sound of raised voices filled the air, rising in volume with each passing second. "That doesn't sound good," he said, pushing to his feet, hand going to his weapon.

"I hope like heck you don't need that," Sarah said,

standing up, fearful they had another obstacle to conquer before they'd even begun to tackle the root problem they faced. "Please, Lord," she whispered. "Don't let it be another bout of craziness overtaking the town. We have enough to deal with without saving them from themselves."

Max started for the door. "Maybe the demon wants to keep us busy," he commented, more to himself than to her.

Reacting to his words, Sarah took a fast sidestep, intercepting him, her hand going to his arm. She ignored the jolt to her stomach the touch created and focused on more important matters than her overactive libido. "What about this archangel? What do you know that I don't?"

He stared down at her, his eyes dark, probing; his big body close; his scent, spicy and all too alluring. "We have a great deal to discuss, Sarah," he said softly.

Something in the way he said her name, the way he looked at her, said he referred to far more than demons and the troubles of this town. Her heart kicked into double time, heat rushing through her limbs. Good Lord, what was it about this man that got to her this way? She had a town to save, people to help.

"So talk," she said, her tone demanding by design. She would not let him see how much he affected her. Better yet, she would tune him out completely, at least on a personal level.

The sound of voices lifted in the air again, demanding attention. "Not now," he said. "We both know we need to deal with whatever is going on out there."

She hesitated and then forced herself to drop her hand from his arm. "Fine." Her lips pursed. "But I want answers, Max. I won't involve you in the investigation if you don't shoot straight with me."

He narrowed his gaze on her. "I know what you want, Sarah."

Though he spoke in a low, almost monotone voice, she could feel an undertone of heat rush through the words and then directly to her cheeks. Quickly, she turned away from him, hiding her reaction, taking the lead down the hallway—or trying to. Max quickly aligned himself next to her, and together they headed toward the source of the noise.

Still, as much as she needed space away from Max to consider why he impacted her as he did, she was also glad to have him by her side. As much of a loner as she considered herself, the idea of being the only person in this town unaffected by whatever was happening here was a bit daunting.

As they followed the sounds of chaos to the outer office, Sarah noted Max's hand on his gun, ready to draw it at the first sign of trouble. She couldn't blame him for being cautious after the way people had gone a bit whacko at the inn earlier. Fortunately, there was no rage and fighting this time and no need for a gun. Just a group of six or seven citizens assembled around the sheriff, all desperate for answers.

Sarah and Max looked at each other, pausing in the doorway as he eased his hand off the gun, the danger they'd feared clearly not present. In silent agreement, they stayed in the background, listening in on the conversation without interference.

A redheaded woman in her mid-to-late thirties

shivered and hugged herself. "I know it sounds crazy, but my doors flew open and shut by themselves."

"That could have been the wind," Sheriff Jenson argued, clearly trying to downplay the paranormal fears feeding the town's panic.

"Three times?" the woman challenged, her chin lifting defiantly. "I don't think so."

"My dog tried to attack me," an elderly man chimed in. "That dog has never so much as growled at me before today."

"It's that Allen Walker," another man said, running his hand over his bald head. Sarah and Max exchanged a quick look at that statement. The man continued, "He's working some kind of voodoo. If that black rain and absence of sunlight aren't proof, I don't know what is."

"He's right," the redhead said. "We've all been worried about Allen."

The bald man spoke again. "He came into the post office the other day to pick up a package, and I swear, his eyes were so black, there weren't any whites around them. It was pure evil I saw in those eyes."

"All right now," the sheriff said, irritated. "That's enough of this talk. We all want answers, and it's easy to look for someone to blame. But none of us need to go persecuting a man who isn't here to defend himself. Anyone who lost his wife, as Allen did, would act funny."

Another woman, with short dark hair and black-rimmed glasses, spoke up then. "You've been telling us that about Allen for a month now, Sheriff, but frankly it's not good enough anymore. We need to know we're safe. That our kids are safe."

A murmur of support for the woman's words filled

the room. "I'll talk to Allen," the sheriff conceded, "but I need all of you to go home and stay inside. We don't know if this rain is over."

The woman with the glasses spoke again. "We don't know anything about what's happening, do we, Sheriff?"

A few more minutes of conversational dodgeball continued, with the sheriff as the target, until finally the lobby was empty.

As the last person exited, Sheriff Jenson leaned against the door, rubbing his temples. "If I don't get some answers soon, I'm going to have a lynch mob on my hands," he said. "I told you. They're convinced Allen is behind this."

"They aren't the only ones. Sarah thinks he's involved, too. I think it's past time we pay Allen a visit."

"Agreed," Sarah said. "I need to go by the hotel and get Cathy and Edward on the way."

"Might be best if I drive out there and bring him into the station," the sheriff inserted, his voice holding authority.

Max beat Sarah to voicing an objection. "You don't even have your deputy and frankly, Sheriff," Max said, "dealing with the paranormal isn't exactly textbook law enforcement. You know that or you wouldn't have called Sarah in the first place."

"He's right, Sheriff," Sarah quickly agreed. "You called me here for a reason. My team is trained to handle this kind of situation. We've studied the paranormal for years and that includes black magic."

"Black magic," the sheriff said flatly. "That's twice now you've mentioned that. Is that what we think is causing all of this? Can black magic create this magnitude of events?"

"I can't say anything with certainty right now," she replied cautiously. "My point is simply that we must be prepared for anything."

The sheriff's lips thinned but he nodded his agreement. "I need to round up my deputy. I'll drop you by the inn and then swing by his house. It won't take more than a few minutes."

Sarah exhaled as she cast Max a frustrated look. They needed time alone to talk before going to see Allen. She would not go into a dangerous situation with him by her side without some answers. And if he didn't like it, she'd tell the sheriff to leave him behind. But as Sheriff Jenson started out the front door, she glanced in Max's direction, noting the way he watched her, the way he seemed to touch her without even moving, without making contact. And she knew…she was in big trouble.

She had no business lusting after a man who could be an enemy, a man she didn't know for certain was friend or foe. She just knew she wanted him in a bad way. A way that defied reason and kept her from thinking straight. She was smarter than this. She had to clear her head, to stop operating in a lust-filled haze—before it got her, or someone else, killed.

Chapter 6

On the short drive from the sheriff's office to the inn, Max rode in the backseat of the patrol car while Sarah sat in front. A good thing because Max needed to think through some things before she had time to question him. Time to think about things like what he was going to tell her about that legend, about how Raphael's connection indicated that his own involvement was far more profound than mere chance.

The answers weren't simple, considering he was partnering with Sarah and her team to some extent, and by doing so, possibly exposing the Knights and their secrets. Which simply wasn't done. If the Beasts thought a human was important to the Knights, or might hold information about the Knights, that human became a target.

By the time the car stopped in front of the inn and

Max got out, he'd settled on the details of a basic cover
story about the Knights being a special-ops group. He
hated lying to Sarah, especially since there could be a
time when he had to face that lie. But this would earn
him enough of Sarah's trust to stay close to her and her
team and keep them safe. The rest he'd deal with later.
Or never. He didn't know. His life might be headed to
hell, and Sarah deserved better than he could offer.
Maybe a lie and goodbye were all there could ever be.

And one kiss. He had to kiss her at least once. Damn,
how he wanted to kiss her. Like he'd never wanted to
kiss a woman before. Hell, the thought of kissing her
got him hotter than having sex would with most other
women. Of course, he knew why. Deep down inside, he
needed no confirmation beyond what he felt. Sarah belonged to him. She was his mate.

The minute Sarah exited the car, she rushed toward the
front of the inn where the van was sitting, its rear doors
standing open. Max followed her, noticing that Cathy already stood at the rear, peering inside. Since Max had
Edward's keys, he assumed they had a spare set.

"Everything okay?" Sarah asked, as she and Max
stopped on either side of Cathy.

Cathy motioned to where Edward sat inside the van
at an equipment panel. "We still can't get anything to
work," Edward muttered, scrubbing his jaw.

"Elaborate setup you have there," Max observed.

"We landed a nice little grant last year," Sarah said.

"Must have been." Max noted the impressive equipment. What he wanted to look at was the circuit board
in the computer, though. He'd snuck a peek at the computers in the sheriff's office right before they left; the

boards had been fried. "I know my way around electronics. Mind if I take a look?"

Edward glanced up, his expression skeptical as he looked to Sarah for approval. "Yes. That's fine," she said. Though his expression carried disbelief at his boss's agreement, Edward climbed out of the van, apparently more than willingly, and motioned Max forward.

"Feel free," Edward said. "I damn sure can't get anything to work."

The sheriff pulled up just then and called out to Sarah.

"I'll be right back," she said, and disappeared.

"I'm choking to death here. I'm going to hunt down a bottle of water," Edward said, excusing himself and leaving Max alone with Cathy.

Max settled into Edward's seat at the panel and began checking out various wires and connections.

"I'm impressed," Cathy said. "Sarah doesn't let anyone inside our group, but she seems to be letting you in. She even seems to be giving you her trust. I wonder why that is."

The hint of suspicion gave Max pause, and he glanced up at her. "I imagine the fact that I was the only person acting sane when the rest of you were trying to kill each other."

"Which makes me even more curious," she said. "Sarah is unique. She talks to dead people. I can see *her* having some weird immunity to all of this, but why are you immune?"

"What are you getting at?" Max asked, starting to get irritated and not one to sidestep an issue.

"I'm just wondering what your story is. Sarah doesn't trust easily. Frankly, I don't want to see her get burned."

His irritation disappeared as he realized Cathy was simply protecting Sarah. "I'm here to help, Cathy," he said, looking her in the eyes and hoping she saw his sincerity. "Nothing more. Nothing less. Help. There are things going on here I don't think any of us have faced before. We need to be united in this, so we can succeed."

Sarah rounded the back of the van with Edward, ending any further conversation between Max and Cathy. "The deputy is hanging back at the sheriff's office," Sarah explained. "Apparently, they are still getting lots of upset citizens there. So whenever we are ready, the sheriff is, too. He's inside juggling more questions and trying to make people feel safe."

"I need a few more minutes to check out the equipment," Max told her, glancing at Cathy and looking for some semblance of approval. She gave him a slow incline of her head, discreet, but definite.

"All right then," Sarah said to Max's request for more time. "I need to bring them up to speed on a few things, anyway."

Max went back to work as Sarah filled Edward and Cathy in on what had happened back at the sheriff's office, including the information about the town legend, her contact with the spirit and her belief that Allen was trying to bring his wife back to life.

"If he is, he's treading on dangerous territory," Cathy commented, her voice full of concern. Clearly, she was their expert on the subject. "The blackest of black magic."

"That's what I said, too," Sarah affirmed. "I was hoping you would know what would be involved."

Cathy considered that a moment. "There are several ways, none of them good."

Max looked up at that, his gaze catching on Sarah's. "Cathy comes from a family rich in magical practices," Sarah explained, unaware that she was answering the question playing in his mind about how Cathy knew that information.

"Magic, demonology, paranormal beings," Cathy inserted. "You name it. I've studied it, or rather study it. There's a lot to learn and know. But what I can tell you for sure is this—even the most experienced dark practitioners don't delve into resurrecting the dead. There is a belief that raising the dead has consequences, a price that would be too horrific for anyone to bear."

In his four centuries of living, Max had crossed paths with a few people who had touched the dark arts. He'd made a fast path in the other direction. He made it his goal to avoid anything to do with it. Which made this little test in Nowhere all the more ironic.

"But if you wanted to bring someone back from the dead," Sarah asked, "it's possible?"

Reluctantly, Cathy inclined her head. "Yes." She listed off several ways this might be done, ending with, "I've also read about certain higher-level demons granting such wishes…for a price."

"Really?" Sarah said, perking up. "Max mentioned a demon, as well." She cast him an expectant look. "Didn't you, Max?"

Max took his time answering, knowing it was time to lay down his cards, but not eager to do so. He hated lying to Sarah. Hated it with a passion.

Stalling, he reported on the laptop. "Its board is fried," he said rotating around to face Sarah and her team. Edward cursed in response to the news. "Just like the one at the sheriff's office. Which isn't a coincidence. I would bet every computer in this town is fried. I don't believe in coincidence."

Max glanced at Sarah and baited her into questioning him. "Nor do the people I work for."

"Which is who?" Sarah asked, just as he had hoped.

Hesitating, Max pretended he didn't want to answer, ready to feed them the cover story. "A special-ops team."

"Military?" Edward asked.

"More covert than that. We fight the kind of wars the military would never claim existed."

Edward wasn't satisfied yet. "As in the supposed alien-research center our government had been covering up for years? That kind of thing?"

"Something like that," Max said, trying to tell as much truth as possible.

Quick to end the questions, he got back on task. "Which brings me back to the problems going on in Nowhere and my statement about there being no such thing as coincidence. We have a man we believe could be evoking a demon, in a town that has a legend about a demon. Seems to me we have two plus two here."

Sarah studied Max a minute, her gaze probing. "I can buy that. But what about the connection to Raphael?"

Max's eyes locked and held with Sarah's. Clearly, she hadn't let go of his reaction to hearing Raphael's name. He didn't want to lie about this. At this point, the truth was definitely not an option. Even if he did tell them that Raphael oversaw an immortal army of demon hunters, and that he himself happened to be one of those immortals, it wasn't as if they would believe him. He needed to do some fast thinking and talking.

Fortunately, Cathy aided his efforts with her own insertion. "Raphael is the healer of humanity, and that is why he is often called upon for healing in prayers and from those who practice angel magic," she said, proving she'd done her homework in this area, as well. "But he's also believed to be a protector of humanity and a mighty warrior when it's demanded of him. If we choose to assume the legend is true, including Raphael's involvement, then that indicates to me that the demon in question is a powerful one, worthy of angelic intervention. In other words, an upper-level demon, which would be required to resurrect the dead. Who knows what a powerful demon such as this one is capable of doing." Her brows dipped. "If Allen Walker is evoking this kind of upper-level demon, he could inadvertently set it free." Cathy looked from Max to Sarah. "I need to do more research for information on this kind of practice. Maybe one of my reference books will help. Did either of you see the name of the demon?"

"No name," Max said. "Part of the page in that book was torn away. Maybe the sheriff can help us there."

His eyes met Sarah's for several long moments. Max could see that she knew there was more to tell that he hadn't shared. Hopefully her instinct to trust her mate would make her tolerant of his silence. Damn it, he hated this need for secrecy. He tore his eyes from hers, exiting the van. "We should go," he grumbled. "I need to grab a room and pull some supplies from my bags."

And then he walked away, feeling Sarah's stare on his back, his heart pounding with the turbulence of his thoughts. He prayed he was making the right choices. What should he tell Sarah and what should he keep to himself? He wanted to tell her everything, but he also knew that too much too fast could push her away. And if that happened, protecting her could become difficult. He needed to keep her close and safe. To do that, like it or not, he had to keep these secrets. And when he did share his world, he wanted it to be forever.

And right now, he wasn't sure he had that to give.

Sarah watched Max depart as she leaned on the door of the van, her stomach twisting into a knot of conflicting emotion. Why did she want to call him back rather than let him walk away? He'd be right back. What was wrong with her?

"I've never seen you trust anyone so quickly," Cathy warned, as if reading Sarah's mind. "The man has secrets. Lots of them. I think we should take everything he gives us with a grain of salt until we can confirm his story."

"How will we do that?" Edward asked with a snort, hand on his hips. "Call the army and ask if they have a covert paranormal team that they pretend doesn't exist?"

"Don't be a smart-ass, Edward," Cathy said, cutting him an irritated glance. "We're dealing with something really evil here. For all we know, Max could be part of it. He was the only other person who didn't go psycho at the inn earlier. Just being a part of some special-ops team wouldn't make him immune to evil."

"What are you suggesting?" Sarah asked, apprehensive as she waited on Cathy's reply, worried about where this might be going.

"We know what makes you different and why you weren't affected by the rage, as the rest of us were," Cathy said, waving her hands around in an animated fashion. "But why wasn't Max? What if it's because evil is immune to evil?" She continued immediately, "If we are going to intimately invite this guy into our investigation, don't you think we need to know more about him?"

"I hate to admit it," Edward said, "but she does have a point."

Satisfaction flickered in Cathy's eyes. She loved being right and Edward rarely allowed her that privilege. Obviously empowered by the approval, she added, "If we think Allen's cabin is the source of evil, or close to that source, taking Max might be a mistake. What if he somehow makes that source stronger?"

"On the other hand," Edward interjected, sitting on the bumper and crossing his booted feet, "if Max is one of the good guys, he might know something we don't. He might be the ticket to beating this thing."

Cathy scowled at Edward while Sarah drew a deep breath. "I'll talk to Max and decide from there," Sarah said after a moment of consideration. "That's the best I can do under the circumstances." She glanced at the stormy sky as the wind kicked up speed, lifting her hair from her shoulders. The change in weather brought with it concern that it somehow signaled some new event about to unfold. "Tell the sheriff I'd like to be out of here in fifteen minutes." Sarah didn't wait for a reply; she started walking toward the inn.

She needed to talk to Max, to figure out what he was really all about. To make a decision about his involvement, though she wasn't really sure how.

Cathy was right to be cautious. Sarah's trust of Max wasn't anywhere close to her normal reaction to strangers. Still, even knowing this, she couldn't shake the nag-

ging feeling that keeping Max by her side had life and
death consequences. If only she could figure out why.

Cathy's suggestion that Max could be connected to
evil came to her mind. Was this connection she felt to
Max a product of evil? She didn't think so, but how
could she be sure? And if she wasn't sure, could she
allow him near the cabin, the place from where they felt
the evil originated? Wouldn't that be pressing their luck?

Thunder rumbled in the background and hail started
to fall. Sarah climbed the steps to the inn at a trot, feeling
a sudden urgency to get a move on things. Time was a
luxury she didn't have. People's lives could well be on
the line in this town, and she had to take action to make
sure everyone was safe—and do so now.

She drew in a labored breath, hating the choice she
knew she had to make. But, she couldn't take risks by
allowing strangers into their inner circle. That's how
she had operated since her parents' death and it had
worked. Max couldn't go with them to the cabin, and he
wasn't going to like it one bit. But if she let him, and
something happened to Edward or Cathy, she'd never
forgive herself.

This was the right decision.

So why did it feel so wrong?

Chapter 7

Max sank down onto the mattress in the center of the cozy little room, with its floral curtains and lacy pillows, feeling like a fish out of water. More so than he'd ever felt. Somehow, the environment emphasized the darkness growing inside him.

The truth was he knew nothing of the softer side of life, of family and love. He'd come from a noble English family, and in those early days, he'd been known as Maxwell Kingsley, "the spare to the heir," the younger of two boys. Despite how belittling his family had been to him, how abusive and downright vicious at times, they had been all he knew, all he had. And they had been taken from him—stripped away by the Beasts and violently bled dry.

The centuries since had done nothing to stop that horrible day from replaying in his head in vivid, sickening color. Keeping others from falling prey to the Beasts had been the only peace his life had held, the only purpose.

He shoved off the bed and flipped open a long suitcase full of weapons, the velvet lining inside hugging several long blades, the tools of his trade. The method of destroying a Darkland Beast. They were tools that held no answers to defeating this new enemy, to finding a path that would deliver him to victory rather than defeat—and victory was the only answer. His hands slid over the silver of one blade; the power he wielded with it was fresh in his memories of battlefield victories.

Whatever meant to harm this town would not succeed, Max silently vowed. He would protect this town. And he would protect Sarah. His mate. He became more confident of their bond with every passing moment, her presence touching him deep in his soul. A knock sounded on the door and he knew who it was without ever opening it. Sarah. She wouldn't be here if not to ask for answers. Answers he wasn't sure he could offer her.

He walked to the door and pressed his hand to the wooden surface, closing his eyes. Damn. She was so close and so far away at the same time. He wanted to rip away the barriers, to open the door and pull her close. To tell her everything and more. "Max?" she called when he didn't respond. "It's me. Sarah."

He forced himself to keep that door shut, that barrier between them. "I'll be down in less than five minutes," he said, hoping she'd accept that and leave.

Nothing. Silence. But he could still hear her breathing. Could feel the turbulence of her emotions, feel them with odd certainty, as if they were his own. He'd heard the mated Knights speak of such things. Even with the heavy wood between them, the warmth of her presence wrapped around him, overwhelming him with its intimacy, with her nearness.

"Max…"

He turned back to the bed, shoving the suitcase lid down to hide the weapons and setting it on the floor. A second later, he yanked the door open, bringing Sarah into focus. Instantly, her green eyes melted into his, his groin tightening with the impact. He grabbed her and pulled her into the room, shutting the door behind them, his actions pure, protective instinct.

He flipped the locks firmly into place and turned to find Sarah directly behind him, barely inches away. He clutched his fists by his sides to keep from reaching for her. "What is it, Sarah? What's wrong? Did something else happen?"

Confusion flickered in her eyes as she searched his face, probing with intense scrutiny. "Nothing. Everything is fine." But it wasn't fine. If he hadn't sensed her turmoil, then her hesitation before continuing would have been enough to make that clear. "I simply wanted to tell you we're headed out to Allen's cabin. I was hoping you'd keep an eye on things back here? Maybe check in on the deputy?"

He'd expected questions, not this. He rejected her words with force. "You're not going out there alone. I'm going with you."

A flash of anger darted through her eyes. "You're not in a position to make demands. The sheriff hired me, not you. I make the rules and I say you're not going with us. That's how this is going to happen."

"No, sweetheart, it's not. I'm going and that is final."

She laughed with disbelief. "You're a piece of work, Max. Your macho, bossy attitude goes over well for about all of one minute." She hardened her voice. "You're not going, Max. That's the bottom line here. My team doesn't trust you."

He didn't miss her reference to her "team's" distrust. What about her trust? "Do *you* trust me?" he asked, knowing she did, knowing their destiny as mates would make that a given.

"I don't even know you, Max."

Those were the wrong words for one mate to utter to another, though he wouldn't have known that before she issued them. Possessiveness rushed through Max with the force of a volcanic eruption. Sarah knew him better than any other person in existence, and he wanted her to realize that, wanted her to know it as she had never known anything else in her life. The fierceness of those emotions sent Max into action. This was his woman, and everything male in him demanded she be clear on that fact.

One minute they were glaring at each other in a standoff, the next she was in his arms, her soft curves molded against his aroused body, her sweet lips pressed to his. He felt her fingers pressed to his shoulders as if she would resist, her body stiff, yet she made no movement to exit the embrace. Nor was Max about to give her the chance to come to her senses.

Wasting no time, his tongue swept past her teeth, gliding along them, and tempting her into response. She moaned, a sensual purr of a sound that drove him wild with desire. His palms flattened on her lower back as her arms slid around his neck, her chest pressing into his.

Never in his life had Max felt as complete as he did

with Sarah in his arms, with the sweet taste of her on his tongue. He belonged to Sarah, with Sarah, as he had never belonged in his entire life. Peace filled him, and when he would have reveled in the purity of it, the feeling was yanked away, the beast flaring to life with vicious intensity. It wanted her. All of her. To claim her. To make her his beyond a simple moment in time. A taste wasn't enough. A touch wasn't enough. Yet the man in him knew it had to be enough. For now, it had to be. He couldn't cave to the urges of his darker side. A war raged inside him as he battled between the right thing to do and what the beast demanded of him.

If there had been any doubt in Max's mind that Sarah was his mate, then those moments where beast and man battled did away with it. Only when answering the mating call did a Knight bear the cuspids of a Beast. And the truth became dangerously obvious as Max's gums tingled, and his teeth threatened to elongate.

In some far corner of his lust-hazed mind, Max knew he should pull away, put distance between them. But the fire coursing through his veins, all-consuming and demanding, wouldn't allow him to set her free. The primal urges of his beast were flaming hot, pushing him to take more. For a moment he did, but he was not alone in this. Sarah took, as well, kissing him with long strokes of her tongue, her hands all over him, torturing him with erotic touches. But it was her hips that did him in, her hips that arched against his erection, teasing him with possibilities, moving against him with a sensual glide up and down his long, hard length. Suddenly, they were on the bed, sharing crazy hot kisses, Sarah beneath him, on her back. Max didn't even remember how they got there. Her legs eased open for him without hesitation, inviting him intimately into her world as Max settled his hips into the V of her body, telling himself to stop before it was too late. Only the beast in him didn't want to stop, it wanted inside her, to feel the warm, wet heat of her surrounding him.

He couldn't get enough of her, couldn't get close enough. His hands were traveling, exploring. She moved beneath him, pressing closer, hips arching into him, driving him crazy as she teased his groin. The room, the danger, the need for anything but each other seemed to slide away as passion consumed and controlled.

More was all he could think of. More. His fingers slid beneath Sarah's flimsy T-shirt, the warmth of her skin inviting him upward, even as a soft moan told of pleasure. He filled his hands with her lush breasts as his mouth found her jaw, her neck, her shoulder. Her nipples pebbled beneath the silky material of her bra, and he shoved down the barrier, his fingers tweaking her nipples, his mouth hungry to do the same. But he found himself hungry with a primal burn, pressing her shirt away, exposing more of her neck, her shoulder. It would be so easy to claim her, to sink his teeth into her shoulder and mark her as his mate. She was the one. His woman. His life. Even her body fit his, perfectly. She was his. The words replayed in his mind as he deepened their kiss.

Wouldn't their mating make him pure? Wouldn't that save him from his potential fate in hell?

"Max," Sarah whispered his name, her voice full of sensual heat, full of surrender. She'd give herself to him, their connection as mates overshadowing everything but her need for him, their need for each other.

Which meant she trusted him. *Trust.* The word dropped into his head like a bomb being unloaded and brought with it a heavy dose of reality. To take Sarah, without her knowing who and what he was, would be wrong. To take her at all in his present situation—his destiny possibly eternal hell—would be unfair in every way.

Somehow, Max managed to tear his lips from hers, staring down at her desire-filled expression, his chest heaving with the effort that his restraint claimed from him. He squeezed his eyes shut, guilt sliding into his gut with a knot of pain. What if he'd lost control? What if he'd claimed her and she couldn't save him? He could have taken her straight to hell with him.

He rolled off of her onto his back, thankful he'd stopped before it was too late. "I'm sorry," he whispered. "I'm so sorry, Sarah."

She didn't move, lying there as if she were as stunned as he was by what had just happened. Seconds passed. "I don't know what's wrong with me," she said, her hand covering her face for a moment before dropping to her chest, as if trying to calm her racing heart. "I lost all sense of the here and now. I…God. People are counting on me and I didn't even care."

Without warning, she sat up and shot off the bed, her fingers running through her hair as she turned to face him. "What just happened to us?" She shook her head, as she appeared to struggle to swallow. "That wasn't normal, Max. I know you know that. It's the demon, isn't it? Doing something to distract us, so we can't stop it."

Max eased to a sitting position on the side of the mattress, shocked by her assessment. "What?" he asked, brows furrowed. "No. It's not the demon, Sarah." He quickly weighed his options and ruled out shooting straight with her. Who knew how she'd react in her present state. But he also couldn't let her dismiss what had happened between them as some sort of evil trick. He repeated his prior declaration for good measure. "It's not the demon. Things just got out of hand. We're under stress and we turned to each other. That's all."

"It's more than that," she insisted. "It was too intense not to be. It's the demon messing with us. I know it is."

There was a real franticness about her expression, in her voice. Max pushed to his feet, grabbing her hand before she could resist and pulling her close. Thankful she didn't back away.

Gently, he eased his hands into her hair, tilting her face to his, making sure she read the truth in his words. "No demon, Sarah. Just two people who want each other. I promise."

"What if it's more?" Her hands went to his wrists, her grip tight. "I've seen demons do things. I've seen—"

He kissed her. A fast, sensual kiss that he forced himself to end quickly, proving the fire between them could be ignited by another kiss at any time, but it could also be ended with the right restraint.

"Max," she whispered breathlessly, as he pulled back to look at her.

"We want each other, Sarah," he said, his voice low, husky, his groin tightening again despite his best efforts to contain himself. "There's nothing evil or unnatural about what we share." His lips smiled teasingly. "And if you keep insisting some demon made us feel this way, I am going to get insulted."

"I'm sorry." Her lashes lowered and then lifted. "It's

just that…well…someone close to me was possessed by a demon and it didn't end well."

Holy crap. Max didn't see that one coming. Thank God, he hadn't told her about the mating ritual. And no telling what she'd do if she knew his soul had once been touched by a demon. He'd scare the hell out of her.

"Talk to me," he urged. "What happened?"

Max searched her face, noting the retreat in her eyes as he waited for answers. She'd withdrawn, shut him out. The door inside her circle of trust had been firmly slammed shut, with him on the wrong side. Silently, he vowed to win his way to the right side.

Sarah drew a long, deep breath and stepped out of Max's arms, shocked she'd let that admission slip out. Shocked at how cold she felt without his touch. It would have been easy to blame the demon for what had happened with Max, but the truth was, she'd needed the escape—the moments of having big strong arms wrapped around her, without the world on her shoulders.

But those moments in his arms were gone now, and there was a demon to deal with. "People died. I won't relive that again."

He stared at her for several intense seconds, appearing frozen in place, without a breath, a blink, a movement. Then, he went into action. "Nothing is going to happen to you, your people or this town." He grabbed a duffel bag and tossed it on the bed, yanking out a holster of some sort and tightening it around his hips. "I'm not going to mince words here. You want to know what I do and why you need me, and I'm going to tell you. I hunt demons, Sarah. We call them Darkland

Beasts because they first appeared in the Mexico deserts. Nasty monsters that have fangs and bad attitudes. Their entire goal in life is to steal human souls. If I'm here, there's a good chance my people knew they would be, too."

Her blood ran cold. Spirits she understood. Fanged monsters, she did not. "When you say steal the souls, what exactly does that mean?"

"If they choose to turn a human to Beast rather than kill them, they strip the soul. There's nothing left then but pure evil. That human becomes a Darkland Beast."

He picked up the suitcase and put it on the bed, opening the lid. Sarah's eyes went wide at the sight of several long swords. The lethal-looking blades made anything she had seen him wearing before look like butter knives.

"They're saber swords," he explained, before she could ask. "They kill the bastards better than any other blade I've found. Guns won't kill them." He grabbed another holster. "Can you fire a gun?"

"Yes. My parents..." She stopped. Damn it, no more of the "personal." "Yes. Why? You said guns don't kill them."

He tossed her a shoulder holster and she caught it. "Put that on," he said, reinstating the bossy attitude he couldn't seem to shed. Still, she did as he bid. She wasn't a fool. She'd take all the protection she could get under present circumstances. He continued, as she tightened the shoulder strap. "Unload the ammo into the demon's head—and I'm talking all of it. You get enough bullets in a Darkland's head, and it will knock him down for a minute or two. Long enough for me to get to you."

He retrieved a gun from his bag and walked over to her, offering her the butt of the weapon.

A sizzle of excitement mingled with fear touched Sarah as she accepted the gun. The same feelings she'd shared with her parents when exploring new forms of the supernatural. Fresh guilt twisted in her gut. How could she derive excitement from a world that had taken their lives? Emotion welled in her chest, and she refocused on survival, sliding the gun into the holster.

Cathy and Edward needed protection, she realized. "Do you have enough to go around?"

"I've got Cathy and Edward covered, too," he promised, reading her mind.

"I've never dealt with a demon that would only die from a sword," she said, swallowing hard as he slid a long saber into a holster at his hip.

"I've never dealt with one who wouldn't," he commented, his fingers brushing her cheek, drawing her gaze to his. "I guess that's why we need each other."

Sarah felt the touch of his eyes, the intimacy of his words, with all the implications, hopes, fears. She hadn't let herself need anyone in years, nor did she want to now. But, deep down, Sarah knew it was already too late. Max had done what she swore nobody would ever do again. He'd made her need him.

Chapter 8

They're coming.

With Vars's words a whisper in his mind, Allen rushed to his truck, keys jiggling nervously in one hand, a small suitcase of supplies in the other. He didn't know who "they" were, only that they intended to stop him from getting his Kate back. No one was going to stop him. No one. His hand shook as he opened the driver's door of his candy-apple-red F-150 pickup. Kate loved red. He thought of her excitement the day they'd brought it home, and his chest tightened with the memory. Now, he had to bring her home. His temples were throbbing, his pulse pounding at double-speed—a product of his jacked-up adrenaline—yet despite the urgency to flee, Allen was careful with the case he held, taking care to slide it securely to the floorboard of the passenger's side and under the seat.

It held valuable supplies that Vars said would be needed for the task before him. Allen had to collect three power sources and bring them back to the cabin. With these sources, he would have everything he needed to free Vars. And with Vars's freedom would come Kate's.

Allen didn't know what these power sources were any more than he knew who "they" were. But it didn't matter. All that mattered was that he act quickly. He started the engine, hitting the accelerator with a heavy foot. As he pulled out from beneath his patio, he noted the eerily dark clouds, and satisfaction filled him. If Vars had the ability to conjure weather from his prison cell, then once he had his freedom, Vars surely had the power to bring back Kate. Soon the demon prince would be free and Kate would live. And finally, Allen would have ended the hell he'd suffered without his wife. The world would be right again.

Still reeling from Sarah's touch, from the implications of the hell that might have become her destiny had he claimed her, Max followed her down the inn stairs to join the others. It had taken some effort, but he'd convinced Sarah to agree to keep his revelations about the demon hunting to herself. Anyone who knew about the Darklands would become a target. He'd only told Sarah to ensure she understood the dangers they faced. That and, ultimately, her destiny lay inside his world and that of the Knights.

Still, there was no doubt that Sarah's crew would have to be prepped for this lethal form of danger, and Max needed a reason for carrying his sabers. The final outcome of these concerns led Max and Sarah to fabricate a story of sword-wielding demon worshippers, which wasn't so far from the truth.

Feeling anxious to get to Allen's cabin, to take action toward resolution, Max hoped to avoid any further delays. Relief washed over him as he noted the lobby was vacant except for Cathy, Edward and Sheriff Jenson. The fewer people present, the less chance of another detour before hitting the road.

The instant they approached the group, Cathy's eyes settled on Max, her expression turning sour. Before Max could comment, Sarah took charge. "He's coming with us," she stated, making her position on Max crystal clear.

Max smiled to himself at the victory, pleased with Sarah's support. He was, after all, only intending to protect them all, Cathy included.

It was a victory that had lasted only a few moments. Suddenly Max found himself being confronted by the sheriff. "You're not going anywhere packing those weapons," Sheriff Jenson said, scowling at Max. "You trying to scare the hell out of my town, or what?"

"I'm trying to save them, Sheriff," Max countered. "Exactly why I'm keeping the weapons."

The sheriff took a step toward Max and appeared to want a confrontation they didn't have time for. Again, Sarah grabbed the reins, placing herself between them. She faced the sheriff, directly in front of Max. "Why don't we take this outside before we draw attention? There are new developments you need to hear about before you demand that Max throw away those weapons." Sheriff Jenson hesitated, but agreed. Sarah cast Cathy and Edward a look. "You'll both want to hear this, as well."

A few minutes later, the trip to Allen's cabin was underway; the story Max and Sarah had fabricated had been accepted with grim regard, and satisfied the sheriff enough to allow Max to remain armed.

With the sheriff riding shotgun, Edward maneuvered the van along a bumpy dirt path. Cathy sat in the back of the vehicle directly across from Max and Sarah, absorbed in a chant she called a "protection spell."

Max doubted that any magic Cathy might manage to muster would touch the category of evil they were obviously up against, but he held his tongue. Who knew? He'd been surprised more than once in his long life, and Cathy certainly seemed to keep herself educated on the magical elements.

Leaning his head against the wall, allowing his eyes to shut, he feigned boredom. In reality, every nerve in his body was charged with Sarah's presence beside him. At the same time, he was on edge, worried for her safety.

Several minutes, and a huge pothole later, Max looked up to find Cathy holding a crossword puzzle book. This hardly seemed the time for games. Sarah apparently noted his expression, and responded. "Crosswords are her way of dealing with stress."

Max glanced at Sarah, and was overcome by their intense connection. The bond between them was growing, carving itself inside him. Did she feel it, too?

"It's crosswords or nonstop talking," Edward commented from the front, jerking Max back to reality. "Trust me. Crosswords are the lesser of two evils."

Max laughed at that, expecting Cathy to jab back at Edward as his fellow Knights would, the sense of friendship evident in the jests shared between the two.

Instead, Cathy tuned Edward out. "I need a five-letter word for a place between heaven and hell." She frowned. "Five letters?"

"Texas," Edward said. "That's five letters, and we're here now and definitely in hell. We need gas. Damn it, I should have filled up."

"It's not much farther up the road," Sheriff Jenson said.

"Limbo," Max said.

"Limbo," Cathy stated. "I think that's it." She frowned and wrote it down. "What is limbo?"

Max shrugged. He'd always kind of figured he was in limbo, but didn't say that. "Depends on who you ask, but the general gist is neither heaven nor hell—it's a place where the unbaptized must stay."

"I've always wondered where the spirits are who talk to me," Sarah said. "I never seem to get that from them."

"Any word from Allen's wife?" Cathy asked.

"Nothing," Sarah said.

Max still wasn't quite used to all the spirit stuff. "Is that good or bad?" he asked.

"Silence is approval," Sarah said, and rolled her eyes. "Believe me. If the spirits don't think I'm getting the message, they find a way to scream louder."

"We're here," Sheriff Jenson called back to them.

Max turned to look through the windshield. A small cabin was now visible on the horizon, and a sizzle of alarm was ringing in his body, the hair on the back of his neck standing on end. The same feeling he got when he was about to face an enemy, about to face war.

They pulled to a stop in front of the cabin. "Well, damn," Sheriff Jenson mumbled. "I don't see his truck."

Sarah reached out and grabbed Max's arm, intent on

stopping his departure; a chill raced down her spine. The ghost of Kate touched her mind, issuing a warning. "Something is wrong," she whispered, frowning as she realized Kate seemed to be fighting against some other energy source. One minute Kate was there in Sarah's head, communicating, and the next, she was gone, almost as if she'd been ripped right out of Sarah's head. Her grip on Max tightened. "Very wrong."

Max narrowed his eyes on her but didn't ask questions. Apparently, her word was enough. Then he took things into his own hands.

"No one leaves this van until I say it's clear," Max ordered, slipping his jacket off, ready to go to war.

"Oh, no, son," Sheriff Jenson said. "I'm not going to put Allen on the defensive. I'll go talk to him, and then see if he'll allow you all in. I can't go accusing him without evidence."

"Sheriff, please," Sarah said. "Listen to Max. I have a bad feeling about this." But it was too late. Sheriff Jenson shoved open the door and exited.

Max cursed and started for the side door. When he got there, he rotated around in a squatting position to look at Sarah. "Stay here until I know it's safe. You remember what I said about the gun?"

"I remember all too well," Sarah said, hoping she wouldn't have the opportunity to unload a weapon into a demon's head.

He shoved open the side door. "Hold it in your hand. It'll make me feel better. And lock the doors."

A second later he was gone, and Cathy didn't hesitate to lock up behind him. Edward did the same up front. They both knew if Sarah said something was wrong, something was wrong. Sarah eyed Cathy who hated guns. "Pull your gun."

"You know how I feel—"

"Pull the damn gun, Cathy," Sarah said, her tone uncharacteristically sharp, but she didn't care. She had Max and Kate feeding her the kind of information that created nightmares. This wasn't the time for coddling Cathy. Better to have her alive and irritated than dead.

Not waiting for Cathy's response, Sarah moved to the front of the van to claim the passenger's seat next to Edward, who had his gun resting on the steering wheel, aimed straight ahead, ready for use.

The sheriff was knocking at the cabin's front door. Max appeared to be scouting the exterior of the place. Sarah drew a breath, her chest tight. All they could do now was wait and pray all hell wasn't about to break loose.

Max met the sheriff at the front door of the cabin after a quick sweep of the perimeter. All might have seemed in order, but instincts, and Sarah's warnings, had urged him to peek inside the windows. The crazy drawing on the floor and half-burned candles confirmed Allen was into some sort of magic.

"We have to go inside, Sheriff," Max said.

"I don't have a search warrant," he countered.

"Then look the other way and I'll go inside."

Max didn't have time to talk in circles with this man. "Look," he said, hands settling on his hips. "Arrest me if you have to, but I'm going inside." He inclined his head toward a window. "You might want to take a look in that window before you make any rash decisions, though." Sheriff Jenson's lips thinned beneath his thick mustache as he huffed and then stomped toward the window, apparently none too happy about the decision put before him. Max rested his weight on one foot, watching Sheriff Jenson survey the inside of the cabin before cursing under his breath.

"Fine," he said, walking toward Max. "We'll go in."

Max didn't have to be told twice. Before the sheriff made it back to his side, Max had popped the lock and shoved the door open. He would have headed inside, but his gut twisted at the idea of allowing Sarah out of his sight for even a moment.

"I'll check it out first," the sheriff said forcefully.

Perfect. Max didn't argue. Let the sheriff ride his power trip. At the moment, it served Max's needs well. "I'll get the others."

Sheriff Jenson hesitated. "Make sure they know this has to be quick. In and out. The last thing I need is for Allen to drive up while we're inside." He turned and entered the cabin.

Max made fast tracks to the van; he stopped at the passenger's window as Sarah rolled it down. "Well?" she asked anxiously.

"No obvious signs of danger," Max said. "But I did find markings on the cabin floor."

"What kind of markings?" Cathy asked, her voice lifting with urgent interest as she poked her head between the seats.

"I'd rather you look for yourself," Max said, casting Edward a glance. "Drive under the carport and park." He wanted them sheltered as long as possible—just to be safe.

"You forget we need gas." Edward patted the dashboard. "This baby is running on fumes. I don't want to power her up again until we leave."

"Damn," Max muttered.

"All's clear inside," the sheriff called from the door, motioning everyone forward.

Max waved his understanding before turning back to the van. "When you get out of the van, don't linger. Run to the cabin and get behind closed doors."

"You said you didn't see any trouble," Cathy countered, her tone full of concern.

"That's true," Max agreed, trying to calm her before she got worked up. "I'm just playing things safe."

"Let's get this over with," Edward said, looking over his shoulder at Cathy.

"All right then," she conceded with a heavy sigh that indicated she wasn't all that sold on the idea.

Max yanked open Sarah's door as Cathy and Edward exited the driver's side.

"Something isn't right here," Sarah said. "Kate was trying to tell me something, and I felt another spirit there, something dark." He watched her swallow, her throat bobbing with the action. "And then she was just gone."

Max wasn't sure what to make of that, but it was clear that Sarah was rattled. All this spirit stuff had him grasping in vain for a game plan that had some semblance of cohesiveness.

Edward and Cathy rounded the van, and Max eyed the Sheriff who stood on alert. "You two go on inside." They didn't argue, moving toward the cabin at a fast walk. Max watched their progress, scanning to ensure they were safe before turning back to Sarah. "Stay behind the door. Once they're inside, we'll follow."

She didn't respond, her expression troubled. "I wish I had the answers," he said. "But we'll find them. We'll get through this. Have faith."

She made a frustrated sound, shoving her hair behind her ears before hugging herself. "I gave up on faith when it burned me years ago." Her gaze slid to the ground. "I'll stick with caution as my guide."

Clearly, something in her past had worked her over in a big way. Max understood pain, Lord only knew. But his reaction to Sarah's emotions delivered a shocking bit of personal introspection. In four hundred years, no matter how dark his world, no matter how hard he struggled against his inner beast, he'd hung on, and he'd never lost his faith. He'd doubted himself plenty. At least once a week, he questioned why he'd been chosen as a Knight, rather than his elder brother. He'd beaten himself up daily for not saving his family. But when he went onto the battlefield, he believed in what he fought for. And that—*that*—was what kept him fighting *off* the battlefield.

He reached out to slide his hand down her hair. To be his mate, her soul had to be pure. She had faith and hope inside her. He'd felt it in her kiss, in her touch, as it had calmed the darkness within him. She simply had to find her way back to her true self. No matter how much he wanted Sarah to be the magic key to save his soul, the truth was, she needed a bit of saving herself.

Max slid his finger under Sarah's chin as he lifted her gaze to his. "Then I'll have enough faith for both of us," he vowed, and motioned toward the cabin.

Her eyes flashed with vulnerability, and he wanted to kiss away her pain. Instead, he forced himself to focus on the imminent need for action. "Let's go find some answers," he said, backing away a step to offer Sarah some space.

His attention turned to the cabin where the sheriff stood waiting at the door, his impatience evident in his glowering look. No doubt he was worried about Allen's return.

Max reached around Sarah and shut her open door. "Once we step out of the shelter of the van's cover, start moving and don't stop until you're inside."

She nodded and they went into action. They started for the cabin, and Max felt a sudden rush of awareness track along his nerve endings, a feeling of being hunted. He held his breath, not daring to let it out until Sarah disappeared inside the doorway of the cabin.

Max paused at the entrance, his senses screaming, on the alert. Beasts. A Knight could sense a Beast from miles away, though a Beast couldn't sense a Knight. A definite edge over his enemies that Max had been thankful for more than a few times. Without question, Max knew his enemy was near. The question was—did the Beast, or Beasts, know he was present? He grabbed his phone from his belt and checked for a signal, hoping to call Jag for backup. Nothing. Still dead. He scanned again but saw nothing, no movement, no Beasts.

The wind picked up with sudden fierceness, and Max realized it had all but disappeared while he and Sarah had been standing at the van. Back now, it packed vicious gusts, seeming almost angry, pounding anything in its path.

One more look around and Max entered the cabin, shutting the door and locking it, his mind racing, adrenaline coursing through his veins. He had three humans to get out of there safely and no idea how many Beasts he faced, let alone what other evil he was up against. He needed backup, and he needed it now.

You'll get it when you're intended to have it, he reminded himself. *Faith. Hang on to your faith. It's gotten you through four hundred years. It'll get you through one more day.*

In the near distance, a spark of fire appeared in the air and took human form. Adrian, leader of the Darkland Beasts, appeared on the outskirts of the small town of Nowhere, Texas. The wind lifted his long blond hair from his leather-clad shoulders as he surveyed the small wooden cabin. He was seething with resentment that his king, Cain, had ordered him to aid Prince Vars's escape. He despised the royal chain of command, despised his inability to rank within those standings. No matter how much hell he brought to earth, Cain would always keep Adrian in his place, hold him one notch beneath in the gifts he was allowed, the powers he wielded.

He didn't give a damn about Vars's promise to help defeat The Knights of White. Adrian had no desire to see his victory credited to Vars.

Adrian crossed his arms in front of his chest. There were a few enticing angles to using Vars's legion of demon spirits to battle the Knights. If those spirits claimed innocent human bodies, the Knights wouldn't want to kill them. And it would shift the power to the dark side. But that power belonged to Adrian, not Vars. Which meant that Vars's legion of demon spirits had to become Adrian's, as well.

If Vars were to be destroyed, his legion of demon

spirits would be inherited by the first power who claimed them. What better time to battle Vars than during his first few moments of freedom when he'd be weak and unpracticed.

Adrian laughed, realizing his king had given him a gift. Cain knew Adrian would not allow Vars to steal his glory. No doubt the king intended Adrian to steal Vars's legion of demons.

Adrian snapped his fingers, and fire once again stroked through the air. Two nameless servants appeared beside him, tall and dark, with dark eyes, and faces chiseled into harsh features—Hell Hounds in human disguise. They were gifts from Cain. Pets who did as he bid without daring to think on their own.

"Secure the cabin and kill anyone who gets in your way," he ordered. His pets instantly responded, shifting into their Hound forms. The two massive animals lunged down the hill, muscled bodies shifting with otherworldly force, their long fangs bared in warning to any who dared approach.

Adrian watched the creatures depart; they were so easily at his command, just as his army of demon soldiers were. He could almost taste the power of owning Vars's legion of demon spirits. He might not possess the royal title he desired, but Adrian was well on his way to being indestructible. He stared at the little cabin, thinking how inconsequential it appeared, but how important it had become. Because inside that cabin, Vars would be set free, and when he was, Adrian would be there to destroy him.

That cabin had become the stage for war, and the stepping-stone to Adrian's next level of power.

Chapter 9

Sarah hesitated as she entered the cabin, finding herself lingering, waiting for Max. Why—she didn't know. Only that keeping him close felt important. As if her safety, and his, somehow depended on it.

Behind her, she heard him push locks into place, sealing them inside the cabin. A momentary feeling of claustrophobia, an impulse to turn to Max and tell him to unlock the door, shot through her body. She shivered and hugged herself against the pure evil that seemed to pour from the walls.

As if he sensed her need, Max stepped to her side, his hand grazing her back; a wave of calm rushed over her. She inhaled, chest expanding, wondering how Max had such an impact on her. How could a man, a stranger, somehow give her a sense of security when people she'd known for years could not?

Together, operating almost as one, Max and Sarah began surveying the room. It was a tiny cabin with a fireplace in the corner, ruffled curtains and framed pictures decorating the walls. Normal enough except that the furniture had been stacked against the walls to make room for the magical circle and triangle in the center of the room. Scented incense laced the air—most likely used for a summoning ritual.

Cathy sat on a big blanket that had been spread out on the ground. It was covered with books and magic supplies. Edward stepped to the center of the circle drawn on the floor and studied the intricate details of the star inside its frame.

"What do all the details inside the circle mean?" Sheriff Jenson asked.

Cathy looked up from the book she held. "There are specific types of circles used for different magical purposes, but the general gist is that the conjurer stands in the circle and evokes to the triangle. The demon or spirit, or whatever it might be, should theoretically be trapped inside the triangle. Unless the conjurer is foolish enough to call on a demon more powerful than they can handle." She held up the book. "This is the *Grand Grimoire*. Black magic in its rawest form. It's bad stuff. Allen didn't start small. Once he dipped his toe, he went all the way, which leads me to believe he was one of the foolish ones who called on powers well beyond his own."

"Your job is starting to make mine look easy," Max said softly, for Sarah's ears only. Somehow, from what Max had described of the Darkland Beasts, she doubted that. She would have replied to that effect, but paused with sudden awareness.

"Kate," she whispered. "Kate, she's trying to find me again, but she's still fighting something. She's—"

Pain shot through Sarah's head with a force she'd never experienced before. She squeezed her eyes shut and found herself reaching for Max to keep from falling. Images charged into her head, violent flashes that cut in and out like a television with static interference, each flash delivering a jolt of pain.

"Oh, God," she gasped with shock. She'd never had a vision come in such a burst of images, never felt trauma of this magnitude from a spiritual communication.

In some remote part of her mind, Sarah felt Max's arms around her, felt herself sink against the wall of his chest, taking comfort in his presence, his protection.

The bit of reality that Sarah tried to cling to, slid into darkness, and there were just the images flashing in her mind, and pain—so much pain. Her head felt like it would explode, but she fought through her discomfort and fixed her mind on what she was being shown. Allen in the circle. A demon in human form—a huge man with long, black hair—standing inside the triangle. A name. The demon's name. Vars. More pain. More images. A blood bond. A promise of one favor for another. Something else. Something important. She reached out, trying to understand, fighting through the blackness. Kate screamed, a horrid wrenching sound that tore through Sarah's mind, her ears, her head. And then, Kate was gone—but not before she gave Sarah one more important detail. Not before telling Sarah what Vars had asked of Allen and how he intended to get it. Sarah clung to that last bit of information as darkness overtook her. Complete, utter darkness.

* * *

Max sat down against the wall, Sarah cradled in his arms. She was in pain, and damn it, he couldn't do anything about it. There had been only one other time in his life when he'd felt this helpless, and that had been when the Beasts were killing his family. He couldn't stand doing nothing.

"You're sure this is a vision?" Max demanded, fixing Cathy in a desperate stare. She kneeled beside Sarah, holding her hand. Edward and the sheriff hovered behind her.

Cathy opened her mouth to speak, but the words were lost in a choked scream of pain as Edward grabbed her hair, dragging her toward the other side of the room.

Max blinked, certain he was seeing wrong. A glance at the Sheriff's shocked expression said he, too, didn't believe what he was seeing. The sheriff acted quickly, pulling his gun and trying to find a shot that wouldn't put Cathy at risk. He shouted orders at Edward, but Edward acted as if he didn't hear him.

Edward's eyes flashed red as he fixed his attention on Sarah before charging at the sheriff, half dragging Cathy with him for cover. A second later, the sheriff was flat on his back, Cathy on top of him, and Edward charging at Max and Sarah.

From there it was a blur. Acting on instinct, Max covered Sarah with his body and rotated at the hip landing a hard foot in Edward's stomach.

He barely had time to face forward and right himself before Edward came at them again, his eyes flashing red—seemingly unaffected by the blow Max had blasted him with. And it had been a hell of a blow, considering Max had supernatural strength. Which could mean only one thing—a demon. That was all it took for Max to let his beast flare, to embrace his darker side.

This *thing,* whatever it was, wanted to kill Sarah. Max had seen it in Edward's glowing red eyes. Max slammed a fist into Edward's jaw. Edward's head snapped back, and Max used the opportunity to slam him to the ground. A split second later, Max straddled Edward, pinning one of the man's hands beneath his knee, holding the other.

Battle instincts in play, Max used his free hand to unsheathe a blade, ready to destroy the demon bastard pretending to be a friend, pretending to protect when he meant to destroy.

"Max!" Sarah's scream pierced the air. "No, Max! No!"

Max heard her voice, reaching for restraint but struggling. He'd handed over control to his beast at some point, and the beast pressed Max to finish this, to take out his enemy. Max's body literally shook with the effort to hold back, the muscles in his neck and shoulders contracting painfully. He wanted to kill Edward. He wanted to kill him in a bad way.

Sarah appeared before him, kneeling above Edward's head, facing Max. Her eyes were imploring, and Lord help him, Max couldn't hide what was inside him, couldn't hide the beast. No telling what she saw in those moments, what she would think of him, how she might fear him.

"Edward's body is possessed by a demon," she explained hoarsely. "But Edward might still be in there. We have to try. *Please.*"

As if denying Sarah's words, Edward started squirming, shouting nasty things at her. Max ground his teeth, holding Edward with ease, but feeling rage bubbling within, threatening to consume him.

"You're sure?" he asked, his teeth clenched. "Sure enough to take a chance with your life, Sarah? He tried to kill you. Even now, he wants you dead."

"We have to try," she said, repeating her words and eyeing the sheriff. "We need something to tie him up with."

Max wasn't convinced Edward was still human, if he ever had been in the first place. "Sarah—" Edward spouted out nasty words, cutting off Max's sentence.

"It's the demon talking," she assured Max. The sheriff came over with some rope and Sarah continued her argument. "We'll tie him up until we can figure out what to do. Cathy comes from a family with deep and varied magical roots. If anyone can figure out how to get Edward back, she can."

He shoved the blade back into his belt holster, still uncomfortable about his actions. "Do it," he ordered the sheriff. "Tie him up, but you'll need more rope. He's unnaturally strong right now."

The sheriff grunted. "You aren't kidding."

"I'll find something," Cathy said.

"Electrical cords," Max said. "They'll be strong."

"Let's tie this bastard up good and tight," Sheriff Jenson said, offering his approval.

Sarah studied the sheriff with a probing gaze. "You okay, Sheriff?"

"No," he said in a grouchy voice, working the rope around Edward's wrist, as Max continued to hold it. "I'm living a nightmare no one is going to believe."

Cathy reappeared with several cords and Sarah surveyed her, as well. "You look pretty beat up," she said.

"I'm fine," Cathy said, touching the scratch on her face. "Nothing that a little Band-Aid and some ointment won't cure."

"He dragged her across the room by her hair," Max commented, moving away from Edward, the restraints secure. "I've seen grown men whimper over less." He gave her tiny frame and cutesy bobbed hair a once-over. "You're tougher than you look."

Cathy's expression registered surprise and appreciation. "I do believe that was a compliment."

Cathy's obvious dedication to knowledge, coupled with her warrior spirit, was beginning to earn his respect. "It is."

Cathy's lips hinted at a smile but Edward threw his head from side to side, drawing her attention, and her expression quickly sobered.

"Actually," she said, "I think I got the good end of this deal. Edward is lost in there somewhere."

"I hope you're right," Sarah whispered, hugging herself, her voice shaking a bit. Max looked at her and realized she was rattled. Not a little. A lot. This thing with Edward had hit some sort of nerve. She wasn't any more certain than he was that Edward was still human. Yet, unlike him, she'd wanted to save him.

Edward mumbled more profanity and ended with, "Bitch!" right before the sheriff gagged him.

Max noted the way Sarah took a solid backward step. Max stared down at Edward, the implications of what had gone down between the two of them starting to take hold. He didn't know what to think about Edward but if Cathy were right, if Edward was still inside that body, then Max had almost killed another human. He'd been so sure that wasn't the case, so driven by the rage of Edward trying to take Sarah from him. The same way he'd seen red when that human had tried to kill Des's mate. The beast had risen and Max had handed over power.

Max squeezed his eyes shut, recognizing that this could have been part of his test, tormented by how close he'd come to failing. Salvador had known Max would face humans such as Edward, possessed and out of control. Had known Max would have to fight to determine right and wrong, to show he still knew the difference. His human side did, indeed, have faith, but how much of the human was left? Enough to be saved? After this, he wasn't sure.

Sarah's hand settled on his arm. "Max?"

The touch slid along his nerve endings and delivered calmness that he wouldn't have believed possible in that moment of turmoil. Slowly, he turned to face her, not sure what to say, or how to explain his actions toward Edward. He'd been ready to convict the man rather than save him.

Touching Max delivered a calmness Sarah didn't quite understand, but she didn't fight the feeling. She needed calm now, needed a bit of comfort. Seeing Edward taken over by a demon brought some demons of the past back to Sarah. She'd seen a friend possessed, seen him kill her family. Was Edward evil? Could a demon control someone truly good? Her gaze went to the turbulent expression on Max's face, and her heart clenched. He'd been so afraid for her.

As if he read her mind, he spoke. "I was afraid he was going to kill you."

Sarah stared at Max and the minute her gaze locked with his, she felt herself at a loss for words, felt her chest tighten with emotion——his emotion. Just as she'd felt his utter fear for her during her vision. How could she feel what he felt? The same way she would feel a spirit sliding into her mind and body.

Somehow, she found her voice, though it was gravelly, and laced with the potency of her feelings. "If you hadn't been here," she whispered, "he might have succeeded."

"And if you hadn't stopped me, I would have killed him."

"But you didn't," she said, uncertain about what to do next. Maybe she should have warned Max about the potential for possession. She'd been so afraid to trust him, to let him know her past, her secrets. Cathy and Edward both knew about her parents, about the friend that had killed them. Her fears of exposing herself to yet another person had impacted Max, left him unprepared. What had just happened to Edward should make her less willing to trust Max, but oddly, she wanted someone to trust right now more than ever. Max shared a connection with her. She sensed his emotions and they didn't feel evil. Besides, Max was involved; he was working with them now. He deserved to be armed with data that could protect him—protect all of them.

Decision made, she leaned closer to him and lowered her voice. "There are things you need to know." She discreetly glanced at the others. "Just not here and now."

"Did you find out anything with that little vision of yours?" Cathy asked, breaking into their private conversation, as she and the sheriff piled books into a box.

Reluctantly, Sarah pulled her attention from Max, their unfinished business bothering her. "I did," Sarah said, snapping back into the imminent danger of their circumstances. "I assume that's why Edward was turned against me. The demon imprisoned beneath the town is directly below the cabin."

"Did you get a name?" Cathy quickly asked, her voice lifting with urgency.

"Why is the name so important?" the sheriff asked.

Cathy explained, "You have to have the true name of the spirit or demon to evoke it or summon any form of control over its actions."

"Right," Sarah agreed. "And it has to be the exact, proper name. Problem is, I'm not sure if I remember it correctly. Prince Vars is what keeps replaying in my head."

"A prince," Cathy said. "Interesting. Royalty in the demon world spells power. Each member of royalty in the Underworld is thought to have an army of evil spirits beneath him. If that's true, then we can assume one of Vars's spirits is inside Edward."

Sarah looked concerned. "I just hope the name is right. When Kate was trying to speak to me, there was some sort of evil entity there, shoving her away. Maybe Vars. Maybe some of his demon army. I don't really know. Bottom line—I couldn't absorb everything the way I normally would in a vision."

Cathy patted one of the leather books in front of her. "I'd venture to say one of Allen's resources here will refer to the name or something similar because he had to find it somewhere. Most likely in a reference to the town legend."

"And the library has the same book that I have in my office," the sheriff offered. "Minus the torn page."

Sarah continued relaying the details of her vision. "Vars—if that is the right name—told Allen he would be strong enough to bring Kate back from the dead once he had his freedom."

Max frowned at that. "Which he achieves how?"

"Honestly, that's where things are a little cloudy." Sarah leaned against the wall, digging deep into her mind, working through the pain still splintering her head. "This is where it gets a little weird."

"It gets weirder than this?" the sheriff asked, motioning to where Edward lay on the floor, tied up. "I doubt that."

"'Fraid it does, Sheriff," she said, her tone grim. "From what I gathered, Allen needs the source of power held by the three Shadow Masters." She frowned. "I'm not sure. There are stones of some sort, I think. The stones have some sort of power and these 'Masters' guard them. I think. Damn it, I'm really not sure. For some reason, that doesn't seem quite right."

"The three Shadow Masters," Cathy repeated, brows dipping. "That's remotely familiar. I think they are part of some sort of cult." She let out a breath. "I could find out if we actually had communication with the outside world."

"Okay," Sheriff Jenson concurred. "Maybe it does get weirder."

Cathy's voice became grim. "I doubt I need to say this, but we need to get to Allen before he gets to these Shadow Masters. He'll come back here, though, once he has them. I'm sure of it. Most likely he intends to return by the next full moon ten days from now. That would be the optimal time for a ritual. This is where Vars is contained and where he must be released. But I need to point out a tiny little problem. Stopping Allen might not be all that simple. Vars could potentially use Allen like a vessel for his own magic, if they made a blood pact. And they did. I see dried blood in the circle."

"Ten days is something at least," Sarah said. "We have some hope of heading this off." She glanced at the sheriff. "Thank goodness you called when you did."

"It's not a lot of time when you consider the implications of Vars escaping," Cathy reminded her.

Max quickly offered support. "My people will help; they'll respond quickly and secure the town." His lips thinned. "But I have to get out of this town and to a working telephone."

"Then we should move on that now," Sarah said. "I get the feeling every second counts."

"Wait now," Sheriff Jenson chimed in, hands going up stop-sign fashion. "Someone is going to stay here in Nowhere to help me, right? As much as I hate admitting I'm over my head, clearly I am. I need help."

"He's right and I'll stay," Cathy said without hesitation. "I think I can bind the demon inside Edward for at least a while, but I need a calm environment and focus to do it. Plus, he's in no condition to travel. That means not moving him beyond the local doctor's office." Her expression turned bleak. "But I don't think I'm strong enough to expel it alone. I'll need you to call for help."

"I don't feel good about leaving town with you and Edward still here," Sarah objected. "I should stay, too. You have no way to contact us if you get into trouble."

"We'll be fine," Cathy assured Sarah. "You and Max

have to go after Allen and those Shadow Masters. Max is the muscles, and you have the connection to Kate. It makes sense for me to stay here and help the sheriff. Just send help. Our people. Max's people. Whoever. I'll take what I can get."

With surprise, Sarah realized this was what she had sensed earlier, she and Max would have to team up to defeat this enemy. But after the situation with Edward, she felt torn. To trust anyone frightened her. But Max was different. She thought. She hoped. She needed it to be so. And it seemed their teaming up was the logical answer to finding Allen.

"I still don't like this," Sarah murmured, half to herself, fretting over the choice put before her, even though she knew there wasn't one. She had to leave Cathy and Edward in town and go after Allen. "But I'll go."

"Obstacle one is getting out of this cabin safely," Max said, spilling the hard-core facts. "Based on what we have seen thus far, I find it hard to believe we are going anywhere without some resistance."

With those words, Sarah thought of the demon directly beneath the cabin, felt the evil within the walls closing in on them. She had no doubt the source of that evil would destroy anything, or anyone, in its path. It had already tried to kill Sarah to keep her from relaying what Kate had shared.

They'd come there determined to find answers, and they had, indeed, found them. But would they get out of there alive?

Chapter 10

Max wasted no time dropping Edward to the floor of the van, right next to the box of books that Cathy had collected from the cabin. The feeling of being watched was still biting at his nerves. He quickly turned to check on the sheriff. He was pouring gas into the van's tank from a can they had found next to the lawn mover in the storage shed out back.

"Done," the sheriff confirmed, tossing the can to the side of the driveway, clearly no longer worried about Allen knowing they'd been there. He joined Max near the front of the van. "Let's get the hell out of here."

"Agreed," Max said, one hand resting on a weapon, in ready position as he motioned Sarah and Cathy forward. The sooner they were out of this place, the better.

The two women darted forward, clearly as eager as the men to get moving. Sarah and Cathy were almost at the van doors—Cathy at the driver's side, Sarah at the passenger's side—when Max felt the hair on the back of his neck prickle and then stand on end. He barely had time to blink before two Hell Hounds darted around the side of the cabin. One headed straight for Sarah; the other charged toward Cathy.

The sheriff pulled his gun at the same moment Max unsheathed his swords. "Shoot between the eyes," Max shouted at him, as Cathy managed to get inside the van and the sheriff slammed the door shut, firing his weapon as he did.

Sarah screamed, yanking at her door which appeared to be jammed. With a full body tug, she managed to jerk it open. But the Hound was stalking her. It had jumped to the hood of the vehicle, and then to the roof to come at her from above. Max went from a fast run to a stealth-like vault on top of the hood. The Hound turned away from Sarah to face off with Max, giving her the time to escape and slam the door shut.

Max leapt at the Hound, knowing the creature would go up in flames when he killed it, concerned about fire making contact with the gas tank. As he shoved the Hound toward the edge, the damn thing sunk its teeth into Max's leg. Pain tore through his body as he went over the edge with the Hound. Swords in hand, Max had to either drop them and risk facing the Hound without protection, or try to control how he fell. He maneuvered the blades, trying to make sure they didn't end up in his body, but with limited success. A slice ripped down his midsection, opening up a gaping wound.

Max shoved aside the pain, survival instincts controlling his actions. He maneuvered to his feet at the same

moment the Hound did. Even wounded, defeating a
Hound was nothing, compared to a Beast, and in a swift
practiced move, Max took the creature's head. The animal burst into flames and crumbled into ash as Max
turned away; he stalked toward the other Hound that had
the sheriff trapped at the driver's side of the van.

Max rounded the hood to find the Sheriff Jenson on
the ground and Sarah hanging out of the window firing
a gun at the Hound. The Hound took several bullets to
the head and stumbled before falling to its side. Max held
up his hand, silently telling Sarah to hold her fire—not
interested in adding a bullet wound to his other injuries.

Once he knew Sarah understood his request, he went
into action, lifting his sword and rearing back. A second
later, Max's blade claimed the creature's head. Fire and
ash consumed the Hound almost instantly, and Max
turned away, not giving himself time to consider what
Sarah might think of his ability to kill so readily. Reminding himself she'd been quick to fire her own gun,
that she understood this world enough not to fear him
for what he'd just done.

He slid his swords back into their holsters and turned
his attention to the sheriff's wounded body lying on the
ground. Max squatted next to him, checking for a pulse
and finding it—weak, but there. At least, he was alive.

"Is he okay?" Sarah asked, her voice urgent, worried,
as she shoved open the van door and darted forward. Her
eyes went wide. "Oh, God. You're hurt, too." She
squatted down next to Max, her hands shaking as she
steadied them on her knees, her gaze raking his leg and
stomach. "You're hurt bad, Max."

"I'm fine," he said, his attention on the sheriff as he

noted numerous cuts and scrapes, but the worst was the huge slit in his wrist spouting blood. "He's losing too much blood." Max reached for the knife inside his boot, the wound on his leg all but numb, though his gut hurt like a son-of-a-bitch. He leaned back to cut off part of his shirt and decided it was too blood soaked.

Sarah gasped, her gaze locked on Max's midsection. "Your stomach is wide-open," Sarah whispered.

Max sliced off some of the sheriff's shirt to make the bandage. "It looks worse than it is," he said, referring to his injuries. Which was the truth. Max, like all Knights, didn't die easily. Beheading or bleeding to death were pretty much the only ways he'd die. He was a long way from bleeding to death, though he couldn't ignore the need for medical attention forever.

Cathy appeared, standing above them, and stared at Max. "Oh, crap," she gasped, just as Sarah had moments before. "You're bleeding as much as he is. What can I do? How can I help? Are you okay?"

Max noted Cathy's rambling. If Edward was right, it was a sign of nerves. Unfortunately, Max wasn't exactly in a position to offer comfort right now. Max tied off Sheriff Jenson's wrist with a tight knot. "I need you to drive, Cathy." He eyed Sarah as he reached under the sheriff to pick him up. "Can you open the side door for me?" She nodded and rushed to do as he asked.

Weakened from his own blood loss, Max forced himself to work through it. Lifting the sheriff took more effort than it should have, the pain in his gut ripening with the movement. But Sheriff Jenson had sacrificed himself to save Cathy, and that made him a hero in Max's book. Guilt added to the pain in his stomach. He should have gotten to him sooner, and maybe he wouldn't be in the shape he was now.

Max settled the sheriff into the back of the van, hating that he had to place him next to Edward. The minute the injured man was on the floor, Max turned and pulled Sarah inside, eager to get her into a secure place, out of the open.

He slid the door shut. "Now, Cathy," Max called to her, sitting down before he fell, and sliding to the wall to use it as a support. "Hit the accelerator and don't stop until you get us to a doctor."

Max knew he needed to tie off his wounds to stop the bleeding before he allowed himself to rest. He reached for his knife and started for the sheriff, needing a piece of his shirt to make a bandage. Sarah held out her hand. "I'll do it." She pointed to the wall. "Sit back and rest."

He started to argue and decided he was in no shape to win. "I was going—"

"—to cut off some of his shirt to make another bandage. I know. I'll do it."

He would have smiled at her determination if not for the dizziness floating around in his head. Instead, he leaned back against the wall as ordered, and let his eyes shut. He healed quickly. Even small bouts of rest would allow his blood to start clotting, the magic of immortality to start taking hold, to start healing his injuries.

He didn't want to sleep, didn't want to let down his guard, but his body demanded attention. A few minutes of rest…and then he could fight again.

Sarah surveyed Sheriff Jenson, quickly checking for a pulse, and for any wound needing attention that hadn't received it yet. Satisfied he was stable, she reported as much to Max and Cathy, certain Max wouldn't let her help him until he knew the sheriff was well taken care of.

She sliced long pieces of material from the man's shirt, ignoring Edward's snorts and grunts behind her, because they spoke with brutal reality about just how close the demon remained to them. How easily it had insinuated itself into their group. Once again, her life had been touched by a demon possession. She hadn't completely gotten her mind around that yet, and she wasn't sure she wanted to. Not now, when she had to stay sharp, ready for the next challenge.

Rotating, she scooted to Max's side and onto her knees. His head was back, eyes shut. Not wanting to startle him, she reached forward and pressed her hand to his jaw. "Max," she whispered, watching his lashes lift as if weighed down. "I'm going to tie off your wound. Okay?"

"The sheriff—"

"Is stable," she assured him, wrapping the cloth around his leg and tying it off as hard as she could. The Hound's fangs had shredded his pants, and she couldn't bear thinking about those nasty teeth in his flesh. "Were those the Darkland Beasts?" she asked.

He laughed but the sound held no humor; his eyes drifted shut. "Those were nothing but pets. Nowhere near as nasty as the Beasts."

"Oh," she said, not happy with that answer. If those were "pets," she didn't want to see the real thing. But one thing was for sure, she knew she had been right to believe Max. Her instincts were on target. Now she had to shoot straight with Max, so neither of them could be taken off guard.

She nudged his legs. "Lay them flat so I can see your stomach."

"As long as you promise not to get all worked up over it," he said.

"I'm already all worked up. I saw how bad it is." She firmed her voice. "Put your legs down."

He did as she ordered and she studied his wound, her chest tight with worry. She didn't want him to die. What if he died? What if Edward died? Everyone around her got hurt. She inhaled and told herself to calm down and take action, rather than fret. She wondered how Max managed to carry the sheriff with that kind of wide-open gaping wound in his gut.

Another inhaled breath and she went to work quickly tying strips of material together. She leaned forward and braced her hand on his chest. Max's eyes shot open, his hand going to hers, covering it. Despite the darkness of their circumstances, the intimacy between them shot to red-hot in an instant.

Sarah cleared her throat, trying to find her voice, her eyes still locked with his. "I need to wrap the bandage around your waist," she explained, leaning forward, worried about the blood he was losing, not wanting to waste time.

She had nothing to soak the blood up with, and her T-shirt was already thickly covered with a combination of the sheriff's and Max's blood. "How close are we to town?" she called to Cathy.

"Another ten minutes," Cathy replied. "I think I saw the doc's office when we first arrived. I'll head straight there and hope someone is home."

"That works," Sarah said, sliding the cloth behind

Max's back and around his waist. She tried not to think about the wave of warmth washing over her body, the sexual awareness well beyond inappropriate at this moment. The way she sensed this man on so many levels, so without reason or rationale, confused her.

Once she finished her work, Sarah found it to be poor at best. Blood was already staining the cloth. "Thank God we're almost there. You need a doctor."

Max grabbed her hand and pulled her close. "I need all right," he murmured, his fingers lacing into her hair, their mouths only an inch apart. "You forgot something."

"What would that be?" Sarah whispered.

"A kiss to make it all better," he replied, a smile hinting on his sexy mouth, pain clearly keeping him from more.

She didn't hesitate, not about to deny a wounded man—especially not one she found so damn appealing. She pressed her lips to his, feeling him inside out with that simple act of intimacy, wishing deep in her soul she could escape with him into that moment. That she would wake up in a warm bed, him by her side, all of this nothing but a bad dream.

When she finally found the will to pull away, she took a few lingering moments to drown in those hazel eyes of his. "Now, damn it," she said, "get well. That's an order."

Adrian watched from a distance as the van sped away, a smile touching his lips. Normally, the presence of a Knight would make him furious. Every time he turned around, those damn Knights got in his way. He wanted their destruction and nothing less would do. But he knew this Knight. Max. He was one of the original Knights—Raphael's first attempt at battling Adrian's army—most of whom had succumbed to their dark sides and now fought for the Beasts. Adrian had been collecting the former Knights, forming a special unit to lead the battle against their present-day counterparts. Max walked near the darkness, barely touching the light. That he had survived so long spoke of his strength. He would be an excellent addition to this unit. Of course, it was a pity Adrian had shown his hand with the Hounds. They would surely alert Max of the Dark-land presence. But he wouldn't know for sure.

His next move must be considered carefully. Or per-haps his next move was to do nothing at all. Though Cain had ordered him to contain the town, to stop any-one from leaving, Cain would appreciate the magnitude of this opportunity. A trap could be set. Max would leave Nowhere and find a phone. He'd call his faithful brothers-in-arms and they'd race to the town's aid. Yes. Adrian rather liked where this was leading. The more the merrier as far as Adrian was concerned. Cain would feel the same. Once the Knights were here in full force, Adrian could put his Beasts and his new legion of spirits to good use in battle.

On the other hand, the last thing Adrian needed was Max, or the woman who he sensed was Max's mate, get-ting in Allen's way. Adrian wanted Vars free so he could steal his powers. The woman would have to die. Which was really quite a perfect idea. Max would then be sealed in darkness. Max would fall to the beast and become one of Adrian's army. Perhaps a little chat with Vars was in order. He'd allow the Vars to feel involved in his little plan to destroy the Knights, use his re-sources, build a little trust with the demon prince. Then, when the time was right, Adrian would destroy Vars just as he would the Knights.

Who would have thought a place called "Nowhere" could deliver such satisfaction?

In fact, this could prove a good test for his high-ranking Beasts, as well. He needed a new second, his last *Segundo* having betrayed him by trying to steal his place with Cain. The Beast who reined supreme on the battlefield against the Knights would begin his training as the new *Segundo*. Adrian smiled at the sheer brilliance of his own mind and then flashed out of the town, fire and malice lacing the air in his aftermath, his destination the Underworld. Cain would be pleased with his plan to destroy the Knights, although he'd leave his plot to destroy Vars out of things. Once he had Vars's powers, Adrian might well be strong enough to overtake Cain.

But first, Nowhere and the Knights who would come to protect it, would fall.

Chapter 11

Ready to leave town, Max followed Sarah down the inn stairs, fresh bandages in place, compliments of his stop by the doc's office. Max still felt like crap, but his natural healing abilities were aiding his efforts at hanging tough or at least faking it well. Though right about now, he wasn't feeling the results of that ability. He'd lost a lot of blood. He needed rest to allow his body to do the job of healing.

After several hours of attention by the doctor, the sheriff was stable—at least for the time being—and Edward was sedated, with Cathy by his side, working on her demon-binding spell.

Sarah paused at the front desk, assuring the innkeeper that help was coming. Max stepped onto the porch, the clouds above black and ominous, though no more rain had fallen. He let his senses reach out, searching, expecting the scent of a Beast, but finding none. The presence of Hounds had to mean they were near. Were they? Max grimaced. He didn't know anything for certain. This was a situation like none he'd ever faced before. Maybe the Hounds belonged to Vars. As soon as the thought crossed his mind, Max dismissed it. He'd sensed Darkland Beasts back at that cabin. Which meant more were near, ready to devour this town and its people.

The faster Max got Sarah out of here, the better he'd feel. In a short window of time, a possessed Edward and a Hell Hound had come after her. Clearly, she'd been marked for death.

The inn door opened behind him and Sarah's voice followed. "The doctor doesn't want you to travel," she said for the fifth time in ten minutes.

Max cast her a sideways glance as she stepped forward. "The doc has his hands full with the sheriff and Edward. He doesn't need to deal with me, too."

She turned to face him, her action showing the determination behind her words. "You've lost too much blood," she said. "I'm worried."

He turned to her then, surprised and warmed by the unfamiliar words of concern. No one worried about him except the Knights, and it wasn't the same as Sarah doing so. He smiled through the dull throb in his gut. "If I don't go, who'll protect you?"

She gave him the evil eye and then lashed out at his male ego. "Oh, please. You're in no shape to protect me. In fact, I'd have to protect you."

Max couldn't help himself, he laughed—it hurt like a bitch, but he laughed. Never before had he known a woman who had the guts this one did. She'd seen those

Hounds, and yet, he believed she'd charge back into danger to save lives. "You have more balls than a lot of men I've known in my life, Sarah Meyers."

She blinked at him, apparently not seeing the humor in any of this. In fact, her moment of taunting and teasing had disappeared completely. Her gaze dropped to his waist, where the bandages bulged beneath his shirt, lingering a moment before lifting to his face again.

With her brows knitting together, her voice quavering ever so slightly, she said, "Don't you dare go and die on me."

His gut tightened but not from pain this time—from the emotion in her voice, from her genuine fear for him. Max took her hand and pressed it to the bandages, determined to convince her that he was okay when that wasn't anywhere near true. The small improvements his body could make without rest weren't enough to overcome the extent of his wounds. He needed sleep and he needed it soon.

"I'm already healing, Sarah," he assured her. "Can't you tell I'm moving around more than before? I'm not like other people. I don't die easily."

She stared at him blankly before making a little huff of a noise. "There is a time and place for the macho—"

"No," he said, interrupting her, covering the hand she had pressed to his stomach with his own. "It's not like that. I'm different, Sarah. Different in ways I can't explain right now. I promise I'll be fine until we can get to a phone line."

Her expression held a hint of well-contained shock. "Are you saying the government did something to you? Kind of like a super soldier of some sort?" Max had never claimed to work for the government and part of him wanted to clarify that, to make sure she didn't think he'd misled her. But his instincts told him to hold back. Inviting more questions meant potential delays they couldn't afford. The time for some honest conversation had come, though.

"I'm not saying anything at this point," he said. "We need to have a heart-to-heart, honest talk, but let's get out of this town first."

"*If* we can get out of here," she said.

"Oh, we're getting out of here," Max declared. "One way or the other, we're leaving." They climbed into the van, Sarah in the driver's seat.

We're getting out of here, one way or the other. Sarah replayed Max's words in her head as she drove over the town bridge—the bridge where Kate had been killed. She glanced in Max's direction, noting his battle-ready position. He held several guns, ready to fire from the window, intent on at least slowing any pursuers. She gripped the steering wheel with a white-knuckled hold, certain they were about to be attacked at any moment. But nothing happened. Nothing. Ten minutes passed and not a peep of trouble.

Max set his guns down, but kept them easily accessible as he started dialing his cell. "No signal yet," he said.

"I can't believe we just drove out of town," Sarah said. "No trouble at all."

"Seems a little too good to be true," Max commented, punching the buttons on his phone again. "Which means it probably is."

Sarah reached for a logical explanation. "Maybe

reaching out to Allen from a distance is draining the demon's powers."

"Maybe," he said, but he didn't sound convinced.

"You don't buy that, do you?" she asked, casting him a quick look.

A frustrated sound slid from his lips as he hit the end button on his cell. "Damn it, we need a phone line." He pressed his eyes shut a minute and then admitted, "In answer to your question, no, I don't think the demon's powers have weakened. I think letting us leave served an agenda we don't understand yet."

"There's a sobering thought," she said dryly. "Thanks for that."

"Better to keep it real and stay on guard," he retorted.

Kate brushed Sarah's mind as a Motel 6 sign came into view and she did a quick turn into the entrance. "What are you doing?" Max asked, his wide-eyed gaze fixed on her, a stunned look on his face.

"The land lines are working here," Sarah explained. "Kate says they're working." She pulled into a parking spot in front of the lobby.

Max gave her a blank look and then cautioned her. "You're a lot more trusting of spirits than I am right about now." He grabbed the door handle and pushed it open, noting only one lone car in the parking lot, no signs of human life anywhere.

Sarah met him at the front of the van, not willing to let his comment go by unanswered. "These spirits aren't evil, Max. They want me to succeed because I'm helping them."

"Just be careful," he said. "We don't know what this Vars is capable of doing. That's all I'm saying."

She inhaled, realizing he was right. They didn't know what Vars could do. It was an unsettling thought. She'd always found the spirits she helped were in her comfort zone. Always assumed she could sense their true essence, just as she'd sensed the evil in that cabin. But what if she couldn't?

"Call me paranoid," Max said, changing the subject, "but I'm not about to part with my weapons, and I doubt they'll be well-received inside. I'll wait by the door where I can see you in case you run into trouble. If the phones work, let's grab a room and we can wait for backup here. If not, let's get in and out, and move onward."

Right, Sarah thought, her adrenaline suddenly spiking. Phone. Room. Alone with Max. Why did she find the latter made her heart pound at triple time in her chest?

Ten minutes later, Max followed Sarah into the hotel room, locked the door and started for the phone but stopped as Sarah seemed to stumble. He caught her with his arm, holding her upright. "Wow. Are you okay?"

Sarah nodded and inhaled. "Kate's trying to communicate, but it's…it's as if there is a battle raging in my head. Like the darkness from the cabin is beating at my mind, as well, trying to stop her."

Max helped her to the bed, noting the way she swayed a bit, the way her skin seemed devoid of color. She'd been through a lot today, and neither of them had eaten or slept in—how many hours was it? He didn't even know.

He eased her onto the edge of the mattress, and he kneeled in front of her, hands on her legs. He wished he could wipe away her pain, take it as his own, but he didn't know how. "What can I do?"

She managed a weak smile and touched his jaw. "Just get help for that town. I'm going to go to the bathroom and splash some water on my face." Her stomach growled. "Okay, so maybe food and a little rest is in order, too."

"I'll call for help and then ask the front desk about the nearest food."

"That sounds good," she said, pushing to her feet and standing there a minute. "The dizziness seems to have passed."

She'd rested all of a minute. Max wasn't convinced she'd recovered. "Just the same, leave the bathroom door open so I can hear you call out if you need me."

"You're the one that's injured," Sarah reminded him. "I have a headache. Nothing more."

He hoped she was right. "At least leave it cracked."

"I'll leave it cracked in case *you* need *me*," she teased.

Max laughed at that and moved to sit on the bed by the nightstand, shaking his head at Sarah's comment. Damn how he loved her spunk. If they both weren't so exhausted and beat up, he'd worry about being alone with her, worry he'd lose his willpower and make use of the bed for much more appealing pleasures than sleep.

He grabbed the phone and the sweet sound of a dial tone slid into his ears a second before Sarah screamed and fell to the bathroom floor. Max dropped the phone. "Sarah!"

Max found her curled up like a child, her hands on her head. "Max," she whispered. "I… My head hurts. It hurts bad. Every time Kate—" Her words disappeared into a sob.

"It's okay, baby," he said, pulling her close. God, she was shaking. "I'll get you help. I promise. I'll get you help."

Lifting her, Max carried Sarah to the bed, and began rubbing her arms and back, trying to calm her down. He knew from experience that the adrenaline and fear a person experienced from pain would intensify their physical reactions.

He leaned against the headboard and pulled her close to his uninjured side and under his arm, reaching for the phone cord with the free hand and tugging. When it was in reach, he dialed Jag's cell, relieved to hear his leader's voice after only two rings.

Jag didn't bother with hello. "We were about to come looking for you," Jag said. "You aren't answering your phone, and Des had one of those new visions of his. He said the Beasts—"

"I need Marisol and I need her now," Max said, cutting off Jag.

"We'll be right there." The line went dead. Max set the phone back in place, telling himself everything would be okay now. Jag's gifts included an ability to locate anyone he made verbal contact with. Jag and Marisol were the only two in their group who could travel by orbing—they could travel through space at light speed. Once Jag had found Marisol, they'd be here in a flash. And Jag had said they were about to come looking for him, which meant he wasn't on his own. In the far corner of his mind, he'd worried that because of his test, there would be limits to what Jag would be allowed to do to help. But deep down, he knew that if innocents were in danger, there were no limits. Whatever test Max had to pass would not put others in danger. Only himself.

Sarah breathed in and out with labored effort, alter-

nating silence with soft murmurs of pain. Max lay there
holding her, minutes passing as if they were hours, fear
for her life tearing him up inside. How long had it been
since he'd cared for someone as he did Sarah? He remembered his family, remembered the emptiness their
deaths had left inside him—he lived with that each day
of his life. But the caring, the worry, the daily emotions
that came with love—these things he didn't remember
at all. Only that what he felt now, with Sarah in pain, in
his arms, touched him deeply. Love bound together two
mates, destiny linked their souls. Love. It hurt. It excited. It scared the hell out of him.

Jag and Marisol appeared in that moment at the foot
of the bed. Max wasn't sure what calmed him more, the
dominating warriorlike confidence of their leader or the
soft promise of hope that clung to their healer. "You two
are a sight for sore eyes," Max said. "She's in pain, and
I don't know how to help."

"You don't look so good yourself, man," Jag said instantly, as Marisol moved forward, easing onto the bed,
tucking her long white skirt under her legs, and shoving
her mass of raven hair behind her ears.

"What the hell happened?" Jag demanded. "Why
couldn't we get through to you?"

Marisol reached out to touch Sarah, but Max gently
shackled her wrist. As much as he wanted her to heal
Sarah, it wouldn't be fair to let her begin without the
facts. "You should know what you're dealing with first."

Max knew Marisol could fight off beastly influences
if she touched a human soon enough after a bite, but
these were not Darkland Beasts they were dealing with.
These demons were demon spirits. He went on to ex-

plain more about the demon spirits, including a condensed version of what had taken place back in Nowhere, his focus shifting between Marisol and Jag.

Drawing to a conclusion, Max shared the sheriff's and Edward's dicey medical conditions before fixing his attention back on Marisol. "Can you help her?"

Marisol's eyes comforted, her presence alone somehow warm and full of healing. She reached out and touched Sarah. "She's not sick. She's exhausted." Her gaze went from Max to Jag. "She's also very special. Her gifts are strong, her mind, too. These evil spirits are draining her, though."

"What does that mean?" Max asked. "If they keep attacking her, will this keep happening?"

"When was the last time either of you slept?" Marisol asked, but didn't give him time to respond.

Sarah murmured something.

"She doesn't seem as if she can rest," he said.

"I'll put her into a deep healing sleep," Marisol said. "After I heal you," she said, her gaze sweeping his stomach.

He quickly rejected that idea. "No. Healing weakens you. The sheriff and Edward are not well and who knows how many others have been injured since we left."

"It takes a lot to drain me, and who will protect her if you die?" Marisol said. "Bleeding to death serves no purpose. She's your mate. It's your duty to protect her."

"Mate?" Jag asked, his brows lifting. "Sarah is your mate?"

"I believe so," Max said, glancing at Marisol. "How did you know?"

"Not with magic or my healing touch," she said. "It's

in your eyes. That same look of utter devotion Jag and Des have for their mates." She gave him a reprimanding look. "Now, let me heal you, so I can get on with taking care of your woman."

Jag chuckled and eyed Max. "The lady has spoken. I think you better listen."

"You're sure you can heal the others if you heal me?"

Marisol rolled her eyes, pushed off the bed and stomped around to Max's side. "Stop asking questions and let me do my job."

"I'll gather a team to go into Nowhere," Jag said, inclining his head at Max and grinning at Marisol's reprimand. "I'll meet you out front so we don't disturb Marisol and Sarah when I return." He didn't wait for an answer before flashing out of the room.

Thirty minutes later, completely healed, though still exhausted, Max stood outside. Fortunately, they seemed to be the only visitors at the hotel, allowing them to engage in open conversation. Des, Rock, Rinehart and Jag surrounded Max. These were the Knights who made him feel as if he belonged, who he hoped would allow him to become a permanent part of their team. To really be a part of their circle of trust. He knew they had doubts about his involvement, but since he'd saved Des's mate, they looked at him differently, with more acceptance. But he also knew that Des, especially, knew how close to the darkness Max walked. Des had been there the day Max had taken that human's life.

With a quick recap of everything that had gone down back in Nowhere, Texas, Max brought the Knights up-to-date on the troubles they faced. When Max finished, Des was the first to interject his opinions.

"Chingado," Des muttered using a familiar Spanish curse word—at least familiar to anyone who spent any amount of time around Des. "I knew something was wrong, man. These damn visions are freaking impossible to understand." He laughed incredulously. "I kept seeing you with a shovel refilling a deep-ass hole in the ground. I guess that was you trying to keep this demon in his underground prison. I don't know how I was supposed to know what that meant and send help."

"They'll get easier to decipher with time," Jag offered, one booted foot resting on a concrete step leading to the second floor of the hotel. The sparse accommodations offered only outdoor entry to the rooms.

"Says Salvador," Des said dryly. He'd never been fond of Salvador's coded messages and vague statements.

Jag narrowed his gaze on Des. "Says me. Every day with Karen, my abilities become stronger."

"You're here now," Max inserted. "That's what counts. And that town needs you." He frowned. "There's something bothering me, though. Why was I allowed to leave? Surely Vars knew I'd bring back help."

"Sounds like a trap," Rinehart reflected, shoving his cowboy hat back from his blue eyes that were sharp with suspicion.

"Oh, yeah," Rock chimed in. "Definitely a trap. But hey—" he shrugged "—we're used to that."

Rinehart snorted, irritated at Rock as usual. "Are you nuts, kid? Going into that town is playing right into their hands. We can't just charge in without any idea what we're dealing with."

Max didn't like it, but Rinehart made sense. He eyed Jag. "The town doctor could only do so much for the

sheriff. He'll die without immediate help." He hesitated. "If it's not too late already. And this Cathy who
works with Sarah. She actually has several people she
wanted me to contact who could help. She's got a lot to
offer. She understands the magical aspects of all of this."

"Let's recap what we all know," Des said, resting a
hand on his hip. "We've got three Shadow Masters, and
three Shadow Stones. Somehow, together they can give
Vars the power to be free. We don't known anything
about these stones or these Masters. Really, we don't
know squat."

"We know we have to get to them before Allen does,"
Rock interjected.

"Or keep Allen from getting back to the cabin with
them in tow," Max added.

"Wait," Jag said. "Allen has to go back to the cabin
to free Vars?"

"Right," Max agreed. "Which makes securing the
cabin critical. If we can't stop Allen from getting the
power he needs to free Vars, we need to stop him from
getting back to Vars."

"Which is likely what they're counting on," Rinehart
inserted. "Get us there and trap us."

Rock nodded his agreement before offering a suggestion. "Why not put a group of Knights on the outskirts of town, ready to aid our efforts in case of attack,
but out of harm's reach?"

Rinehart, a military man in his human life, quickly
axed that. "That's expected. The Beasts could simply
come up behind them and push them forward."

Jag considered a minute. "Okay. Here is what we'll
do. I'll talk to Salvador. Des will go back to the ranch

and make contact with Cathy's people and come up with a list of targets Allen might be after. From there he will communicate with Max and Sarah to go after Allen. Rock, Rinehart, you two head into Nowhere and investigate. Take Marisol so she can heal the sheriff and attempt to help Edward."

As if on queue, Marisol opened the door and motioned Max and Jag forward. The two of them joined her in the room. "She's resting now." Marisol looked at Max. "She should sleep awhile now. Let her. She needs it. You do, too. I know you don't want to but you need to. Let us take over long enough for you to recuperate."

"You're sure she's okay?" Max asked, staring at Sarah's pale face, dark circles coloring the skin beneath her eyes.

"She just needs rest," Marisol said.

"We can take her to the ranch where she'll be safe," Jag offered.

"No," Max said quickly. "I haven't explained everything about our world to her." He paused, torn about saying more than he had to. Jag might not agree with his handling of Sarah. Reluctantly, he added, "I don't know if I am going to."

Jag narrowed his eyes on Max and then cast Marisol a look. She quickly picked up on what he wanted. "I'll leave you two to talk, so I can attend to the others who need me."

"Marisol," Max said, as she walked to the door. She turned back to him and he added, "Thank you and be careful."

A sad look flashed in her eyes. "I'd tell you to do the same, but I know you won't listen." She glanced at Sarah as if she wanted to say more, but didn't, turning away and exiting without another word.

"I've never asked a favor before," Max said the minute the door shut, "but I need one now. I need to know if I don't pass this test, if I don't survive, that Sarah will be looked after."

Jag tilted his head, his gaze probing Max's face. "You've decided your fate already." It wasn't a question.

"I almost killed Edward today," Max said. "I *wanted* to kill him."

"But you didn't."

"Didn't you hear what I said? I wanted to. I could damn near taste his blood. He tried to kill Sarah and I lost it." His lips thinned. "Just like before. Just like with the other human. The beast took control."

"If the beast had control, you would have killed Edward."

"I stopped because of Sarah." He hesitated. "Because I didn't want her to see what I really am. Not because I wanted to spare the human." And he realized, it was also because he'd felt her fear, her guilt. She would have blamed herself for Edward's death, for not saving him, for not protecting him from the demon.

"A Beast wouldn't have stopped for any reason. You know that as well as I do."

"And if you're wrong?" Max asked. "She has enough demons in her world without dealing with mine. I have to find a way to come through this or leave her without her ever knowing who and what I truly am."

Jag glanced at Sarah and then back at Max. "She has no more peace than you at present. I feel...loss in her. She's lost much in her life. She's afraid to lose more." His gaze went back to Max. "She needs you as much as you need her. Give her a chance to help."

"If I claim her and then fail this test, will her destiny be the same as mine is—in hell?"

"Yes," Jag said. "Once your souls are linked through mating, she will share your future. Which leaves you with only one option." He paused for obvious effect. "Don't fail this test. She is your incentive to succeed."

Jag inclined his head as he often did before departing a room. "I will contact you with an update soon." And then he was gone, leaving Max no chance to respond. No chance to ask questions.

Max scrubbed his jaw and walked to the bed, staring down at Sarah. He wanted to live for her, wanted to succeed. But what if he didn't? What if he let her down as he had his family? What if he failed?

He couldn't risk that. He couldn't. No matter what—he would see Sarah and this town through this danger. But he'd do it without claiming her or telling her who and what he was.

She murmured a soft something in her sleep. God, he loved her, he realized. He'd always heard a mate's love was instant, and he knew, in that moment, that it was true. He wouldn't cause her pain or put her in jeopardy for his own comfort, his own hope.

But Jag was right. Sarah was incentive enough to keep him fighting. New resolve formed and he vowed to defeat his beast and pass this test.

Vars heard Adrian's summons and it infuriated him. He'd called on Cain for hours with no response and now he was being called by the idiotic fool he wanted to destroy. Vars materialized in the cabin at Adrian's summons, but given the circumstances, found these confines more frustrating than his prison below. Fury consumed Vars as he brought the blond-haired, leather-clad, arrogant bastard into his sights.

"I asked one thing of you," he ground out, with anger lacing the words. "One. You were to ensure no one left this town. Cain will hear of this, and he will know you for the idiot you are!"

Adrian laughed, a mocking sound that bit at Vars's nerve endings. "I am not the one who is imprisoned beneath the ground, begging for my freedom like some pitiful dog begs for a bone. Consider yourself lucky I've lowered myself to dealing with the likes of you. Cain knows what I have done and it serves a purpose. One broader than your small mind can apparently wrap around. The man is no man, he is one of Raphael's Knights of White. The woman is his mate. The Knight will lead his army here to their own destruction."

Vars would have choked the life out of Adrian if he wasn't stuck in his pathetic shrine of powerless confinement, his abilities drained by the magic he was pumping into Allen right now. He bit back his anger and ground out a nasty reply. "The woman has connections to the other side, you fool. She will try to stop Allen before I get my energy sources."

Adrian waved off the words. "The woman will be dead in a few hours. Now—" he crossed his arms in front of his body "—I understand you need these energy sources by the next full moon. You have only ten days. Do I need to fetch your Shadow Stones for you so we are sure it gets done right?"

Adrian couldn't do the job if he wanted to, and Vars took pleasure in that knowledge. "For centuries now, each eldest son of the Shadow Masters' families have placed their souls in a magical Shadow Stone. In exchange, I endowed them with great health and wealth. The Masters will not release their souls from the stones to anyone but me, their *royal* master. They will find me through my bond with Allen, and he, and he alone, will receive their souls. Quite simply, you are not worthy of the stones. So, do your job. Protect this town. Protect Allen. Or is that too much for you?"

A sudden rush of menace filled the air, Adrian's eyes flashing yellow and red. "Do not test my limits, Vars, or you will remain beneath the ground." A second later Vars found himself thrown back into the pit of his prison, fire consuming him, pain—however momentary—scorching his every muscle. When the flames subsided, Vars pushed to his feet, vowing to make Adrian pay for his actions.

Adrian flashed to his home deep below the Mexican mountains where he lived in luxury and housed his sex slaves and army of Beasts. Rage burned inside him, rage directed at Vars. He was beneath no one, beneath nothing.

He snapped his fingers and a brunette beauty appeared. The sheer pink gown she wore showed the bright red of her puckered nipples. She was bound to him by the marks on her shoulder, her soul stuck between dimensions, allowing him to control her every need. He kissed her, savoring the sweetness of her taste, sex an outlet for the thunder raging inside. But one human would not sate this rage. He snapped his fingers and another slave appeared—this one blond, voluptuous, full breasted. She wore the same pink gown. Pink

was a favorite of Adrian's. It made him think of the in-
nocence he'd stolen from them. He tasted the second
female's lips, his cock throbbing with need. Then he
waved his hand and flashed them into the king-sized bed
behind him, discarding their gowns with his magic.

He had a business matter to attend to before he could
devour his prey. With another wave of his hand three
Beasts appeared in their demon forms, half their faces
distorted, their yellowish red eyes alert with the call of
their master.

They were part of the Unit of his prior second-in-
charge. U1, U2 and U3 were the only names they
deserved—for now. "Each of you have the chance to
earn the spot of my next *Segundo*. How you perform
your next assignments will decide your futures. One of
you will achieve greatness by my side. The other two—"
Adrian paused for effect, an evil smile playing on his
lips "—will be beheaded."

Fear crackled in the air at the words and Adrian drank
it in, reveling in the power he had over the Beasts.
Adrenaline and lust spiked within him, as he continued
to speak. "U1 will ensure the Shadow Stones are recovered. Take a team and follow the human called Allen
Walker. Kill any Knight or human who dares to interfere." He flashed U1 out of the room.

Adrian focused on U2. "You have a special as-
signment. You will kill the human called Sarah Meyers.
I've come to understand she is the mate of your former
brother. You are not to kill him. I want him on our
special-forces team." Adrian could feel U2's edginess,
his desire to see his brother dead. "Destroying her will
ensure he crosses over to the dark side. Have your way

with the woman, torture her, torture him for all I care. I really don't care. Just make sure she's dead and he watches her die. I want her blood spilled by the next dawn." He touched U2's chest, heat flaming from his palm to the Beast's skin, painfully reminding him who had control. "Fail me and die." He didn't give U2 time to respond, flashing the Beast from the room.

One final Beast remained, U3. "You will handpick the Beasts that are the strongest. Use them to defeat the Knights who gather in Nowhere, Texas." The final Beast was flashed from the room, and Adrian thought of Vars. "I will destroy the demon prince myself and enjoy doing so."

Now that he had his Beasts after blood, he turned back to the naked beauties in his bed, ready to explore the pleasures they represented. Ready to sate at least one of the desires burning within him. Satisfied to know his other needs would soon be fulfilled, as well.

Chapter 12

With Rock at her heels, Marisol walked toward the door of the exam room where Cathy and Edward were resting. He was scared to death to leave her alone, afraid the Beasts would attack. The young Knight acted like her keeper, as if she couldn't simply shimmer out of the room and away from danger. Secretly, she loved his protectiveness, just as she knew she loved him. But it was forbidden that she ever act on those feelings. Her love for Rock worked against her duty, her vows as a healer. She was not of this world, she simply served it.

She turned to him, silently telling him she needed privacy to talk with Cathy. He stepped to the side of the entrance. "I'll be right here if you need me."

Her heart clenched with his words and she resisted the urge to reach out and touch him. "Thank you," she said, softly, not daring to look into his eyes for fear he would see how much his concern touched her.

She stepped around Rock and opened the door, pausing as she took in the sight before her. The man she assumed to be Edward was strapped to a table and sedated, yet still he tossed about, driven by the demon possessing him.

Beside the table, sleeping in a chair, was the woman called Cathy. Poor thing was exhausted and Marisol could feel her turbulent emotions. Cathy didn't know help had arrived, didn't even know Marisol had healed the sheriff who was now talking with Jag and Rinehart.

Marisol walked toward Cathy, surprised at the charge of energy that flowed from the female. She was gifted with magic beyond what she practiced, born into powers she had yet to realize. Jag would find this interesting. For he had learned what Marisol's centuries in another realm had taught her well—nothing happened without a reason. Cathy had been delivered to them to play a role in this battle against evil, a battle that would most likely transcend the one fought in this town.

Kneeling in front of Cathy, Marisol touched her leg. "Cathy," she whispered.

The woman blinked and lifted her head, staring at Marisol. "My God, you have beautiful green eyes."

Marisol smiled at the compliment, which wasn't uncommon. "Green is the color of healing," Cathy said. "You're the healer Max spoke of," Cathy said, her hands going to the sides of the chair. "The sheriff—"

"Is as good as new," Marisol said. "He's chatting with the others in my group."

Cathy went a little pale. "That's impossible."

"You're welcome to go see for yourself," Marisol

offered, pushing to her feet. She spotted a mirror on the wall and inclined her head. "Or you can stand in front of that mirror while I heal that cut on your face."

A moment passed as Cathy cocked her head to the side and studied Marisol. "All right." She stood and walked to the mirror. "Let's see what you've got."

Marisol smiled and approached the other woman, touching her face. The wound was small, and took little effort to wipe away. A second later, she pulled her hand from Cathy's face and smiled. "Good as new."

Cathy stared in the mirror and moved closer to the surface, inspecting her face. She whirled and faced Marisol. "You know what's the most amazing part of this?" She didn't give Marisol time to answer. "It's not what you did but what I felt when you did it." She touched her chest. "I felt warm and…touched by, well, something special."

"You know what's the most amazing thing to me?" Marisol asked.

"What?" Cathy asked, her eyes wide with interest.

"That you know what you felt was special. That you are close enough to the source of my power to feel it. That makes you special, Cathy."

She snorted at that. "I'm not special." Edward made a low growling noise and her expression turned serious. "Can you help him? I've tried everything I know to do."

Marisol walked over to Edward and touched his hand. Evil rocketed through her body, and she gasped, stepping back and breaking contact.

"That didn't look good," Jag said, leaning on the doorjamb.

"It wasn't," Marisol said. "Whatever is inside him is

far more evil than a Beast. I need to consult my *Book of Knowledge*."

"Book of Knowledge?" Cathy asked.

Marisol eyed Cathy. "It's my reference…it's special. It may hold the answer to saving Edward." She looked toward the doorway. "This is Jag, the leader of The Knights of White."

Cathy did what all women do in Jag's rather intimidating masculine presence. She stared. Besides being gorgeous, with shoulder-length black hair and a body that would set any woman on fire, Jag carried an air of power and sexuality. He also adored the mate who waited for him at home more than life itself.

"You're Max's boss then?" Cathy asked. "He called you here to help?"

"We are here to help, and yes, Max called us." Jag's lips twisted in a hint of a smile. "As for being his boss, I don't know that anyone can claim to being Max's boss. I am, however, honored to have him on our team."

"Glad to meet you," Cathy said. "I have a feeling I owe Max an apology for doubting him." She frowned. "Or two or three." She glanced between Jag and Marisol. "Did Sarah talk to my people? Are they coming here, too?"

"It's too dangerous for your people to come here, Cathy," Jag said. "We can go to them."

"They won't talk to you," she insisted. "I wasn't completely sure they'd talk to Sarah but at least my mother has met her and liked her. The world of magic is a private one. There are secrets that simply aren't shared—not without consequences from those in the circle."

Jag considered her words. "We can take you to your people."

"I can't leave Edward," Cathy said, her arms crossing in front of her body. She shook her head. "That's simply not an option."

"Cathy has some gifts I can harness to heal Edward," Marisol said, "and perhaps others who might be afflicted as he is. Perhaps her gifts may even help us fight some of the evil we are faced with. I really need her to stay, so we can figure out what we are capable of together."

"What are her abilities?" Jag asked.

"I know a little magic," Cathy answered, casting Marisol a curious gaze.

Marisol, in turn, gave Jag a look that was meant to tell him she had more to say on the subject later—when they were alone. His eyes narrowed and then he gave her a barely discernible nod. "Where does that leave us then?" he asked. "My men are researching, but so far we have nothing on these Shadow Masters."

"And my guess is you won't find anything," Cathy inserted with confidence. "We are talking about the blackest of magic here. No one talks about this kind of evil openly for fear they will be punished by those using it. They certainly don't write it down nor do they discuss it over the phone. Nor do they talk to strangers. My family knows the magical world. They have connections. That's why we need to get them involved. But you can't do that without me."

Marisol gave Jag a pointed look. "Can I talk with you?" He inclined his head and Marisol glanced at Cathy. "Give us one minute."

Jag and Marisol stepped into the hall to join Rock. "Let's go outside so we can speak freely," Jag said.

A few seconds later they stepped onto the porch, the

sky black despite the fact that the dawn hour had come and gone. Rock and Jag framed Marisol, their big bodies almost like a shield to the outer world.

The two men turned to her, Jag speaking first. "What's Cathy's story?"

"She's unique, gifted with inbred magic she doesn't even know she has. I really think we have a better chance at saving Edward together than if I go it alone. I can use her magical energy to strengthen mine. And if we can figure out how, maybe we can turn that combined energy on Vars in some way."

Jag ran his fingers over his goatee. "Well, then," he said. "That's an interesting twist of events. Any idea what the source of her power is?"

"I'm seeing a familiar pattern to the women who enter our world," Marisol said. "I'm guessing a little research will find her tied to that list of angelic bloodlines we recently discovered. In other words, I think she is part of our world and someone's future mate."

Jag's eyes lit with that explanation. "A Knight's salvation."

"Or perhaps a future Knight," Marisol suggested.

Jag took a sudden step forward, his eyes traveling the horizon. "Beasts," he murmured. "Do you feel them, Rock?"

Rock stepped to his side. "I do," he said quietly. "Our men should arrive soon."

"Not soon enough, I fear," Jag said, turning back to them. "There is a distinct flavor of power in the air. Adrian, I think."

"Adrian?" Rock said. "As in, the leader of the Darklands? I didn't think he came into the trenches."

"He doesn't," Jag said. "Which is exactly why I'm worried. Both of you be on guard and warn the others to do the same." He looked at Marisol. "Perhaps Cathy came to us for a reason. Her powers may be needed. Do what you can to help her awaken them." He didn't wait for a reply. "I need to speak with Salvador and then I'll take Sarah to meet with Cathy's mother. I'll update you soon." He inclined his head and vanished without another word.

Marisol drew in a breath and focused on Rock. "I need to get my *Book of Knowledge,*" Marisol said, eyeing Rock. "Can you stay with Cathy while I'm gone? I can't shake the feeling she will be important in the future. I don't want to risk someone else figuring that out and coming after her."

"I'll protect her with my life," Rock said, willing as always to meet Marisol's needs.

She rolled her eyes at his over-the-top gallant words. "You're laying it on thick today, Rock."

He grinned. "Just making sure you know I'm here for you."

Her expression turned serious. "I know you are, Rock," she said, and shimmered into air, disappearing before he could respond.

Allen pulled up to the gate of the fancy Houston mansion and hit the buzzer, knowing he'd be expected. He checked the name on the marble plate beneath the buzzer and confirmed he had, indeed, found the one he sought—Caden Neil, a dark sorcerer who'd be bringing together the Shadow Masters in the Stone Ceremony.

Vars had arranged his visit, though he didn't know

how and didn't really care. The rich bastard who owned this place had apparently come by his money with help from the dark side. Figured. Allen used to wonder how some people had an overabundance of luck and money. Now he knew. They used magic. The Shadow Masters certainly had. But they'd also sold their souls for all they possessed. A bargain that would now destroy them. But that didn't matter to Allen; his only concern was getting Kate back. These Shadow Masters were evil. In truth, he was doing the world a favor. He'd be ridding it of the black sorcerers, and bringing back into it a lovely, wonderful woman. A good woman.

He touched the vial hanging from his neck, the one he'd created with the magic Vars had given him. A vial that would soon hold the souls of the Shadow Masters. And those souls would wield the power to free Vars. Allen simply needed this Caden to extract the souls from the stones. He wondered what Caden got in return for all of this, and how Caden had been connected to Vars. It was clear everything in this world operated on trade. Give me this and I give you that. Not that Allen cared. He just wanted this done.

A camera swung around to fix on him, and he stared into it. Seconds passed and the big steel gate slid open. Allen smiled and put the truck into Drive. Soon the Shadow Masters would be no more—soon Kate would come home to him.

Chapter 13

Sarah tossed and turned in the bed, screaming out in her mind as the cold bitterness of the familiar nightmare claimed her. Once again locked inside those moments so many years before when someone close to her—someone she trusted like a brother—had pulled the trigger of a gun two times, two deadly bullets hitting their targets and stealing her parents' lives.

Sarah lived that moment again, collapsing over her parents' bodies, touching them, searching for life that wasn't there to be found. "No," she whispered, shaking, her gaze lifting to the one who held the gun—to Kevin, a man who'd worked closely with her family for years. Had he always been this…this evil thing? Had she missed the signs? "Why?" she sobbed, her voice and hands shaking. "Why?"

But what she saw when she looked at Kevin wasn't

Kevin at all. Red eyes, evil and full of malice, stared back at her. "Who are you?" she demanded, but she knew already. She knew this was the demon they'd been hunting, the one the police thought was a serial killer. How long had Kevin been controlled by that demon? How long?

She let her lashes flutter, eyes shut. She would die next. But seconds passed and nothing happened. "Do it!" she screamed, wanting to die. She'd lost everything; she'd failed her family.

When she fixed her gaze on Kevin, for a moment she saw the man she'd known—or she thought she did. She couldn't be sure. And then, before she could stop it, before she even knew what was happening, the gun turned on Kevin.

"No!" Sarah shrieked, pushing to her feet, not sure if Kevin was really Kevin anymore—if he could be saved—just that she had to try. But it was too late.

The shot rang in the air, a loud thunder that made her jerk, and Kevin crumpled to the ground. Slowly, Sarah fell to her knees, tears pouring from her eyes. Why was she alive? Why? Would this demon come for her later? Was he taunting her? Why was she alive? She looked at her mother's pale face, and rocked back and forth. Why couldn't it be her and not her mother? Her gaze went to her father, and she screamed from the injustice of it all. Screamed until it hurt, until it felt as if her throat bled. Until everything went black.

The nightmare shifted to a hospital room, the smell of medicine lacing her nostrils. She blinked awake and memories flooded her, the pain of loss filling her. God, how it hurt. She'd failed everyone she loved. She'd let the demon take them. Let the demon get inside their world and destroy it from the inside out. Why hadn't she sensed it? Why? Had Kevin ever been their friend? Or had he always been possessed, a part of that demon? Tears spilled from her eyes, tears so full of self-hatred, they burned her cheeks. She wanted to destroy that demon one moment; the next, she wanted to die. She shivered, cold, alone, empty—so very empty.

Abruptly the cold began to fade, shift, move. Warmth surrounded Sarah and she moved closer to it, needing it, desperate for it. A soft masculine voice slid into her mind, her name a baritone murmur. She blinked and her lashes lifted. Sarah was awake for real this time, outside her nightmare, and strong arms held her, absorbing the emptiness, making her feel whole again.

"Max?" she whispered, as she stared into his rich hazel eyes. Reality began to register and she vaguely remembered passing out.

"Yes," he said softly, his voice full of gentle comfort that so contrasted with the strength in his masculine features, in the powerful body holding her. He rested against the headboard, legs stretched out in front of him, shirt off, his bare chest cradling her body. "I'm here."

She shivered, and he rubbed her arm, tugging the blanket over her. "Are you cold?"

"No." Not anymore. Not with him here, holding her, somehow making the nightmare fade when nothing else would. "I had a nightmare." She leaned up on an elbow, taking in the surroundings, trying to remember how she got in bed. She was dressed but her shoes were off. The room was dimly lit, only a small corner lamp on; a glance at the window confirmed night had fallen.

She swallowed hard. "You took care of me." Then another thought followed before she could digest that one. "How long was I out? Did we call for help? The sheriff and Edward—are they okay?" Her mind was racing now. Max was hurt! What if he'd looked out for her and waited too long for care? "Oh, God! You need a doctor."

She tried to yank back the blanket and sit up to inspect his injuries, but Max pulled her back down; her chest was pressed to his side, one of his legs grabbing hers and pulling it beneath him, holding her in place. Shock mixed with pure fire surged through her body.

"Max!" she objected, confused by his actions. "What are you doing?" His mouth was close to hers, the air crackling with tension—charged with sexual energy, with attraction—but there was more there, too. She tried to identify the feeling. Apprehension perhaps?

"Everything is in order," he said. "You slept for six hours. My people have gone to Nowhere to offer aid, and they're researching the Shadow Masters. They will protect your team. I promise."

She would have felt relief, but for the look of tension on Max's face. A fizzle of fear raced through her and started to spin out of control. Her hands dug into his arm. "What's wrong? Just tell me. What's wrong?"

"Nothing that wasn't wrong when you went to sleep," Max said.

"I don't believe you," she whispered vehemently. "Tell me."

He shut his eyes and his torment washed over her. Suddenly, Sarah felt his sorrow, his pain. The connection she shared with him was so intense, so alive, it was almost as if he moved inside her. She'd never felt anything like this with another person. Nothing remotely close.

Her hand went to his jaw. "Max?" she softly prodded. "Talk to me."

"I need to show you something, but I need to know you won't freak out on me. I'm not like other people, Sarah. I don't want you to be afraid of me." Fear fluttered in her chest and she stiffened ever so slightly. After that nightmare, the unknown set her on edge. Max didn't, though, she reminded herself. Max calmed and comforted her. He needed acceptance now, too, she realized. Just as she often wanted acceptance, but rarely found it from those around her. And, my God, the man had saved her life several times already. He deserved her support.

She wanted to be there for him as he had been for her when she'd collapsed. "I understand being different. I live it each day of my life."

His throat bobbed. "Not like me, Sarah." He hesitated and then yanked the sheets back and exposed his bare abdominals.

Sarah blinked and blinked again. She couldn't be seeing what she thought she was seeing. His wound had disappeared, healed completely. He reached out and took her hand, pressing it to his stomach, the touch intimate, and packed with a punch. Heat darted up her arm and then coiled low in her stomach.

Her fingers itched to move and explore while her mind warned of her need for answers. "How can this be?"

"When you collapsed you were in a great deal of pain. I was desperate to take away your pain. I summoned Marisol. She is special, Sarah. She heals by touch. She eased your pain and helped you rest. Then, she took care of me. Hopefully, she's aided the sheriff and Edward by now, as well."

"I don't even remember her being here," Sarah said, frightened that so much was going on out of her control. Errors happened when she didn't keep things well under thumb. People died. But then, if what Max said was true, maybe people had been saved—her people. The sheriff. "When will we know if she helped them?"

"Soon I hope," he said, but offered nothing more, his attention turning back to the prior conversation. "My world is different from yours, Sarah." Something in his voice drew her gaze to his. "I'm not like other humans." His hand flattened on hers with more force. "But I need you to know I am one of the good guys. I'll fight to my death to protect you. I won't leave you to deal with this challenge alone." More conviction slid into his voice. "I won't."

For the first time in years, Sarah trusted someone at their word. She looked into Max's tormented eyes, and she let herself be lost. Lost to him, to the moment, to the whirlwind of emotions taking hold of her. She wanted him as she had never wanted a man, beyond reason, beyond explanation. The world was crumbling only a few miles away, but for just the briefest of times, she wanted to escape, to pretend nothing existed but the two of them.

"I believe you," she whispered, her body turning toward his, her hand sliding from beneath his, to the sprinkle of dark hair on his chest.

Max felt the brush of Sarah's lips on his and it was all he could do to remain still, to hold back. But he had to hold back. Had to. If he dared to explore where this could lead, he risked breaking the promise he'd just made. Because attached to him, mated to him, she would not be protected. She would share his destiny, his potential hell.

"Sarah—"

She pressed a finger to his lips. "Don't talk. I need you, Max. Make love to me."

Her mouth pressed to his, her tongue sliding past his lips, inviting him into a seductive game, dangerous and enticing, impossible to resist. Neither man nor Beast had enough willpower.

Suddenly, Max was kissing her, passion exploding within him, the completeness of his desire for this woman, his mate, consuming him at all levels—heart, soul, body. His fingers laced through her hair, her taste as addictive as her touch. And she was definitely touching him, showing no hesitation to explore his body. Her hands were everywhere, fingers tracing his muscles with tantalizing results, her leg over his, as his had been over hers earlier. As if she was the one who feared *he* would escape. But the only escape he wanted was inside her, his body intimately bound to hers. She was the sweetest thing life had ever given him, and for this one night, he was going to be strong enough to enjoy her without losing control.

"Max," Sarah whispered, easing her body on top of his, straddling his hips, the V of her body teasing his groin, thickening his cock. His hands gripped her hips, pressing her more firmly against him, pelvis lifting upward.

She moaned and pulled her blood-stained shirt—stained with his blood from when she'd taken care of him—over her head. The thought warmed him for an instant before fading away, as Sarah tossed her bra to the floor and leaned forward, pressing her chest to his chest, skin intimately touching skin.

Her lips lingered above his, her nipples pebbled against him. "I meant what I said earlier," she said, her voice barely audible.

"Which was what?" he asked, having a hard time remembering anything beyond the present, his hands skimming the softness of her bare back, to ease up her sides.

"I don't make a habit of getting naked with strangers."

He brushed the sides of her breasts and she moaned. "We might have only just met, Sarah," he murmured, his lips caressing hers for a quick moment, fingers sliding around the lush fullness of her breasts to tease her nipples. "But we aren't strangers." His teeth tugged on her bottom lip ever so gently. "Haven't you figured that out by now?"

She didn't immediately respond. Their breathing mingled, the air crackling with sensual tension. Slowly, Sarah eased back a bit, staring down at him, her eyes heavy with passion, with questions. "I've never felt this before."

He didn't ask what she meant by *this* because he understood. "That makes two of us," Max replied, his voice leaden with desire, with tenderness he hadn't known he possessed. But as quickly as that tenderness had consumed him, so did other, darker emotions.

Primal instincts flared inside Max, pushing him to take Sarah, driving him to claim. The need to control the pace, to control Sarah's actions rang in his mind as important. He couldn't risk her taking him beyond the place where man contained beast. If Sarah pressed him over the edge, he might not make it back. There was no option—he had to dominate. Had to control.

Max responded to the growing demands of his beast,

rolling Sarah onto her back, spreading her legs as he had back at the inn, and settling between them. The beast clawed at him, making its presence known, but Max suppressed it, dominated, pressed it back into the deep depths of his soul. He'd fought his darker side for centuries, and he would fight it now. Control belonged to the man, not the beast.

His mouth closed down on Sarah's softer one, as he forced himself to be gentle, to reach inside to calm himself. But that kiss quickly went from tender to fiery hot. Their tongues tangled in a seductive dance that turned into a full body sway. The kiss he'd meant to help him slow down, to put restraint in place, simply wasn't enough to satisfy either of them.

"I want you, Max," Sarah announced against his lips, fingers entwined in his hair, urgency lacing her words. "All of you." She reached between their bodies and slid her fingers over his erection before working his zipper with no success. "Take them off."

He hesitated, wanting this, but aware he was about to cross into the land of no return. This was where his willpower would be stretched, his limits strained.

"Now, Max," she ordered, her voice lifting.

Her demands drew laughter from him when he'd never have believed that possible. Not when he felt this depth of passion, not with the beast so close to the surface. No woman had ever done that to him, but Sarah could. Sarah was special. He nipped her lips. "You're very bossy."

She didn't laugh, but her eyes sparkled with mischief. "You haven't seen anything yet," she countered. "Now, get rid of the pants."

His cock pulsed with those words. Sarah had this knack for being both sweet and sexy, meek and powerful, all in one moment. It got him hotter than hot.

Max brushed his lips over hers. "Your wish is my command," he replied, pushing off the bed to stand and undoing the button on his pants. He would have demanded she undress, but she was already doing it; the sight of her jeans sliding down her legs, panties in tow, stilled his actions. She was beautiful, her silky white skin a direct contrast to the ripe red of her aroused nipples, her breasts high and full, stomach flat, hips rounded with womanly curves.

"What's taking so long?" she asked, easing toward him on her knees until she stopped directly in front of him. "And please tell me you have a condom packed in one of those pockets."

"Old battle injury," he said, his eyes tracking the hard peeks of her nipples, the lift of her full breasts. "I shoot blanks."

"Really?" she asked, surprise in her voice.

"Disappointed?" he asked, watching for her reaction his chest tightening as he realized he could never give her a normal life. No kids, no white picket fence.

Her response came quickly. "Not at all," she said, smiling, her gaze sliding up and down his body. "It's perfect. You're perfect."

Max sensed no remorse in her, no loss at the implications of his words. "*You're* perfect," he told her, meaning it. Her body was perfect, but even more so, she was perfect. Perfect for him.

Her hand went to his zipper again but this time with success. Together they shoved his pants and boxers down his legs. Max made quick work of kicking away his clothing, thankful his boots were long gone.

Before he knew her intent, Sarah's soft touch closed around his erection, stealing his breath with the bold action. And with that touch any hope he had of keeping their joining on his terms slid to oblivion, and he didn't give a damn. Sarah leaned into him and tilted her mouth up in an invitation, and he devoured her with greedy pleasure.

He ravished her with his kiss, tasting her deeply, his tongue growing more demanding with each stroke of her hand along his hard length. When he thought he could take no more, Max reached for restraint by claiming control. He filled his hands with her breasts, thumbing her nipples, before pressing her back onto the mattress. Leaning over her, he lapped at her nipples, teasing them with his tongue and teeth, licking and tasting. She moaned, arching her back, murmuring his name with raspy sensuality. So sexy, so alluring. The sound pressed him further to the edge, made him see fire and heat and possessiveness.

For a fleeting moment, he considered lifting her legs over his shoulders and sliding inside her, keeping their bodies distant, his mouth away from the temptation of marking her. But another second flashed by and he couldn't bear moving away from her, couldn't bear separating skin from skin. One instant he was lapping at her nipples, the next he was sliding his cock along the silky wet core of her body, seeking entrance. He sunk into the warm, wet heat that pulled him into the depths of blind passion—passion born of the joining of two mates. Their mutual sighs filled the room as he hit her core, a tantalizing sound of merging pleasures.

His forehead settled against hers, and he drew a shaky breath, emotion rushing over him, a feeling of belonging with Sarah. Their lips lingered close, their bodies intimately joined, unmoving. His chest was tight, his body on fire. He leaned back to look in her eyes, seeking the confirmation that she felt what he did and finding it. Their gazes held and locked, the contact intensifying the connection, the love shared naturally by mates radiating between them. He ran a gentle finger down her cheek and whispered her name. She took his hand in hers and brought it to her lips. Their stares fired into desire, and what was softness and sensuality turned red-hot, combustible.

Suddenly, they were kissing, bodies moving, rocking, swaying. He wanted to go slow, wanted to explore, linger, enjoy what might be the only time he'd ever make love to Sarah. But he couldn't slow down; he couldn't hold back. She was driving him crazy with need. Her body arched into him, her legs wrapping around his thighs to get closer, higher, pull him deeper.

Max thrust into her, harder, faster, and with the build of passion, with the build of release, the beast grew stronger. He felt it, but he couldn't seem to stop moving, couldn't seem to hold back. Sarah. He simply had to have more, had to get deeper. Had to touch her breasts, her hips, her face, her hair. All of her. Any of her. He simply had to have her. Long minutes passed, their lovemaking intense, passionate.

"Max," she gasped between moans, arching into him and stiffening.

He knew she was about to climax and he wanted her pleasure, wanted it as he'd never wanted another woman's pleasure. He kissed her jaw, her lips, her nose. "Come for me, baby," he urged.

"I'm, oh, I'm—" She lost the words as her body erupted in spasms that grabbed at his cock with erotic pressure, tantalizing and explosive. In that moment of pure, white-hot pleasure, Max's teeth elongated, his willpower dissolving. Damn it. Knights only had fangs during mating. He knew this but he'd been sure he could stop it from happening, been sure that centuries of suppressing the beast wouldn't fail him now.

He buried his face in the bed by her neck, fighting the urge to sink his teeth into her shoulder. No! The beast didn't listen. The beast wanted Sarah. Demanded her. He just needed one taste of her. One. Taste.

No! He screamed the word in his head over and over. No!

Max fought the primal urge to claim, fought it with other desires, with the burn of his body's need for release. He plunged deeper into her core, thrusting harder—thrusting faster. But it wasn't enough. The beast kept him on the edge, unable to find completion, wanting him to take more than pleasure. If he didn't find release soon, he'd lose the battle with the beast; he would lose control. He was close to the edge, close to explosion. He just needed a little deeper. Needed to move a little faster.

Desperate, Max raised up on his hands and plunged hard and deep. Once. Twice. And there it was, there was relief, control, satisfaction. He spilled himself inside the depths of her core, her heat consuming him, shaking with the intensity of orgasm. But in that moment, he also forgot those fangs, forgot the monster that passion had brought to life.

Suddenly Sarah's sigh of satisfaction became a scream. Max had shown her the beast within himself, and there was no way to hide the truth.

Chapter 14

"Get off me!" Sarah screamed, her heart about to explode out of her chest. Max had fangs. Fangs! She'd let her guard down and been fooled. She never let down her guard. Not since the day a friend had turned demon and killed her family.

Max held her, his big body still on top of hers; good God, he was still inside her. "Wait. Sarah. Please."

"No!" She kicked and squirmed, but found movement near impossible. Grinding her teeth, she stared up at him. "Let me up."

"Not until you hear me out," he said. "I told you I'm different. I tried to explain before…before we made love."

"Had sex! Just sex!" she shouted, refusing the feelings she had for him. She kicked some more. He grunted and rolled off of her.

Sarah grabbed the sheet and yanked it around her

body, turning to square off with him. "Who are you, Max? What are you?"

"I mean you no harm, Sarah," he said, standing there naked and glorious, his big body powerfully male. "I know you feel that. I know you trust me."

"How can I?" she asked. "How?" But the truth was, even now, she wanted to. Desperately, Sarah prayed Max would give her a reason to make those fangs not matter. But how could he? What would make this better? Nothing. Nothing at all, and damn, it hurt. His betrayal, her past, her life—it all hurt. So she did all she ever knew how to do when that pain bit into her. She pushed back. "My parents were killed by a friend we trusted who was possessed by a demon. You want me to trust a man who tells me he fights demons and then shows signs of being one himself? Tell me how I can do that? Tell me! I'd be a fool to trust you. I was a fool once in my life, and that cost me everything. How can I trust you? Tell me that. How?"

Max digested that news as he would a solid punch to the gut. She'd lost her family to a demon just as he had. He understood that pain, understood the loneliness. To have a close friend be the killer, well, he certainly understood why that would breed distrust. That had to be hell to live with. He wanted to be there for her, to ease her pain. But almost certainly, this demon connection assured that Sarah could never accept him as her mate. Even if he passed this test, his time was short-lived. He couldn't fight the darkness without a mate much longer, and he wouldn't go to the other side. He'd die first. He'd let a Beast take his head and end this before he'd go to the other side.

A decision became clear. Leaving this world with lies between them or even with unspoken words simply wasn't an option. They would only feed the fear and distrust she obviously harbored toward others after the death of her parents.

He stared at her, wanting to speak, but tormented by what he found in her face. Her eyes were wary, accusing. Her back pressed against the wall as if she couldn't get far enough away, the sheet clutched in front of her body. She covered herself as if he were an enemy rather than her mate, her lover. Damn it! Frustration and anger formed within him. Why did it have to be this way?

Snagging his boxers, he pulled them on, trying to make her more comfortable. "This is exactly what I didn't want. I didn't want you to be afraid of me, Sarah. I told you, I'm different, but I'm not dangerous." Okay, that might not be the truth so he added, "Not to you. I'd sooner die than hurt you." That was the truth. The complete truth. He let out a heavy breath. "I was trying to tell you about me, about my people." He held his hand up in frustration. "Things just got out of control."

Her hand shook where it held the sheet in place. "How can I know that, Max? How?"

"Think back to what we've been through. How many times could I have hurt you if I meant you harm? How many times did I save you and your friends?"

"Don't you see?" she asked. "It's not about what you did. It's about secrets. The friend who killed my family—to this day I have no idea if he was ever a friend. Was he always possessed? He seemed normal up to the minute he pulled a gun and shot my family." Her lips pressed together, and she continued as if she couldn't rein in her thoughts, "How do I know you're not with Vars? How do I know you aren't supposed to earn my trust and turn it on me? The demon my family hunted was a serial killer. He possessed human bodies, changing forms with each murder. The police never had a chance of catching him. For all I know, my friend was always working for this demon, telling him every step we took. I've been through too much to see what I just saw and ignore the risks. I've had someone close to me steal everything I knew and loved, and I won't be foolish like that again."

Max's gut clenched at the pain in her voice, in her face. "What happened to the demon?"

"I destroyed that bastard," she said. "And, Max, as much as I've wanted to trust you, if I find out you want to hurt people I care about, hurt anyone for that matter, I'll find a way to stop you."

As much as her need to threaten him tore him up inside, he admired her courage.

He hated the story he had to tell. Inhaling deeply, he made an effort to distance himself from his words. "I lost my parents to the Darkland Beasts. Watched them die right in front of me. They didn't bother converting my parents. They just killed them, drained them dry. My brother was another story. They took his soul, and he became one of them. I watched the transformation. One minute he was my brother—the next, something so evil I didn't even recognize him. I would have turned out like that, too, evil and beyond salvation. But a man came then. He killed the Beasts that didn't run, and gave me back my soul. That was how I became what I am now. How I became a Knight of White. We aren't military, Sarah. We aren't even human. We exist to fight evil."

His chest filled with emotion, and it took him a minute to continue. "That was four hundred years ago. I've spent those long years fighting the Beasts…and finding that battle the reason to keep going." But now, with no hope of light, no hope of Sarah to save his soul, there was no reason to continue. "My journey has been long and it's about to end. Once I see you through this, it's over for me."

Tormented by the prospect of Sarah's rejection, of never having her in his life, his impervious shell threatened to crack. He cut his gaze from Sarah and grabbed his pants and shirt. "I'm going to take a shower. You can leave, but I don't advise it. There have been several attempts on your life. Obviously, the Darklands are partnering with Vars. They'll hunt you down, Sarah. I'll keep you safe if you let me. I told you back at the cabin, I'd have enough faith for both of us. Now I'm afraid you're going to have to find some of your own. But if you do, Sarah, if you reach deep and you find that faith, I won't fail you."

He headed into the bathroom, leaving her alone, knowing she might walk out the door. It was one of the hardest things Max had ever done in his life. He wanted to tie her down and force her to let him protect her, but that wasn't the answer. Not yet at least. He didn't know what he'd do if she walked out that door.

A demon. She had been in the arms of a demon. Sarah laughed, a choked, nervous sound even to her own ears. That was impossible. Max wasn't a demon.

But she'd seen the fangs, she reminded herself. He might feel human and even look human, but so had Kevin, the friend who'd killed her parents. Fangs! Damn it, Max had fangs. Her hand pressed to her stomach, nerves fluttering. She'd never been so confused in her life.

Have faith, Max had said. Her parents had said that often. Every time they'd headed into an investigation, every time things seemed grim. Sarah wasn't sure she knew what faith was anymore. Where had faith gotten her in life? Alone, that was where—looking over her shoulder and afraid of the shadows. Pretending she was afraid of nothing, when she was afraid of everything. Every investigation terrified her. Having others close to her was a two-fold terror. Who would get hurt? Who would turn evil? If someone became possessed, were they evil to start with? Had Kevin been evil? Was Edward? No. She refused to believe that Edward was evil. So where did that leave her?

She inhaled, thinking of what Max had been through in his past. If he was telling the truth, he'd lost his parents as she had lost hers. Or was he simply an enemy playing with her, dragging her into a seductive game to distract her from finding Allen?

She felt as if she was going to be sick. She didn't want Max to be an enemy. He was the first person, in what felt like forever, that she actually wanted to let into her life. With Max, she had the oddest sense of belonging. It didn't matter that they'd just met. Thinking back to the moment he'd walked into the inn, she realized the feeling had been instant.

The very fact that he'd given her the chance to leave spoke volumes. Fangs or no fangs, Max felt safe. He felt right.

Her hand went to her chest, her throat dry, her heart drumming at a fast beat. What had he meant when he'd said his journey was about to end? Why did the idea of his departure bother her so much?

Faith. She rolled the word over in her mind and reached deeper inside than she had in a very long time. Max had protected her and her friends. He'd been hurt doing it, too. He deserved the benefit of the doubt—no, a little faith. He deserved a little faith.

Her eyes slid shut, and for the first time in years, she prayed. She prayed for the strength to act, for the wisdom to know what to do. Seconds passed and she let that prayer take root in her mind, let it slide through her body and soothe. She opened her heart and her soul; she prayed that it was the right thing to do.

And when she was done, she acted. She didn't give herself time to think, not even time to dress. If she did either of those things, she might talk herself out of what she was about to do. Instead, she wrapped the sheet snugly around her and marched to the bathroom.

She needed answers and she intended to get them.

The water was running. Perfect. Somehow, his being in the shower made him the prisoner and offered her control. And control was exactly what she was after right now. She reached for the doorknob and turned, letting out a sigh as it opened. Steam poured out of the room and clung to her skin. She swatted it away and moved forward, sitting down on the toilet.

"Max," she said, struggling a bit for her voice.

The curtain moved instantly, his head appearing around the side. "Sarah?" He disappeared again and the water turned off.

An instant concern formed. She'd meant for him to stay in the shower. Of course, he wouldn't. Maybe she should have done a little thinking before acting after all. A naked Max would mean distraction in a big way. She grabbed a towel and shoved it behind the barrier. He snatched it, and a second later the curtain moved back to expose him, dripping wet, in a too-small towel. Wet hair clung to his high cheekbones, to his muscular chest. A droplet of water ran down his stellar abdominals, and her gaze followed it as it disappeared inside his sunken belly button.

"Sarah?" He repeated her name as a question, and the one word held vulnerability she didn't think a man so strong could show.

The emotion in his voice drew her attention, and she searched his face, probing for the true man beneath the warrior shell. What she found in his eyes took her breath away. Torment and pain laced those hazel eyes. Eyes speckled with yellow. Eyes she loved, she realized.

Lonely hurt eyes that still held warmth where another's might be cold. Hope flooded her body then— hope that touched deep in her soul. Hope that her trust in Max hadn't been wrong.

A surprising realization took hold. "I'm not afraid of you. I should be, but I'm not."

He reached for her and she held up a staying hand, afraid now, but not of him. Of herself. Of forgetting what she'd seen in that bedroom, and forgetting her caution, her questions.

Frustration flashed across his face and a hint of fresh pain. It was almost enough to send her into his arms, but she forced herself to remain in her seat. "I would have

walked—no run—out the door and never looked back
if I didn't find a little of that faith you asked for." Her
voice softened, holding a bit of defeat over the obvious.
"But, Max. You have to know this fang thing is messing
with my head. If you aren't a demon and you aren't
human, what are you?"

He closed his eyes, his lips tight. She could feel his
hesitation to the point of almost tasting it. He didn't
want to explain. He didn't want to tell her. That meant
whatever he had to say wasn't good. She hugged herself,
seconds passing as she waited, before his lashes lifted,
water clinging to them.

"Immortal, Sarah. I belong to Raphael's army of
demon hunters."

She could barely breathe when she heard those
words. "Raphael."

He nodded. "Yes. That's why I knew that legend had
to be relevant to what was going on in that town."

His urgency to know which archangel was involved
in the legend made sense now. Still, this seemed a fairy
tale, not reality. But then, fangs and Hell Hounds
seemed a nightmare. Fangs. Max had fangs.

"Why would an archangel give his army fangs?"

"There is only one time when a Knight possesses
fangs."

No way. "Are you telling me every time you have
sex—"

"Not sex," he said, his voice lower, his eyes hotter.
"Mating."

She sucked in a breath at the sound of that word. Unbidden, a hint of excitement fluttered in her chest that she
couldn't begin to understand. "What does that mean?"

"There is only one mate for our kind, and we know that person when we find them. The desire to bind them to us for all of time is primal, instinctive—a matter of survival. The male marks the female's shoulder with his teeth, and with that bite comes the melding of souls. The two are linked together for all eternity."

Her body reacted to his words of its own accord, completely out of her control. Heat pooled low in her limbs and her nipples tingled. The images she played in her head were erotic, seductive, far more appealing than they should be. Most of all, they felt right. They felt like what was supposed to happen between her and Max.

This was crazy. Insane. Mating? Bound for all of eternity. Or was it? She knew there were things beyond this realm of existence. She dealt with spirits all the time. And there was no doubt she felt a connection to Max. Lord help her, she felt as if she knew him beyond time. As if they'd been lovers in another life, or something. She knew him. She was Max's mate? Maybe it was true. Maybe that explained the need to trust him. The idea of having someone close to her, someone to fill the emptiness, both excited and frightened her. But someone to love was someone to lose, as well.

"So if you bite me…" she said, hugging herself, her teeth worrying her bottom lip. Had she ever been this confused in her life? "What exactly happens?"

His response came fast and hard. "Nothing, because I won't damn you to my future, Sarah. I won't. I only told you this because you saw the fangs, and as long as I'm around you I can't promise I won't feel the urge to take you again." Without warning, he stepped out of the tub and stared down at her. "Which means I can't touch you again."

An emotional door slammed shut in Max, and she felt it like a punch, but she saw the look in his eyes a second before he walked away. He wanted her, even needed her. She jumped to her feet, following him, not about to be dismissed that easily. She didn't know if she wanted to be Max's mate; it was all too overwhelming. But one thing was for sure—she wanted all the facts. She rounded the corner to find him already buttoning his jeans and started to confront him. He didn't give her time.

His hand ran over his wet hair, pressing it away from his face. "Don't ask anything else, because I don't even know how to answer you."

"You have to answer me," she argued. "I deserve answers and you know it. Damn it, Max. Tell me what is going on!"

"Fine," he said. "You want to know?" He didn't give her time to answer. "When I was saved, my soul retained a dark stain. I've battled that stain for longer than most. These Knights I fight with are not the original Knights. Almost all of those who were first created eventually fell to the darkness inside them."

"What does that mean?"

"It means they turned into the very thing they battled—they became Darkland Beasts. Since then, a new breed of Knights has been formed, and they now have a chance to erase the stain on their souls. If they find their one chosen mate in time, the mating will imprison the demon side of the Knight and save him forever. But I have fought this battle four centuries now. More and more, I can't control my dark side." His chest expanded as he looked away from her as if ashamed. "I couldn't control myself when we were together. I don't know what I am capable of." He looked at her again, his eyes stormy with emotion. "One of the biggest fears a Knight has when he finds his mate is biting her and killing her. I'm hundreds of years older than any of these Knights I fight with. There is far less human in me than there was in them when they claimed their mates."

She sucked in a breath. "You're telling me I could save your life if we mate, but you could kill me in the process?"

"Don't worry, Sarah. I won't be biting you. Mating is not an option. It's simply too late for me, anyway. I broke a sacred rule and now I'm being tested. If I fail this test, I go to hell. If you are linked to me, you will, too. Which is exactly why I can't touch you again. And I'll want to, Sarah, just as you will want to touch me. Passion between mates is as natural as breathing."

If she believed all of this, and the fangs seemed to make it pretty believable, then the passion between mates made sense. It explained why she couldn't keep her mind on her job. Sarah swallowed hard, trying to take all of this in. As for going to hell, she didn't know if Max meant literally or not, but she knew she didn't want to find out. And where the biting her shoulder thing had seemed rather erotic a moment before, possible death-by-fangs certainly zapped the passion out of the idea.

"Tell me about the test and the rule you broke."

Max didn't respond. His body tensing, his expression registered alertness. A second passed and he turned away from her, his attention fixed on the door as if he knew something she didn't. "Get dressed," he said without looking at her, a second before a knock sounded.

Max walked to the window and looked outside.

Sarah's heart pounded as she ran to do as he said, fear making her heart race. "Who is it?"

"It's Jag," he said, tapping the window and holding up a finger. "Our leader."

Sarah had her clothes in her hand. "That's good then, right?"

He laughed at that, though it sounded a bit forced. "Yes. He's one of the good guys."

"I'll go into the bathroom and change so you can let him in." A thought occurred. "Wait. Was he in town? Will he know about Edward and Cathy? About the sheriff?"

"Probably, yes."

She rushed at him then, almost tripping over the sheet. Max grabbed her and kept her from going down. "Ask him for an update. Please." Her hands clung to his arms. "I'll wait right here."

He looked as if he might argue and then he nodded. "Give me a second."

"Thank you, Max," she said, her stomach in knots. "I just really need to know they're okay."

His knuckle gently brushed her cheek. "I understand."

The act was tender, sweet. It touched Sarah inside, beyond simple skin-to-skin contact. She watched as he turned and exited, rocking on her heels and hugging herself as she waited. Thankful when he returned after only a minute.

"Cathy and Marisol are working together on Edward's situation, and the sheriff is healed."

Relief washed over her at the news. Cathy and Edward were still alive. "Sheriff Jenson is healed?" she asked, surprised. "Completely?"

"Marisol is good."

She blinked. "Yes. I can't quite get my mind wrapped around such a talent. I don't know if I will believe it until I see it." Her gaze went to his stomach where the injury had disappeared. "Okay, I believe it, but I'll still feel better when I see the sheriff up and about myself."

"So far no one has anything on the Shadow Masters. I worked the Net myself while you were sleeping and found nothing. Cathy sent word to remind you to call her mother. But she said not to bring up the Shadow Masters on the phone. It's too dangerous. We need to go see her."

"I hope she can help," Sarah said, worry etching her features. "I'll call as soon as I get dressed."

"Your shirt has blood all over it," Max told her and inclined his head at the closet. "I brought your bag in while you were sleeping."

She hadn't been taken care of in, well, forever. It was a small gesture, but it meant something to her. "Thank you," she said, her eyes locking with his. She started to turn and hesitated. "There can't be double standards in this relationship."

A frowned touched his eyes. "What?"

"If I'm going to have faith, you can't go losing yours. It doesn't work that way." She didn't wait for a response, pushing to her toes and brushing her lips quickly over his. Then she headed to the closet to grab her bag before disappearing into the bathroom.

She shut the door and stared into the mirror. Her hair was a mess, and aside from the smudged mascara under her right eye, her face bore no makeup. She was a mess on the outside and confused on the inside. But she also felt a sense of belonging she hadn't felt for a long time. A sense of needing and being needed.

They'd figure out this test he faced, just as they'd figure out how to save Allen, and the town of Nowhere. They had to. Failure wasn't an option.

Suddenly, she realized Kate had been silent since she woke, despite previously desperate attempts to communicate with Sarah. Her mind stretched to that communication. Kate had told her something—something important. A place maybe. A location. Somewhere Allen was going. Sarah dropped her sheet and stepped into the shower. By the time the hot water poured over her, she was lost in her thoughts, desperate to find the clue lurking in the depths of her mind. She had to remember…before it was too late.

Chapter 15

Once Sarah entered the bathroom, Max spent the next few minutes pacing the room. Jag had disappeared, no doubt orbing to some distant place, his return certain at any moment. Frustration welled in Max's gut over his situation. Damn this test. Why give him some secret test that could doom him to hell and deliver him to his mate at the same time? Why? And the thought of dooming his mate to hell, as well, was unbearable. He began pacing again, scrubbing the now overgrown stubble on his jaw.

A knock sounded on the door and Max reached for it, his frustrations funneled into the action as he yanked it open, biting back angry words of confrontation. A good thing because Jag was no longer alone. Karen, his mate, stood beside him.

"We thought you might be hungry," Karen said, smiling as if she didn't notice the scowl on Max's face, her blue eyes twinkling. Blond and beautiful, she was strikingly light in appearance and personality—a direct contrast to the dark edge that clung to Jag's presence—yet somehow the perfect match for him. She held up the bag to make sure he saw the name on the side, and added, "I know how you love Big Macs."

Max cast Jag a disgruntled look. He didn't make a habit of confronting Jag—he respected him too damn much—but right now this test and Jag's Big Mac party were pushing the wrong buttons. Very personal buttons. "I know what you're doing and it's not okay." Max ground out the words between his teeth. "I don't want to pull Sarah into my world when I don't even know if I'm going to be here for her."

"You will be," Jag said, "because I refuse to let you fail this test."

"That makes two of us," Karen said, shooing him with her dainty little hand. "Now, step aside. I'm hungry and I want to eat." She grinned. "And meet Sarah."

Max slid his teeth together and obediently did as he was instructed, easing back into the room, allowing Jag and Karen to enter. But then his restraint snapped; the agitation that had pushed him to pace only moments before bubbled over into actions. Max shut the door in a near slam and whirled around to find Karen on the bed pulling food from the bag, and Jag leaning on the dresser.

"How am I going to pass this damn test when I don't even know what it is?"

"By believing you can."

The softly spoken answer came not from Jag, but from Sarah, who had entered the room as he spoke. She paused just outside the bathroom wearing slim-cut black jeans and a red T-shirt. Freshly showered, her hair damp, her face fresh, she looked lovely—like an angel. His angel. Max felt his frustration melt away as he looked at her. Felt the calmness take hold. She did that to him. She brought him a peace he hadn't felt in centuries.

He watched her closely, expecting her to focus on Jag in awe as most people did when they first met him. Jag had a way of drawing both male and female attention. It was an aura of power he oozed, a bit of magic even. But Sarah wasn't looking at Jag. She was staring at Max, as lost in him as he was in her. God, this connection he shared with her made him whole. He felt it as surely as he knew this was what had been missing all his life. He wanted to believe he could pass this test. He did. Wanted to believe there was enough human left in him to deserve to stand beside his fellow Knights, as well. To deserve Sarah and mate without harming her. But he'd killed a human; his beast had dictated that action. Four hundred years of fighting the beast had taken its toll and beaten down the man.

Out of his peripheral vision, Max saw Jag cross one booted foot over the other, and he knew Jag's action was meant to gain his attention. "Smart woman," his leader murmured softly.

Sarah glanced at Jag. "Actually," she corrected him, "my mother was the smart one." Her attention went back to Max. "She said that doubt breeds weakness and bad choices."

Without warning, Sarah's stomach rumbled rather loudly, shifting the mood in the room. Sarah's cheeks flushed red as her hand pressed to her middle. She laughed, the sound laced with embarrassment. "Sorry about that. I guess the smell of food is getting to me."

Karen started laughing, too. "I heard that. Sounds urgent." She patted the bed. "I'm Karen, Sarah. Jag's mate and wife."

Jag offered a tiny bow. "Nice to meet you, Sarah."

"Nice to meet you," Sarah said, studying him a moment with interest.

"Come sit with me," Karen ordered playfully, bringing Sarah's attention back to her. "I won't have you starving on my clock."

A smile touched Sarah's lips. "I love McDonald's," she confessed, claiming the spot next to Karen and reaching in a bag for a fry. "Hmm. I don't know if they are really good or I'm just really hungry."

"I brought choices," Karen offered. "Nuggets, double cheeseburgers or Big Macs."

"Big Mac," Sarah said, accepting a burger and inhaling the smell. "Love these things."

Karen smiled and eyed Max, a Big Mac in his hand. "You know you want it." She turned to Sarah. "He loves them, too."

"I'll grab some drinks," Jag said. "I know what everyone else likes. Any preferences, Sarah?"

"Coke," Sarah, "but I'll settle for Pepsi."

Jag looked at Max. "Why don't you help me?"

Max glanced at Jag and silently told him again, he knew what his leader was up to. Jag wanted to give the women some alone time. At this point, Max didn't see the point in arguing. Jag had expertly orchestrated Operation Bring Sarah Into The Inner Circle, and it was working like magic. Sarah and Karen were getting along as if they were longtime friends.

Max took a minute to fully dress, and for any Knight, that included arming himself with blades. Once outside, he expected Jag to corner him about Sarah. He quickly learned that assessment was wrong.

Jag pulled out his phone. "I need to check in with Des one last time before he's in Nowhere and I can't reach him. Right before I left, I sensed Adrian's presence."

Two things instantly crossed Max's mind. (1) He was damn impressed that Jag could sense Adrian's presence. Jag couldn't have done that before now. Their leader was growing stronger each day, and that meant the Knights were, as well. (2) He'd been around four centuries, and he knew the rules that guided those not of this world.

Max gave Jag a puzzled expression. "He's not allowed to interfere with activity in this realm any more than Salvador is," Max pointed out. "So what's he up to?"

"His usual no good, but at least I have Salvador alerted. If Adrian crosses any lines, Salvador will be watching. Salvador can't intervene unless certain lines are crossed. He has to work through us."

"Did he offer any insight into Vars's history?" Max asked, ready for any bit of information he could sink his teeth into.

"He uses humans for personal entertainment, subjugates them to stroke his ego," Jag offered. "He's concerned about us being lured to Nowhere by Adrian."

Max filled in the blanks. "I guess we all are. It's pretty obvious Adrian had chosen it as his battlefield."

"Exactly," Jag said. "Which means we need to turn the tables on the enemy and turn their trap into our trap."

Max grinned. "I like the way you think, Great White leader."

Jag punched the buttons on the phone, and Max moved toward the soda machine, allowing Jag the privacy to talk to his second-in-charge. He gave himself a moment to think about what had to be done. A great battle faced them all. He had to make some tough choices and ensure that Sarah was safe if he didn't make it to the other side of this war. And he damn sure wouldn't take her to hell with him if that was where he ended up. Nor would he let her live here on earth blaming herself for not saving him. He wasn't a fool. He could see she lived her life with the guilt of her parents' death.

No. Max had to get this under control and focus on the battle ahead. He'd push Sarah firmly away, but not so far that he couldn't protect her. There wasn't another option. He had to do this. But damn, he wasn't going to like it. This was going to be a little taste of living hell.

Sarah watched the door shut as the men exited the room and immediately turned to Karen. "What can you tell me about this test Max has to face?"

"Regretfully," Karen said, "not much. The test comes from above Jag, and neither of us were told the details." She held up a finger. "But I can tell you Max will be asked to do nothing he is not capable of achieving. His success, not his failure, is the goal. And frankly, I believe that you, as his mate, came to him now as a guide, to support him and help him conquer this test. If that's not proof he's intended to succeed, I don't know what is."

"So you believe I'm Max's mate, too?"

Karen gave her a curious look. "Don't you?"

Sarah hesitated only an instant, deciding there wasn't time for anything but directness, her heart telling her all she had to know. "I do," she admitted. "It's a little overwhelming to believe something like this is real, but I know it is. I felt the connection the minute I met him." She considered the situation a minute, and then asked, "If you can't tell me what this test is—can you tell me why Max is being tested? He said he broke a rule, but didn't seem inclined to explain the details."

A conflicted look flashed across Karen's features. "I'm afraid I'd be out of line to comment. I think this needs to be something Max tells you."

"But you know."

Karen nodded. "Yes. I know what he did. I just shouldn't say."

Sarah's shoulders slumped in defeat. "I suspected you would say that." Still, she wasn't willing to give up without some form of information. "Can you confirm he goes to hell if he fails the test?"

"That's true," Karen replied softly, the words touched with regret.

Sarah felt that confirmation like someone ripping her heart out. "I just barely met the man and the idea of losing him feels like torture."

"Time is irrelevant," Karen explained. "Your soul is connected to his. Max is your other half. In this lifetime or another, you would never have felt complete satisfaction without him. Don't run from the connection. He needs you too much. Accept your bond and you'll save him."

Karen tugged her shirt to the side to expose her shoulder. "This is the mating mark you will receive after he bites you." She quickly added, "If you make the choice to mate."

Sarah blinked, shocked at the star which not only looked like a tattoo but seemed familiar in a very personal way. "That star—it's related to King Solomon, right?"

Karen let her shirt slide back into place as surprise registered on her face. "It is. We call it Solomon's Star, though in his time it was named after his father, David."

"The Star of David," Sarah said.

"Right," Karen confirmed. "Unfortunately, Solomon's service ended with betrayal and he turned to dark powers. We call it *The Star of Solomon* as a reminder that Jag must protect humanity without corruption."

Sarah could barely believe what she was hearing. "I...this is crazy." Karen gave her an inquisitive look and Sarah continued, "My parents were killed by a demon. When I finally destroyed it, I used Solomon's magical writings to do it." Her chest tightened. "Just not soon enough to save my family." She shook her head. "This is so strange. The connection to Solomon seems too big to be a coincidence."

Karen's expression held certainty. "Everything happens for a reason, though you may not know that reason until much later. You were guided to Solomon's writings for a reason. I have no doubt you deserved justice and you received it. I've found the higher powers can't always stop the evil forces, but they can guide us to do it. I don't pretend to understand all of this but I know this. Your destiny is with us. We are your family now, Sarah. In time I hope you feel that, too." She touched Sarah's arm. "One day I'll share with you how the Knights became my family."

Family. She forgot what that felt like. All these years of doubting, of losing that faith Max had spoken of, and there seemed to be a higher force guiding her all along. Her mother had always said there was. Deep inside, Sarah knew that all along.

Male voices rumbled outside, signaling the men could be returning. Quickly, Sarah blurted out a rather embarrassing question weighing on her mind. "One more thing. Max said he was worried about the mating process. He said he could kill me. That there isn't enough human left in him to bite me and not turn into a Beast."

Karen rolled her eyes. "They all think that and it's simply not the case. And, yes, I know Max is an old, old man." She crinkled her nose. "He acts like it sometimes, too. He hovers over everyone in protective mode all the time. Especially the younger Knights." Her expression turned thoughtful and she continued before Sarah could ask more about Max's "old man" tendencies. "I've given some consideration to why mating requires they bite their intended mate, considering biting a human and taking blood could turn them into a Beast for good."

Sarah absorbed the last bit of information with some apprehension. Once the Knight bit a human, he converted to demon. She suppressed a shiver. "And what did you come up with?"

"I think it's because they must believe they are worthy of their duty to continue this journey they are on. If they can't believe in themselves, why should anyone else? He's been through a lot and so have you. But you have each other now. It will work out. He can't hurt you. He'd die to save your life."

She believed that. All of it. Max had already saved

her too many times to count. "This all makes sense,"
Sarah said, thinking of just how much Max didn't be-
lieve in his worthiness, relieved he wasn't possessed.
That he couldn't turn on her. She smiled. "Thank you.
I feel better already." She blushed a bit and then asked
one last thing, "Those teeth of Max's are pretty long.
Does it hurt? Were you worried at all when he bit you?"

"Not at all," Karen said, and grinned. "It's actually
quite sexy. It's a sensual bonding of body and soul you
only get to live once. Enjoy it."

Sarah smiled. "I guess that explains why I got all
warm all over when he described the process."

"Oh, yeah," Karen agreed. "That's why, all right. The
natural attraction between mates is quite yummy, isn't it?"

The door opened, and Karen and Sarah quickly ended
their private conversation, sharing a female look of understanding, two kindred spirits. They'd become fast
friends, and Sarah couldn't be more pleased about that fact.
Suddenly, in the middle of a firestorm of danger, Sarah felt
a bit of hope. The kind she hadn't felt in a very long time.
Max wasn't a demon. He was connected to an archangel,
in fact. And he needed her. If there had been anything she'd
gotten out of this talk with Karen, it was that.

Max's ears filled with the women's laughter as he
pushed open the door to the room. His eyes caught on
Sarah's, his heart squeezing because he'd just made a
hard decision. One that forced him to pull away from her.

He cut his gaze away, afraid she would read the distress in his eyes. Intentionally Max settled on the floor,
against the wall, putting distance between them. Jag
passed out drinks and then joined him.

The two men sat there, eating in silence, listening to the women bond as Karen shared details about Jaguar Ranch. Changing subjects, Karen shifted the conversation to Sarah's personal life. "How long have you been able to talk to spirits?"

"Actually, they talk to me," Sarah said. "I can't really talk back, though I try. I was twelve when it started. The same age as my mother and her mother before her. I have an older brother, but he's normal and, believe me, he likes it that way."

"Interesting that only the females carry the gift," Karen said. "Des's mate, Jessica, can sense evil. A person you and I might think seems perfectly nice will put her nerves on edge. She's remarkably accurate, too."

"Really?" Sarah said. "She'd be great to have around on an investigation."

"You won't get her without Des right by her side," Karen commented and eyed Jag. "Like Jag, he's quite protective."

Max watched Sarah closely as Karen talked, understanding how Des felt. He wanted to protect Sarah. Exactly the reason he had to push her away. Part of him said claiming her would contain his dark side, and that passing the test would then be ensured. But the other part of him, the part that logic ruled, knew he couldn't take a risk with Sarah's future.

"You've heard nothing from Kate since Marisol helped you sleep?" Jag asked, his long legs stretched in front of him as he reached for a bag and pulled out a second burger.

Sarah shook her head. "Nothing yet."

"What does that mean?" Karen questioned, her expression concerned. "Is something wrong with her? Did the demon spirits get to her?"

"I don't think it's anything like that," Sarah assured her. "Spirits only communicate when they have something important to say. My guess is the information she had before was time-sensitive. It's too late for it to matter now."

"That doesn't sound good," Karen mused. "It must have been important. Why else would demon spirits try to stop the communication?"

"You think Allen has the stones already?" Jag asked.

"I don't know," Sarah said, leaning forward to set her drink on the nightstand. "But Cathy mentioned that the ritual Vars would need to perform should be held on a full moon. That gives us only a little more than a week to track down Allen. Between Cathy's mother and Kate, I'm praying we get some leads." Her lips thinned slightly. "Kate was trying to tell me something about a location last night. I remember that much, but nothing more. And even if I remember the location, I don't remember the relevance it has."

"If it were still important, Kate would tell you again though, right?" Max asked.

"That's usually how it works," she confirmed. "The spirits are quite forceful and determined when they want me to understand a particular detail. Then again, I have this nagging feeling whatever she told me last night was important, and she can't, or won't, contact me again right now. She might be afraid these demon spirits will hurt me again."

"The full moon will be here before we know it," Jag pointed out. "We have nothing to go on and only a short time to find answers." He discarded half a burger into a bag, and pushed to his feet. "We should get going."

"I hope Cathy is right about the full moon," Karen said. "It seems that Vars has left us more time to counter his threat than I would have expected."

"It's not a long time when we have no clues," Max reminded her. "And Vars didn't intend for anyone to catch on to his plan."

"I'll call Cathy's mom," Sarah offered. "We can talk to her about the timelines to confirm Cathy's thoughts. I'll try to get her to talk on the phone, though. I think it's about a three-hour drive to Dallas from here."

Karen reached out and touched Sarah's hand. "Jag has a few special talents himself. When you make that call tell her you'll be right over. As in *right* over. No travel time. No drive."

Sarah blinked. "What? How?"

A smile touched Karen's lips. "Jag has this nifty little ability to transport through space in a blink of an eye. Unfortunately, he can transport only two at once. I'll get back to the ranch and help research the Shadow Masters while Jag takes you two to see Cathy's mother. I believe Des and a team of Knights should already be in Nowhere by now, so you can feel confident your friends will be well looked after. Des is one of our best Knights."

Sarah's eyes were wide as she glanced at Max. "Can *you* do that?"

"Ah, no," he said. "If I could, I'd have gotten us the hell out of Nowhere a long time before I did."

"You know," she commented, "it's kind of nice not to be the only one who's different. Around you all, I feel almost normal." Max's eyes held hers, and beside him, he could feel Jag's approval. Jag had done this on purpose, trying to motivate Max to conquer this test by letting him see what life could be like when the test was behind him. But what Jag didn't understand was that Max had to look out for Sarah—in best case and worst case scenarios. He had to be sure he was on the other side of this test before he pulled her close and kept her there.

Karen and Jag departed, leaving a file behind with all the research Karen and Jessica had done so far on Vars and various other topics that they thought might be helpful. Max rested against the door, keeping his distance from Sarah as she spoke on the phone with Cathy's mother, Sheryl.

"Okay," Sarah said after ending the call. "We're set. She expects us and she's willing to help. Of course, she's worried about Cathy. If we don't convince Sheryl that her daughter is safe, she'll take off after her." Her gaze probed his features. "You look tired. You didn't sleep at all, did you?"

He shrugged. "I wanted to be alert in case I needed to call Marisol back for you."

"Thank you, Max," she said softly. "I hate that you did that, though. I can see you're tired. You need rest."

She stood and he prayed she'd keep her distance. Especially since her concern touched him, weakening his resolve to push her away. No one worried about him. No one. Not even in his human life. It had always been his brother, the heir to his father's title, that his parents had worried for.

"I'll rest when this is over," he said, his voice low, a bit gruff from emotion. She took another step—she was too close. He held up a staying hand. "Stop. Sarah." He inhaled her soft feminine scent. It wasn't perfume that teased his senses, it was the sweetness of Sarah, his mate, his woman. "I told you I can't be near you."

"And I told you I'm not afraid of you."

She took another step and he acted out of desperation to keep his resolve, acted before he talked himself out of it. He gently shackled her arms with enough force to startle her, maneuvering her so that he placed her back against the wall.

Max pinned Sarah's hands over her head, his thighs framing hers, trapping her legs, his hips pressed snugly against hers. Instantly, his groin tightened, desire licking at his limbs, at his cock—his willpower fading away. But he had to be strong, to let her see his dark side, and not allow himself to cave to temptation.

His mouth lingered above her ear, his primal side alive, hungry for her. "Fear me or you're a fool," he rasped softly.

"You can't hurt me," she countered, her voice quivering ever so slightly. "You said so. Karen said so, too."

He leaned back and looked her in the eyes. "I lied. Think about it, Sarah. What if there isn't enough human left in me to properly mate? What if I bite you and the beast takes too much blood and kills you?"

Seconds ticked by. She narrowed her gaze on him, her eyes full of confusion, her scrutiny intense. Her voice low, taut. "This isn't working, Max. I told you I can sense your emotions, just like I do the spirits that communicate with me. You're lying and you hate yourself for it. Why? Why are you doing this?"

"You might know the human, little Sarah," he purred, nipping her lobe with his teeth, "but you don't know the beast."

Her chin lifted in defiance, but her voice quavered. "You're not a Beast."

"Are you sure?" he asked, leaning back to let her see the challenge in his expression. "I don't know what Karen told you but look into my eyes, Sarah. See the yellow? Did you know many of the Beasts have yellow in their red eyes? I'm so close to my dark side, even my physical appearance is changing."

She shook her head, rejecting his words. "Lots of people—*human* people—have yellow in their eyes, Max."

"But those humans aren't four hundred years old with a soul as black as hell. You want to know why I'm being tested?" He felt a muscle jump in his jaw, his admission hard to muster. "I killed a human, Sarah." He gave her no time to respond. "I killed a man and I don't even remember doing it. The beast had total, complete control. I. Don't. Remember."

He dropped her arms, forcing himself to take a step back from her, hating the tears he saw welling in her eyes. "So now you know. I'm no different than the demon that took your parents and your friend. I killed, too."

She hugged herself, her body shaking, though she gave him a steady look, her eyes pinning his in a probing stare. "Why did you kill this person?"

"Who and why doesn't matter."

Her voice raised in demand. "Why, Max?"

A knock sounded on the door. "Jag's back. We need to go."

Awareness rushed over Max—Beasts. They never attacked in a public place without killing all witnesses. The hotel was in the middle of open country, which left them exposed to a Darkland attack.

"Who, Max?" Sarah persisted, unaware of Max's shift of attention to the imminent threat. She turned to the door as she said, "I'll ask Jag."

Sarah flipped the lock and Max grabbed her, tossing her behind him, and not as gently as he would have liked. He simply wanted her alive and well, out of harm's way.

He flung open the door, blades already drawn, finding Jag in heavy combat with the Beasts. Max didn't hesitate. This is what he did—what he was born to do. He attacked.

Chapter 16

Sarah found herself stumbling and falling to the hotel floor, stunned to have been shoved away by Max. Even more stunned to see him pull his blades and charge out the door. Something told her she was about to meet a Beast up close and personal, and after those Hounds, she didn't want to do it unarmed.

Pushing to her feet, she scrambled toward the closet where she'd seen Max's bag. He'd have weapons, she was sure of it. She had taken only a few steps when a snarl drew her attention. She turned, her eyes going wide at the creature standing in the doorway—with half its face distorted, and one eye bigger than the other. She noted the yellowish red eyes, and her stomach clenched as she recalled Max's yellow-flecked eyes. She barely had time to take in the vinyl-looking suit the Beast wore, the long fangs, and wild mass of hair, before the Beast stumbled forward, Max on its back.

"Lock yourself in the bathroom," Max yelled, as he landed on the ground, on top of the Beast.

Sarah darted to the closet, instead, to search for a gun. Adrenaline pumped through her body with such force she could feel her stomach in her chest. She couldn't imagine how Max could take the Beast's head in this tiny room. He'd never have the room to swing wide enough. A gun would at least slow the Beast down long enough to drag it out of here. She hoped.

With desperation in her actions, she grabbed the bag in the closet and dug, relief washing over her as she found a loaded Glock. Her relief faded as she turned to find Max's back to her. She couldn't fire at the Beast without hitting Max. Sarah held the gun in ready position, searching for an opportunity; there just wasn't one.

"Jag!" she screamed, and repeated his name several times, praying for help. A good move because suddenly Jag was there. He came up behind the Beast and wrapped his arms around him. A second later he orbed out of the room, taking the Beast with him.

Max whirled around, eyes wild with concern as he focused on Sarah. "Tell me you're okay."

"I am!" She pointed. "Go help Jag!"

Max was on the move before she ever finished her sentence. She ran after him, clutching the gun—a tiny comfort she embraced wholeheartedly. But, thankfully, she didn't need it. When she joined them, Max and Jag had already destroyed the enemies, the last one going up in flames as she watched, before turning to ash. Her eyes went wide as she realized their fancy vinyl-looking suits turned to ash, too. She didn't ask how. She knew how. Magic.

Jag scanned the surrounding area as he and Max quickly sheathed their weapons. "I don't see any witnesses, but I'm going to check closer to be certain. We may need Marisol to wipe some memories."

Max inhaled and scrubbed his jaw. His voice was low, tense. "I know it's crazy, but I had the distinct feeling William was here."

Jag considered Max for a moment. Sarah didn't know who William was, but she could tell he was important to Max.

"Never ignore your senses," Jag responded, offering no further insight to clear up William's identity for Sarah.

Jag continued, "They came for your woman."

The sound of Jag calling her Max's woman sent a dart of heat through her limbs, despite her confused emotions about Max right now. She'd seen the Beasts, seen their eyes. She'd endured Max's assurance that he, too, was a Beast. It was hard not to feel a bit of apprehension, even fear.

She inhaled and forced herself to focus on the reason for the attack, not the personal side of this situation. She could see why the Beasts would want her dead. "They don't want Kate to talk to me," she whispered, the gun easing to her side.

Jag's eyes narrowed on Sarah, his stare potent, packing a punch. "Know this, Sarah," he said softly. "You are far more than a link to information. Max has resisted the call of his beast when others have not. His soul is a prize to our enemy. Destroying you would take away his hope of ever escaping the darkness—it would destroy him." His gaze shifted back to Max. "Which is why you had to save Jessica that day, Max. Had you let her die, Des would be gone now. We both know he lived too close to his beast." A second passed, then another, tension crackling in the air. "Don't forget what you did for your fellow Knight, your brother-in-arms. I won't, nor will Des. And I assure you, Salvador won't, either."

Jag walked away then, leaving Sarah and Max to face each other. Their eyes locked. Sarah felt the contact from head to toe and deeper—in her soul. He didn't speak, and she knew he was waiting for some sort of reaction from her. She couldn't find words no matter how hard she tried. There was so much to take in and try to understand. She didn't want to say the wrong thing.

Moments ticked by, and Max made a frustrated sound. "Pack up," he said. "I want the van loaded so we're mobile if needed." She felt the bitterness lacing his words and stepped backward with the impact. He'd wanted something from her, though she wasn't sure what. Something she hadn't given. He was confusing her. One minute, he made love to her, the next he pushed her away. Now, he seemed to want her to come to him.

Breaking eye contact, she turned away to do as he said, heading to the room to be alone with her internal struggles. She had to think. It was as simple as that. Images of those Beasts taunted her. The idea of one of them controlling Max made her almost sick. She could see that he was close to the edge; she'd even sensed it while he was fighting. There had been a primal ferocity to him while he fought, whereas Jag had seemed to be more warrior than Beast. Deep in her heart, Sarah knew that if she didn't complete this mating soon, it would be too late for Max. He wouldn't last much longer.

God, how she wanted to talk to Karen again, to understand more about mating. She needed more time to get to know Max, too, to understand him and his world. Sarah looked skyward. *Give me a little time. Please. And then let me make the right choices.* Sarah let her hands fall to her lap and ran her palms down her jeans. If she caused anyone else to get hurt, she'd be the one who deserved to be in the ground. She'd certainly be living in her own personal form of hell.

With Jag in between her and Max, his hand on each of their arms, the three of them appeared at their destination—Cathy's mother's home, on the front porch.

As Jag had promised Sarah, their travel experience was uneventful, and she found herself staring at the door of Sheryl's home. Despite the ease of the experience, her nerves were still rattled from the events back at the hotel. And despite Max being a big part of what caused those nerves, her first reaction was to look at Max, to share this new experience with him. She received a guarded look in return, an expression that was shielded, but no doubt cold. She'd pushed him away; now he pushed her away. They seemed to be having a tug-of-war, and she didn't like it. Unbidden, a feeling of loss washed over her—fear that she'd lost him when she'd not even found him fully yet. This didn't work for her. She had to clear the air and soon.

Doing her best to shake off the way his coldness bothered her, Sarah quickly eyed her surroundings, concerned that the neighbors might have seen them "pop" into view. But no worries—she found the porch enclosed and hidden from easy viewing.

"Has anyone ever caught you doing this?" she asked Jag. "You know—one minute you aren't here and the next you are?"

Amusement danced in Jag's eyes. "No, and I don't plan to be caught. I choose my landing spots with care."

"I'd ask how you do that, but I'm sure the answer would be as unbelievable as the gift." She stepped to the door, making a mental note to ask him the question another time when they weren't in peril.

Sarah started to knock when the door flew open to reveal an older version of Cathy with much longer dark hair, but the same big brown eyes and adorable features. Sheryl Wilburt wore a long, cream-colored, fitted dress that flattered her slim figure, showing off her curves without being too snug.

"Sarah!" Sheryl said, pulling her into a hug. Sarah had met Sheryl once before and often took her calls at the office, so they had a comfort level together. "Tell me what's going on. I've been worried sick." She leaned back to look at Sarah, her voice cracking a bit. "Tell me Cathy is okay. I need to hear it again. And Edward? Is he any better?"

"Cathy is fine," Sarah said, hoping it was still true. "And there is no change in Edward. Both are well guarded." She hesitated, as she indicated the two men framing her with their big bodies. "Just as you can see I am."

"Absolutely, ma'am," Max said, surprising Sarah. She got the feeling he really understood Sheryl's fear for her daughter as he added, "We have some of our best men with Cathy and Edward. They'll be taken care of."

Sheryl shifted her attention to Max, feminine appreciation flashing in her eyes, and Sarah introduced him. They shook hands and murmured a greeting. "Max has been working closely with our team on this particular case." Sarah motioned to Jag next. "And this is Jag. He heads the team that Max works for."

Sheryl's gaze narrowed just a bit on Jag, before she accepted his hand. "What kind of team would that be?"

"Similar to mine," Sarah responded, smiling, quick to ease Sheryl's mind of any concerns and take the pressure off the men to respond. "Only with a lot more brawn."

A tiny laugh bubbled from Sheryl's throat. "I can see that." She lowered her voice for Sarah's ears only and added, "Interesting company you're keeping these days." Then to all of them she said, "Come in." Motioning them forward as she stepped back into the house, she gave them room to enter.

Sarah went first, with Max and Jag behind her. Once in the hallway, they followed Sheryl into a living room decorated in warm blues with a brick fireplace in the center. Sarah sat on the couch next to Sheryl and Max sat on the matching love seat to her direct left. Jag walked to the mantel and looked up at the picture of a mighty-looking archangel hanging as the centerpiece.

He glanced over his shoulder at Sheryl. "You like Michael, I see."

"Michael is a brave warrior," Sheryl explained. "I feel safe with him around."

"I'm a bit partial to Raphael myself," Jag said, leaning an elbow on the ledge beneath the picture. "Raphael is a healer of earth and humanity."

Sarah and Max exchanged a look and she almost thought she saw a hint of a smile on his lips, his dark mood seeming to lighten a bit. "But Raphael isn't a warrior by nature," Sheryl countered.

"That's true," Jag agreed, looking impressed with her knowledge. "He raises his sword reluctantly, but no less efficiently."

Sheryl tilted her head. "You know your archangels."

"As do you," Jag replied. "You practice angel magic." It wasn't a question.

"My family is rich in inbred magic, though how we practice those gifts may vary. Angel magic just happens to be what speaks to me." She directed a grave look at Sarah and directed the conversation to her obvious worries. "Talk to me, Sarah. What was so dangerous that it couldn't be discussed on the phone?"

Sarah took a moment to explain the situation with Vars and Allen. The minute Sarah said Shadow Masters, Sheryl paled.

"There are stories," she said. "None of them good. Some from sources that make me believe it's true. Three men who sold their souls for wealth and power, even immortality. Their souls are said to be locked inside the magical stones. These Masters are said to be dark powers in the magic world, all able to kill you with a mere spoken word."

"I'm remembering something," Sarah said, shutting her eyes, trying to focus on what Kate had tried to communicate in the cabin. "The stones hold the souls. The demon wants the souls released from the stones so he can use them somehow to free himself." She looked at Sheryl. "Does that sound right?"

Sheryl nodded. "I've heard stories that seem to support that conclusion. It's also said that the Masters use the stones to perform black magic, and that the power collected by those stones is immense. If their souls are released, the demon would have that power to use for his own purposes."

"Such as freeing himself," Jag stated. "Any idea how Allen would be involved? How he would get the Masters to release their souls?"

"None," Sheryl said. "And honestly, I can't be certain of any of this. I am simply making educated guesses. I would conclude that the Masters will die when their souls are freed, though. Allen must be the carrier who delivers them to this demon." Sadness flashed across her face. "Poor Allen. It sounds like all he really wants is his wife back. The pain of losing a loved one can be a dangerous thing."

Sarah barely kept her eyes from Max's but she knew Sheryl's words had to touch him as much as they did her. They'd both felt that pain. Both had felt the desperation of grief, too.

"Do you have any idea who these Masters are?" Sarah asked, hoping for some semblance of a lead.

Sheryl shook her head, her lips tight. "You can't go asking questions about these men. If they're real—and I believe they are—they'll kill you before you get any-where near them."

Sarah grabbed Sheryl's hand. "If we don't find them, a lot more people will die than just us. There has to be someone we can go to who can help? Someone who can be trusted?"

Sheryl swallowed hard, her apprehension palpable. Seconds passed, and somehow they all knew to leave her be, not to press. Finally, she pushed to her feet and left the room. Sarah glanced at the men, their expressions seeming to indicate they were feeling the same uncertainty she was. Her gaze lingered on Max. His hair had a windblown look, a bit too long, a bit too wild. A bit too sexy and distracting. And as his eyes met hers, she saw through the cold shell he had enclosed himself in, saw a moment of tenderness.

Sheryl returned in a scurry of movement, and handed Sarah a piece of paper. "This is opening a door I shut tight, but if you go to this man and tell him I sent you, he will help you. I'm sure he will call me to confirm and that's…expected." She hesitated. "He is dangerous, Sarah, but he wants to please me." Her gaze went to Max who now stood behind Sarah. "Still, he's volatile. His mood can turn dark quickly. Get in and get out." She shut her eyes. "There was a time when the dark side of magic touched me more than I like to admit. I'd appreciate it if you didn't share that with Cathy. I've taught her to learn about the dark side of magic as a way of defending herself against it, and that's the right reason. She has no idea I learned about it for the wrong reasons. After her father left us, I needed someone who actually accepted our world. Someone who embraced magic. I swear, I didn't know—"

Sarah squeezed her hand. "Don't do this to yourself," she said. "You have nothing to be ashamed of. Honestly, I think you should tell Cathy because she loves you and she'll be there for you. But I won't break your trust." Concerned for Sheryl's safety, Sarah asked, "What will happen once you open this door?"

"You just stop this demon from rising," she said, stiffening her spine, her resolve firming as Sarah watched. "I can handle myself. Don't underestimate Caden, though. He knew my family had a strong foot in magic. He wanted the power he thought us joining could bring him. The man is gifted with dark magic no human should possess. It's downright frightening. But if these Shadow Masters exist, he'll know how to find them."

Sarah had the feeling Sheryl was opening herself to painful repercussions by letting them use her name with Caden. "Thank you."

"Thank me by getting my daughter out of that town safely." She eyed the men at that point. "I'm talking to all of you now."

The men were quick to promise their protection as Sheryl walked them all to the door. After hugging Sheryl goodbye, Sarah stood on the porch with Jag and Max by her side. She looked at the piece of paper that held the name *Caden Neil* and a Houston address.

"Houston," Sarah said holding up the paper for them to see.

"This could get us no place fast," Max said. "I know you're worried about the men, Jag. Houston's only a few hours from the inn. Sarah and I can drive it."

"Once I'm inside Nowhere, we can't guarantee communication," Jag cautioned. "You'll be on your own."

"Just make sure Allen doesn't get back to that cabin if he makes it back to town," Max said. "What we're doing may or may not lead anywhere."

Jag gave a slow nod of approval and looked at Sarah, offering her his arm so he could orb them back to the van. "Ready to go?"

She remembered the conversation she'd had with Karen about Max believing in himself. And she thought of the care he'd shown for Sheryl, for her team, for everyone but himself. Suddenly, it felt very important he know she saw the human in him, not the beast.

Sarah reached for Max's hand, her gaze finding his. Without words, she hoped he saw the message in her eyes—that she was with him, ready to fight. He couldn't push her away.

When she saw the ice of his stare melting, she knew she'd at least touched some part of his emotions. She turned to Jag and took his arm. "Now I am."

Jag's eyes warmed and she took strength in his obvious approval. She turned back to Max, the man who'd taken her life by storm. Her hand tightened on his, as his did on hers, their palms melting together as their bodies had only hours before.

And in that moment, as Jag orbed them back to the van, they were united, no barriers, no worries—just the two of them, no matter what the future held.

As they stood beside the van, Max knew he should let go of Sarah's hand and push her away. After all, his plan was to scare her off, not draw her close. But as he wished Jag a farewell, he couldn't seem to find the will.

"I'll check in with Karen every twelve hours and you do the same," Jag instructed Max. "If I don't hear from you, I'll try to find you based on the last update you left. At least that leaves us with some form of communication."

"And if you don't check in?"

"Karen will contact Salvador and give you instructions," Jag replied. "Unless you're told otherwise, stay your path if it feels productive." He grabbed Max's shoulder. "Be safe, my friend." With a nod, he indicated Sarah. "And take good care of our newest recruit here." He stepped back from them and disappeared.

Max turned to face Sarah, not sure what to say. She let go of his hand and stepped back from him, grabbing the keys from her pocket. "I'm driving so you can sleep."

For a moment he considered insisting that he drive, but decided she'd call him macho and she'd be right. He was exhausted, plain and simple. "A little shut-eye would do me good." She smiled her approval and climbed in the van. Once Max was inside, he leaned his seat back. "If anything seems wrong, if you get even a slight vibe of trouble—"

Sarah inserted the key and turned on the engine. "I'll scream, you'll jerk away and draw your blades, and we'll do battle. Got it." She cast him a warning look. "Lie down and go to sleep."

He did as she said, secretly smiling at her bossy attitude, enjoying it more than he should. Enjoying it because she was once again genuinely concerned about him.

And with that secret smile, he drifted off to sleep, hoping to wake with a clear mind and a solution to all their problems. A way to save lives, including his own. A way to make him and Sarah more than a fantasy.

Chapter 17

They'd been on the road about two hours when the sun set. A traffic jam had caused them to lose an hour sitting on the highway. Max had been in and out of sleep the entire time, occasionally sitting up to check on things and then sliding back into a nightmare. She knew they were nightmares because of the way she felt his emotions. It really was quite hard to get used to her sensitivity to him. Being sensitive to spirits had become a way of life, and it only came during their brief visits. But with Max, she got his emotional feed pretty much all the time. And boy, was it intense. He still had plenty of human in him. She didn't doubt that now. He also had a lot of pain that needed healing.

Another rush of feelings came over her, and this

time it was so turbulent, so full of anguish and hurt, that she tensed, fingers turning white as she gripped the steering wheel.

"William," Max murmured, his head tossing from side to side. "No!"

Her chest tightened, stomach queasy. He was dreaming of the day his family was murdered. She knew because this is what she felt when she dreamt of hers dying. He quieted, but he made a jerky movement with his hand. "William!" Then he shouted louder as he sat up and grabbed the dash, "William!"

They'd entered a tiny town and were about to pass a small ice-cream and burger joint on the right. Sarah whipped into the driveway and stopped the car.

She quickly reached for him. "Max," Sarah whispered, careful not to startle him, not sure how he would react. "You're having a nightmare. Just a nightmare." Her hand stroked his arm, offering comfort.

He blinked and turned to look at her, his eyes narrowing, focusing. "What happened?" Surveying the surroundings, he shook his head as if to clear the cobwebs and ran a rough hand through his hair. "I didn't even know we'd stopped. I should have been more alert."

"You had a nightmare," she said softly, her hand moving up and down his arm. "One of many in the past two hours. You were screaming a name—William."

Darkness flashed across his handsome features, and he dropped back on the seat. "My brother."

"I assumed as much," she said. "You answered a question for me today."

He glanced her way. "What would that be?"

"The nightmares never end. I had hoped with enough time they would."

"No," he agreed, turning away again. "They never end."

"Want to talk about it?"

Max laughed at her question, the sound bitter even to his own ears. "No. Reliving that day every time I sleep is enough."

Beside him, Sarah reclined her seat, and he glanced over to see her lean back and shut her eyes. She didn't press him for more information, didn't press him period. She simply lay there with him, for him, and he knew it. No one had ever been there for him. Not even in his human life.

He stared up at the roof of the van, replaying the nightmare, and somehow he just started talking. Still, he didn't look at her. He kept his focus on the plain black ceiling.

"I grew up in England, a part of the English nobility. My brother was the oldest, the one who'd inherit my father's title. I never cared about titles and social functions as they did." He made a frustrated sound. "That's something I've never missed."

"You don't have an English accent," she observed.

"I've had centuries to shed that accent," he reminded her, eyeing the ceiling again. In a corner of his mind, he knew this conversation compromised his plans to push her away. He should be cold, quiet, working to keep her at a distance where he couldn't hurt her. Instead, he kept talking.

Her voice was soft, gently prodding. "I think you mentioned your brother became a Beast?"

"We both did, but William wasn't saved. Salvador…"

He cast her a sideways look and explained, "That's the one who created the Knights—he's a direct descendant to Raphael." He continued, "Salvador said it wasn't William's destiny to join me. Nothing more. No matter how many times I ask, that's what I get. Everyone loved William. It makes no sense. None."

Sarah reached for his hand. "Max." He turned to look at her, sucking in a breath at the tenderness in her gaze as she sympathized, "I understand how you feel. Why didn't the demon kill me? Why my family? My friend? Not knowing tears me up inside." Darkness enclosed the van as nighttime fell around them, shadowing her expression. But he heard the anguish in her voice. "Deep down I want to believe my survival had a purpose, but it's been hard. You're part of the Knights, and they give you a purpose."

More than anything, he wanted to pull her close and kiss her, to believe he would beat this test, to believe he could be with his Sarah and control his inner beast.

"Sarah," he murmured, his body turning toward hers, his willpower fading. The air crackled with their shared attraction, the moments that passed potent as they leaned toward each other. They froze as Max's cell phone rang.

Max eyed the screen caller ID. "It's Karen." He hit the answer button and listened a minute. "Cathy?" His gaze went to Sarah. "Before you ask, she's fine. Nothing has changed."

Sarah visibly relaxed. Max held up a finger and listened. A few seconds later he hung up. He motioned to the restaurant. "Let's grab some food before we get back on the road, and I'll fill you in."

"All right then," she said, and reached for her door.

They walked side by side toward the restaurant, and he wished like hell they could be that way for a lifetime.

A few minutes later they sat together in a tiny booth eating burgers and fries again. Sarah listened as Max explained the details of Karen's call, which had been badly timed. She'd wanted him to kiss her—one more second and he would have.

"Marisol can sense magical abilities. Not the kind a human creates but inborn talents. The minute she met Cathy, she knew she was special. Most of the women who come into our circle come from certain bloodlines. Angelic bloodlines. Karen is researching to see if either or both of you are on the list we hold. Des's mate is on the list."

Sarah's eyes went wide. "Angelic bloodlines?" She shook her head. "Unbelievable." She would have asked more questions, but there were simply too many and too little time. "Does Cathy know any of this?"

Max dipped a fry in ketchup. "Marisol has talked to her." He leaned back in his seat. "Marisol hopes she can funnel Cathy's abilities into her own and dispel the demon that is possessing Edward. So far no go, but they're working on it."

"Do we know what Cathy's abilities are?"

"Not yet." He drew a sip off his straw and swallowed. "The good news is that Karen felt Cathy and Marisol were making progress on how to help Edward."

This made Sarah think of Vars. "Anything going on inside the town?"

"Jag visited Karen right after he reviewed the town's situation. It's quiet there—eerily so. He's convinced the Sheriff to keep the town on lockdown, so the residents won't be walking targets for the Beasts. He confirmed the Beasts have taken positions on the outskirts, intending to trap us inside the perimeter of the populated area. But we're ready. We have Knights in position behind their Beasts. We'll know when they move, and we'll hit them from behind."

"So we're talking an all-out war zone forming," Sarah said, a chill racing up her spine at the thought of how many might die.

"We'll try to keep the battle away from populated areas," he said, and eyed their food. "Right now, we better finish up and get on the road. I'd like to talk to this Caden person tonight. The sooner we get answers, the better."

Sarah nodded her head and reached for her burger. She couldn't agree more. It seemed that everyone she cared for had somehow become linked to the destiny of a town called Nowhere.

Adrian appeared in the back of the underground temple, a shrine to the royalty of the Underworld. Unbeknownst to those inside the temple, his Beasts surrounded the upstairs club, ensuring the property was secure from unwanted visitors.

Low chants filled the air, evil enough to be downright sensual as far as Adrian was concerned. Caden Neil, a sorcerer dark enough to be murmured about in the Underworld, stood in the front of the room, speaking to hundreds of humans who wore long black robes, their hoods covering their faces. To the humans who followed him, he was "The Dark One" capable of inhuman acts no man should be allowed to perform.

It didn't surprise Adrian that Vars had chosen Caden

to aid Allen's efforts to free him. Century after century, Caden's ancestors had made pacts with the Underworld.

Caden called out to the room of eager listeners. "The Shadow Masters are delivering to us the ultimate power of a great Underworld leader," he announced. "This leader will soon be with us.

"He will bring wrath on those foolish enough to turn away from him. Bring wealth and pleasure to those who whisper his name with praise and devotion. Vars is the name of this great demon prince."

The chants changed to the name. "Vars, Vars, Vars…"

Adrian ground his teeth. He wanted those chants to be for him, not for Vars. These people would know the truth of who had the power, he vowed, and they would know soon. He would take Vars's legion of demon spirits and make these people, every last one of them, know his name. Right after he made The Knights of White wish they hadn't raised a blade to fight his Beasts. Adrian would destroy the Knights just as he would destroy Vars.

As for Caden Neil, he served the wrong master and for that there was only one solution—when this was over, Caden would die.

He watched as the three Shadow Masters stepped forward, taking center stage, the ritual beginning. For six days, they would be treated as gods, worshipped, prepared, pleasured—the sexual magic feeding the stones' powers, feeding the stones' magic. By the end of day six, the stones would glow with energy, ready to transfer the souls of their masters into the vial around Allen's neck. The Shadow Masters let their robes drop to the floor, all displaying the naked muscular bodies of thirty-year-old men, when none of them were a day younger than fifty. They'd bargained with their souls for a life of luxury, a life where youth never ended nor did the money and sex. They thought their life in hell would be the same, but they knew not what they were dealing with. They would live in a prison, sex slaves for the Underworld royalty, used to service their wants and desires. Three robed women stepped forward, untying their garments and letting them fall to the floor, displaying their sensual curves. Adrian leaned against the wall; his anger faded as he prepared to watch the orgy. Perhaps he'd even join in.

He might not be a king in the Underworld, not even a prince, but here on earth, he could have anything, or anyone he wanted. He pointed at two hooded figures, knowing instinctively they were beautiful women. They turned to him, his magic controlling their minds. Their robes fell to the ground, lush curves, full breasts, displayed for his enjoyment. He pointed at a third female, drawing her forward. He would need more than two women this night, perhaps more than three. Because, yes, he could have anyone, anything, he wanted here on earth, but it simply wasn't enough anymore.

He drew the women close and then flashed them out of the room, refusing to take his pleasure in a place where Vars was being worshipped.

Allen stood in the corner of the room, watching as the robes fell to the ground, watching as bodies pressed to bodies. He didn't want to be aroused, didn't want to be involved. But he was here, and he *was* aroused—and he hated himself for it. Hated how disloyal to Kate that made him. He'd not touched another woman since her death. Yet, despite his guilt, his eyes fixed on a particular woman as she rubbed her voluptuous curves against her partner's body like a cat in heat.

Caden appeared before him then, blocking his view, still wearing his robe, his short dark hair covered by a hood. His black eyes piercing as they fixed Allen in a stare. He and Allen were the only ones among hundreds who remained clothed.

"The stones won't work without feeding their power," Caden proclaimed. "If you want your precious Kate back, forget your guilt and find pleasure." He stepped to the side, giving Allen a view of the woman again, just in time to see the man fondling her breast, her long red hair spread over creamy-white shoulders. "If you want her, she is yours."

Caden narrowed his gaze on Allen's features. "And you do want her. I can damn near taste your lust. This isn't a game. This is about power. The power to give life to those stones. If you want Kate, then fuck the woman and do it well."

Caden snapped his fingers and the woman looked at him. She was too far away to have heard the snap. Allen knew Caden had somehow bidden her attention with magic. The gorgeous beauty stared at Caden for several seconds, and then smiled, pushing out of the arms of her lover and walking toward Allen.

Allen damn near choked on his tongue trying to object, but no words would come. He glanced at Caden and saw the evil smile on his thin lips. He'd done something to Allen to silence him. And it was too late to object, anyway. The woman leaned into him and took

his hands, filling his palms with her breasts. "Tell me
what you want," she purred, her lips brushing his jaw.

"Kate," he whispered in his mind, but as the woman
started to rub against him, he found himself kissing the
redheaded seductress, fighting an internal battle to push
her away, to cling to Kate. But as seconds passed, so did
his memories. All he could think about was here and
now. Kate began to fade, and he fought the cries of his
body for satisfaction. And when his robe came off and
he could fight no more, he promised himself this was
for Kate. This was to empower the stones. To bring
back Kate. She'd understand. She always understood
him. She was Kate.

Chapter 18

Caden was no place to be found. A visit to his house had found no one present, aside from the two armed guards outside the grounds, which sent a pretty clear message—Caden had something to hide.

Now, near midnight, Max pushed open the door to the high-rise hotel room and tried not to think about the single bed the overbooked hotel had offered.

Seemingly unaffected by the intimate setting, Sarah went straight to the bed and sat down, her scent lifting in her wake, taunting him with its sweetness. Max inhaled that soft smell despite his best efforts not to, his body warming, firing his desire to reach for her. They'd only just entered the room, and he was already fighting temptation. It was going to be one hell of a long night.

Max hesitated by the closet, staring at Sarah as she reached for the menu lying on the bedside table. Thinking of what it would be like to be in that bed with her, naked, making love. His groin tightened and his gums tingled. Damn. His mating instincts were wildly out of control if a simple fantasy could make his cuspids start to emerge. He squeezed his eyes shut as though that would block the images playing in his head. But there was no blocking them. No hiding.

He would not touch her, would not make love to her— absolutely would not claim her as his mate. Max murmured these words in his head as he tracked across the hotel room. Sliding into the chair behind a tiny corner desk, he cut his gaze from Sarah. *Focus on work,* he told himself. *Focus on work.*

Trying to distract himself, he cataloged the room as he booted up his computer: blue drapes; blue floral comforter; tan rugs; and a nightstand by the bed. Tight confined quarters. Intimate lighting perfect for making love. He ground his teeth and looked back at his computer. Work. He needed to get lost in work.

Needed to get lost in anything but Sarah.

"They have a twenty-four-hour menu that amounts to pizza," she commented. "Is that okay?" He nodded stiffly and she asked hopefully, "Pepperoni?"

He managed a smile despite the rage of desire pumping through his body. "My favorite."

"Excellent," she said, her eyes lighting up as she reached for the phone.

Max inhaled and turned away from her, trying to make the act of powering up his computer absorbing enough to block out his desire for Sarah. A feat that proved impossible as he listened to her talk on the phone, her soft voice sensual and far too arousing.

When she finished placing the order, he could feel her attention, feel her eyes on him. But he didn't look up, didn't dare invite further contact until he'd reined in his lust. Only when the knock sounded on the door, to indicate their order had arrived, did he dare turn in Sarah's direction and push to his feet. He made fast work of paying for the order and returned to set the pizza on the bed.

And then he sat down at the desk and drew a deep breath, forcing logic into his mind. Finding Caden and stopping Vars were his objectives. These things were imperative if he wanted a future with Sarah, a part of his test—he felt it in his core. He had to pull himself together. Clarity came with those conclusions, and slowly the tension in his body eased enough for him to eat.

The next hour was filled with remarkably comfortable silence; their fingers tapping the keyboards were the only sounds between them. On some level, Sarah seemed to sense, and even understand, his need to keep to himself. A good hour after they'd finished off the last of the pizza, Sarah straightened a bit and began tapping the keyboard more rapidly, explaining her sudden spike of energy as she typed. "I've been scanning these occult sites and several of them referenced 'The Dark One,'" she commented, hitting a few more keys and then looking up at him. "After some digging, I found another reference—this one to 'Caden—The Dark One.'"

Max rotated in his chair to face her, his attention piqued. "Sheryl made it clear this guy is involved in the dark arts. That doesn't seem surprising."

"Not until you hear the rest," Sarah said. "There's a reference related to Caden and some underground worship ceremony that is invitation only. I don't have a location or any details, but—" she raised a finger, her voice lifting as she added, "here's the kicker. It's this week. I think Caden is more than a source of information. I think he's the one helping Allen."

"It makes sense," Max agreed. "And no matter how much Sheryl swore Caden would talk to us, the fear I saw in that woman's face spoke a warning beyond her words." Which brought him back to the need to find Caden. "He's not going to be at work tomorrow. He'd be smarter than that. He'll be in hiding until this is over."

Sarah nodded her agreement and started working on her computer again. "We have to find a location for the ceremony." Her voice lowered to a murmur as she seemed to think out loud. "Maybe an occult chat room."

"I had a little success myself," Max offered, drawing her hopeful gaze. "Caden owns a variety of businesses around the state, but most of them are here in Houston. They seem like obvious locations to check out for this ceremony. There's a restaurant, an antique store, a large number of bars, and the list goes on. I'll shoot the names to your e-mail so you can cross-reference them with the occult Web sites." Sarah gave him her address and he punched a few keys.

They worked on the list a good hour and ranked each of Caden's businesses based on probable ceremony sites. They were ready with a plan of attack for the next day. "I think we're set," Max announced at last, the final outline of Caden's business locations mapped out.

"Finally," Sarah said. Her gaze slowly lifted from the computer as she blinked a couple of times. Her eyes were heavy, weariness in her expression.

"We should sleep a few hours while we can," he said, worried about her ability to ward off another mental attack if she were exhausted.

"Yes," she agreed. "Sleep would be really good."

But neither moved. They sat there, silent, the implications of the one bed hanging in the air.

Max's body began a fast burn to arousal and he pushed to his feet, quick to distance himself from Sarah and temptation. He walked to the closet and pulled the extra pillow and blanket from the top shelf, aware that Sarah's attention was on him. He didn't look at her as he found a spot beside the wall and lay down, clothes and boots still in place, the blanket on top of him. Next, Max grabbed his cell phone from his belt and set the alarm for seven. That was only a few hours of sleep, but it had to be enough.

In his peripheral vision, he saw Sarah clear the bed and turn to face him. "Please don't do this, Max. You need some real rest. Share the bed with me."

He shut his eyes. "Turn off the light, Sarah, and go to sleep."

"Max—"

His lashes snapped open. "This isn't a debate. I'm sleeping here. Turn off the light."

Several seconds passed before she pounded the pillow and murmured, "This is crazy." The light went out.

No, it's torture, he thought to himself as the silence fell again, this time laced with discomfort, with sexual tension.

"Max?"

"Yes."

"I'm not afraid of you."

"You should be."

"I did a lot of thinking while we traveled." A few seconds of silence. "You said Darkland Beasts have no soul, right?"

"Yes."

"But you have a soul."

"A dark one."

"I lived those nightmares with you. I feel your feelings like I do the spirits. And no one would feel the guilt you do if they were evil. Evil people don't care about anything but themselves. I imagine soulless, evil Beasts care even less. You care. You aren't evil."

Max wanted her acceptance and her approval more than anything in that moment, and she was giving it to him. But he couldn't take what she offered and it was killing him. There was a reason he'd tried to scare her away, and he couldn't lose sight of that fact. He was protecting her.

He had to make her understand. "You've seen my eyes, Sarah. You've seen how much they resemble the eyes of a Beast. I'm on the edge. I could hurt you. I could hurt someone you love. I won't let you go through that again." Frustration rolled inside, his words laden with emotion. "Why are you trying to make me human when I'm not?"

"Because you are, Max. Immortal, yes, but still human beyond that. Just like Edward is. As was the friend I lost to that demon possession. We have to fight, Max. *You* have to fight."

Why couldn't she just be scared? He'd given her every reason to be afraid of him.

As if she read his mind, she added, "I realized something else today. When that demon took the people I loved, it destroyed a part of me, too. I forgot the higher purpose that is served when I use my gifts to help people. I've lived in fear and I refuse to do it anymore. I know what I feel when I'm with you. I know how comfortable I felt with Karen and Jag. Everything in my life has come back to right now, with you. Did you know the demon that killed my family had a connection to Solomon?"

"What?" Max asked in surprise.

"Yes." She went on to explain how they'd hunted the demon, and how Solomon's writings had helped her destroy it. "So you see, finding you has to be part of my destiny. That means you are supposed to pass this test and fight by my side. I feel it. I choose to believe it. I won't let fear of history repeating itself make me hide. Not anymore."

Admiration filled Max. "I knew you'd find that purpose again, Sarah. And I know if I'm not here, you'll make a difference in this war."

Her voice reached through the darkness. "You have to be here. It was meant to be. Why else would we find each other if you weren't?"

He wanted to be here. He did. "Maybe I am supposed to see you through this battle in Nowhere and lead you to the Knights for protection and guidance. Or maybe I was just supposed to help you find your place in this world again, Sarah."

"Do you believe that?" she asked. "Because I don't."

The truth was he didn't know what to believe, but he knew he couldn't risk her future for his. Maybe Sarah would do something great in this lifetime, and he had to make sure she survived to do it. There were so many possibilities he could think of, but he saw no point in sharing them with Sarah.

The fact was he had to get them both through this present battle before he could look for a future with her.

And he wasn't sure he had enough willpower to resist Sarah if she kept trying to pull him closer—enough to fight his inner Beast and her. Now came the big question. How did he keep her at a distance, away from him, so he couldn't adversely affect her destiny, without destroying her newfound purpose?

He knew of only one thing that might work—the one thing that might show her they'd met too late. And that was the cold, hard truth he hated with all of his being. The truth about what he'd done, why he was being tested. "Sarah." He hesitated, forcing out the words he'd spoken before, but now with the truth behind them. "I killed a man. I *killed* him." His thoughts flashed back to that day. "He was trying to give the list of angelic bloodlines to the Beasts, so they could hunt them. Jessica, Des's intended mate, tried to stop him. I saw him draw a knife—he was going to stab her. I charged after him, but I was too late. The blade had pierced Jessica's side. And then I just lost it. I don't know what happened. I blacked out. The next thing I knew, I was leaning over his dead body, a bloody blade in my hand."

Seconds ticked by and Sarah said nothing. Nothing. Pain ripped through his chest. He'd succeeded in doing what he needed to do. He'd scared her, pushed her away. He turned onto his back and stared into the dark room, moonlight illuminating the ceiling above. He willed himself to be pleased with his results, to sleep and be ready to fight this war again tomorrow. That's what he did. He fought. Alone.

He heard Sarah moving around, perhaps settling

beneath the blankets. He didn't look. He couldn't look. He inhaled. A mistake. Her scent was everywhere. All around him. Tempting him.

But then the most amazing thing happened. Sarah was there, lying down on the floor with him. "What are you doing?" he asked, objecting, and then turned to face her, on his side as she was, his back to the wall— putting distance between them.

"Relax," she said. "I'm on top of the blanket, and we have our clothes on."

She reached over the distance and her fingers brushed his jaw. Max's breath lodged in his chest at the gentle touch. He'd felt few of those in his lifetime. He'd had women, had plenty of sex. Tenderness he didn't even remember. He needed this, he realized. He wasn't strong enough to push her away right now. He hated himself for that, but he wasn't. "Sarah," he whispered. "I don't want to hurt you."

"You won't," she assured him. "I don't know what happened that day, Max, but I know you were trying to save Jessica's life. Obviously Jessica is alive, and you rescued that list of bloodlines. The way I see it, you saved a lot of lives that day."

"I killed him."

"You must have had no other option."

"There is always another option."

"If only that were true," Sarah said. "But it's not, Max. We both know that. If it were, neither of us would have let our families die." With those profound and painful words, she snuggled up as close to him as the blankets would allow, her hand going to his hip. "Go to sleep, Max."

He didn't sleep, though. Not for a long time. He was

afraid of hurting her, of losing control in his sleep. But his eyes were heavy, as were his thoughts. And soon he drifted into sleep....

Sarah woke to the throbbing in her head—Kate was trying to communicate with her, and once again, the demon spirits were trying to stop her. A shooting pain pierced Sarah's temple and Max scooped her into his arms, cradling her against his body. In some remote corner of her mind she heard him talking to her, heard his worry.

"Kate," she whispered, clinging to him. "Kate is—" The barely-there words were cut off as Sarah was hit with flashes of images with moments of blackness as the demon spirits worked to defeat the vision Kate was delivering.

Sarah felt Max near her, felt his strength. She reached through the pain, searched the images. Three men wearing robes—no—they dropped the robes. They were the Shadow Masters and they were naked. So were hundreds of others. Another black spot. Lots of blackness. Then Sarah saw Allen in a corner, watching the people as they pleasured each other. Waiting on something. The Shadow Masters. Yes. He was there for the Shadow Masters. Suddenly loud music came from somewhere. Dance music. Overhead. A club maybe. The music got louder as if Kate wanted her to know it was important. Flash to a man—he wore a robe and spoke to Allen. He was evil—pure evil. Kate fed her a name—Caden. And then everything went blank.

Sarah collapsed against Max, not realizing until that moment that every muscle in her body had been tense and now burned like fire. She swallowed against the dryness in her throat and slid her fingers along her scalp.

"Caden," she said, sitting up despite the dizziness that came along with the action. "He's using some sort of sex ritual to activate the stones."

Max followed her to a sitting position and he ignored her words. His palms framed her face. "Forget Caden for the moment. You scared the hell out of me. Are you okay?"

"Fine," she said, her hands going to his wrist. "Nothing a bottle of aspirin and caffeine won't cure." She made an attempt to smile that didn't quite work out. "We don't do mornings very well, do we? Yesterday I saw your fangs. Today this."

His expression softened and he brushed hair from her brow. "We do mornings fine. These are extraordinary circumstances."

"At least you didn't lecture me about sleeping with you and tell me we shouldn't be doing mornings together at all."

"We're supposed to do a lot more than mornings together," he said, his words laced with regret. "But like I said—extraordinary circumstances."

The alarm on his cell went off and Max ignored it. He pressed his forehead to hers. "I don't know how to protect you, Sarah. I've spent centuries fighting demons, yet, I can't destroy the ones attacking you during these visions."

Her heart clenched at the words and she leaned back to look at him. "We will destroy them with Vars, but you're right. You can't use a sword and slay the evil that touches the spirit world. But, Max," she said, her voice laced with a plea, her fingers tracing his lips, "you *can* stop trying to push me away."

His hands slid from her face and he eased his back

against the wall. "That's the one thing I can't do. Not now. Not until this is over and we know the outcome."

"Of the test," she said, exhaling against the throbbing of her head.

"Are you—"

Her lashes lifted. "I'm fine," she assured him. "Jag talked about you saving Jessica back at the other hotel. About how he'd never forget that. Think about it, Max. I have. He was telling you something. Telling *me* something."

His brows furrowed. "Like what?"

"I don't know but my guess is that everything isn't as you assume it is. You have to remember."

Frustration laced his response. "You think I haven't tried?"

"Try harder," she countered, knowing he wouldn't like her words, but knowing, too, that he needed to hear them. "If this test is based on that incident, then your life depends on it. Maybe mine, too. You fight for everyone but yourself. Fine. Fight for me."

"I am fighting for you," he said. "That's why I can't touch you again. Not now."

This time she was the one who was frustrated. "Fight, Max. Fight for yourself. Do it for me if you won't do it for you."

Sarah pushed to her feet, ignoring the slight dizziness overtaking her and walking to the phone. She ordered aspirin and coffee and then covered the phone to ask if he liked waffles. He did. That didn't surprise her. They seemed to share a lot of likes. Too bad he seemed determined to make sure he spent eternity in hell and wouldn't be sharing any of them with her. He was stubborn and making her mad. She wanted to shake sense into his big, burly ass. He could see only one way of dealing with his test—alone.

By the time she hung up the phone, she'd reined in her heated mood. Max did alone so well because it's all he knew. That wasn't the case for her. She'd been alone, yes, but for far less time than Max. And she had been close to her family. She could feel the distance Max had with his family. He'd been hungry for the love he'd never received. She'd just have to show him he didn't have to do this alone. Somehow. Some way. She'd figure it out.

He'd taken a seat behind the desk and she turned to him. "About Caden and this ritual," she said, shifting back into the current challenge of finding Allen. "Sexual energy can be quite powerful. I've read about rituals that last for days." She thought a moment, her lashes lowering, her mind reaching for the details of her vision. "Six days. This one is six days. Two for each stone and then they are empowered. Somehow that allows the souls to be extracted from the stones. I think…yes. We have some time. If we can find a location where all of this is happening, then maybe we can stop it. So what do you think?" She remembered something. "Music. There was loud music. A club. A club is above the ritual ground. Yes. It's underground."

"I'd say it's a good thing we didn't find him last night. Now that we know he's involved, I'd say questioning him would only put him on guard."

"My guess is he isn't even in his office. Not with this ritual going on." She grabbed the phone. "Let's find out." Sure enough, a quick call later, and she'd confirmed he was out for the rest of the week. "Now we have to figure out which club."

"Maybe if you see the locations, you'll remember something?" Max asked.

"I hope so," she said. "Because the full moon is fast approaching."

Chapter 19

Seventy-two grueling hours of searching for answers had passed for Sarah and Max.

It was just past ten o'clock, with the full moon closing in on them in a matter of a few days, when Max and Sarah walked up a red-carpeted sidewalk leading to the Red Room, one of the many clubs Caden owned.

Visiting several clubs a night had been a stretch, considering they were spread out from one end of the city to the next. And working the employees and patrons for information took an effort to fit in which couldn't be made by darting in and out. Nor could searches of private areas be done without some tricky side steps.

The time with Sarah had been both heaven and hell for Max. Heaven because he'd listened to stories about her life, and shared some of his own even—he'd learned about Sarah and he liked what he'd found. It had also been hell—keeping his hands off her was damn near killing him. Sarah wouldn't sleep without him. She wouldn't let him run from her, or push her away. Lord only knew, he'd tried.

They neared the entrance to the club, and Max kept Sarah close, her arm linked under his, her body pressed to his side. The closer they got to the entrance, the more his skin warmed, the more aware he became of Sarah's soft curves against his body. The feeling of sexual need formed rapidly, and Max knew he was in trouble.

Lust carved its way into his limbs, hungry for his complete submission. He was in trouble. Even his weakest moments of temptation with Sarah hadn't come close to this. The beast was alive, threatening to consume him. If he'd thought he had reclaimed control, he now knew that control to be a facade. He didn't want this to happen around Sarah. His worst fear was a blackout, like the one he'd had when he killed that human. He had no idea what he was capable of in that state, and he didn't want to find out.

Before he could even begin to consider warning Sarah, the hostess smiled and motioned them forward. He greeted her, beating down his beast. This was important. They had to find Caden.

The entry into the club was pricey for nonmembers—obviously meant to discourage anyone who wasn't a high roller.

They'd made a trip to the mall earlier today for clothes to fit the part. Max wore Ralph Lauren slacks and a sleek blue button-down with a matching tie. He didn't much like dressing up. It reminded him of the social affairs back in England. The fluff meant for nothing but upward movement. He did, however, enjoy seeing Sarah in her knee-length, figure-hugging black dress. Simple yet elegant, it matched her personality to perfection.

Max was about to hand his gold card to the hostess when a red phone buzzed, claiming the hostess's attention. She picked up the receiver, listened a moment, and cut a look at Max and Sarah that was meant to be discreet, but wasn't.

"I'll handle it," she said into the receiver, and replaced it on the base.

The woman ran Max's card and then handed it back to him, avoiding eye contact. Bingo. She was nervous. That call had been about them. Someone had caught on to their hunt for Caden.

"Your visit to The Red Room will start in the lounge on the second floor. It's a private room that overlooks the club as you enjoy beverages. It will allow you to see the various flavors we have to offer here." She motioned to another woman to cover her post. "Follow me."

Max glanced at Sarah to confirm she'd picked up on the potential trouble they were in and confirmed she had. He pulled her closer as they exited the entry hall and entered the club, her safety the most important thing. If he got any vibe of real danger, they were leaving.

The instant they entered the heart of the crowd, Max could feel the sexual charge. Music pounded through speakers with a sensual rhythm; dim lighting cast a red glow on the room. The low thrum of arousal he'd felt outside escalated. The dance floor held couples pressed together in highly suggestive undulations. Heat vibrated through his body in an unnatural way.

Sarah's hand tightened on his arm, and he felt the movement in every nerve ending he owned. What the hell was happening to him? His heart was pounding in his chest, his groin tightening. His desire for Sarah was to the point of complete, utter distraction. This wasn't just mating instinct. It was something more. If this continued, he might well be the danger to Sarah, rather than this place.

The hostess started up a winding stairwell, and Sarah hesitated at the bottom, pushing to her toes to whisper in Max's ear. "This is it. Don't you feel the sexual energy?"

He didn't look at her, not wanting her to know just how much the atmosphere was affecting him. The need to mate was obviously intensifying his sensitivity. "I feel it," Max murmured, taking her hand as he started up the stairs.

The hostess stood at the top of the landing and waved them through an open door. Max went in first, leading Sarah, prepared to inspect their destination before Sarah entered harm's way. Inside he found a room with a long, red love seat and a marble, art deco-looking black table that held two oversized red martini glasses filled to the rim. Candles flickered around the room, and in the corners on tall pedestals. The candlelight almost seeming to dance to the music being funneled through ceiling-mounted speakers.

The walls directly in front of the seating area held television screens, each displaying various locations within the club, including private areas not visible upon entry. Several of the visuals were quite erotic. Max turned toward the hostess to ask a question, finding her still in the doorway. Before he could issue his question, she departed. "Enjoy," she said, and shut them in the room.

Max immediately turned to Sarah, intending to warn her to be silent, that they were being watched. But the minute he looked at her, the minute he saw those big green eyes and full red lips, he was on fire. He pulled her close, molding her hips to his, his hand splayed on her lower back.

In some far corner of his mind, he recognized his actions—what he felt wasn't right. "Sarah," he murmured, his voice low, full of sexual intent. One hand slid into her hair, angling her mouth to his, lips a breath away from hers. "We're being watched."

"I know," she whispered, a soft little sound of pleasure sliding from her lips. "The ritual is close… The magic. It's close. Acting like a drug." But still, her arms wrapped around his neck, her actions defying the warning of her words. "We should g—"

Max kissed her, swallowing the last of her words. He hadn't kissed her in days. He told himself he just wanted a taste of her, one little taste. And, God, it was good. He savored the moment of that first intimate contact—tongue against tongue. She tasted so pure, so sweet.

He deepened the kiss and suddenly it turned passionate, hot, wild. Max couldn't get enough of her, hungry for more, desperate for all of her. In those moments, life was perfect and nothing else mattered. He wanted her, his mate, and damn it, he would take her. The beast began to flare, his teeth elongating, and he didn't care. He was done waiting. He'd take her here and now.

"It's time, Sarah," he murmured near her ear. "Time to become mine."

His teeth scraped her neck, and she cried out. "Yes. Now."

But a moment later she stiffened, her cry of pleasure turning to something different. Her fingers dug into his shoulders, and Max shook his head, trying to clear the fog in his mind. What the hell had he almost done?

Her knees started to give way, and he wrapped his arm around her waist, holding her up. "Sarah!"

"Kate says…" She squeezed her eyes shut. "She says we are…in danger. Get out." Her lashes lifted. "Your brother is here."

The shock of her words shot through him a second before the door was flung open. Max stepped in front of Sarah, protecting her with his body. "Tell Kate a little more warning would be nice!"

Just as Kate said, William walked into the room, looking every bit Max's brother in human form. Max inhaled, jolted by the sight of the Beast who'd once been family.

He'd hoped to never face this day—the day when he might well have to kill the Beast who was once his brother. "William."

"Hello, Maxwell," William said, an evil laugh following the greeting. "All that mating heat is a bitch, isn't it? None of your other senses work worth a crap when you have that pretty little thing all over you. A shame you didn't know I was coming. Maybe you should reconsider your priorities. Play for the right side of this war."

Understanding filled Max. Somehow, they knew Sarah was his mate. They'd funneled the ritual magic through this room somehow, drugging him as Sarah had suggested, dulling his ability to know his enemy was near. His hand inched toward his belt, and he silently cursed as he remembered his only weapons were hidden, beyond reach.

"Looking for something, brother?" William asked. "Tsk. Tsk. Hunting 'The Dark One' unarmed. That really wasn't bright. How did you think you'd protect your woman?" He laughed again and snapped his fingers at the two Beasts behind him. They grabbed Max's arms, shackling him from behind. William reached to his pant leg, pulling it upward to display an ankle holster. He pulled out a small, sharp blade—a blade useless against a Knight, but not against a human such as Sarah.

In his peripheral vision, Max could see that Sarah had backed against the wall, but he didn't dare make eye contact with her. He didn't dare look away from his enemy. He could take the two Beasts holding him, but he wasn't sure he could do it fast enough to get to Sarah before William did. He had to be cautious, to strategize his move.

"Join us and she goes free," William offered, holding the weapon so that the candles flickered against the shiny silver blade.

"You're without your armor," Max pointed out, knowing a Beast without his protective gear could feel a great deal of pain. They couldn't bleed but they could be tortured. "Let her go and I'll kill you fast. I promise you'll feel no pain."

William smiled, seemingly pleased with that answer. "I figured you'd make this a challenge." His eyes raked over Sarah's body. "But something tells me, with Sarah around, I might enjoy convincing you." He winked. "She's a nice choice, brother."

The words cut through Max's heart for too many reasons to pin down in that moment. Right now, all that mattered was freeing Sarah. "You aren't my brother, and I swear to God, if you touch her, I will take your head."

"It's not nice to make promises you can't keep." He slid two fingers down the blade and turned to Sarah. "Maybe we'll join the others downstairs and play a while." He grimaced. "No. I want you all to myself." He glanced over his shoulder at Max. "But you can watch." With the threatening words he inched forward, closer to Sarah.

She slid along the wall, retreating until she bumped into a tall pillar that held a flaming, three-wick candle.

"William, he's your brother," Sarah said. "Help us and maybe we can save you. Maybe Salvador will have mercy on you."

His reply was instant, his words steely with hatred. "It is my mercy you should pray for."

Max ground his teeth at William's words. God, how he wanted William to exist beyond the shell of the man he once was—he had always held on to that hope despite Salvador's insistence that he let William go.

William's eyes lit with contempt as they settled on Max. "I offer you a chance for conversion because I am ordered to do so. If you are smart, you will do what you always failed to do in our human lives—follow my leadership."

He moved then, fast and without warning. His blade touched Sarah's neck, his attention still riveted to Max. "I'd hate to kill her before I show her who the better brother is, but don't doubt for a second I will." He paused. "So here are the hard-core facts, Maxwell. You must choose. Your soul, or your mate's life. Which will it be?"

Max wasn't a fool. He'd gladly sacrifice himself for Sarah, but to do so now would be for nothing. The Beasts would see her dead anyway. He could stand here and pretend he didn't know that or he could take action.

He was tired of playing captive to the two Beasts holding his arms. As for the knife at Sarah's throat, that had to go. Now.

With heavy thoughts, Max surrendered to the inevitable. For the first time since he killed that human to save Des's mate, he had to allow his inner beast to fully take control.

His resolve thickened, his eyes lingering on the knife at his mate's neck; he let the raw emotions, the fury, take hold. Max embraced the heavy pulse of adrenaline pumping through his veins, welcomed the power of his beast as it rose to the surface—clawing its way upward, from the depths of his soul. Soon, man and beast existed as one.

The time to do battle had arrived.

Sarah watched in horror as the room erupted in chaos, the knife at her throat a constant threat. Since she wasn't dead yet, she had to assume there was a reason to keep her alive—perhaps simply to torture her and make Max watch. Either way, she had a chance to survive, which meant she had to fight.

She watched as Max wrenched one arm free from one of the Beasts and smashed his fists into the same Beast's jaw. The blow packed so much force that the Beast stumbled backward. Immediately, the second captor hit Max; the sound of knuckles cracking against bone filled the air. Sarah cringed, thankful that Max recovered quickly and returned the blow. She couldn't believe Max had gone on the attack. He was outnumbered, in tight quarters. Her heart pounded so hard, she thought her chest would explode. She had to help. Think, damn it!

Max somehow freed himself from his two attackers and charged at his brother. William turned to face Max, shoving Sarah behind him, the blade finally lifted from her skin. Sarah stumbled into the candle pillar to her right, and it wobbled. Instinctively Sarah reached out to steady the candle. But then an idea hit her. Fire. Alarm. The people downstairs panicking. That might just work.

She shoved the candle to the ground, praying the carpet would go up in flames. It did. Well, one flame. A small one, but it would grow. That little success didn't offer much comfort, though, because Max was in trouble. All three of the Beasts were pounding on him.

Sarah clung to the hope her plan offered and went into action, taking advantage of the attention being off her for now. She grabbed candles from anywhere she could find them, tossing them to the ground. Fire was beginning to form a circle around the battle, smoke rising, lifting, hopefully touching the alarm sensors. When one of the Beasts tumbled back into her, Sarah barely sidestepped the flames as she found herself crushed against the wall. Somehow, she held on to the candle in her hand, seeing it as a weapon.

Taking opportunity where it presented itself, she pressed the flame into the back side of the Beast's long hair. The strands ignited with quick speed and the creature screamed as flames traveled up his head, jumping around in the center. He was now a live weapon ready to set anything in its path on fire.

William and the other Beast backed away from the fire and finally the alarm sounded. Water erupted from the ceiling almost instantly, screams filling the air as the customers felt its downpour. Apparently, this signaled a temporary retreat to William; he darted out the door, disappearing into the club. But she'd seen how determined he was to destroy Max and how devious he was about achieving it. He was most likely regrouping, planning another strike upon their attempt to depart. His uninjured Beast followed in his wake. The one that was on fire dropped to his knees as if he were submitting to the fire licking at his body, the water barely dulling the flames. In shock, she watched as the creature seemed to be melting into the fire, proving beheading wasn't the only method of destroying these monsters.

Suddenly Sarah was in Max's arms and being carried out of the room. He dodged the growing fire as if it required no effort, charging out the door and down the stairs toward the bottom floor. Sarah searched the crowd for William, the sound of sirens touching her ears. People were pushing and shoving their way to the front door. They had to find Allen now—before he was gone, before their hope of stopping his plans faded.

She tried to say as much, but the shrill alarm drowned out her voice.

Max weaved through the crowd, and before Sarah could object, they were outside the club. Still, he didn't stop moving. "Max! Stop! We have to find Allen."

Max didn't stop. No matter how many times she screamed, ordered, pleaded, he stayed his path. They were blocks away from the club when she found herself on the sidewalk watching as Max flagged the cab that had apparently been the reason for his sudden stop. The cab responded, pulling to the curb.

Max yanked open the door and Sarah stared at

him. "We have to go back," she argued, not understanding his plan.

"I *am* going back," he said, and handed her his cell,
barely looking at her in the process. "Jag and Karen are
both on speed dial. Jag will protect you. Have him orb
you to his location and have him do it now. Then tell him
I need backup. The immediate kind."

He opened the front door and gave the driver the
hotel address and tossed money onto the seat. He
slammed the door. "Go to the room and stay there, so I
know you're safe."

"Max—"

His gaze caught hers midair, and her throat went dry
at what she saw. Yellow eyes…predator eyes. His voice
was low, thick. "Just do as I say, Sarah."

Answering wasn't an option, not that she could find
words in that moment.

And then he was running, leaving her behind. She'd
never seen Max seem quite so on edge, so dangerous.
She watched his departure, his muscular body, long and
sleek, traveling at inhuman speed.

Her mind raced with thoughts, fear pressing into her
consciousness. She rejected it as a useless emotion.
She'd seen how powerful those three Beasts had been.
There were probably many more back at that club. Max
couldn't face them alone.

The cabdriver honked, and she slammed the door
shut and waved him forward without her. A second later,
she hit the speed dial for Jag, praying he would answer.
He didn't. Next she tried Karen, pacing as the phone
rang in her ear.

She didn't bother with hello. "Tell me Jag is there."

"No," Karen said. "What's wrong?"

Five minutes later, Sarah hung up the line, discouraged. Jag's next call-in time was almost an hour away. A lot could happen in an hour. Max could be dead in an hour. Sarah didn't know what to do but go after him herself. At least, she could tell Jag exactly where he was when he called. Doing nothing wasn't an option, because she wasn't sitting back and waiting while Max got himself killed.

So she did the only thing she could. She took off running—back to the nightclub. Back to Max.

Chapter 20

Allen stood in the corner of the ritual room, naked, without his prior reservations about being a part of what went on here—about the sexual explorations required by Caden. His duty to contribute to the power of the stones could not be questioned—not when Kate would be the reward for his actions. Two women clung to him, touching him, kissing him. For days now, he'd shoved aside guilt, promising himself this was for Kate, that it did not betray his love for her. This was to bring her back. To bring her home.

Murmurs filled the room, and Allen pried one woman's lips from his to see what was going on. The Shadow Masters had returned after a short rest, and they now stood center stage. The robes they wore pooled at their feet, and all eyes turned to them, all activity stilled.

Each time they returned, Caden tested the stones

with some magical spell, and so far he'd been pleased with their progress, which was ahead of schedule. That progress kept Allen going, kept him focused on the magic that could bring back Kate.

He held his breath as he awaited Caden's update... but it never came.

Without warning an alarm sounded and the sprinklers came on, raining water down on the crowd. Allen's heart slammed against his chest, and he shoved aside the two women, storming toward the stage, taking the stairs two at a time. He stopped just behind Caden, who directed the Shadow Masters to depart. "Where are they going?" Allen demanded.

Caden turned to face him. "The same place you are. Away from here. We are compromised."

"It's a fire alarm. It might not even be real."

Irritation touched Caden's eyes. "You fool," he spat. "The sprinklers are on. That means smoke."

"That can quickly be dealt with," Allen countered.

"We are exposed," Caden reiterated. "We leave, and we do it now."

Allen wasn't accepting that answer. "We can't leave. The ritual can't be delayed. The full moon is coming. And what if this is a ruse? What if someone is trying to use the fire to get us out of here?"

"We are leaving," Caden said, the bite to his words telling of his growing impatience. "We have escape tunnels. Vars didn't choose a fool in me. You, though, I am beginning to wonder about."

Panic formed and Allen exploded. He couldn't let this happen. Not with Kate's future on the line. "I am the one who controls this vial." His fist closed around the glass that hung from a string around his neck—the vial that would hold the souls of the Shadow Masters once the stones had enough power to make it happen. "I am the one who can give Vars what he wants. Without me Vars cannot be a part of this ceremony. He speaks through me. And I say we stay and finish the ritual. I say—"

Caden waved his hand and Allen's words were magically lodged in his throat. "*You* say nothing, and if you aren't careful, I'll silence you permanently. You are nothing but a useful puppet that Vars needs right now to free himself. A tool to aid my efforts in this ritual. I, however, am bound to Vars, his eternal blood servant, gifted with abilities that would make you wet your prissy little pants." He pointed to the end of the stage. "Now walk. We are leaving. Before we find trouble I can't fix."

Hatred crept into Allen's heart in that moment, and it scared him. He'd never been one to feel such things, but he did now. He hated this man for claiming his control. This was his journey, his path, launched for Kate, not this man. Stiffly, he turned and walked to the edge of the stage, wishing he had the magic to make Caden eat his words. And just as he'd never been a man full of hatred, Allen had never sought vengeance on anyone. But if Caden failed to perform this ritual properly, if he cost Allen his Kate, he would deliver vengeance against Caden.

The air crackled with Adrian's fury a second before he appeared on the stairwell of the club in front of U2— or William as he was once known. Adrian pointed at U2 and the Beast flew against the wall, back plastered to the concrete with magic, feet dangling in the air.

"How much pain your future holds is up to you," Adrian snarled between his clenched teeth. Irritation wracked his nerves, the sound of the fire alarm screeching with warning and reminding him of U2's stupidity. If Vars didn't escape his prison, Adrian couldn't claim his demon army. Vars had to be freed, yet the ritual to aid that escape was now being interrupted and he had U2 to thank for that. "If this fire destroys my plans, you will wish you were dead. And make no mistake—I am allowing you to continue for only one reason. I want what is Salvador's and your brother is his. I suggest you deliver him to me."

Adrian sliced his hand through the air and U2 fell to the ground. "Don't make me come to you again. Next time you will not get off so easily."

He shot a dart of electricity through U2's body. The Beast shook with the jolt, his eyes rolling back in his head. Adrian inhaled with pleasure; U2's fear and pain were almost as sweet as sex. Yes. He felt calmer now.

But what he wanted was not calm—it was power. The power he would soon take from Vars. With his own army and that of Vars, Adrian would be unstoppable. He would destroy The Knights of White with ease, ridding himself of the hindrance they had become in his quest for power. His power would allow him to overtake Cain, and Adrian would then be king in his place. He would finally find his position within the royalty of the Underworld. And then, one by one, he would overtake and destroy the other leaders—until he ruled all of hell.

Chapter 21

Max sprinted toward the club, determined to get there before Allen took flight. He found the front door as the fire trucks pulled up. Flames flickered through the front entrance, energized now, spreading through the structure. Searching for a discreet entry point, Max darted around to the back of the building.

Even as he scouted for trouble, on alert as his senses picked up the presence of Beasts, his thoughts were dimly fixed on Sarah. Leaving her worried him. Towing her along with him worried him more. Protecting her from an army of Beasts—which could well be the case—would be damn near impossible. Not to mention his present state of internal struggle. He'd barely reined in his beast after that last battle. He was clinging to a proverbial limb, barely holding on to reality. Days ago, he'd wanted to scare her away. Now, he was terrified he might really do it. He couldn't let her see him like this. Not if he wanted her in his life. And he did. More than anything he'd ever wanted in four centuries of living.

Kneeling by a window, Max yanked up his pant leg and removed the gun he had strapped to his calf. The compact Glock wasn't his preferred weapon considering it wouldn't kill a Beast. At least a few well-placed bullets would stun his enemy long enough for Max to steal a real weapon. Using the butt of the gun, Max broke the glass that blocked his entry into the building and then cleared the opening of the remaining jagged pieces. He slid through the tight space and found himself on a smoky industrial stairwell. Sucking in the thick air, he adjusted his breathing, appreciative that he was far less affected by such things than a normal human.

Not wasting any time, Max charged down one flight of concrete stairs and found a closed door in his path. Cautiously, he opened it, finding no resistance and no enemies. Just another set of stairs. These were narrow and winding in a snakelike path. He trotted down their distance and found himself at the edge of a dark, empty auditorium, with a stage overlooking the room.

Using his exceptional night vision, Max assessed his surroundings. Chairs were folded at the sides of the room; silk blankets and cushions were covered in water from the spray of overhead sprinklers. The scent of sex and perfume lingered in the air, telling of how recently the occupants had fled.

"Damn," Max murmured, his instincts flaring with the warning of Beasts. He surveyed the room, finding no movement, but that didn't fool him.

Max went into action—the idea of being a sitting

duck holding no appeal. He plowed across the room, the water soaking his already damp clothing. Somehow, this room had another exit, different from the way Max had come in. The fire up above would have stopped their departure.

A search turned up no departure points, but Max knew, damn good and well, there was another exit somewhere. Obviously high-tech and well-hidden. And the darkness wasn't helping matters.

A low sound had Max whirling around, his weapon in front of him.

"Max." It was Sarah. He saw her the same moment he heard her voice, and she immediately started running toward him. "Thank God, you're okay."

His heart lurched at the idea of her being here, at the epicenter of danger. "Damn it, Sarah, it's not safe here."

"For either of us," she countered, leaping across an overturned chair in her path. "You're one against many. I couldn't leave you alone."

Alone. He was used to alone, though he didn't like it. Softening with her words, Max motioned her forward, wanting her by his side so he could protect her. He couldn't quite get used to someone looking out for him, but if that someone was Sarah, he'd easily adapt.

Still, she needed to learn to listen. He almost laughed at that. She would never listen. Neither Jag's nor Des's mate did. Why would Sarah? The Knights drew strong-willed mates.

"I should have known you wouldn't go back to the hotel," he commented, moving to meet her halfway.

"I don't generally take orders well," she said. "Especially when someone I care about is in danger. I—"

The rest of her words faded as Max saw William dart across the stage and leap off the edge. He was after Sarah and he was well-armed.

"Run!" Max screamed at Sarah as he launched himself forward, a bull after his target. His body collided with William's not a second too soon, because Sarah was almost in his brother's grasp. Max and William went into a clench hold, arms locked with arms, and Max's gun landed in a splash on the wet floor. The two brothers rotated around in circles as each tried to get the upper hand. A battle of wills and strength ensued, the floor slick beneath their feet, leftover chairs crashing around them as they became obstacles.

With each shove, each push, the idea of his brother hurting his mate became the ultimate betrayal for Max. It fed his anger, and he managed to rip himself free of William's hold and throw several hard blows. He took some, too, but he didn't feel them. He was driven, angry, in primal fighting mode. And when opportunity presented itself, he seized one of the blades at William's hip. That same instant, William drew the other blade he wore.

The two brothers sliced the weapons through the air, blades held at each other's throats. William laughed and dropped his weapon, fearless of Max. "You can't do it and you know it."

"Don't count on that," Max growled, his hand shaking, his fingers clutching the sword's handle.

"I'm your brother. If you can kill me, maybe you're more like me than I gave you credit for. That's it, isn't it?" William smiled. "You're more like me, Maxwell, than you want to admit. Accept it. Seize what you are. The time to accept your true calling has come."

Max's gut clenched at those words. He felt dark, he felt dangerous. He felt every bit like the beast who pressed him now to take William's head for trying to hurt Sarah. He didn't see his brother. He saw only red, saw only the Beast who wanted to kill his mate. He drew a deep, calming breath. Yet… Damn it! Why? Why had he stopped when he could have killed this Beast and ended this? Dimly, he saw the truth. His beast didn't have as much control as he had thought. The control that he would have sworn was gone, remained loosely in place. And his human side recognized William, his brother, as the only piece of his past that still lived.

He reached for reason, for rationale. This wasn't William. This was a Beast who killed humans without concern, smashing them as if they were mere flies. He couldn't let this Beast live just because it looked like his long gone brother. He had to end this. He had to do this—and not as the beast. He had to do this as Max, as the man who understood good versus evil. Salvador wouldn't save William. The truth was hard to swallow, but deep down, Max understood why. As a human, William hadn't known right from wrong. He would never be a Knight. He would always be a Beast.

"You're thinking about it." William dropped to his knees, daring Max with his actions. "Do it! Kill me or join me!"

Painfully, Max lifted his sword, preparing to do what he'd always known he'd have to do one day—just accept that William was gone. He would have acted, would have swung his sword, but voices echoed in the hall. Close. Too close. Damn it. They couldn't do this in front of humans.

Laughter bubbled from William's lips, and he pushed to his feet, backing away. "Think about what I've said." And then he turned away, taking long strides and jumping up on the stage with agility and ease before detouring to an exit behind the stage.

Sarah swiped at the tears streaming down her cheeks. Emotion welled inside her for Max; she was riveted by the torment she'd witnessed him endure as he'd faced killing his brother. But there was more to what she felt, so much more. As she'd watched Max's face, the fierce, primal desire to kill contorted into raw human agony. She'd known the minute he'd accepted the loss of his brother. And she'd had a flashback to the day her parents had died. The demon hadn't spared Sarah's life. Her friend had. He'd fought that demon possessing him and killed himself rather than Sarah. Her friend had beaten that demon, and he'd deserved the trust she'd questioned all these years. The trust she'd denied everyone around her since that day—including Max. But he had it now. He had her trust, and he had her.

Sarah walked to Max's side, where she belonged. She touched his arm and his gaze found hers. The angst in his eyes was almost too much to bear. God, how she ached to ease his hurt. To tell him that what he felt made him human.

Instead, she said, "I love you, Max. There was an empty spot in my life that I've never understood. Now I do. I was waiting for you. I don't want to do any of this alone anymore."

Shock registered in his face before he pulled her close and kissed her. His forehead rested against hers, his arms wrapping around her waist. "You have no idea how much I needed to hear that right now."

Her hands went to his face, her surroundings forgotten, her heart and body warm with the moment, with the emotion that this man, her mate, drew from her. "I believe in you. Just make sure you believe in you."

"You won't ever be alone again, Sarah. I promise. I *will* conquer this test, so we can be together. I love you and I need you. So damn much. You have no idea."

Sarah never got to tell him how much *she* had needed to hear those words. Firemen charged through the door. They were rescued.

Near sunrise, Sarah and Max returned to the town of Nowhere with the aid of Jag's travel abilities. Hours of searching the tunnels discovered beneath the club had delivered no results. A standoff at the cabin appeared more and more likely.

Sarah walked into the deserted lobby of the inn. Cathy flew down the stairs, obviously aware of their arrival. It took only a moment for Sarah to find herself wrapped in a big hug.

"I've been worried about you," Cathy said, easing back and looking them both over, her gaze taking in their muddy, damp clothing. "You two are a mess. You should clean up and get some rest."

Max stepped closer, by Sarah's side. "Any news on Edward?"

Cathy crossed her arms in front of her chest, instantly tense. She wore no makeup. Only faded jeans, a T-shirt and Keds tennis shoes. Dark circles tinted the pale skin under her eyes. "No change. I'm headed over to the doctor's office now. I took a shower and slept for an hour. Or tried to at least."

"What happened to you and Marisol trying to combine your magic to expel the demon?" Max asked.

Cathy's tone went flat. "Nothing. This stuff about me having the ability to use magic beyond what I've learned from books isn't flying. So far, I got nothing."

"You've been focused on expelling the demon from Edward, right?"

"Right," Cathy agreed.

Sarah continued, "I think we need to give Edward the power to defeat the demon himself. Somehow, focus the magic to empower Edward. Let the man defeat the demon. Don't use the magic ourselves. Direct it to Edward."

"Let the man defeat the demon," Cathy said, repeating the words. "That's actually quite brilliant. I have to go." She sidestepped Sarah and Max and reached for the door.

Sarah turned to Max, their eyes locked, warmth spreading through her limbs at the connection they shared. They didn't speak. They didn't have to. They knew tonight had been life changing. Each of them had faced their pasts and it had brought them closer. Their fingers linked, and Max eased them into motion, up the stairs. Neither questioned whose room they were going to. That they would be together was simply expected.

The minute the door shut to Max's room and the lights were on, he and Sarah turned to each other, bodies joined in an embrace, eyes locked. There was no doubt in her expression, no fear. Only love, passion, hope. He bent his head, his cheek brushing hers, the contact soft, perfect. His body heated, limbs fired with a burn for Sarah. *Pull away,* he told himself. She meant more to him than one night. Than this night. *You can't have her yet.* Pass the test first.

As good as his intentions were, when her lips brushed his jaw and then his lips, her fingers caressing his neck, he somehow lost himself in the moment. He pressed Sarah against the door and kissed her. Kissed her as if there was no tomorrow because there might not be. She tasted like honey and felt like heaven. His version of heaven. Possessiveness rose from within Max, intense, sudden. Somehow, he reined in the heat spreading through his body, shoved aside the haze of passion threatening to claim control of him. Her tongue slid against his in delicious hungry strokes, her arms wrapping his neck, her breasts pressed to his chest, soft curves melting into him.

"Max," she whispered, her lips dissolving into his again, her hands pushing his shirt off his shoulders.

When had she unbuttoned it? He let the material fall to the floor, her soft touch pulling him into a seductive spell. He had to stop. Why? He had to remember why. His body defined his mind, his groin tight, cock thickening with the promise of Sarah's slick, wet heat.

He ached for his mate. To be inside her again, this time with acceptance...but the test. He reached for honor, for reason. He tried to pull away. "Sarah—"

Her hands went to his cheeks, her teeth nipped his lip, tongue tracing it, delving into his mouth and stroking. "Don't tell me we can't do this," she ordered in a raspy reply, answering his unspoken objection. "I need you. I need you so much, Max."

Urgency resonated in her voice and her hands were everywhere. His nostrils flared with the scent of her desire, with his own desire. She leaned back to look at him, a dare flashing in her eyes an instant before she peeled her shirt off. Immediately, her bra followed. His gaze dropped, eyes devouring the sight of her high breasts and perfect red nipples. He reached out and brushed the peaks with his fingers, watching them respond before rolling them with his thumbs. The shuddered breath she drew told of her pleasure, fueling his actions, begging him for more without words.

He kissed her, filling his hands with her breasts, hard peaks of her nipples pressed against his palms. He bent at the knees, fitting his hips against the V of her body. They fit together perfectly, their limbs molded together, promising pleasure beyond anything either had imagined before now. She arched into the touch of his hands, her hips sliding against his.

She tore her mouth from his. "There's no reason to wait," she whispered.

No reason. No reason to wait. A jolt of reality rocked Max. Calling on every ounce of willpower he owned, he leaned back, forcing his hands from the woman he burned to touch, pressing them against the door behind her. His chest heaved with the effort to contain his urges, his burn for Sarah.

"The test, Sarah." The words came out a tormented hiss. "We aren't doing this. Not yet."

"You are going to pass the test," she said. "Maybe you already have. Maybe that's what happened tonight with your brother." Her finger brushed his bottom lip. "We need each other."

It would be so easy to listen to her, but Max had to love her enough to wait. "It's not time yet."

"What if something happens to one of us? I want to know we had one time together without anything between us."

"Nothing's going to happen to you, damn it," he said. "I won't let it. And there is something between us now."

Seconds ticked, Sarah's gaze searching his. "This is what you want." Her voice held defeat.

"No, but it's how it has to be. It's killing me, baby, I swear. But I want us to do this right. I want to make love to you. I want you to choose an eternity with me without regret. You should see the ranch, see my life. Know you want what I can offer you. To be my mate, my wife."

Emotion rushed into her eyes and she wrapped her arms around him, her nipples pressed into his chest. Her lips brushed his. "I don't need to see the ranch. Just pass this test and let's get on with eternity."

His heart warmed with her words, his hands sliding up her bare back. He kissed her, torturing himself with the sweet taste of her. Knowing a very long, cold shower was as much his destiny as Sarah.

Hours later Sarah lay with her head on Max's chest. They'd been talking for hours, and she'd told him about how her memory of the night of her parent's death had sparked the idea to save Edward. How it had given her new perspective on life, on her future.

When finally they fell silent, each trying to sleep, the comfort his arms delivered did nothing to deliver peace of mind. As perfect as lying with Max had become, she couldn't fight the ominous foreboding that rested heavily in her thoughts. The fact that they had fully dressed after showering, ready for trouble, only added to the darkness clinging to her mood.

She was so close to finding her way in this world again. Would the rug get pulled out from under her? No matter how much she tried to control the outcome of the next few days' events, she couldn't. Would she lose Max before she truly found him? No, she promised herself. They would get through this. They had to.

But as soon as she said the words in her head, pounding started on the door. "Sarah!" It was Cathy's voice.

Sarah and Max darted from the bed at the same time. Sarah rushed to door, Max for a weapon.

Flinging open the door, Sarah could barely believe what she saw. Cathy wasn't alone. Edward stood by her side. He was okay. She smiled and hugged him. She was taking this as a sign. She'd started to have faith again and she wasn't going to stop now.

They were winning one demon at a time. Her chest tightened. Too bad it sounded as if an entire army was on the way.

A message from the Underworld had reached Salvador. Innocents would die if Salvador did not meet Adrian immediately. The location of the meeting—a residential home in Nowhere, Texas. In other words, Salvador was being led into a trap. After great consideration, he refused the meeting, with the support of those he answered to. But when the pain of a young child began to play in his mind, Salvador reconsidered.

Salvador appeared on the front lawn of the home designated for the meeting, a child's cry sounding in his mind. Eager to act, but not foolish, he took a moment to allow the home to speak to him.

The history of the people who lived there automatically came to him. It was his gift of sight, the ability to see the past and the present—though at times, the higher powers withheld information. He didn't question why. It wasn't his place to question.

The information flowed freely now. A young couple lived within these walls. They'd lost their youngest child to cancer, and their eldest child, a daughter now ten, became a treasure they feared would also be taken from them. Each night they had prayed for her safety.

Sensing Adrian was at the rear of the house, Salvador disappeared from the front lawn and reappeared in the backyard beside a whirlpool. The child was inside the tub, her face contorted in pain, her body submerged in the Water of the Damned—water that would create such pain in a human, it would rip their hearts to shreds.

The parents were tied to chairs and gagged; a Beast was standing guard, ready to kill. The woman cried, tears streaming down her cheeks. Without hesitation, he pointed at the Beast and sent it flying across the lawn. A wave of his hands and the parents were untied. He waved his hands and flashed them across town, where they couldn't do anything foolish.

Fire singed the air and Adrian appeared a few feet from Salvador. "If you don't go in and save her, she will die."

"You know the rules. You are not to touch a human." Long ago, the Laws of Existence had been established. The higher powers allowed evil to exist within limits. It served a purpose well beyond human comprehension. And for those who had crossed over, who no longer held a human essence, there were severe penalties for breaking those laws.

Adrian smiled. Evil. Pleased with himself. "I didn't. My Beast did."

Salvador had latitude to undo the injustice done to humans by the evil that visited this realm. But that latitude came with strict guidelines. To abuse his power would come with a penalty.

"Semantics," Salvador said. "And we both know it. You did this. I can undo it."

"Feel free," Adrian offered, motioning to the child. "Save her."

Salvador showed no outward signs of reaction, though the decision before him tore him up inside.

If he went in after that child, into the water, his powers would temporarily be stripped. He'd be able to transport himself to safety, before Adrian could attack him, but nothing more. The Water of the Damned was the opposite of holy water, a hazard to all those of the higher realm, and this wasn't his first experience with it. Salvador had worked to build immunity to the water, expecting it would be used as a weapon against him again. There had been a time when the water would have ensured that he was useless for a week. But not now. Now, he would recover rapidly. He might even be ready in time for the full moon. Might. There was always the risk he would not. Not that he would interfere. The rules were clear. He kept the balance of power in proper alignment. He acted to protect the balance and enforce the rules.

Just his presence alone in Nowhere would ensure Adrian didn't break their laws. He knew it and so did

Adrian. Which was why Adrian wanted Salvador out of the picture.

The child cried out, screaming with a sharp pain; the sound wrapped around Salvador and stabbed his heart. He could not let the child die. Salvador fixed Adrian in a hard stare.

"If I find out you have violated the laws of our kind, I will ensure you pay and pay well." He said nothing more, accepting what had to be done. Salvador waded into the water.

It was time for the final Stone ceremony.

Adrian laughed as Salvador waded into the water before reluctantly flashing away from the scene of his enemy's demise, and into one of the many caverns Caden had prepared as the possible ceremonial location. Once again, Adrian became an observer, standing in the back of the lust-laden room filled with naked humans, candles flickering across bare skin. Everywhere he looked, bodies were pressed together in pleasure. Only one man stood without a partner, and that man was Allen. He sat in a corner, rocking back and forth. Adrian could feel guilt coming off the man. How pathetic. He'd come this far to bring his wife back, and now he felt guilty for the three lives that would be lost to empower the stones.

Disgusted at the sight of such weakness, Adrian jerked his gaze away, focusing on the podium in the center of the room, several feel above the collage of bodies. The three robed Stone Masters stood center stage on top of it, waiting, even welcoming, their final moments of life in this realm. A stone lay at each man's feet.

Excitement flared inside Adrian as Caden weaved his way through the crowd and stopped at the bottom of the stairs leading to the podium. Adrian was so close to embracing Vars's powers he could almost taste the pleasure of it. Caden spoke into a small microphone and began an underworld chant that Adrian knew well. It was meant to taint the souls of humans, meant to hypnotize. And it worked. It always worked. The humans quickly joined the chant, repeating his words, their desire for one another lost as they walked toward the podium, joining hands and forming a circle. The Stone Masters disrobed, giving their bodies to their cause, as they would soon give their souls. Caden began a slow walk up the stairs, the magic within already called to life, crackling in the air.

Adrian watched as Caden stepped to the center of the podium, watched as blue lightning shot from one stone to its master. Seconds passed, and the master crumbled to the ground. The two others quickly followed. The stones crackled with electricity, glowing blue.

Pleasure filled Adrian. Things were going his way. With the ceremony complete and Salvador out of the way, nothing would stop Adrian from claiming Vars's magic and his rightful place in the Underworld. Pleasure filled Adrian. Things were going his way.

Chapter 22

For two days the town had been silent, almost normal. A facade that no one believed. And now, the night of the full moon had arrived.

Max stood on the porch of the inn, Des by his side. "You don't have to do this," Max reminded Des. "You have a mate now to think about. Go back to the ranch and take care of her."

Des snorted. "Right. Like me leaving is really going to happen." His hand went to Max's shoulder before he leaned on the railing. "Jessica would kick my ass if I deserted you in your time of need. Not to mention I'd never miss a fight like this one." He sobered. "You helped me save Jessica's life, man. I am in your debt for eternity."

"If I have an eternity left," Max said, his gaze traveling the dark horizon where lightning struck, searching for the trouble, his senses raw with warning.

"You still don't remember what happened that day, do you?" Des asked.

Max's gaze shot to Des. "Do you?"

"I was freaking out over Jessica being stabbed. I didn't see what happened. I wish I had because, man, I don't believe you went all dark and just killed that man. Not for a minute. You believed in me when I thought I couldn't be saved. Back at you, *brother.*" He emphasized the last word, letting Max know he had a new brother, he had Des. "I choose to believe in you now, too."

His eyes lifted, searched, and he pushed off the railing, tense and alert. "You getting that vibe I'm getting?"

Before Max could say, "Hell yes," an army of Beasts appeared in the far distance. Jag orbed onto the porch. Rinehart and Rock rushed through the door of the inn. The Knights stood side by side, swords drawn. They all knew a team of their own army would close in from behind the Beasts. Just as they had Knights at the outskirts of the cabin, waiting, ready.

Cathy, Sarah and Edward appeared on the porch. Sarah stepped to Max's side. "Oh, my God," she whispered. "There are so many of them."

"They're early," Cathy said. "They shouldn't be able to do the ritual until midnight. It's not even nightfall."

"Apparently, they have other ideas," Edward commented dryly, back to his normal form.

"Max," Jag said, his tone clipped, short. "The minute our men attack, you and Des hit the road. Take Sarah and the others to the cabin."

Max nodded. As much as he didn't want Sarah at the cabin, her team could stop Allen and Caden from liberating Vars if they worked together with Marisol to counter the magic.

Jag turned to Rinehart and Rock. "Get the humans under cover. I'll come back for you, with Marisol in tow."

Black rain began to fall. Hell was calling. Max and Des looked at each other, their shared look saying they were ready to answer that call; they were ready to fight.

And they planned to win.

The van hit a pothole and flew into the air, crashing down to the road with a heavy thud that threw Sarah against Max. Des reached for a handle on the door; Max grabbed Sarah, righting her before she hit the wall of the van. His gut wrenched. He wasn't going to be able to protect her so easily. Her eyes lifted to his and her hand went to his where it rested on her shoulder. She laced her fingers with his. This was it and they both knew it. Live or die, eternally together, or forever separated. This town, their lives, their futures were on the line. Somehow, Max was certain his test ended here, today, along with this battle to stop Vars—both outcomes uncertain.

"Holy shit!" Edward yelled from the driver's seat.

Cathy shouted a similar proclamation from beside him. Max pulled away from Sarah to look out the front window, the cabin in their sights. Knights and Beasts were heavy in combat. A Mercedes sat beside the cabin.

Sarah pushed to Max's side. "They're here already. Please don't let us be too late."

Jag and Marisol appeared in the van. "Stop the van," Jag ordered.

Edward slammed on the brakes. Marisol moved

between Cathy and Edward and took their hands. Jag did the same with Max and Sarah and issued a warning. "We have no idea what we're headed into. Be ready for anything."

Marisol offered a grave reminder. "Take your positions around the triangle where Vars will appear, and let Max and Jag deal with Caden and Allen."

"Right," Max said. "We'll break the magic circle and end the ceremony."

"And get the vial," Jag added.

"But if they fail," Marisol said, "we have to be ready to send Vars back to his prison."

"Looks like I'm the fifth wheel," Des said. "I'll be outside kicking ass." His gaze settled on Max. "I've got your back, man. Nothing is getting inside that isn't already there. Be safe, brother."

Jag eyed the group. "Ready?"

Sarah and Max stared at each other. "Ready," they said at once.

Max had barely set foot in the cabin before things spun out of control. The pure evil lacing the air damn near stole his breath, and he knew Vars was stronger now, ready for the freedom they'd come to prevent him from receiving. Caden and Allen were both there already, both wearing black robes, both holding knives. And they were not without protection.

Four Beasts stepped between their team and the ritual area. The drawings on the floor were ready for use. Max wasn't surprised to find William was one of those Beasts; he'd expected another confrontation. Even welcomed it. Well-armed, the Beasts wore their vinyl-looking armored suits. There was no facade of humanity; the Beasts bared their fangs as quickly as they did their swords. Max wrestled down his fear for Sarah, willing himself to stay focused on the battle. There was no turning back now.

He and Jag placed themselves in front of their group, both drawing their weapons. The Beasts charged forward. With practiced precision, Max and Jag took on two enemies each, both quickly beheading the first of their foes. The heads tumbled to the ground in flames that quickly turned to ash.

As Jag dealt with his second opponent, William darted toward Sarah. Edward grabbed her and shoved her behind him. William growled and yanked Edward forward, his fangs sinking into his neck, Edward's feet dangling from the ground.

Sarah screamed, and the sound sent guilt rocketing through Max's body. He should have killed William while he had the chance. Rage ripped through him, and Max attacked William's back. Jag appeared in front of William, pulling Edward from his grip. Max threw William with all his might, and William stumbled, a loud angry sound erupting from his throat. He turned to face Max at the same moment that Max's sword cut through the air. William's head tumbled to the ground, turning to ash within seconds.

Without warning, wind erupted in the room, throwing things everywhere, hissing with evil bliss. You could feel its menacing quality, its impatience for the demon prince to be freed.

"The ritual has started!" Cathy yelled over the chaos from where she leaned over Edward's limp body. "Break the circle."

Max turned to see Caden and Allen slice their palms, bleeding into the circle. Vars appeared inside the triangle, one step closer to freedom. His deep, evil laugh resonated eerily through the room.

Before Max could stop her, Sarah dashed toward the circle, brave, without hesitation. Max's heart kicked into double time, concern for Sarah pushing him forward. She crossed the line of the circle before he could get to her and Vars roared with anger.

"Adrian!" he shouted, and then faded away, back into his hell hole.

The circle broken, the ritual had temporarily come to a halt. But they needed the vial to stop it permanently and Sarah grabbed it from Allen's neck and yanked. Max appeared at the edge of the circle and ripped Sarah from its confines an instant before Caden's blade would have claimed her. She stumbled backward onto the ground. Max stripped Caden of his knife, and shoved him far out of the circle, his peripheral vision catching Allen diving for Sarah and the vial.

Sarah. He had to save Sarah.

Max turned to find her on her back, Allen crouched over her as they struggled for the vial. Max bent over Allen and grabbed his shirt, the blade he'd just removed from Caden in his hand—throwing it down would be handing it over to Caden again. Before he could get a good grip on Allen, Caden pounced on his back. Max tried to hold the weight, fearful of all three men falling on top of Sarah. He saw Jag's boots, knew he was going after Caden. But Allen panicked and shoved upward. To Max's horror the blade he held ripped through Allen's back.

Everything seemed to fade into slow motion. Memories assailed Max. Memories of the day he killed the human. The man had turned into his blade much as Allen had now. The entire scene replayed in his mind with brilliant clarity. Max squeezed his eyes shut, realizing for the first time that killing the human had indeed been an accident. He hadn't lost control, hadn't allowed his dark side to kill.

Feeling the weight of Caden yanked off his back, Max rolled off Allen. Briefly, his gaze flicked to Jag as he shoved Caden out the front door, into the mix of the battle still raging beyond these walls. Then Max's attention returned to Allen.

Max lifted Allen off of Sarah. The knife was deep in his back. Max's eyes locked with Sarah's and relief flooded him when he noted she was unhurt. The vial remained in her hand, crushed, glass splintered in her palm.

Assured of Sarah's safety, his concerns returned to Allen. *Please, God. Don't let him die. Not again. Not Allen.* "Marisol!" he shouted, bending down over Allen, desperate to somehow make this right.

Sarah tossed the vial aside, scrambling to her knees, ignoring any pain she might feel as she crouched next to Max.

Her good hand went to Max's back. "It was an accident Max. An accident." She called out as he had. "Marisol!"

Marisol was finally there kneeling beside Allen. She touched his head as if she would find answers there. Max held his breath as he waited for her conclusion and he sensed Sarah did the same.

She glanced up at Max. "Remove the knife."

He nodded and did as she said. "Please tell me you can fix him."

"I can."

Max exhaled, relief washing over him. Relief that lasted only a minute as Adrian appeared beside the ritual circle, four Beasts by his side. "You will pay for interfering in my plans," he said. "The Knights will lose their leader this day. Jag will die." Two more Beasts appeared in the room. Then two more.

Max shoved to his feet, stepping to Jag's side. Neither Knight looked at the other, both ready for battle.

Sarah took in the sight of the man who'd promised Jag's death. He wore black leather, his long blond hair and muscular body making him look more Sex God than demon. But there was no mistaking the pure evil surrounding him. She pushed to her feet, sick to her stomach, certain that death would follow.

In astonishment, she watched another man appear in front of Jag and Max; his presence was like a shield. She could see only his back, his long black hair, his simple clothing of jeans and T-shirt. But just as there was no mistaking the other man's evil, there was no mistaking this man's power. "Hello, Adrian," the newcomer said. "Sorry I'm late. Did I miss anything?"

The man, Adrian, contorted into a beastly image. "Salvador! You can't be here. I stripped your powers."

"You should never underestimate me, Adrian. Your Water of the Damned was nothing but a temporary thorn in my side. Consequently, I've sealed Vars's prison. He won't be coming out anytime soon. And I believe one of your Beasts already dealt with Caden. You seem to be the only loose end. I'd suggest you and your Beasts retreat before I send you to join Vars. I filled him in on your plan to steal his demon legions. I'm certain he'd welcome a visit from you right about now."

Adrian pointed at Salvador, the act ominous, threatening. A laugh bubbled from Salvador's throat. Rich. Pure. It rippled down Sarah's spine. *Was he an angel?* Sarah wondered.

"Please do give me a reason to strike back," Salvador challenged, his voice laced with a taunt. Adrian hesitated before his hands balled by his sides. A second later, he thrust his fist forward and fire shot at Salvador. Palm up, Salvador received the fire, throwing it back at Adrian. A wild eruption of fireballs went back and forth, one after the other until Salvador and Adrian stood in a face-off, neither a victor nor a failure. With red, blazing eyes, Adrian glared at Salvador, the entire room crackling with his menace. There was no doubt a vicious battle could evolve from this confrontation, no doubt the danger of just that was but a hair from conception.

Abruptly, Adrian thrust his head back in the air and roared, the entire building shaking with the impact. When he finally calmed, his chin tilted downward and his stare fixed once again on Salvador. "This isn't over. Mark my words—in the not-so-distant future your Knights will fall to my Beasts. And I will revel in watching you suffer through their pain."

Fire erupted around him, and he and his Beasts disappeared. Max turned to Sarah and pulled her close. She clung to him, seeing the tension in his face. The worry in his eyes spoke volumes. He thought this was it. His final moments.

Salvador rotated around to face those who observed him but he appeared to see only Max and Sarah. That's when she saw his eyes. Green, serene, devastating in their impact. His features were not handsome, yet he was beautiful beyond belief. She shook as he approached, but not from fear.

"Hello, Sarah. I'm Salvador."

"Hello," she replied, at a loss for anything more brilliant to say.

"You've done well," he said. "Your parents are proud. They want you to know they are always with you."

Tears came instantly, because Sarah knew, absolutely knew, he had spoken to them. She collapsed against Max, shaken to the core.

"Max," Salvador said. "You, too, have done well. You selflessly refused to find the peace Sarah would have given you. You put her first. Over and over, I have watched you fight your darkness. Even when you thought you had no hope of survival, you fought to help Des find his. You had faith in everyone but yourself, and I couldn't allow that. Ultimately, it weakened you and it would have led to your destruction."

He smiled. "Now you have Sarah. I'm quite certain you have another four centuries to give me, don't you?"

"As long as you will have me," Max said, his voice cracking.

"I'd say an eternity should do," Salvador said, smiling. Sarah's heart swelled and she hugged Max tighter than she'd ever hugged anyone.

He kissed her, his hands framing her face, his finger wiping the tears from her cheeks. "And as long as you will have me."

"An eternity should do," she whispered.

"One more thing," Salvador said, drawing their attention. "Cathy is the mate of a future Knight. I'd like you both to look out for her, though I've arranged a big brother of sorts for her." His gaze shifted to Sarah. "Edward will be joining the Knights. I trust you can deal with mediating Cathy and Edward's arguments a little longer?"

Sarah smiled, laughter bubbling from her throat. "Oh, yes. I believe I can."

"Good. Good. And don't worry about Allen. Marisol will wipe his memories and he will live a long life. How he spends the afterlife comes down to how he lives that long life. But he still has hope of seeing his wife again one day." He winked at Sarah. "Kate is quite appreciative by the way." He motioned Jag forward. "Jag and I will ease the town back into their comfort zone. I thought the two of you might enjoy heading to the ranch and settling in."

Sarah looked up at Max, happiness shining in his eyes. "Yes," they said together.

Salvador touched them both, filling them with warmth. Sarah and Max disappeared and reappeared on the front lawn of a house.

Max smiled down at her. "Welcome to the ranch. The home of The Knights of White, and your home— our home together—if you decide to make it so." He pressed his fingers to her lips before she could respond. "And don't say you've already decided. I've waited four centuries for you, Sarah. I can wait a little longer. I need to know you come to me not out of duress, not out of the heat of danger. Be here. Be with me. Then make your choice."

"Max," she whispered, her hand brushing his cheek. She loved him so much in that moment. He was a man of honor, unwilling to take what wasn't his. But she was his. She always had been. She'd been waiting for him all her life.

Epilogue

Two weeks later

Breakfast at the ranch was a big event and it drew a crowd that had now finally thinned. Sarah and Max sat across from each other, at the kitchen table. In some corner of her mind, she was aware of Edward and Cathy arguing. Again. But Sarah had no idea about what. Nor did she care. The two of them were happy here. Cathy was already planning ways their operation could aid the Knights' work. No. Cathy and Edward were not her concern right now. She and Max were.

Sarah stared at her plate, afraid to look at Max for fear she might explode into flames—that's how damn aroused and on edge she was these days. She and Max had been getting to know each other for far too long now. She understood why he'd wanted to wait, why he wanted her full acceptance of his life, his world, but he had that. The ranch was wonderful. The little cottage to the east of the main house that Jag had offered to make theirs was perfect. But so far they were still staying in an upstairs bedroom—together, but not quite. It was time to solidify their mating.

She shoved her chair back and stood, her eyes lifting to Max's. "Can I see you a moment?" Heat curled in her stomach the instant their eyes connected, no doubt desire flared in her eyes. She hoped so. Hoped he saw what she felt. Hoped he knew what she wanted.

Slowly, he rose from his seat, a primal edge clinging to him. He burned for her as much as she did for him. He had to know they could wait no longer. "Of course," he said.

Sarah didn't say anything to Cathy or Edward. She rounded the table and Max followed. In silence they climbed the stairs to the second level of the house, the air crackling with sexual tension.

The minute they were in the guest bedroom they'd been occupying, Sarah whirled on Max. "Do you want to spend forever with me?"

Instantly, he reached for her. Her hands settled on his chest, the heat of his body pressed to her. His voice was low, husky, laced with fire and desire, with love. "I love you more than I could ever express and, yes, I want you forever, Sarah. I want you to be my wife, my mate. You're already my everything."

"Then make it so, Max." Her voice lowered to a soft plea. "Make it so."

He kissed her then, a long deep kiss full of tenderness. Kissed her until a firestorm of passion erupted between them.

Long minutes later, they were in the bed, clothing piled on the floor. Sarah was on top of Max, straddling him, their bodies intimately connected. She lay on top of him, their lips joined, her breasts pressed to his chest. Their hips rocked, their movements a sensual sway. The pleasure almost more than she could bear yet it still wasn't enough.

When she thought she might cry out for him, Max sat up, his arms around her back, holding her. Yellow tinged his eyes and she smiled. For she saw the beast in him—her beast.

Her lips brushed his. "Max," she whispered.

"I love you, Sarah." And with those precious words he bent his head, his teeth claiming her shoulder. Sarah gasped with the contact, a sigh quickly following, the pleasure of the moment darting straight to her core. The happiness filling her heart.

Now she was home.

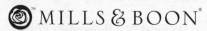

INTRIGUE

Coming next month

2-IN-1 ANTHOLOGY

A SOLDIER CAGED by Rebecca York

Kept in a military bunker, Jonah is a damaged war hero looking for a way out. Sophia is his only chance of escape yet she also inspires his most fiery desires!

SEDUCING THE MERCENARY by Loreth Anne White

To the rest of the world, Jean-Charles is a dangerous tyrant. But only Dr Emily Carlin knows his true self – which leaves her powerless to resist his seductive spell.

2-IN-1 ANTHOLOGY

THE BODYGUARD'S RETURN by Carla Cassidy

When Savannah is attacked, her only hope is to hire bodyguard Joshua to keep her safe. He's the perfect protector, but could he be something more?

INTIMATE ENEMY by Marilyn Pappano

A stalker sends Jamie into hiding in the least likely of places – the home of ex-lover Russ. Yet will being with Russ bring up emotions that may be just as dangerous…?

SINGLE TITLE

HOLIDAY WITH A VAMPIRE
by Maureen Child and Caridad Piñeiro
Nocturne™

Celebrate this winter with two chilling tales and two seriously sensual heroes who are fighting the ultimate temptation!

On sale 20th November 2009

Available at WHSmith, Tesco, ASDA, Eason and all good bookshops.
For full Mills & Boon range including eBooks visit
www.millsandboon.co.uk

millsandboon.co.uk Community

Join Us!

The Community is the perfect place to meet and chat to kindred spirits who love books and reading as much as you do, but it's also the place to:

- Get the inside scoop from authors about their latest books
- Learn how to write a romance book with advice from our editors
- Help us to continue publishing the best in women's fiction
- Share your thoughts on the books we publish
- Befriend other users

Forums: Interact with each other as well as authors, editors and a whole host of other users worldwide.

Blogs: Every registered community member has their own blog to tell the world what they're up to and what's on their mind.

Book Challenge: We're aiming to read 5,000 books and have joined forces with The Reading Agency in our inaugural Book Challenge.

Profile Page: Showcase yourself and keep a record of your recent community activity.

Social Networking: We've added buttons at the end of every post to share via digg, Facebook, Google, Yahoo, technorati and de.licio.us.

www.millsandboon.co.uk

2 FREE BOOKS
AND A SURPRISE GIFT

We would like to take this opportunity to thank you for reading this Mills & Boon® book by offering you the chance to take TWO more specially selected books from the Intrigue series absolutely FREE! We're also making this offer to introduce you to the benefits of the Mills & Boon® Book Club™—

- **FREE home delivery**
- **FREE gifts and competitions**
- **FREE monthly Newsletter**
- **Exclusive Mills & Boon Book Club offers**
- **Books available before they're in the shops**

Accepting these FREE books and gift places you under no obligation to buy, you may cancel at any time, even after receiving your free books. Simply complete your details below and return the entire page to the address below. You don't even need a stamp!

YES Please send me 2 free Intrigue books and a surprise gift. I understand that unless you hear from me, I will receive 5 superb new stories every month, including two 2-in-1 books priced at £4.99 each and a single book priced at £3.19, postage and packing free. I am under no obligation to purchase any books and may cancel my subscription at any time. The free books and gift will be mine to keep in any case.

Ms/Mrs/Miss/Mr _____ Initials _____

_____

Surname _____

Address _____

_____

_____ Postcode _____

Send this whole page to: Mills & Boon Book Club, Free Book Offer, FREEPOST NAT 10298, Richmond, TW9 1BR